Dynevor Terrace
Or The Clue Of Life
Vol. II

by

Charlotte M. Yonge

Dynevor Terrace
Or The Clue Of Life
Vol. II

by Charlotte M. Yonge

Copyright © 2024

All Rights reserved.

No part of this publication may be reproduced, stored in a retrieval system, or transmitted in any form or by any means, electronic, mechanical, photocopying or Otherwise, without the written permission of the publisher.
The author/editor asserts the moral right to be identified as the author/editor of this work.

ISBN: 978-93-63050-97-6

Published by

DOUBLE 9 BOOKS

2/13-B, Ansari Road
Daryaganj, New Delhi – 110002
info@double9books.com
www.double9books.com
Tel. 011-40042856

This book is under public domain

ABOUT THE AUTHOR

Charlotte M. Yonge was an English novelist and historian, born on August 11, 1823, in Otterbourne, Hampshire, England. She is best known for her prolific writing career, which spanned over 60 years and produced more than 160 works, including novels, children's books, and historical studies. Yonge's writing was strongly influenced by her deep religious beliefs and her interest in history and education. Many of her novels, such as "The Heir of Redclyffe" and "Heartsease," explore moral and religious themes and are known for their wholesome and uplifting tone. She also wrote numerous works for children, including the popular "Book of Golden Deeds," which features stories of heroism and selflessness. In addition to her writing, Yonge was a prominent figure in the Church of England and was involved in various philanthropic and educational endeavours. She founded a school for girls in her hometown and was a supporter of the National Society for Promoting Religious Education. Yonge died on May 24, 1901, in Otterbourne, Hampshire, England. Her legacy as a writer and educator continues to be celebrated, and her works remain popular with readers today.

CONTENTS

CHAPTER I
THE TRYSTE 7

CHAPTER II
THE THIRD TIME 17

CHAPTER III
MISTS 26

CHAPTER IV
OUTWARD BOUND 35

CHAPTER V
THE NEW WORLD 51

CHAPTER VI
THE TWO PENDRAGONS 65

CHAPTER VII
ROLAND AND OLIVER 83

CHAPTER VIII
THE RESTORATION 91

CHAPTER IX
THE GIANT OF THE WESTERN STAR 104

CHAPTER X
THE WRONG WOMAN IN THE WRONG PLACE 116

CHAPTER XI
AUNT CATHARINE'S HOME 123

CHAPTER XII
THE FROST HOUSEHOLD 137

CHAPTER XIII
THE CONWAY HOUSEHOLD 149

CHAPTER XIV
THE TRUSTEES' MEETING 158

CHAPTER XV
SWEET USES OF ADVERSITY 174

CHAPTER XVI
THE VALLEY OF HUMILIATION 188

CHAPTER XVII
'BIDE A WEE.' 204

CHAPTER XVIII
THE CRASH 214

CHAPTER XIX
FAREWELL TO GREATNESS 228

CHAPTER XX
WESTERN TIDINGS 237

CHAPTER XXI
STEPPING WESTWARD 250

CHAPTER XXII
RATHER SUDDEN 257

CHAPTER XXIII
THE MARVEL OF PERU 275

CHAPTER I
THE TRYSTE

> One single flash of glad surprise
> Just glanced from Isabel's dark eyes,
> Then vanished in the blush of shame
> That as its penance instant came—
> 'O thought unworthy of my race!'
> The Lord of the Isles.

As little recked Fitzjocelyn of the murmurs which he had provoked, as he guessed the true secret of his victory. In his eyes, it was the triumph of merit over prejudice, and Mrs. Frost espoused the same gratifying view, though ascribing much to her nephew's activity, and James himself, flushed with hope and success, was not likely to dissent.

Next they had to make their conquest available. Apart from Louis's magnificent prognostications, at the lowest computation, the head master's income amounted to a sum which to James appeared affluence; and though there was no house provided, it mattered the less since there were five to choose from in the Terrace, even if his grandmother had not wished that their household should be still the same. With Miss Conway's own fortune and the Terrace settled on herself, where could be any risk?

Would Lady Conway think so? and how should the communication be made? James at first proposed writing to her, enclosing a letter to Isabel; but he changed his mind, unable to satisfy himself that, when absent from restraint, she might not send a refusal without affording her daughter the option. He begged his grandmother to write to Isabel; but she thought her letter might carry too much weight, and, whatever might be her hopes, it was not for her to tell the young lady that such means were sufficient.

Louis begged to be the bearer of the letter. His aunt would certainly keep terms with him, and he could insure that the case was properly laid before Isabel; and, as there could be no doubt at present of his persuasive powers, James caught at the offer. The party were still at Beauchastel, and he devised going to his old quarters at Ebbscreek, and making a descent upon them from thence.

When he came to take up his credentials, he found James and his little black leathern bag, determined to come at least to Ebbscreek with him, and declaring it made him frantic to stay at home and leave his cause in other hands, and that he could not exist anywhere but close to the scene of action.

Captain Hannaford was smoking in his demi-boat, and gave his former lodgers a hearty welcome, but he twinkled knowingly with his eye, and so significantly volunteered to inform them that the ladies were still at Beauchastel, that James's wrath at the old skipper's impudence began to revive, and he walked off to the remotest end of the garden.

The Captain, remaining with Louis, with whom he was always on far more easy terms, looked after the other gentleman, winked again, and confessed that he had suspected one or other of them might be coming that way this summer, though he could not say he had expected to see them both together.

'Mind, Captain,' said Louis,' it wasn't *I* that made the boat late this time last year.'

'Well! I might be wrong, I fancied you cast an eye that way. Then maybe it ain't true what's all over the place here.'

Louis pressed to hear what. 'Why, that when the French were going on like Robert Spear and them old times, he had convoyed the young lady right through the midst of them, and they would both have been shot, if my Lady's butler hadn't come down with a revolver, killed half-a-dozen of the mob, and rescued them out of it, but that Lord Fitzjocelyn had been desperately wounded in going back to fetch her bracelet, and Mr. Delaford had carried him out in his arms.'

'Well!' said Louis, coolly, without altering a muscle of his face, as the Captain looked for an angry negative.

'And when they got home,—so the story went,—Mr. Frost, the tutor, was so mad with jealousy and rage, that my Lady declared those moorings would not suit her no longer, but had let go, and laid her head right for Beauchastel.'

'Pray what was the young lady supposed to think of the matter?'

'Stories appeared to vary. One version said that Mr. Delaford had found him on his knees to her; and that my Lady had snatched her cruelly away, because she would not have her married before her own daughters, and looked over all the post, for fear there should be a letter for her. Another declared that Miss Conway would not have him at any price, and was set upon the poor tutor, and that he was lying dangerously ill of a low fever. — The women will have it so,' observed the Captain, 'the story's everywhere, except maybe in the parlour at Beauchastel, and I wouldn't wonder if Mrs. Mansell knew it all herself, for her maid has a tongue a yard long. I won't say but I thought there might be some grain of truth at the bottom—'

'And you shall hear it by-and-by, when I know what it is myself.'

'I'd not say I would have believed it the more if that fine gentleman had taken his oath of it—a fellow that ain't to be trusted,' observed the Captain.

This might have led to a revelation, if Louis had had time to attend to it; but he had pity on James's impatient misery, and proceeded to ask the loan of the boat. The tide would not, however, serve; and as waiting till it would was not to be endured, the two cousins set off to walk together through the woods, Louis beguiling the way by chaffing James, as far as he would bear, with the idea of Isabel's name being trifled with by the profane crowd.

He left James at the gate of the park, prowling about like a panther to try for a glimpse of Isabel's window, and feeding his despair and jealousy that Louis should boldly walk up to the door, while he, with so much better a right, was excluded by his unguarded promise to Lady Conway. All the tumultuary emotions of his mind were endlessly repeated, and many a slow and pealing note of the church-clock had added fuel to his impatience, and spurred him to rush up to the door and claim his rights, before Louis came bounding past the lodge-gates, flourishing his cap, and crying, 'Hurrah, Jem! All right!'

'I'm going to her at once!' cried Jem, beginning to rush off; but Louis caught and imprisoned his arm.

'Not so fast, sir! You are to see her. I promise you shall see her if you wish it, but it must be in my aunt's way.'

'Let me go, I say!'

'When I have walked five miles in your service, you won't afford me an arm to help me back. I am not a horse with wings, and I won't be Cupid's post except on my own terms. Come back.'

'I don't stir till I have heard the state of the case.'

'Yes, you do; for all the sportsmen will be coming home, and my aunt would not for all the world that Mr. Mansell caught you on the forbidden ground.'

'How can you give in to such shuffling nonsense! If I am to claim Isabel openly, why am I not to visit her openly? You have yielded to that woman's crooked policy. I don't trust you!'

'When you are her son, you may manage her as you please. Just now she has us in her power, and can impose conditions. Come on; and if you are good, you shall hear.'

Drawing James along with him through the beechwood glades, he began, 'You would have been more insane still if you had guessed at my luck. I found Isabel alone. Mrs. Mansell had taken the girls to some juvenile fete, and Delaford was discreet enough not to rouse my aunt from her letters. I augured well from the happy conjunction.'

'Go on; don't waste time in stuff.'

'Barkis is willing, then. Is that enough to the point?'

'Fitzjocelyn, you never had any feelings yourself, and therefore you trifle with those of others.'

'I beg your pardon. It was a shame! Jem, you may be proud. She trusts you completely, and whatever you think sufficient, she regards as ample.'

'Like her! Only too like her. Such confidence makes one feel a redoubled responsibility.'

'I thought I had found something at which you could not grumble.'

'How does she look? How do they treat her?'

'Apparently they have not yet fed her on bread and water. No; seriously, I must confess that she looked uncommonly well and lovely! Never mind, Jem; I verily believe that, in spite of absence and all that, she had never been so happy in her life. If any description could convey the sweetness of voice and manner when she spoke of you! I could not look in her face. Those looks can only be for you. We talked it over, but she heeded no ways and means; it was enough that you were satisfied. She says the subject has never been broached since the flight from Northwold, and that Lady Conway's kindness never varies; and she told me she had little fear but that her dear mamma would be prevailed on to give sanction enough to hinder her from feeling as if she were doing wrong, or setting a bad example to her sisters. They know nothing of it; but Walter, who learnt it no one knows how, draws the exemplary moral, that it serves his mother right for inflicting a tutor on him.'

'Has she had my letter? Does she know I am here?'

'Wait! All this settled, and luncheon being ready, down came my Lady, and we played unconsciousness to our best ability. I must confess my aunt beat us hollow! Isabel then left us to our conference, which we conducted with the gravity of a tailor and an old woman making a match in Brittany.'

'You came out with that valuable improvable freehold, the Terrace, I suppose?'

'I told the mere facts! My aunt was rather grand about a grammar-school; she said even a curacy would sound better, and she must talk it over with Isabel. I gave your letter, conjuring her to let Isabel have it, and though she declared that it was no kindness, and would put the poor darling into needless perplexity, she was touched with my forbearance, in not having given it before, when I had such an opportunity. So she went away, and stayed a weary while: but when she came, it was worth the waiting. She said Isabel was old enough to know her own mind, and the attachment being so strong, and you so unexceptionable, she did not think it possible to object: she had great delight in seeing you made happy, and fulfilling the dictates of her own heart, now that it could be done with moderate prudence. They go to Scarborough in a fortnight, and you will be welcome there. There's for you!'

'Louis, you are the best fellow living! But you said I was to see her at once.'

'I asked, why wait for Scarborough?' and depicted you hovering disconsolately round the precincts. Never mind, Jem, I did not make you more ridiculous than human nature must needs paint a lover, and it was all to melt her heart. I was starting off to fetch you, when I found she was in great terror. She had never told the Mansells of the matter, and they must be prepared. She cannot have it transpire while she is in their house, and, in fact, is excessively afraid of Mr. Mansell, and wants to tell her story by letter. Now, I think, considering all things, she has a right to take her own way.'

'You said I was not to go without meeting her!'

'I had assented, and was devising how to march off my lunatic quietly, when the feminine goodnatured heart that is in her began to relent, and she looked up in my face with a smile, and said the poor dears were really exemplary, and if Isabel should walk to the beach and should meet any one there, she need know nothing about it.'

'What says Isabel?'

'She held up her stately head, and thought it would be a better return for Mr. Mansell's kindness to tell him herself before leaving Beauchastel; but Lady Conway entreated her not to be hasty, and protested that her fears were of Mr. Mansell's displeasure with her for not having taken better care of her—she dreaded a break, and so on,—till the end of it was, that though we agree that prudence would carry us off to-morrow morning, yet her ladyship will look the other way, if you happen to be on the southern beach at eleven o'clock to-morrow morning. I suppose you were very headlong and peremptory in your note, for I could not imagine Isabel consenting to a secret tryste even so authorized.'

'I never asked for any such thing! I would not for worlds see her led to do anything underhand.'

'She will honour you! That's right, Jem!'

'Neither as a clergyman, nor as a Dynevor, can I consent to trick even those who have no claim to her duty!'

'Neither as a gentleman, nor as a human creature,' added Louis, in the same tone. 'Shall I go back and give your answer?'

'No; you are walking lame enough already.'

'No matter for that.'

'To tell you the truth, I can't stand your being with her again, while I am made a fool of by that woman. If I'm not to see her, I'll be off. I'll send her a note; we will cross to Bickleypool, and start by the mail-train this very night.'

Louis made no objection, and James hurried him into the little parlour, where in ten minutes the note was dashed off:—

> My Own Most Precious One!—(as, thanks to my most unselfish of cousins, I may dare to call you,)—I regret my fervency and urgency for an interview, since it led you to think I could purchase even such happiness by a subterfuge unworthy of my calling, and an ill return of the hospitality to which we owed our first meeting. We will meet when I claim you in the face of day, without the sense of stolen felicity, which is a charm to common-place minds. My glory is in the assurance that you understand my letter, approve, and are relieved. With such sanction, and with ardour before you like mine, I see that you could do no other than consent, and there is not a shadow of censure in my mind; but if, without compromising your sense of obedience, you could openly avow our engagement to Mr. Mansell, I own that I should feel that we were not drawn into a compromise of sincerity. What this costs me I will not say; it will be bare existence till we meet at Scarborough.
>
> 'Your own, J. E. F. D.'

Having written this and deposited it in the Ebbscreek post-office, James bethought himself that his submissive cousin had thrown himself on the floor, with his bag for a pillow, trying to make the most of the few moments of rest before the midnight journey. Seized with compunction, James exclaimed, 'There, old fellow, we will stay to-night.'

'Thank you—' He was too sleepy for more.

The delay was recompensed. James was trying to persuade Louis to rouse himself to be revived by bread-and-cheese and beer, and could extort nothing but a drowsy repetition of the rhyme, in old days the war-cry of the Grammar-school against the present headmaster,—

'The Welshman had liked to be choked by a mouse,
But he pulled him out by the tail,'—

when an alarum came in the shape of a little grinning boy from Beauchastel, with a note on which James had nearly laid hands, as he saw the writing, though the address was to the Viscount Fitzjocelyn.

'You may have it,' said Louis. 'If anything were wanting, the coincidence proves that you were cut out for one another. I rejoice that the moon does not stoop from her sphere.'

> 'My Dear Cousin,—I trust to you to prevent Mr. F. Dynevor from being hurt or disappointed; and, indeed, I scarcely think he will, though I should not avail myself of the permission for meeting him so kindly intended. I saw at once that you felt as I did, and as I know he will. He would not like me to have cause to blush before my kind friends—to know that I had acted a deceit, nor to set an example to my sisters for which they might not understand the justification. I know that you will obtain my pardon, if needed; and to be assured of it, would be all that would be required to complete the grateful happiness of
> 'Isabel.'

The boy had orders not to wait; and these being seconded by fears of something that 'walked' in Ebbscreek wood after dark, he was gone before an answer could be thought of. It mattered the less, since Isabel must receive James's note early in the morning; and so, in fact, she did—and she was blushing over it, and feeling as if she could never have borne to meet his eye but for the part she had fortunately taken, when Louisa tapped at her door, with a message that Mr. Mansell wished to speak with her, if she were ready.

She went down-stairs still in a glow; and her old friend's first words were a compliment on her roses, so pointed, that she doubted for a moment whether he did not think them suspicious, especially as he put his hands behind his back, and paced up and down the room, for some moments. He then came towards her, and said, in a very kind tone, 'Isabel, my dear, I sent for you first, because I knew your own mother very well, my dear; and though Lady Conway is very kind, and has always done you justice,—that I will always say for her,—yet there are times when it may make a difference to a young woman whether she has her own mother or not.'

Isabel's heart was beating. She was certain that some discovery had been made, and longed to explain; but she was wise enough not to speak in haste, and waited to see how the old gentleman would finally break it to her. He blundered on a little longer, becoming more confused and distressed every minute, and at last came to the point abruptly. 'In short, Isabel, my dear, what can you have done to set people saying that you have been corresponding with the young men at Ebbscreek?'

'I sent a note to my cousin Fitzjocelyn last night,' said Isabel, with such calmness, that the old gentleman fairly stood with his mouth open, looking at her aghast.

'Fitzjocelyn! Then it is Fitzjocelyn, is it?' he exclaimed. 'Then, why could he not set about it openly and honourably? Does his father object? I would not have thought it of you, Isabel, nor of the lad neither!'

'You need not think it, dear Mr. Mansell. There is nothing between Lord Fitzjocelyn and myself but the warmest friendship.'

'Isabel! Isabel! why are you making mysteries? I do not wish to pry into your affairs. I would have trusted you anywhere; but when it comes round to me that you have been sending a private messenger to one of the young gentlemen there, I don't know what to be at! I would not believe Mrs. Mansell at first; but I saw the boy, and he said you had sent him yourself. My dear, you may mean, very rightly—I am sure you do, but you must not set people talking! It is not acting rightly by me, Isabel; but I would not care for that, if it were acting rightly by yourself.' And he gazed at her with a piteous, perplexed expression.

'Let me call mamma,' said Isabel.

'As you will, my dear, but cannot you let the simple truth come out between you and your own blood-relation, without all her words to come between? Can't you, Isabel? I am sure you and I shall understand each other.'

'That we shall,' replied Isabel, warmly. 'I have given her no promise. Dear Mr. Mansell, I have wished all along that you should know that I am engaged, with her full consent, to Mr. Frost Dynevor.'

'To the little black tutor!' cried Mr. Mansell, recoiling, but recollecting himself. 'I beg your pardon, my dear, he may be a very good man, but what becomes of all this scrambling over barricades with the young Lord?'

Isabel described the true history of her engagement; and it was received with a long, low whistle, by no means too complimentary.

'And what makes him come and hide in holes and corners, if this is all with your mamma's good will?'

'Mamma thought you would be displeased; she insisted on taking her own time for breaking it to you,' said Isabel.

'Was there ever a woman but must have her mystery? Well, I should have liked him better if he had not given into it!'

'He never did!' said Isabel, indignant enough to disclose in full the whole arrangement made by Lady Conway's manoeuvres and lax good-nature. 'I knew it would never do,' she added, 'though I could not say so before her and Fitzjocelyn. My note was to tell them so: and look here, Mr. Mansell, this is what Mr. Dynevor had already written before receiving mine.'

She held it out proudly; and Mr. Mansell, making an unwilling sound between his teeth, took it from her; but, as he read, his countenance changed, and he exclaimed, 'Ha! very well! This is something like! So that's it, is it? You and he would not combine to cheat the old man, like a pair of lovers in a trumpery novel!'

'No, indeed!' said Isabel, 'that would be a bad way of beginning.'

'Where is the young fellow?—at Ebbscreek, did you say? I'll tell you what, Isabel,' with his hand on the bell, 'I'll have out the dogcart this minute, and fetch him home to breakfast, to meet my Lady when she comes down stairs, if it be only for the sake of showing that I like plain dealing!'

'Isabel could only blush, smile, look doubtful, and yet so very happy and grateful, that Mr. Mansell became cautious, lest his impulse should have carried him too far, and, after having ordered the vehicle to be prepared, he caught her by the hand, and detained her, saying, 'Mind you, Miss, you are not to take this for over-much. I'm afraid it is a silly business, and I did not want you to throw yourself away on a schoolmaster. I must see and talk to the man myself; but I won't have anything that's not open and above-board, and that my Lady shall see for once in her life!'

'I'm not afraid,' said Isabel, smiling. 'James will make his own way with you.'

Isabel ran away to excuse and explain her confession to Lady Conway; while Mr. Mansell indulged in another whistle, and then went to inform his wife that he was afraid the girl had been making a fool of herself; but it was not Lady Conway's fault that she was nothing worse, and he was resolved, whatever he did, to show that honesty was the only thing that would go down with him.

The boat was rocking on the green waves, and Louis was in the act of waving an adieu to deaf Mrs. Hannaford, when a huntsman's halloo caused James to look round and behold Mr. Mansell standing up in his dogcart, making energetic signals with his whip.

He had meant to be very guarded, and wait to judge of James before showing that he approved, but the excitement of the chase betrayed him into a glow of cordiality, and he shook hands with vehemence.

'That's right!—just in time! Jump in, and come home to breakfast. So you wouldn't be a party to my Lady's tricks!—just like her—just as she wheedled poor Conway. I will let her see how I esteem plain dealing! I don't say that I see my way through this business; but we'll talk it over together, and settle matters without my Lady.'

James hardly knew where he was, between joy and surprise. The invitation was extended to his companion; but Fitzjocelyn discerned that both James and Mr. Mansell would prefer being left to themselves; he had a repugnance to an immediate discussion with the one aunt, and was in haste to carry the tidings to the other: and besides, it was becoming possible that letters might arrive from the travellers. Actuated by all these motives, he declined the offer of hospitality, and rowed across to Bickleypool, enlightening the Captain on the state of affairs as far as he desired.

CHAPTER II
THE THIRD TIME

> Tho' this was fair, and that was braw,
> And you the toast of all the town,
> I sighed and said, amang them a',
> Ye are not Mary Morison.
> BURNS.

Mrs. Frost and Louis were very merry over the result of Lady Conway's stratagems, and sat up indulging in bright anticipations until so late an hour, that Louis was compelled to relinquish his purpose of going home that night, but he persisted in walking to Ormersfield before breakfast, that he might satisfy himself whether there were any letters.

It was a brisk October morning, the sportsman's gun and whistle re-echoing from the hill sides; where here and there appeared the dogs careering along over green turnip-fields or across amber stubble. The Little Northwold trees, in dark, sober tints of brown and purple, hung over the grey wall, tinted by hoary lichen; and as Louis entered the Ormersfield field paths, and plunged into his own Ferny dell, the long grass and brackens hung over the path, weighed down with silvery dew, and the large cavernous web of the autumnal spider was all one thick flake of wet.

If he could not enter the ravine without thankfulness for his past escape, neither could he forget gratitude to her who had come to his relief from hopeless agony! He quickened his pace, in the earnest longing for tidings, which had seized him, even to heart sickness.

It was the reaction of the ardour and excitement that had so long possessed him. The victory had been gained—he had been obliged to leave James to work in his own cause, and would be no longer wanted in the same manner by his cousin. The sense of loneliness, and of the want of an object, came strongly upon him as he walked through the prim old solitary garden, and looked up at the dreary windows of the house, almost reluctant to enter, as long as it was without Mary's own serene atmosphere of sympathy and good sense, her precious offices of love, her clear steady eyes, even in babyhood his trustworthy counsellors.

Was it a delusion of fancy, acting on reflections in the glass, that, as he mounted the steps from the lawn, depicted Mary's figure through the dining-room windows? Nay, the table was really laid for breakfast—a female figure was actually standing over the tea-chest.

'A scene from the Vicar of Wakefield deluding me,' decided Louis, advancing to the third window, which was open.

It was Mary Ponsonby.

'Mary!'

'You here?—They said you were not at home!'

'My father!—Where?'

'He is not come down. He is as well as possible. We came at eleven last night. I found I was not wanted,' added Mary, with a degree of agitation, that made him conclude that she had lost her father.

One step he made to find the Earl, but too much excited to move away or to stand still, he came towards her, wrung her hand in a more real way than in his first bewildered surprise, and exclaimed in transport, 'O Mary! Mary! to have you back again!' then, remembering his inference, added, low and gravely, 'It makes me selfish—I was not thinking of your grief.'

'Never mind,' said Mary, smiling, though her eyes overflowed, 'I must be glad to be at home again, and such a welcome as this—'

'O Mary, Mary!' he cried, nearly beside himself, 'I have not known what to do without you! You will believe it now, won't you?'—oh, won't you?'

Mary would have been a wonderful person had she not instantly and utterly forgotten all her conclusions from Frampton's having declared him gone to Beauchastel for an unlimited time; but all she did was to turn away her crimson tearful face, and reply, 'Your father would not wish it now.'

'Then the speculations have failed? So much the better!'

'No, no! he must tell you—'

She was trying to withdraw her hand, when Lord Ormersfield opened the door, and in the moment of his amazed 'Louis!' Mary had fled.

'What is it? oh! what is it, father? cried Louis for all greeting, 'why can she say you would not wish it now?'

'Wish it? wish what?' asked the Earl, without the intuitive perception of the meaning of the pronoun.

'What you have always wished—Mary and me—What is the only happiness that life can offer me!'

'If I wished it a year ago, I could only wish it the more now,' said the Earl. 'But how is this?—I fully believed you committed to Miss Conway.'

'Miss Conway! Miss Conway!' burst out Louis, in a frenzy. 'Because Jem Frost was in love with her himself, he fancied every one else must be the same, and now he will be married to her before Christmas, so that's disposed of. As to my feeling for her a particle, a shred of what I do for Mary, it was a mere fiction—a romance, an impossibility.'

'I do not understand you, Louis. Why did you not find this out before?'

'Mrs. Ponsonby called it my duty to test my feelings, and I have tested them. That one is a beautiful poet's dream. Mary is a woman, the only woman I can ever love. Not an hour but I have felt it, and now, father, what does she mean?'

'She means, poor girl, what only her own scrupulous delicacy could regard as an objection, but what renders me still more desirous to have a right to protect her. The cause of our return—'

'How? I thought her father was dead.'

'Far worse. At Valparaiso we met Robson, the confidential agent. I learnt from him that Mr. Ponsonby had hardly waited for her mother's death to marry a Limenian, a person whom everything pointed out as unfit to associate with his daughter. Even Robson, cautious as he was, said he could not undertake to recommend Miss Ponsonby to continue her journey.'

'And this was all?' exclaimed Louis, too intent on his own views for anything but relief.

'All? Is it not enough to set her free? She acquiesced in my judgment that she could do no otherwise than return. She wrote to her father, and I sent three lines to inform him that, under the circumstances, I fulfilled my promise to her mother by taking her home. I had nearly made her promise that, should we find you about to form an establishment of your own, she would consider herself as my child; but—'

'Oh, father! how shall we make her believe you care nothing for her scruple? The wretched man! But—oh! where is she?'

'It does not amount to a scruple in her case,' deliberately resumed the Earl. 'I always knew what Ponsonby was, and nothing from him could surprise me—even such an outrage on feeling and decency. Besides, he has effectually shut himself out of society, and degraded himself beyond the power of interfering with you. For the rest, Mary is already, in feeling, so entirely my child, that to have the right to call her so has always been my fondest wish. And, Louis, the months I have spent with her have not diminished my regard. My Mary! she will have a happier lot than her mother!'

The end of the speech rewarded Louis for the conflict by which he had kept himself still to listen to the beginning. Lord Ormersfield had pity on him, and went in search of Mary; while he, remembering former passages, felt that his father might be less startling and more persuasive, but began to understand what James must have suffered in committing his affairs to another.

The Earl found Mary in what had been her mother's sitting-room, striving to brace her resolution by recalling the conversation that had taken place there on a like occasion. But alas! how much more the heart had now to say! How much it felt as if the only shelter or rest in the desolate world was in the light of the blue eyes whose tender sunshine had been on her for one instant!

Yet she began firmly—'If you please, would you be so kind as to let me go to Aunt Melicent?'

'By-and-by, my dear, when you think fit.'

'Oh, then, at once, and without seeing any one, please!'

'Nay, Mary,' with redoubled gentleness, 'there is one who cannot let you go without seeing him. Mary, you will not disappoint my poor boy again. You will let him be an amendment in my scheme.'

'You have been always most kind to me, but you cannot really like this.'

'You forget that it has been my most ardent wish from the moment I saw you what only your mother's child could be.'

'That was before— No, I ought not! Yours is not a family to bring disgrace into.'

'I cannot allow you to speak thus. I knew your trials at home when first I wished you to be my son's wife, and my opinion is unchanged, except by my increased wish to have the first claim to you.'

'Lord Ormersfield,' said Mary, collecting herself 'only one thing. Tell me, as if we were indifferent persons, is this a connexion such as would do Louis any harm? I trust you to answer.'

He paced along the room, and she tried to control her trembling. He came back and spoke: No, Mary. If he were a stranger, I should give the same advice. Your father's own family is unexceptionable; and those kind of things, so far off—few will ever hear of them, and no one will attach consequence to them. If that be your only scruple, it does you infinite credit; but I can entirely remove it. What might be an injury to you, single, would be of comparatively little importance to him.'

'Miss Conway,' faltered Mary, who could never remember her, when in Louis's presence.

'A mere delusion, of our own. There was nothing in it. He calls you the only woman who can make him happy, as I always knew you were. He must explain all. You will come to him, my dear child.'

Mary resisted no more; he led her down stairs, and left her within the dining-room door.

'Mary, you will now—' was all Louis said; but she let him draw her into his arms, and she rested against his breast, as when he had come to comfort her in the great thunderstorm in auld lang-syne. She felt herself come at length to the shelter and repose for which her heart had so long yearned, in spite of her efforts, and as if the world had nothing more to offer of peace or joy.

'Oh, Mary, how I have wanted you! You believe in me now!'

'I am sure mamma would!' murmured Mary.

He could have poured forth a torrent of affection, but the suspicion of a footstep made her start from him; and the next moment she was herself, glowing, indeed, and half crying with happiness, but alarmed at her own agitation, and struggling to resume her common-place manner.

'There's your father not had a morsel of breakfast!' she exclaimed, hurrying back to her teacups, whose ringing betrayed her trembling hand. 'Call him, Louis.'

'Must I go?' said Louis, coming to assist in a manner that threatened deluge and destruction.

'Oh yes, go! I shall be able to speak to you when you come back.'

He had only to go into the verandah. His father was watching at the library window, and they wrung each other's hand in gladness beyond utterance.

Mary had seated herself in the solid stately chair, with the whole entrenchment of tea equipage before her. They knew it signified that she was to be unmolested; they took their places, and the Earl carved ham, and Louis cut bread, and Mary poured out tea in the most matter-of-fact manner, hazarding nothing beyond such questions as, 'May I give you an egg?'

Then curiosity began to revive: Louis ventured, 'Where did you land?' and his father made answer, 'At Liverpool, yesterday,' and how the Custom-house had detained them, and he had, therefore, brought Mary straight home, instead of stopping with her at Northwold, at eleven o'clock, to disturb Mrs. Frost.

'You would have found us up,' said Louis.

'You were sleeping at the Terrace?'

'Yes, I walked here this morning.'

'Then your ankle must be pretty well,' was Mary's first contribution to the conversation.

'Quite well for all useful purposes,' said Louis, availing himself of the implied permission to turn towards her.

'But, Louis,' suddenly exclaimed the Earl, 'did you not tell me something extraordinary about James Frost? Whom did you say he was going to marry?'

'Isabel Conway.'

Never was his love of electrifying more fully gratified! Lord Ormersfield was surprised into an emphatic interjection, and inquiry whether they were all gone mad.

'Not that I am aware of,' said Louis. 'Perhaps you have not heard that Mr. Lester is going to retire, and Jem has the school?'

'Then, it must be Calcott and the trustees who are out of their senses.'

'Do you not consider it an excellent appointment?'

'It might be so some years hence,' said the Earl. 'I am afraid it will tie him down to a second-rate affair, when he might be doing better; and the choice is the last thing I should have expected from Calcott.'

'He opposed it. He wanted to bring in a very ordinary style of person, from — — School, but Jem's superiority and the general esteem for my aunt carried the day.'

'What did Ramsbotham and his set do?'

'They were better than could have been hoped; they gave us their votes when they found their man could not get in.'

'Ha? As long as that fellow is against Calcott, he cares little whom he supports. I am sorry that Calcott should be defeated, even for James's sake. How did Richardson vote?'

'He was doubtful at first, but I brought him over.'

Lord Ormersfield gave a quick, searching glance as he said,' James Frost did not make use of our interest in this matter.'

'Jem never did. He and my aunt held back, and were unwilling to oppose the Squire. They would have given it up, but for me. Father, I never supposed you could be averse to my doing my utmost for Jem, when all his prospects were at stake.'

'I should have imagined that James was too well aware of my sentiments to allow it.'

What a cloud on the happy morning!

Louis eagerly exclaimed: 'James is the last person to be blamed! He and my aunt were always trying to stop me, but I would not listen to their scruples. I knew his happiness depended on his success, and I worked for him, in spite of himself. If I did wrong, I can only be very sorry; but I cannot readily believe that I transgressed by setting the question before people in a right light. Only, whose fault soever it was, it was not Jem's.'

Lord Ormersfield had not the heart to see one error in his son on such a day as this, more especially as Mary peeped out behind the urn to judge of his countenance, and he met her pleading eyes, swimming in tears.

'No, I find no fault,' he kindly said. 'Young, ardent spirits may be excused for outrunning the bounds that their elders might impose. But you have not removed my amazement. James intending to marry on the grammar-school!—it cannot be worth 300 pounds a year.'

'Isabel is satisfied. She never desired anything but a quiet, simple, useful life.'

'Your Aunt Catharine delighted, of course? No doubt of that; but what has come to Lady Conway?'

'She cannot help it, and makes the best of it. She gave us very little trouble.'

'Ah! her own daughter is growing up,' said the Earl, significantly.

'Isabel is very fond of Northwold,' said Mary, feeling that Louis was wanting her sympathy. 'She used to wish she could settle there—with how little consciousness!'

'If I had to judge in such a case,' said Lord Ormersfield, thoughtfully, 'I should hesitate to risk a woman's happiness with a temper such as that of James Frost.'

'Oh, father!' cried Louis, indignantly.

'I suspect,' said Lord Ormersfield, smiling, 'that of late years, James's temper has been more often displayed towards me than towards you.'

'A certain proof how safe his wife will be,' returned Louis.

His father shook his head, and looking from one to the other of the young people, congratulated himself that here, at least, there were no perils of that description. He asked how long the attachment had existed.

'From the moment of first sight,' said Louis; 'the fine spark was lighted on the Euston Square platform; and it was not much later with her. He filled up her beau ideal of goodness—'

'And, in effect, all Lady Conway's pursuit of you threw them together,' said Lord Ormersfield, much entertained.

'Lady Conway has been their very best friend, without intending it. It would not have come to a crisis by this time, if she had not taken me to Paris. It would have been a pity if the catastrophe of the barricades had been all for nothing.'

Lord Ormersfield and Mary here broke out in amazement at themselves, for having hitherto been oblivious of the intelligence that had greeted them on their first arrival, when Frampton had informed them of Lord Fitzjocelyn's wound and gallant conduct, and his father had listened to the story like the fastening of a rivet in Miss Conway's chains, and Mary with a flush of unselfish pride that Isabel had been taught to value her hero. They both claimed the true and detailed account, as if they had hitherto been defrauded of it, and insisted on hearing what had happened to him.

'I dare say you know best,' said Louis, lazily. 'I have heard so many different accounts of late, that I really am beginning to forget which is the right one, and rather incline to the belief that Delaford brought a rescue or two with his revolver, and carried us into a fortress where my aunt had secured the windows with feather-beds—'

'You had better make haste and tell, that the true edition may be preserved,' said Mary, rallying her spirits in her eagerness.

'I have begun to understand why there never yet has been an authentic account of a great battle,' said Louis. 'Life would make me coincide with Sir Robert Walpole's judgment on history. All I am clear about is, that even a Red Republican is less red than he is painted; that Isabel Conway is fit to visit the sentinels in a beleaguered castle—a noble being— But oh, Mary! did I not long sorely after you when it came to the wounded knight part of the affair! I am more sure of that than of anything else!'

Mary blushed, but her tender heart was chiefly caring to know how much he had been hurt, and so the whole story was unfolded by due questioning; and the Earl had full and secret enjoyment of the signal defeat of his dear sister-in-law, the one satisfaction on which every one seemed agreed.

It was a melancholy certainty that Mary must go to Mrs. Frost, but the Earl deferred the moment by sending the carriage with an entreaty that she would come herself to fetch her guest. Mary talked of writing a note; but the autumn sun shone cheerily on the steps, and Louis wiled her into seating herself on the upper step, while he reclined on the lower ones, as they had so often been placed when this was his only way of enjoying the air. The sky was clear, the air had the still calm of autumn, the evergreens and the yellow-fringed elms did not stir a leaf—only a large heavy yellow plane leaf now and then detached itself by its own weight and silently floated downwards. Mary sat, without wishing to utter a word to disturb the unwonted tranquillity, the rest so precious after her months of sea-voyage, her journey, her agitations. But Louis wanted her seal of approval to all his past doings, and soon began on their inner and deeper story, ending with, 'Tell me whether you think I was right, my own dear governess—'

'Oh no, you must never call me that any more.'

'It is a name belonging to my happiest days.'

'It was only in play. It reverses the order of things. I must look up to you.'

'If you can!' said Louis, playfully, slipping down to a lower step.

A tear burst out as Mary said, 'Mamma said it must never be that way.' Then recovering, she added, 'I beg your pardon, Louis; I was treating it as earnest. I think I am not quite myself to-day, I will go to my room!'

'No, no, don't,' he said; 'I will not harass you with my gladness, dearest.' He stepped in-doors, brought out a book, and when Mrs. Frost arrived to congratulate and be congratulated, she found Mary still on the step, gazing on without seeing the trees and flowers, listening without attending to the rich, soothing flow of Lope de Vega's beautiful devotional sonnets, in majestic Spanish, in Louis's low, sweet voice.

CHAPTER III
MISTS

> Therefore thine eye through mist of many days
>   Shines bright; and beauty, like a lingering rose,
> Sits on thy cheek, and in thy laughter plays;
>   While wintry frosts have fallen on thy foes,
> And, like a vale that breathes the western sky,
> Thy heart is green, though summer is gone by.
>   F. TENNYSON.

Happy Aunt Kitty!—the centre, the confidante of so much love! Perhaps her enjoyment was the most keen and pure of all, because the most free from self—the most devoid of those cares for the morrow, which, after besetting middle life, often so desert old age as to render it as free and fresh as childhood. She had known the worst: she had been borne through by heart-whole faith and love, she had seen how often frettings for the future were vain, and experienced that anticipation is worse than reality. Where there was true affection and sound trust, she could not, would not, and did not fear for those she loved.

James went backwards and forwards in stormy happiness. He had come to a comfortable understanding with old Mr. Mansell, who had treated him with respect and cordiality from the first, giving him to understand that Isabel's further expectations only amounted to a legacy of a couple of thousands on his own death, and that meantime he had little or no hope of helping him in his profession. He spoke of Isabel's expensive habits, and the danger of her finding it difficult to adapt herself to a small income; and though, of course, he might as well have talked to the wind as to either of the lovers, his remonstrance was so evidently conscientious as not to be in the least offensive, and Mr. Frost Dynevor was graciously pleased to accept him as a worthy relation.

All was smooth likewise with Lady Conway. She and Mr. Mansell outwardly appeared utterly unconscious of each other's proceedings, remained on the most civil terms, and committed their comments and explanations to Mrs. Mansell, who administered them according to her own goodnatured, gossiping humour, and sided with whichever was speaking to her. There was in Lady Conway much kindness and good-humour, always ready to find satisfaction in what was inevitable, and willing to see all at ease and happy around her—a quality which she shared with Louis, and which rendered her as warm and even caressing to 'our dear James' as if he had been the most welcome suitor in the world; and she often sincerely congratulated herself on the acquisition of a sensible gentleman to consult on business, and so excellent a brother for Walter. It was not falsehood, it was real amiability; and it was an infinite comfort in the courtship, especially the courtship of a Pendragon. As to the two young sisters, their ecstasy was beyond description, only alloyed by the grief of losing Isabel, and this greatly mitigated by schemes of visits to Northwold.

The marriage was fixed for the end of November, so as to give time for a little tranquillity before the commencement of James's new duties. As soon as this intelligence arrived, Mrs. Frost removed herself, Mary, and her goods into the House Beautiful, that No. 5 might undergo the renovations which, poor thing! had been planned twenty years since, when poor Henry's increasing family and growing difficulties had decided her that she could 'do without them' one year more.

'Even should Miss Conway not like to keep house with the old woman,' said she, by way of persuading herself she had no such expectation, 'it was her duty to keep the place in repair.'

That question was soon at rest: Isabel would be but too happy to be allowed to share her home, and truly James would hardly have attached himself to a woman who could not regard it as a privilege to be with the noble old lady. Clara was likewise to be taken home; Isabel undertook to complete her education, and school and tuition were both to be removed from the contemplation of the happy girl, whose letters had become an unintelligible rhapsody of joy and affection.

Isabel had three thousand pounds of her own, which, with that valuable freehold, Dynevor Terrace, James resolved should be settled on herself, speaking of it with such solemn importance as to provoke the gravity of those accustomed to deal with larger sums. With the interest of her fortune he meant to insure his life, that, as he told Louis, with gratified prudence, there might be no repetition of his own case, and his family might never be a burden on any one.

The income of the school, with their former well-husbanded means, was affluence for the style to which he aspired; and his grandmother, though her menus plaisirs had once doubled her present revenue, regarded it as the same magnificent advance, and was ready to launch into the extravagance of an additional servant, and of fitting up the long-disused drawing-room, and the dining-parlour, hitherto called the school-room, and kicked and hacked by thirty years of boys. She and Clara would betake themselves to their present little sitting-room, and make the drawing-room pleasant and beautiful for the bride.

And in what a world of upholstery did not the dear old lady spend the autumn months! How surpassingly happy was Jane, and how communicative about Cheveleigh! and how pleased and delighted in little Charlotte's promotion!

And Charlotte! She ought to have been happy, with her higher wages and emancipation from the more unpleasant work, with the expectation of one whom she admired so enthusiastically as Miss Conway, and, above all, with the long, open-hearted, affectionate letter, which Miss Ponsonby had put into her hand with so kind a smile. Somehow, it made her do nothing but cry; she felt unwilling to sit down and answer it; and, as if it were out of perverseness, when she was in Mrs. Martha's very house, and when there was so much to be done, she took the most violent fit of novel-reading that had ever been known; and when engaged in working or cleaning alone, chanted dismal ballads of the type of 'Alonzo the brave and the fair Imogens,' till Mrs. Martha declared that she was just as bad as an old dumbledore, and not worth half so much.

One day, however, Miss Ponsonby called her into her room, to tell her that a parcel was going to Lima, in case she wished to send anything by it. Miss Ponsonby spoke so kindly, and yet so delicately, and Charlotte blushed and faltered, and felt that she must write now!

'I have been wishing to tell you, Charlotte,' added Mary, kindly, 'how much we like Mr. Madison. There were some very undesirable people among the passengers, who might easily have led him astray; but the captain and mate both spoke to Lord Ormersfield in the highest terms of his behaviour. He never missed attending prayers on the Sundays; and, from all I could see, I do fully believe that he is a sincerely good, religions man; and, if he keeps on as he has begun, I think you are very happy in belonging to him.'

Charlotte only curtsied and thanked; but it was wonderful how those kind, sympathizing words blew off at once the whole mists of nonsense and fancy. Tom was the sound, good, religious man to whom her heart and her troth were given; the other was no such thing, a mere flatterer, and she had known it all along. She would never think of him again, and she was sure he would not think of her. Truth had dispelled all the fancied sense of hypocrisy and double-dealing: she sat down and wrote to Tom as if Delaford had never existed, and forthwith returned to be herself again, at least for the present.

Poor Mary! she might speak cheerfully, but her despatches were made up with a trembling heart. Louis and Mary missed the security and felicity that seemed so perfect with James and Isabel. In the first place, nothing could be fixed without further letters, although the Earl had tried to persuade Mary that her father had virtually forfeited all claim to her obedience, and that she ought to proceed as if in fact an orphan, and secure herself from being harassed by him, by hastening her marriage. Of this she would not hear, and she was exceedingly grateful to Louis for abstaining from pressing her, as well as for writing to Mr. Ponsonby in terms against which no exception could be taken.

Till secure of his consent, she would not consider her engagement as more than conditional, nor consent to its being mentioned to any one. If Isabel knew it, that was James's fault. Even the Faithfull sisters were kept in ignorance; and she trusted thus to diminish the wrong that she felt her secrecy to be doing to Aunt Melicent, who was so much vexed and annoyed at her return, that she dreaded exceedingly the effect of the knowledge of her engagement. Miss Ponsonby was convinced that the news had been exaggerated, and insisted that but for Lord Ormersfield's dislike, it would have been further sifted; and she wrote to Mary to urge her coming to her to await the full tidings, instead of delaying among her father's avowed enemies.

Mary settled this point by mentioning her promise to Mrs. Frost to remain with her until her grandchildren should be with her; and Miss Ponsonby's correspondence ceased after a dry, though still kind letter, which did not make Mary more willing to bestow her confidence, but left her feeling in her honest heart as if she were dealing insincerely by Aunt Melicent.

The discretion and reserve rendered requisite by the concealment were such as to be very tormenting even to so gentle a temper as that of Louis, since they took from him all the privileges openly granted to the cousin, and scarcely left him those of the friend. She, on whose arm he had leant all last summer, would not now walk with him without an escort, and, even with Mrs. Frost beside her, shrank from Ormersfield like forbidden ground. Her lively, frank tone of playful command had passed away; nay, she almost shrank from his confidence, withheld her counsel, and discouraged his constant visits. He could not win from her one of her broad, fearless comments on his past doings; and in his present business, the taking possession of Inglewood, the choice of stock, and the appointment of a bailiff, though she listened and sympathized, and answered questions, she volunteered no opinions, ahe expressed no wishes, she would not come to see.

Poor Louis was often mortified into doubts of his own ability to interest or make her happy; but he was very patient. If disappointed one day, he was equally eager the next; he submitted obediently to her restrictions, and was remorseful when he forgot or transgressed; and they had real, soothing, comforting talks just often enough to be tantalizing, and yet to convince him that all the other unsatisfactory meetings and partings were either his own fault, or that of some untoward circumstance.

He saw, as did the rest, that Mary's spirits had received a shock not easily to be recovered. The loss of her mother was weighing on her more painfully than in the first excitement; and the step her father had taken, insulting her mother, degrading himself, and rending away her veil of filial honour, had exceedingly overwhelmed and depressed her; while sorrow hung upon her with the greater permanence and oppression from her strong self-control, and dislike to manifestation.

All this he well understood; and, reverent to her feeling, he laid aside all trifling, and waited on her mood with the tenderest watchfulness. When she could bear it, they would dwell together on the precious recollections of her mother; and sometimes she could even speak of her father, and relate instances of his affection for herself, and all his other redeeming traits of character; most thankful to Louis for accepting him on her word, and never uttering one word of him which she could wish unsaid.

What Louis did not see, was that the very force of her own affection was what alarmed Mary, and caused her reserve. To a mind used to balance and regulation, any sensation so mighty and engrossing appeared wrong; and repressed as her attachment had been, it was the more absorbing now that he was all that was left to her. Admiration, honour, gratitude, old childish affection, and caressing elder-sisterly protection, all flowed in one deep, strong current; but the very depth made her diffident. She could imagine the whole reciprocated, and she feared to be importunate. If the day was no better than a weary turmoil, save when his voice was in her ear, his eyes wistfully bent on her, the more carefully did she restrain all expression of hope of seeing him to-morrow, lest she should be exacting and detain him from projects of his own. If it was pride and delight to her to watch his graceful, agile figure spring on horseback, she would keep herself from the window, lest he should feel oppressed by her pursuing him; and when she found her advice sought after as his law, she did not venture to proffer it.

She was uncomfortable in finding the rule committed to her, and all the more because Lord Ormersfield, who had learnt to talk to her so openly that she sometimes thought he confounded her with her mother, used in all his schemes to appear to take it for granted that she should share with him in the managing, consulting headship of the house, leaving Louis as something to be cared for and petted like a child, without a voice in their decisions. These conversations used to make her almost jealous on Louis's account, and painfully recall some of her mother's apprehensions.

That was the real secret source of all her discomfort—namely, the misgiving lest she had been too ready to follow the dictates of her own heart. Would her mother have been satisfied? Had not her fondness and her desolation prevailed, where, for Louis's own sake, she should have held back! Every time she felt herself the elder in heart, every time she feared to have disappointed him, every time she saw that his liveliness was repressed by her mournfulness, she feared that she was letting him sacrifice himself. And still more did she question her conduct towards her father. She had only gradually become aware of the extent of the mutual aversion between him and the Earl; and Miss Ponsonby's reproaches awakened her to the fear that she had too lightly given credence to hostile evidence. Her affection would fain have justified him; and, forgetting the difficulties of personal investigation in such a case, she blamed herself for having omitted herself to question the confidential clerk, and having left all to Lord Ormersfield, who, cool and wary as he ordinarily was, would be less likely to palliate Mr. Ponsonby's errors than those of any other person. Her heart grew sick as she counted the weeks ere she could hear from Lima.

None of her troubles were allowed to interfere with Mrs. Frost's peace. Outwardly, she was cheerful and helpful; equable, though less lively. Those carpets and curtains, tables and chairs, which were the grand topics at the House Beautiful, were neither neglected nor treated with resigned impatience. Mary's taste, counsel, and needle did good service; her hearty interest and consideration were given to the often-turned volume of designs for bedsteads, sofas, and window-curtains; and Miss Mercy herself had hardly so many resources for making old furniture new. Many of her happiest half-hours with Louis were spent as she sewed the stiff slippery chintz, and he held the curtain rings, while Aunt Catharine went to inspect the workmen, and many a time were her cares forgotten, and her active spirits resumed, while Louis acted carpenter under her directions, and rectified errors of the workmen. It might not be poetical, but the French sky-blue paper, covered with silvery fern-leaves, that Louis took such pains to procure, and the china door-handles that he brought over in his pockets, and the great map which Mary pasted over the obstinate spot of damp in the vestibule, were the occasions of the greatest blitheness and merriment that they shared together. Much did they enjoy the prediction that James would not know his own house; greatly did they delight in sowing surprises, and in obtaining Aunt Catharine's never-failing start of well-pleased astonishment. Each wedding present was an event;—Mr. Mansell's piano, which disconcerted all previous designs; Lord Ormersfield's handsome plate; and many a minor gift from old scholars, delighted to find an occasion when an offering would not be an offence. Even Mr. Calcott gave a valuable inkstand, in which Mrs. Frost and Louis beheld something of forgiveness.

Isabel had expressed a wish that Mary should be one of her bridesmaids. A wedding was not the scene which poor Mary wished to witness at present; but she saw Louis bent on having her with him, and would not vex him by reluctance. He had also prevailed on his father to be present, though the Earl was much afraid of establishing a precedent, and being asked to act the part of father on future contingencies. There was only one bride, as he told Louis, whom he could ever wish to give away. However, that trouble was spared him by Mr. Mansell; but still Louis would not let him off, on the plea that James's side of the house should make as imposing a demonstration as possible.

Mrs. Frost was less manageable. Though warmly invited by the Conways, and fondly entreated by her grandson, she shook her head, and said she was past those things, and that the old mother always stayed at home to cook the wedding dinner. She should hear all when Clara came home the next day, and should be ready for the happy pair when they would return for Christmas, after a brief stay at Thornton Conway, which Isabel wished James to see, that he might share in all her old associations.

All the rest of the party journeyed to London on a November day; and, in gaslight and gloom, they deposited Mary at her aunt's house in Bryanston Square.

Gaslight was the staple of Hymen's torch the next morning. London was under one of the fogs, of which it is popularly said you may cut them with a knife. The church was in dim twilight; the bride and bridegroom loomed through the haze, and the indistinctness made Clara's fine tall figure appear quite majestic above the heads of the other bridesmaids.

The breakfast was by lamp-light, and the mist looked lurid and grim over the white cake, and no one talked of anything but the comparative density of fogs; and Mr. Mansell's asthma had come on, and his speech was devolved upon Lord Ormersfield, to whom Louis had imprudently promised exemption.

What was worse, Lady Conway had paired them off in the order of precedence; and Louis was a victim to two dowagers, between whom he could neither see nor speak to Mary. He was the more concerned, because he had thought her looking depressed and avoiding his eye.

He tried to believe this caution, but he thought she was also eluding his father, and her whole air gave him a vague uneasiness. The whole party were to dine with Lady Conway; and, trusting in the meantime to discover what was on her spirits, he tried to resign himself to the order of the day, without a farther glimpse of her.

When the married pair took leave, Walter gave his sister a great hug, but had no perception of his office of handing her downstairs; and it was Fitzjocelyn who gave her his arm, and put her into the carriage, with an augury that the weather would be beautiful when once they had left the fog in London.

She smiled dreamily, and repeated, 'beautiful,' as though all were so beautiful already to her that she did not so much as perceive the fog.

James pressed his hand, saying, 'I am glad you are to be the one to be happy next.'

'You do not look so,' said Clara, earnestly.

The two sisters had come partly downstairs, but their London habits had restrained them from following to the street-door, as Clara had done; and now they had rushed up again, while Clara, with one foot on the staircase, looked in her cousin's face, as he tried to smile in answer, and repeated, 'Louis, I hoped you were quite happy.'

'I am,' said Louis, quickly.

'Then why do you look so grave and uneasy?'

'Louis!' said an entreating voice above, and there stood Mary—'Pray say nothing, but call a cab for me, please. No, I am not ill—indeed, I am not—but I cannot stay!'

'You look ill! It has been too much for you! Clara, take her—let her lie down quietly,' cried Louis, springing to her side.

'Oh no, thank you—no,' said Mary, decidedly, though very low; 'I told Lady Conway that I could not stay. I settled it with Aunt Melicent.'

'That aunt of yours—'

'Hush! No, it is for my own sake—my own doing. I cannot bear it any longer! Please let me go!'

'Then I will take you. I saw the brougham waiting. We will go quietly together.'

'No, that must not be.'

'I was thoughtless in urging you to come. The turmoil has been too much. My poor Mary! That is what comes of doing what I like instead of what you like. Why don't you always have your own way? Let me come; nay, if you will not, at least let Clara go with you, and come back.'

Mary roused herself at last to speak, as she moved downstairs—'You need not think of me; there is nothing the matter with me. I promised Aunt Melicent to come home. She is very kind—it is not that.'

'You must not tell me not to think. I shall come to inquire. I shall be with you the first thing tomorrow.'

'Yes, you must come to-morrow,' said Mary, in a tone he could not interpret, and a tight lingering grasp on his hand, as he put her into his father's carriage.

He stood hesitating for a moment as it drove off; then, instead of entering the house, walked off quickly in the same direction.

Clara had stood all the time like a statue on the stairs, waiting to see if she were wanted, and gazing intently, with her fingers clasped. When both were gone she drew a long breath, and nodded with her head, whispering to herself, in a grave and critical voice—'That is love!'

She did not see Fitzjocelyn again till nearly dinner-time; and, as he caught her anxious interrogating eye, he came to her and said, very low, 'I was not let in; Miss Ponsonby was engaged. Miss Mary lying down—I believe they never told her I was there.'

'It is all that aunt—horrid woman!'

'Don't talk of it now. I *will* see her to-morrow.'

Clara grieved for him whenever she saw him called on to exert himself to talk; and she even guarded him from the sallies of his young cousins. Once, when much music and talk was going on, he came and sat by her, and made her tell him how fondly and affectionately she had parted with her schoolfellows; and how some of her old foes had become, as she hoped, friends for life; but she saw his eye fixed and absent even while she spoke, and she left off suddenly. 'Go on,' he said, 'I like to hear;' and with a manifest effort he bent his mind to attend.

'Oh!' thought Clara, as she went up that night—'why will the days one most expects to be happy turn out so much otherwise? However, he will manage to tell me all about it when he and his father take me home to-morrow.'

CHAPTER IV
OUTWARD BOUND

> The voice which I did more esteem
> Than music in her sweetest key—
> Those eyes which unto me did seem
> More comfortable than the day—
> Those now by me, as they have been,
> Shall never more be heard or seen.
> GEORGE WITHER.

In suspense and impatience, Fitzjocelyn awaited the end of his father's breakfast, that he might hasten to learn what ailed Mary. The post came in, vexing him at first merely as an additional delay, but presently a sound of dissatisfaction attracted his notice to the foreign air of two envelopes which had been forwarded from home.

'Hem!' said the Earl, gravely, 'I am afraid this fellow Ponsonby will give us some trouble.'

'Then Mary had heard from him!' cried Louis. 'She was keeping it from me, not to spoil the day. I must go to her this moment—'but pausing again, 'What is it? He cannot have had my letter!'

'No, but he seems to have anticipated it. Puffed up as they are about these speculations, he imagines me to have brought Mary home for no purpose but to repair our fortunes; and informs me that, in the event of your marriage, she will receive not a farthing beyond her mother's settlements. I am much obliged! It is all I ever thought you would receive; and but for me, it would have been in the bottom of some mine long ago! Do you wish to see what he says?'

Louis caught up the missive. It was the letter of a very angry man, too violent to retain the cold formality which he tried to assume. 'He was beholden to his lordship for his solicitude about his daughter. It was of a piece with other assistance formerly rendered to him in his domestic arrangements, for which he was equally obliged. He was happy to inform his lordship that, in this instance, his precautions had been uncalled for; and referred him to a letter which he would receive from Mr. Dynevor by the same mail, for an explanation of the circumstances to which he referred. He had been informed, by undoubted authority, that Lord Fitzjocelyn had done his daughter the honour of soliciting her hand. It might console his lordship to learn that, should the union take place, the whole of his property would be secured to Mrs. Ponsonby, and his daughter's sole fortune would be that which she inherited by her mother's marriage settlements. Possibly this intelligence might lead to a cessation of these flattering attentions.'

'Mrs. Ponsonby! he can mention her in the same sentence with Mary's mother!' said the Earl.

Louis turned pale as he read, and scarcely breathed as he looked up at his father, dreading that he might so resent the studied affronts as to wish to break off the connexion, and that he might have him likewise to contend with; but on that score he was set at rest. The Earl replied to his exclamation of angry dismay, 'It is little more than I looked for. It is not the first letter I have had from him. I find he has some just cause for offence. The marriage is less disgraceful than I had been led to believe. Here is Oliver Dynevor's testimony.'

Oliver Dynevor's was a succinct business-like letter, certifying his cousin that he had been mistaken in his view of the marriage. Dona Rosita de Guzman was an orphan of a very respectable family, who had come to spend the year before her intended noviciate at the house of an uncle. She was very young, and Mr. Dynevor believed that the marriage had been hastened by her relations making her feel herself unwelcome, and her own reluctance to return to her convent, and that she might not be aware how very recently Mr. Ponsonby had become a widower. For his own part, he was little used to ladies' society, and could form no judgment of the bride; but he could assure Lord Ormersfield that she had been guilty of no impropriety; she was visited by every one; and that there was no reason against Mary Ponsonby associating with her.

'What could the clerk be thinking of?' exclaimed Louis.

'My first impression was not taken from the clerk. What I heard first, and in the strongest terms, was from the captain of a ship at Valparaiso. In fact, it was in the mouth of all who had known the family. Robson neither confirmed nor contradicted, and gave me the notion of withholding much from regard for his employer. He lamented the precipitation, but seemed willing to make excuses. He distinctly said, he would not take it on himself to recommend Miss Ponsonby's continuing her journey. He was right. If I had known all this, I should still have brought her home. I must write an apology, as far as her character is concerned; but, be that as it may, the marriage is atrocious—an insult—a disgrace! He could not have waited six weeks—'

'But I must go to Mary!' cried Louis, as though reproaching himself for the delay. 'Oh! that she should have forced herself to that wedding, and spared me!'

'I am coming with you,' said the Earl. 'She will require my personal assurance that all this makes no difference to me.'

'I am more afraid of the difference it may make to her,' said Louis. 'You have never believed how fond she is of her father.'

On arriving, they were ushered into the room where Miss Ponsonby was at breakfast, and a cup of tea and untasted roll showed where her niece had been. She received them with stiff, upright chillness; and to their hope that Mary was not unwell, replied—'Not very well. She had been overfatigued yesterday, and had followed her advice in going to lie down.'

Louis began to imagine a determination to exclude him, and was eagerly beginning to say that she had asked him to come that morning—could she not see him? when the lady continued, with the same severity—'Until yesterday, I was not aware how much concern Lord Fitzjocelyn had taken in what related to my niece.'

At that moment, when Louis's face was crimson with confusion and impatience, the door was softly pushed ajar, and he heard himself called in low, hoarse tones. Miss Ponsonby was rising with an air of vexed surprise, but he never saw her, and, hastily crossing the room, he shut the door behind him, and followed the form that flitted up the stairs so fast, that he did not come up with her till she had entered the drawing-room, and stood leaning against a chair to gather breath. She was very pale, and her eyes looked as if she had cried all night, but she controlled her voice to say, 'I could not bear that you should hear it from Aunt Melicent.'

'We had letters this morning, dearest. Always thinking for me! But I must think for you. You can hardly stand—'

He would have supported her to the sofa, but she shrank from him; and, leaning more heavily on the chair, said—'Do you not know, Louis, all that must be at an end?'

'I know no such thing. My father is here on purpose to assure you that it makes not the slightest difference to him.'

'Yours! Yes! But oh, Louis!' with a voice that, in its faintness and steadiness, had a sound of anguish—'only think what I allowed him to make me do! To insult my father and his choice! It was a mistake, I know,' she continued, fearing to be unjust and to grieve Louis; 'but a most dreadful one!'

'He says he should have brought you home all the same—' began Louis. 'Mary, you must sit down!' he cried, interrupting himself to come nearer; and she obeyed, sinking into the chair. 'What a state you are in! How could you go through yesterday? How could you be distressed, and not let me know?'

'I could not spoil their wedding-day, that we had wished for so long.'

'Then you had the letter?'

'In the morning. Oh, that I had examined farther! Oh, that I had never come home!'

'Mary! I cannot hear you say so.'

'You would have been spared all this. You were doing very well without me—as you will—'

He cried out with deprecating horror.

'Louis!' she said, imploringly. 'Oh, Louis! do not make it harder for me to do right.'

'Why—what? I don't understand! Your father has not so much as heard how we stand together. He cannot be desiring you to give me up.'

'He—he forbids me to enter on anything of the sort with you. I don't know what made him think it possible, but he does. And—' again Mary waited for the power of utterance, 'he orders me to come out with Mrs. Willis, in the Valdivia, and it sails on the 12th of December!'

'But Mary, Mary! you cannot be bound by this. It is only fair towards him, towards all of us, to give him time to answer our letters.'

Mary shook her head. 'The only condition, he says, on which he could allow me to remain, would be if I were engaged to James Frost.'

'Too late for that, certainly,' said Louis; and the smile was a relief to both. 'At any rate, it shows that he can spare you. Only give him time. When he has my father's explanation—and my father is certain to be so concerned at having cast any imputation on a lady. His first thought was to apologize—'

'That is not all! I remember now that dear mamma always said she did not know whether he would consent. Oh! how weak I was ever to listen—'

'No, Mary, that must not be said. It was my presumptuous, inveterate folly that prevented you from trusting my affection when she might have helped us.'

'I don't know. It would have caused her anxiety and distress when she was in no state for them. I don't think it did,' said Mary, considering; 'I don't think she ever knew how much I cared.'

The admission could only do Louis's heart good, and he recurred to his arguments that her father could be persuaded by such a letter as he felt it in him to write.

'You do not know all,' said Mary. 'I could not show you his letter; but, from it and from my aunt, I better understand what impressions he has of you all, and how hopeless it is.'

'Tell me!'

She could not help giving herself the relief, when that most loving, sympathizing face was pleading with her to let him comfort her. She knew there was no fiery nor rancorous temper to take umbrage, and it was best for him to know the completeness of the death-blow.

'Oh, Louis! he fancies that my dear mother's fondness for her own family destroyed his domestic peace. He says their pride and narrow notions poisoned—yes, that is the word—poisoned her mind against him; and that was the reason he insisted on my being brought up here, and kept from you all.'

'But I don't understand why he let you come straight home to us, and live in Dynevor Terrace?'

'Then he was really sorry mamma was so ill; and—and for all that was past; I am sure he felt it was the last parting, and only wished to do anything that could make up to her. He freely gave her leave to go wherever she pleased, and said not a word against Northwold. It was one of her great comforts that he never seemed in the least vexed at anything she had done since we went home. Besides, my aunt says that he and Mr. Dynevor had some plans about James and me.'

'He will have that out of his head. He will come to reason. Fond of you, and sorry for the past, he will listen. No wonder he was in a passion; but just imagine what it would be to heed half Jem Frost says when he is well worked up!'

'Papa is not like James,' said Mary; 'things go deeper with him. He never forgets! I shall never forgive myself for not having spoken to Robson! I know his manner, seeming to assent and never committing himself, and I ought to have gone through anything rather than have taken such an accusation for granted.'

To hinder his pleading against her self-conviction, she re-opened her letter to prove the cruelty of the injustice. Mr. Ponsonby professed to have been unwilling to enter so speedily on the new tie; but to have been compelled, by the species of persecution which was exercised on Rosita, in order to make her return to her nunnery. He dwelt on her timid affection and simplicity, and her exceeding mortification at the slur which Mary had been induced to cast upon her; though, he said, her innocent mind could not comprehend the full extent of the injury; since the step his daughter had taken would, when known, seriously affect the lady's reception into society, in a manner only to be repaired by Mary's immediately joining them at Lima. He peremptorily indicated the ship and the escort—a merchant's wife, well known to her and charged her, on her duty, as the only proof of obedience or affection which could remedy the past, to allow no influence nor consideration whatever to detain her. 'You see?' said Mary.

'I see!' was the answer. 'Mary, you are right, you must go.'

The words restored her confiding look, and her face lost almost all the restless wretchedness which had so transformed it. 'Thank you,' she said, with a long breath; 'I knew you would see it so.'

'It will be a very pretty new style of wedding tour. Andes for Alps! No, Mary, you need not suspect me of trifling now! I really mean it, and, seriously, our going in that way would set this Rosita straight with society much more handsomely and effectually. Don't doubt my father—I will fetch him.'

'Stop, Louis! You forget! Did I not tell you that he expressly warns me against you? He must have heard of what happened before: he says I had prudence once to withstand, and he trusts to my spirit and discretion to—' Mary stopped short of the phrase before her eyes—to resist the interested solicitations of necessitous nobility, and the allurements of a beggarly coronet. 'No,' she concluded; 'he says that you are the last person whom he could think of allowing me to accept.' She hid her face in her hands, and her voice died away.

'Happily that is done,' said Louis, not yet disconcerted; 'but if you go, as I own you must, it shall be with a letter of mine, explaining all. You will plead for me—I think you will, and when he is satisfied that we are no rebels, then the first ship that sails for Peru—Say that will do, Mary.'

'No, Louis, I know my father.' She roused herself and sat upright, speaking resolutely, but not daring to look at him—'I made up my mind last night. It was weak and selfish in me to enter into this engagement, and it must be broken off. You must be left free—not bound for years and years.'

'Oh, Mary! Mary! this is too much. I deserved distrust by my wretched folly and fickleness last year, but I did not know what you were to me then—my most precious one! Can you not trust me! Do you not know how I would wait?'

'You would wait,' said poor Mary, striving with choking tears, 'and be sorry you had waited.'

'Are you talking madness, Mary? I should live for the moment to compensate for all.'

'You would waste your best years, and when the time came, you would still be young, and I grown into an old careworn woman. You would find you had waited for what was nothing worth!'

'How can you talk so!' cried Louis, wounded, 'when you know that to cherish and make up to you would be my dearest, fondest wish! No, don't shake your head! You know it is not a young rose and lily beauty that I love,—it is the honest, earnest glance in my Mary's eyes, the rest, and trust, and peace, whenever I do but come near her. Time can't take that away!'

'Pray,' said Mary, feebly, 'don't let us discuss it now. I know it is right. I was determined to say it to-day, that the worst might be over, but I can't argue, nor bear your kindness now. Please let it wait.'

'Yes, let it wait. It is depression. You will see it in a true light when you have recovered the shock, and don't fancy all must be given up together. Lie down and rest; I am sure you have been awake all night.'

'I may rest now I have told you, and seen you not angry with poor papa, nor with me. Oh! Louis—the gratitude to you, the weight off my mind!'

'I don't think any one could help taking the same view,' said Louis. 'It seems to me one of the cases where the immediate duty is the more clear because it is so very painful. Mary, I think that you are committing your way unto the Lord, and you know 'He shall bring it to pass.''

As he spoke there was a tap at the door, and Miss Ponsonby, stiffly entering, said, 'Excuse my interruption, but I hope Lord Fitzjocelyn will be considerate enough not to harass you any longer with solicitations to act against your conscience.'

'He is not persuading me,' said Mary, turning towards her aunt a face which, through all her dejection, proved her peace in his support and approval, 'he is helping me.'

'Yes,' said Louis to the astonished aunt; 'since I have heard the true state of the case, I have been convinced that there is no choice for her but to go out, to repair the injustice so unfortunately done to this poor lady. It is a noble resolution, and I perfectly concur with her.'

'I am glad you think so properly, sir,' returned Miss Ponsonby. 'Lord Ormersfield seems quite of another opinion. He was desirous of seeing you, Mary; but I have been telling him I could permit no more interviews to-day.'

'Oh no,' said Mary, putting her hand to her head, as if it could bear no more; 'not to-day! Louis, tell him how it is. Make him forgive me; but do not let me see him yet.'

'You shall see no one,' said Louis, tenderly; 'you shall rest. There—' and, as if he had the sole right to her, he arranged the cushions, placed her on the sofa, and hung over her to chafe her hands, and bathe her forehead with eau de Cologne; while, as he detected signs of hasty preparations about the room, he added, 'Don't trouble yourself with your arrangements; I will see about all I can to help you. Only rest, and cure your head.'

'Say that one thing to me again,' whispered Mary, ere letting his hand go.

Again he murmured the words, 'Commit thy way unto the Lord, and He shall bring it to pass.'

Then Mary felt her hand pressed to his lips, but she would not unclose her burning eyes; she would fain sleep beneath the impress of that spell of patient confidence.

The gentle authority of his manner had deprived Miss Ponsonby of all notion of interfering. This 'odious, frivolous young man of fashion,' so entirely disconcerted her ideas of ardent lovers, or of self-interested puppies, that she gazed at him, surprised and softened; and when he looked at her anxiously, to judge whether Mary would find in her a kind comforter, her eyes were full of tears, and she said as they left the room, 'It must be a great relief to my poor Mary that you see it so sensibly. She has been suffering much in anticipation of this meeting.'

'Her unselfishness goes to one's heart!' said Louis, almost overcome. 'If she would but have spared herself yesterday!'

'Ah! she said she could not bear that you should be pained on your friend's wedding-day. I am much comforted to find that you appreciate the effort.'

This was not what Miss Ponsonby had intended to say, but there was something about the young man that touched her exceedingly; even when fresh from a very civil and decorous combat with his father, and a ripping-up of all the ancient grievances of the married life of their two relations, rendering wider than ever the breach between the houses of Ponsonby and Fitzjocelyn.

Lord Ormersfield came forward to learn whether he might see Mary, and was met by assurances that she must be kept as quiet as possible; upon which he took leave, making a stately bend of the head, while Louis shook Miss Ponsonby's hand, and said he should come to the door to inquire before the day was over.

'I never saw her so broken down,' he said, in answer to his father's compassionate but indignant exclamation as they walked home. 'Yesterday was a terrible strain on her.'

'I wish we had never brought her here,' said Lord Ormersfield. 'The aunt is your enemy, as she always was that of Mary's mother. She nearly avowed that she set her brother on making this premature prohibition.'

'I do not think she is unkind to Mary,' said Louis; 'I could be almost glad that the dear Aunt Kitty is spared all this worry. It would make her so very miserable.'

'Her influence would be in your favour, whereas this woman is perfectly unreasonable. She justifies her brother in everything, and is actually working on that poor girl's scruples of conscience to send her out by this ship.'

'Nay,' said Louis, 'after hearing her father's letter, I do not see that it is possible for her to do otherwise.'

Lord Ormersfield hastily turned to look at his son's countenance,—it was flushed and melancholy, but fully in earnest; nevertheless the Earl would not believe his ears, and made a sound as if he had missed the words.

'I am grieved enough to say so,' repeated Louis; 'but, as he puts it, I do not see how Mary can refuse to obey him.'

'I declare, Fitzjocelyn,' exclaimed his father, with some anger, 'any one who takes the trouble, may talk you into anything imaginable!'

'Not into believing her wrong.'

'I did not think you so weak!' continued his father. 'It is the very case where a woman's exaggerated notions of right may be wrought on to do her infinite harm! They become quite ridiculous without some one to show that such things may be carried too far! I must say, I did expect strength of mind and common sense for your own interest. I esteem it a mere matter of duty to put an end to such nonsense.'

'My dear father,' said Louis, 'it was Mary and her mother who first taught me my own obligations. I should never dare to interfere with any one's filial duty—above all, where my own happiness is so deeply concerned.'

'Yours! I am not talking of yours. What is to become of Mary with such a man as that? and this Spanish woman, who, if she does not deserve all that has been said of her, no doubt soon will?—no education, no principles, breaking out of her convent! And you let yourself be drawn into calling it Mary's duty to run into such company as that! You are not fit to protect her.'

'From all I have heard of Mr. Ponsonby, I am convinced he has too much regard for his daughter to summon her into any improper society. I do not hear that he has been to blame as a father. I wish I could see it as you do; but not only do I know that Mary could not have an instant's peace under the sense of his displeasure, but it seems to me that this is one of the express commands which could not be disobeyed without setting aside the law of Heaven. If I gave my voice against it, I should fear to bring on us a curse, and not a blessing.'

'Fitzjocelyn, I always knew how it would be if you took to being one of those very good people. Nothing is so weak, and yet so unmanageable. Any rational being would look on it as a duty to rescue her from such a man as that; but that is too ordinary a virtue for you. You must go higher.'

Louis made no answer. Never had his father pained him so much, and he could ill brook additional suffering.

'However,' said the Earl, recovering, 'I shall see her. I shall put the matter in a just light. She is a sensible girl, and will understand me when she has recovered the shock. On one head I shall give warning. She must choose between us and her father. If she persist in going out to join this establishment, I will have your engagement given up.'

'Father! father! you would not be so cruel!'

'I know what I am saying. Am I to allow you to be encumbered all the time she is on the other side of the world, waiting Ponsonby's pleasure, to come home at last, in ten or fifteen years' time, worried and fretted to death, like her poor mother? No, Louis, it must be now or never.'

'You are only saying what I would not hear from her. She has been insisting on breaking off, and all my hope was in you.'

'She has? That is like her! The only reasonable thing I have heard yet.'

'Then you will not help me? You, who I thought loved her like your own daughter, and wished for nothing so much!'

'So I might; but that is a different thing from allowing you to wear out your life in a hopeless engagement. If she cast off her family, nothing could be better, otherwise, I would never connect you with them.'

It did not occur to his lordship that he was straining pretty hard the filial duty of his own son, while he was arguing that Mary should snap asunder the same towards her father.

The fresh discomfiture made poor Louis feel utterly dejected and almost hopeless, but lest silence should seem to consent, he said, 'When you see Mary, you will be willing for me to do anything rather than lose what is so dear and so noble.'

'Yes, I will see Mary. We will settle it between us, and have it right yet; but we must give her to-day to think it over, and get over the first shock. When she has had a little time for reflection, a few cool arguments from me will bring her to reason.'

So it was all to be settled over Louis's passive head; and thus satisfied, his father, who was exceedingly sorry for him, forgot his anger, and offered to go home alone as Clara's escort, promising to return on the Monday, to bring the full force of his remonstrances to bear down Mary's scruples.

Lord Ormersfield believed Clara too much of a child to have any ideas on what was passing; and had it depended on him, she must have gone home in an agony of ignorance on the cause of her cousin's trouble, but Louis came with them to the station, and contrived to say to her while walking up and down the platform, 'Her father is bitter against me. He has sent for her, and she is going!'

Clara looked mutely in his face, with a sort of inquiring dismay.

'You'll hear all about it when my father has told Aunt Kitty,' said Louis. 'Clara,'—he paused, and spoke lower—'tell her I see what is right now; tell her to—to pray for me, that I may not be talked into tampering with my conscience or with hers. Don't let it dwell on you or on my aunt,' he added, cheerfully. 'No, it won't; you will be thinking of Jem and Isabel.' And as his father came up, his last words were, in his own bright tone, 'Tell granny from me that giraffes ought always to be seen by gaslight.'

Clara's countenance returned him a look of sorrowful reproach, for thinking her capable of being amused when he was in distress; and she sat in silent musings all the way home—pondering over his words, speculating on his future, wondering what Mary felt, and becoming blunt and almost angry, when her grave escort in the opposite corner consulted civility by addressing some indifferent remark to her, as if, she said to herself, 'she were no better than a stuffed giraffe, and knew and cared nothing about anybody!'

He might have guessed that she understood something by the sudden way in which she curtailed her grandmother's rapturous and affectionate inquiries about the wedding, ran upstairs on the plea of taking off her bonnet, and appeared no more till he had gone home; when, coming down, she found granny, with tearful eyes, lamenting that Mr. Ponsonby was so harsh and unkind, and fully possessed with the rational view which her nephew had been impressing on her.

'Ha!' said Clara, 'that is what Louis meant. I'll tell you what, granny, Lord Ormersfield never knew in his life what was right, half as well as Louis does. I wish he would let him alone. If Mary is good enough for him, she will go out and wait till her father comes round. If she is not, she won't; and Lord Ormersfield has no business to tease her.'

'Then you would like her to go out?' said Mrs. Frost.

'I like anything that makes Louis happy. I thought it would have been delightful to have him married—one could be so much more at Ormersfield, and Mary would be so nice; but as to their being over-persuaded, and thinking themselves half wrong! why, they would never be happy in their lives; and Louis would be always half-asleep or half mad, to save himself the trouble of thinking. But he'll never do it!'

On the Saturday morning Mary's healthy and vigorous spirit had quite resumed its tone. The worst was over when she had inflicted the stroke on Louis, and seen him ready to support instead of adding to her distress. He found her pale and sorrowful, but calm, collected, and ready for exertion. By tacit consent, they avoided all discussion of the terms on which they were to stand. Greatly touched by her consideration for him on the wedding-day, he would not torture her with pleadings, and was only too grateful for every service that he was allowed to render her without protest, as still her chief and most natural dependence.

She did not scruple to allow him to assist her; she understood the gratification to him, and it was only too sweet to her to be still his object. She could trust him not to presume, his approval made her almost happy; and yet it was hard that his very patience and acquiescence should endear him so much as to render the parting so much the more painful. The day was spent in business. He facilitated much that would have been arduous for two solitary women, and did little all day but go about for Mary, fulfilling the commissions which her father had sent home; and though he did it with a sore heart, it was still a privilege to be at work for Mary.

Rigid as Miss Ponsonby was, she began to be touched. There was a doubt as to his admission when he came on Sunday morning—'Mistress saw no one on Sunday,' but when his name was carried in, Miss Ponsonby could not withstand Mary's face. She took care to tell him her rule; but that, considering the circumstances, she had made an exception in his favour, on the understanding that nothing was to break in upon the observance of the Sabbath.

Louis bent his head, with the heartfelt answer that he was but too glad to be permitted to go to church once more with Mary.

Aunt Melicent's Sunday was not quite their own Sunday, but all that they could desire was to be quietly together, and restricted from all those agitating topics and arrangements. It was a day of rest, and they valued it accordingly. In fact, Miss Ponsonby found the young Lord so good and inoffensive, that she broke her morning's resolution, invited him to partake of the cold dinner, let him go to church with them again in the evening, and remain to tea; and when he took leave, she expressed such surprised admiration at his having come and gone on his own feet, his church-going, and his conduct generally, that Mary could not help suspecting that her good aunt had supposed that he had never heard of the Fourth Commandment.

Miss Ponsonby was one of the many good women given to hard judgments on slight grounds, and to sudden reactions still more violent; and the sight of Lord Fitzjocelyn spending a quiet, respectable Sunday, had such an effect on her, that she transgressed her own mandate, and broached 'the distressing subject.'

'Mary, my dear, I suppose this young gentleman is an improved character?'

'He is always improving,' said Mary.

'I mean, that an important change must have taken place since I understood you to say you had refused him. I thought you acted most properly then; and, as I see him now, I think you equally right in accepting him.'

'He was very much what he is now,' said Mary.

'Then it was from no doubt of his being a serious character?'

'None whatever,' said Mary, emphatically.

'Well, my dear, I must confess his appearance, his family, and your refusal, misled me. I fear I did him great injustice.'

A silence, and then Miss Ponsonby said, 'After all, my dear, though I thought quite otherwise at first, I do believe that, considering what the youth is, and how much attached he seems, you might safely continue the engagement.'

Mary's heart glowed to her aunt for having been thus conquered by Louis—she who, three nights back, had been so severely incredulous, so deeply disappointed in her niece for having been deluded into endurance of him. But her resolution was fixed. 'It would not be right,' she said; 'his father would not allow it. There is so little chance of papa's relenting, or of my coming home, that it would be wrong to keep him in suspense. He had better turn his thoughts elsewhere while he is young enough to begin again.'

'It might save him from marrying some mere fine lady.'

'That will never be, whatever woman he chooses will—' She could not go on, but presently cleared her voice—'No; I should like to leave him quite free. I was less his choice than his father's; and, though I thought we should have been very happy, it does not seem to be the leading of Heaven. I am so far his inferior in cleverness, and everything attractive, and have been made so like his elder sister, that it might not have been best for him. I want him to feel that, in beginning afresh, he is doing me no injury; and then in time, whenever I come home, it may be such a friendship as there was between our elders. That is what I try to look forward to,—no, I don't think I look forward to anything. Good night, Aunt Melicent—I am so glad you like him!'

In this mind Mary met Lord Ormersfield. The delay had been an advantage, for he was less irritated, and she had regained self-possession. Her passage had been taken, and this was an argument that told on the Earl, though he refused to call it irrevocable. He found that there was no staggering her on the score of the life that awaited her; she knew more on that subject than he did, had confidence in her father, and no dread of Rosita; and she was too much ashamed and grieved at the former effect of his persuasions to attend to any more of a like description. He found her sense of duty more stubborn than he had anticipated, and soon had no more to say. She might carry it too far; but the principle was sound, and a father could not well controvert it. He had designed the rupture with Louis as a penalty to drive her into his measures; but he could not so propound it, and was wondering how to bring it in, when Mary relieved him by beginning herself, and stating the grounds with such sensible, unselfish, almost motherly care of Louis's happiness, that he was more unwilling than ever to let him resign her, and was on the point of begging her to re-consider, and let Louis wait for ever rather than lose her. But he knew they ought not to be bound, under such uncertainties, and his conviction was too strong to give way to emotion. He thanked her, and praised her with unwonted agitation, and regretted more than ever; and so they closed the conference by deciding that, unless Mr. Ponsonby should be induced to relent by his daughter's representations on her arrival, Mary and Louis must consider themselves as mutually released.

That loophole—forlorn, most forlorn hope, as they knew it to be—was an infinite solace to the young people, by sparing them a formal parting, and permitting them still to feel that they belonged to each other. If he began declaring that nothing would ever make him feel disconnected with Mary, he was told that it was not time to think of that, and they must not waste their time. And once Mary reminded him how much worse it would be if they had been separated by a quarrel. 'Anger might give one spirits,' he said, smiling mournfully.

'At the time; but think what it would be not to be able to remember happy times without remorse.'

'Then you do mean to recollect, Mary?'

'I trust to bring myself to remember rightly and wisely. I shall try to set it for a reward for myself to cure me of repinings,' said Mary, looking into his face, as if the remembrance of it must bring cheerfulness and refreshment.

'And when shall I not think, Mary! When I leave off work, I shall want you for a companion; when I go to work, the thought must stir me up. Your judgment must try my own.'

'Oh, hush, Louis! this is not good. Be yourself, and be more than yourself, and only think of the past as a time when we had a great deal of pleasantness, and you did me much good.'

'Did I?'

'Yes; I see it now I am with Aunt Melicent. You put so many more thoughts in my head, and showed me that so much more was good and wholesome than I used to fancy. Dear mamma once said you were educating me; and I hope to go on, and not let your lessons waste away.'

'Nay, Mary, you won good everywhere. If you had not been Mary, I might have made you a great goose. But you taught me all the perseverance I ever had. And oh! Mary, I don't wonder you do not trust it.'

'There is the forbidden subject,' said Mary, firmly.

That was the sort of conversation into which they fell now and then during those last days of busy sadness.

Truly it could have been worse. Suffering by their own fault would have rent them asunder more harshly, and Louis's freedom from all fierceness and violence softened all ineffably to Mary. James Frost's letter of fiery indignation, almost of denunciation, made her thankful that he was not the party concerned; and Louis made her smile at Isabel's copy of all his sentiments in ladylike phrases.

The last day came. Louis would not be denied seeing Mary on board the Valdivia; and, in spite of all Miss Ponsonby's horror of railways, he persuaded her to trust herself under his care to Liverpool. She augured great things from the letter which she had entrusted to Mary, and in which she had spoken of Lord Fitzjocelyn in the highest terms her vocabulary could furnish.

They parted bravely. Spectators hindered all display of feeling, and no one cried, except Miss Ponsonby.

'Good-bye, Louis; I will not forget your messages to Tom Madison. My love to your father and Aunt Catharine.'

'Good-bye, Mary; I shall see Tom and Chimborazo yet.'

CHAPTER V
THE NEW WORLD

> Still onward, as to southern skies,
> We spread our sails, new stars arise,
> New lights upon the glancing tide,
> Fresh hues where pearl and coral hide:
> What are they all but tokens true
> Of grace for ever fresh and new!
> > Prayers for Emigrants.

There are some days in the early year, devoid indeed of spring brilliance, but full of soft, heavy, steaming fragrance, pervading the grey air with sweet odours, and fostering the growth of tender bud and fragile stem with an unseen influence, more mild and kindly than even the smiling sunbeam or the gushing shower. 'A growing day,' as the country-people term such genial, gentle weather, might not be without analogy to the brief betrothal of Louis and Mary.

Subdued and anxious, there had been little of the ordinary light of joy, hope, or gaiety, and their pleasures had been less their own than in preparing the happiness of their two friends. It was a time such as to be more sweet in memory than it was in the present; and the shade which had hung over it, the self-restraint and the forbearance which it had elicited, had unconsciously conduced to the development of the characters of both, preparing them to endure the parting far more effectually than unmixed enjoyment could have done. The check upon Louis's love of trifling, the restraint on his spirits, the being thrown back on his own judgment when he wanted to lean upon Mary, had given him a habit of controlling his boyish ways.

It was a call to train himself in manliness and self-reliance. It changed him from the unstable reed he once had been, and helped him to take one steady and consistent view of the trial required of him and of Mary, and then to act upon it resolutely and submissively. With Mary gone, he cared little what became of him until her letters could arrive; and his father, with more attention to his supposed benefit than to his wishes, carried him at once, without returning home, to a round of visits among all his acquaintance most likely to furnish a distracting amount of Christmas gaieties. In the midst of these, there occurred a vacancy in the representation of a borough chiefly under the influence of Sir Miles Oakstead; and, as it was considered expedient that he should be brought into Parliament, his father repaired with him at once to Oakstead, and involved him in all the business of the election. On his success, he went with his father to London for the session, and this was all that his friends at Northwold knew of him. He wrote hurried notes to James or to Mr. Holdsworth on necessary affairs connected with his farm and improvements, mentioning facts instead of feelings, and promising to write to Aunt Catharine when he should have time; but the time did not seem to come, and it was easy to believe that his passiveness of will, increased by the recent stroke, had caused him to be hurried into a condition of involuntary practical activity.

Mary, meanwhile, was retracing her voyage, in the lull of spirits which, after long straining, had nothing to do but to wait in patience, bracing themselves for a fresh trial. Never suffering herself, at sea, her first feelings, after the final wrench of parting, were interrupted by the necessity of attending to her friend, a young mother, with children enough to require all the services that the indefatigable Mary could perform. If Mrs. Willis always averred that she never could have gone through the voyage without Miss Ponsonby, Mary felt, in return, that the little fretful boy and girl, who would never let her sit and think, except when both were asleep, had been no small blessing to her.

Yet Mary was not so much absorbed and satisfied with the visible and practical as had once been the case. The growth had not been all on Louis's side. If her steadfast spirit had strengthened his wavering resolution, the intercourse and sympathy with him had opened and unfolded many a perception and quality in her, which had been as tightly and hardly cased up as leaf-buds in their gummy envelopes. A wider range had been given to her thoughts; there was a swelling of heart, a vividness of sensation, such as she had not known in earlier times; she had been taught the mystery of creation, the strange connexion with the Unseen, and even with her fellow-men. Beyond the ordinary practical kind offices, for which she had been always ready, there was now mingled something of Louis's more comprehensive spirit of questioning what would do them good, and drawing food for reflection from their diverse ways.

She was sensible of the change again and again, when sights recurred which once had only spoken to her eye. That luminous sea, sparkling like floods of stars, had been little more than 'How pretty! how funny!' at her first voyage. Now, it was not only 'How Louis would admire it!' but 'How profusely, how gloriously has the Creator spread the globe with mysterious beauty! how marvellously has He caused His creatures to hold forth this light, to attract others to their needful food!' And the furrow of fire left by their vessel's wake spoke to her of that path 'like a shining light, shining more and more unto the perfect day.' If with it came the remembrance of his vision of the threads of light, it was not a recollection which would lead to repining.

And when at Cape Horn, a mighty ice mountain drifted within view, spired, pinnacled, encrusted with whiteness, rivalled only by the glory of the summer cloud, caverned here and there into hollows of sapphire blue, too deeply dazzling to behold, or rising into peaks of clear, hard, chill green; the wild fantastic points sometimes glimmering with fragments of the rainbow arch; the rich variety, endless beyond measure in form and colouring, and not only magnificent and terrible in the whole mass, but lovely beyond imagination in each crystal too minute for the eye. Mary had once, on a like occasion, only said, 'it was very cold;' and looked to see whether the captain expected the monster to bear down on the ship. But the present iceberg put her in mind of the sublime aspirations which gothic cathedrals seem as if they would fain embody. And then, she thought of the marvellous interminable waste of beauty of those untrodden regions, whence yonder enormous iceberg was but a small fragment—a petty messenger—regions unseen by human eye—beauty untouched by human hand-the glory, the sameness, yet the infinite variety of perfect purity. Did it not seem, with all the associations of cold, of peril, of dreariness, to be a visible token that indeed He who fashioned it could prepare 'good things past man's understanding!'

It was well for Mary that southern constellations, snowy, white-winged albatross, leaping flying-fish, and white-capped mountain-coast, had been joined in her mind with something higher, deeper, and less personal, or their recurrence would have brought her nothing but pain unmitigated in the contrast with the time when first she had beheld them six years ago.

Then she was full of hope and eager ardour to arrive, longing for the parental presence of which she had so long been deprived, hailing every novel scene as a proof that she was nearer home, and without the anticipation of one cloud, only expecting to be loved, to love, and to be useful. And now, all fond illusions as to her father had been snatched away, her very love for him rendering the perception doubly cruel; her mother, her precious mother, far away in Ormersfield churchyard—her life probably shortened by his harshness—her place occupied by a young girl, differing in language, in Church, in everything—Mary's own pardon uncertain, after all her sacrifices—A sense of having deeply offended, hung upon her; and her heart was so entirely in England, that had her home been perfect, her voyage must still have been a cruel effort. That one anticipation of being set at rest by her father's forgiveness, and the forlorn despairing hope of his relenting towards Louis, were all she dared to dwell on; and when Mrs. Willis counted the days till she could arrive and meet her husband, poor Mary felt as if, but for these two chances of comfort, she could gladly have prolonged the voyage for the rest of her life.

But one burning tropical noon, the Valdivia was entering Callao harbour, and Mary, sick and faint at heart, was arraying herself in a coloured dress, lest her mourning should seem to upbraid her father. The voyage was over, the ship was anchored, boats were coming offshore, the luggage was being hoisted out of the hold, the passengers were congregated on deck, eager to land, some gazing with curious and enterprising eyes on the new country, others scanning every boat in hopes of meeting a familiar face. Mrs. Willis stood trembling with hope, excitement, and the strange dread often rushing in upon the last moment of expectation. She clung to Mary for support, and once said—

'Oh, Miss Ponsonby, how composed you are!' Mary's feelings were too deep—too much concentrated for trembling. She calmed and soothed the wife's sudden fright, lest 'something should have happened to George;' and she even smiled when the children's scream of ecstacy infected their mother, when the papa and uncle they had been watching for with straining eyes proved to be standing on deck close beside them.

Mary cast her eyes round, and saw nothing of her own. She stood apart, while the Willis family were in all the rapture of the meeting; she saw them moving off, too happy and sufficient for themselves even to remember her. She had a dull, heavy sensation that she must bear all, and this was the beginning; and she was about to begin her arrangements for her dreary landing, when Mrs. Willis's brother, Mr. Ward, turned back. He was a middle-aged merchant, whom her mother had much liked and esteemed, and there was something cheering in his frank, hearty greeting, and satisfaction in seeing her. It was more like a welcome, and it brought the Willises back, shocked at having forgotten her in the selfishness of their own joy; but they had made sure that she had been met. Mr. Ward did not think that she was expected by the Valdivia; Mr. Ponsonby had not mentioned it as likely. So they were all seated in the boat, with the black rowers; and while the Willises fondled their children, and exchanged home-news, Mr. Ward sat by Mary, and spoke to her kindly, not openly referring to the state of her home, but showing a warmth and consideration which evinced much delicate sympathy.

They all drove together in the Willises' carriage up the sloping road from Callao to Lima, and Mary heard astonishment, such as she had once felt, breaking out in screams from the children at the sight of omnibuses filled with gaily-dressed negroes, and brown horsewomen in Panama hats and lace-edged trousers careering down the road. But then, her father had come and fetched her from on board, and that dear mamma was waiting in the carriage! They entered the old walled town when twilight had already closed in, and Mrs. Willis was anxious to take her tired little ones home at once. They were set down at their own door; but Mr. Ward, with protecting anxious kindness, insisted on seeing Miss Ponsonby safely home before he would join them. As they drove through the dark streets, Mary heard a little restless movement, betraying some embarrassment; and at last, with an evident desire of reassuring her, he said, 'Senora Rosita is thought very pleasing and engaging;' and then, as if willing to change the subject, he hastily added, 'I suppose you did not speak the Pizarro?'

'No.'

'She has sailed about three weeks. She takes home your cousin, Mr. Dynevor.'

Mary cried out with surprise.

'I thought him a complete fixture, but he is gone home for a year. It seems his family property was in the market, and he was anxious to secure it.'

'How glad his mother will be!' was all Mary could say, as there rushed over her the thought of the wonderful changes this would make in Dynevor Terrace. Her first feeling was that she must tell Louis; her second, that two oceans were between them; and then she thought of Aunt Catharine having lived, after all, to see her son.

She had forgotten to expect the turn when the carriage wheeled under the arched entry of her father's house. All was gloom and stillness, except where a little light shone in a sort of porter's lodge upon the eager negro features of two blacks, with much gesticulation, playing at dice. They came out hastily at the sound of the carriage; and as Mr. Ward handed out Mary, and inquired for Mr. Ponsonby, she recognised and addressed the white-woolled old Xavier, the mayor domo. Poor old Xavier! Often had she hunted and teased him, and tried to make him understand 'cosas de Inglaterra,' and to make him cease from his beloved dice; but no sooner did he see her face than, with a cry of joy, 'La Senorita Maria! la Senorita Maria!' down he went upon his knees, and began kissing the hem of her dress.

All the rest of the negro establishment came round, capering and chattering Spanish; and, in the confusion, Mary could not get her question heard—Where was her father? and Xavier's vehement threats and commands to the others to be silent, did not produce a calm. At last, bearing a light, there came forward a faded, sallow dame, with a candle in her hand, who might have sat for the picture of the Duena Rodriguez, and at her appearance the negroes subsided. She was an addition to the establishment since Mary's departure; but in her might be easily recognised the Tia, the individual who in Limenian households holds a position between companion and housekeeper. She introduced herself by the lugubrious appellation of Senora Dolores, and, receiving Mary with obsequious courtesy, explained that the Senor and Senora were at a tertulia, or evening party. She lighted Mary and Mr. Ward into the quadra; and there Mr. Ward, shaking hands with her as if he would thereby compensate for all that was wanting in her welcome, promised to go and inform her father of her arrival.

Mary stood in the large dark room, with the soft matted floor, and the windows high up near the carved timbered ceiling, the single lamp, burning in rum, casting a dim gleam over the well-known furniture, by which her mother had striven to give an English appearance to the room. It was very dreary, and she would have given the world to be alone with her throbbing head, her dull heartache, and the weariness of spirits over-long wound up for the meeting; but her own apartment could be no refuge until it had been cleansed and made ready, and Dolores and Xavier were persecuting her every moment with their hospitality and their inquiries. Then came a quick, manly tread, and for a moment her heart almost seemed to stand still, in the belief that it was her father; but it was only Robson, hurrying in to offer his services and apologies. Perhaps he was the very last person she could bear to see, feeling, as she did, that if he had been more explicit all the offence would have been spared. He was so much aware of all family matters, and was accustomed to so much confidence from her father, that she could not believe him unconscious; and there was something hateful to her in the plausible frankness and deferential familiarity of his manners, as, brushing up his sandy hair upon his forehead, he poured forth explanations that Mr. Ponsonby would be delighted, but grieved that no one had met her—Valdivia not expected so soon—not anticipated the pleasure—if they had imagined that Miss Ponsonby was a passenger—

'My father desired that I would come out by her,' said Mary.

'Ay, true—so he informed me; but since later intelligence'—and he cast a glance at Mary, to judge how much further to go; but meeting with nothing but severity, he covered the impertinence by saying, 'In fact, though the Valdivia was mentioned, and Mrs. Willis, Mr. Ponsonby had reason to suppose you would not receive his letters in time to avail yourself of the escort.'

'I did so, however,' said Mary, coldly.

'Most gratifying. Mr. and Mrs. Ponsonby will be highly gratified. In fact, Miss Ponsonby, I must confess that was a most unfortunate blunder of mine last August. I should not have fallen into the error had I not been so long absent at Guayaquil that I had had no opportunity of judging of the amiable lady; and I will own to much natural surprise and some indignation, before I had had the pleasure of personal acquaintance with the charms and the graces—Hem! In effect, it was a step that no one could have recommended; and when your noble relative put it to me in so many words whether I would counsel your continuing your journey, I could not take it on me to urge a measure so painful to your feelings, unaware as I was then of the amiable qualities of the lady who occupies the situation of the highly beloved and esteemed—'

Mary could not bear to hear her mother's name in his mouth, so she cut him short by saying, 'I suppose you thought you acted for the best, Mr. Robson; it was very unfortunate, but it cannot be helped. Pray can you tell me where the lad Madison is?' she added, resolved to show him that she would not discuss these matters with him; 'I have a parcel for him.'

'He is at the San Benito mine, Miss Ponsonby.'

'How does he go on?'

'Well—I may say very well, allowing for inexperience. He appears a steady, intelligent lad, and I have no doubt will answer the purpose well.'

There was one gratification for Mary, at least, in the pleasure this would afford at home; but Robson continued making conversation about Mr. Dynevor's visit to England, and the quantity of work this temporary absence entailed on him; and then on the surprise it would be to his patron to find her, and Senora Rosita's interest in her, and the numerous gaieties of the bride, and the admiration she excited, and his own desire to be useful. This afforded Mary an opportunity for getting rid of him at last, by sending him to make arrangements for her baggage to be sent from Callao the next morning.

Ten minutes more, half spent in conquering her disgust, half in sick anticipation, and other feet were crossing the matted sala, the curtain over the doorway was drawn aside, and there stood her father, and a lady, all white and diamonds, by his side. He held out his arms, Mary fell into them, and it was the same kind rough kiss which had greeted her six years back. It seemed to be forgiveness, consolation, strength, all at once; and their words mingled—'Papa, you forgive me'—'Mary, my good girl, I did not think they would have let you come back to me. This was but a dreary coming home for you, my dear.' And then, instantly changing his language to Spanish, he added, appealing to his wife, that had they guessed she was on board, they would have come to meet her.

Rosita replied earnestly to that effect, and warmly embraced Mary, pitying her for such an arrival, and hoping that Dolores had made her comfortable. The rest of the conversation was carried on in the same tongue. Rosita was much what Mary had expected—of a beautiful figure, with fine eyes, and splendid raven hair, but without much feature or expression. She looked almost like a dream to-night, however, with her snowy robes, and the diamonds sparkling with their dewdrop flashes in her hair and on her arms, with the fitful light caught from the insufficient candles. All she ventured to say had a timid gracefulness and simplicity that were very winning; and her husband glanced more than once to see if she were not gaining upon his daughter; and so in truth she was, personally, though it was exceedingly painful to see her where Mary had been used to see that dear suffering face; and it was impossible not to feel the contrast with her father as painfully incongruous. Mr. Ponsonby was a large man, with the jovial manner of one never accustomed to self-restraint; good birth and breeding making him still a gentleman, in spite of his loud voice and the traces of self-indulgence. He was ruddy and bronzed, and his eyebrows and hair looked as if touched by hoar frost; altogether as dissimilar a partner as could be devised for the slender girlish being by his side.

After a little Spanish conversation, all kind on his aide, and thus infinitely relieving Mary, they parted for the night. She laid before him the packet of letters, which she had held all this time as the last link to Louis, and sought his eye as she did so with a look of appeal; but he carefully averted his glance, and she could read nothing.

Weary as she was, Mary heard again and again, through her unglazed windows, the watchman's musical cry of 'Ave Maria purisima, las—es temblado!' 'Viva Peru y sereno!' and chid herself for foolish anticipations that Louis would hear and admire all the strange sounds of the New World. The kindness of her welcome gave her a little hope; and she went over and over again her own part of the discussion which she expected, almost persuading herself, that Louis's own conduct and her aunt's testimony must win the day.

She need not have spent so many hours in preparation for the morning. She was up early, in hopes of seeing her father before he went to his office, but he was gone for a ride. The English breakfast, which had been established, much to his content, by her own exertions, had quite vanished, each of the family had a cup of chocolate in private, and there was no meeting till, late in the morning, Rosita sauntered into her room, embraced her, made inquiries as to her rest, informed her that she was going to the Opera that night, and begged her to accompany her. To appear in public with Rosita was the tribute for which Mary had come out, so she readily agreed; and thereupon the Senora digressed into the subject of dress, and required of Mary a display of all her robes, and an account of the newest fashions of the English ladies. It was all with such innocent, earnest pleasure, that Mary could not be annoyed, and good-naturedly made all her disappointing display.

The midday meal brought her father—still kind and affectionate, but never dropping the Spanish, nor manifesting any consciousness of her letters. She had hopes of the period allotted to the siesta, to which custom, in old days, she had never acceded, but had always spent the interval on any special occupation—above all, to writing for him; but he went off without any notice of her, and she was in no condition to dispense with the repose, for her frame was tired out, though her hopes and fears could not even let her dreams rest.

Then came a drive with Rosita, resplendent in French millinery, then supper; then the Opera, to which her father accompanied them, still without a word. Another day was nearly the same, only that this time she had to do her best to explain the newest fashions in behalf of a dress of Rosita's, then being made, and in the evening to go to a party at the Consul's, where she met Mr. Ward, and had some talk which she might have enjoyed but for her suspense.

On the third, Rosita was made happy by unpacking an elegant little black papier mache table, a present from Miss Ponsonby. Good Melicent! were ever two sisters-in-law more unlike? But Lord Ormersfield had done Rosita and her husband good service. If Aunt Melicent had first learned the real facts, her wrath would have been extreme—a mere child, a foreigner, a Roman Catholic, a nun! Her horror would have known no bounds, and she would, perhaps, have broken with her brother forever. But by making the newly-married pair victims of injustice, the Earl had made the reality a relief, and Melicent had written civilly to her brother, and a sisterly sort of stiff letter to the bride—of which the Limenian could not understand one word; so that Mary had to render it all into Spanish, even to her good aunt's hopes that Rosita would be kind to her, and use all her influence in favour of her happiness.

Whether Rosita would have comprehended this without Mary's blushes might be questioned, but she did say, 'Ah! yes! you were to have married the Visconde, were you not? El Senor was so angry! Did his father forbid when your father refused your portion?'

'Oh no, he would receive me if I brought nothing.'

'And you wish to marry?' said Rosita.

'If my father would only consent.'

'But why did you come here then?' said Rosita, opening her large eyes.

'My father commanded me.'

'England is a long way off,' said Rosita, languidly, 'he could not have reached you there. You would have been a great lady and noble! How could you come away, if he would still have you?'

'Because it would have been wrong. We could not have been happy in disobeying my father.'

'Ah! but you could have done penance. I had many penances to do for quitting my convent; Padre Inigo was very severe, but they are over at last, and I am free for giving alms twice a week, and the Sisters have forgiven me, and send me so many silver flowers and dulces; I will show them to you some day. Could you not have done penance?'

'I am afraid not.'

'Ah! I forgot you were a heretic, poor thing! How inconvenient! And so you will not come with me to the bull-fight next Sunday?'

Such being Rosita's ideas on the point, Mary gave up much hope in her influence, and tried what a good-humoured announcement of her re-establishment of the English breakfast would effect towards bringing her father to a tete-a-tete, but he never came near it. The waiting in silence was miserable enough for herself, but she would have continued to bear it except for the injustice to Louis, who must not be kept in suspense. The departure of the next English mail should be the limit of her endurance, and after a day of watching, she finally went up to her father when he would have bidden her good night, and said, in English, 'Papa, if you please, I must speak to you.'

'So you shall, my dear, but we are all tired; we must have our night's rest.'

'No, papa, it must be to-night, if you please. It is necessary for me to know before to-morrow how I am to write to Lord Fitzjocelyn.'

'Pshaw! Mary, I've settled that young fellow!'

'Papa, I don't think you know—'

'I've written him a civil answer, if that's what you mean, much civiller than he or his father deserve,' he said, speaking loud, and trying to fling away from her, but she stood her ground, and spoke calmly and steadily, though her heart beat violently.

'You do not understand the true state of the case, papa; and without doing so, you cannot write such an answer as they deserve.'

'I know this, that old Ormersfield has been the curse of my life!' and out poured one of those torrents of fierce passion which had been slowly but surely the death of his wife. Mary had never heard one in the full tide before, but she stood firm; there were none of the tears, auch as, in her mother, had been wont to exasperate him further, but with pale cheeks, compressed lips, and hands locked together, her heart was one silent entreaty that it might be forgiven him above. Thus she stood while the storm of anger raged, and when at last it had exhausted itself, he said, in a lower voice, 'And so you are still taken with this fellow's son, this young puppy! I thought you had more spirit and sense, Mary, or I never would have trusted you among them.'

'There are very few people in this world half so good or so right-minded as Fitzjocelyn,' said Mary, earnestly and deliberately. 'It was he who bade me come to you, well knowing that we could never be happy without your consent.'

'Oh! he did so, did he? He is deeper than I thought would not risk your fortune. Why, Mary, I did not think a girl of your sense could be so taken in! It is transparent, I tell you. They get you there, flatter you up with their attentions, but when they find you too wise for them the first time, off goes this youth to Miss Conway, finds her a bad speculation, no heiress at all, and disposes of her to his cousin. I wonder if he'll find old Dynevor grateful. Meanwhile the old Lord must needs come out here, finds our gains a better prize than he expected, trumps up this story at Valparaiso, takes you in, and brings you home to this precious youth. And you, and your aunt too, are ready to believe it all! I always knew that women were fools whenever a title came in their way, I see it more than ever now, since you and Melicent are both like the rest of 'em.'

'Papa,' said Mary, again rallying her firmness, 'we have found sadly how easy it is to be deceived when one is not on the spot. Will you listen to me, who saw it all?'

'No, Mary, I will not hear the nonsense they have put into your head, my poor girl. No! I tell you it is of no use! It is my resolute purpose that not one farthing of mine shall go to patch up the broken-down Ormersfield property! The man is my enemy, and has sown dissension in my family from the first moment I connected myself with him. I'll never see my daughter his son's wife. I wonder he had the impudence to propose it! I shall think you lost to all feeling for your father, if you say another word about it.'

'Very well,' said Mary, with steady submission. 'Then I will only write one more letter to Fitzjocelyn, and tell him that your objections are insuperable, and that he must think of it no more.'

'That's right, Mary! you are a good girl, after all! You'll stand by your father, in spite of all the House of Peers! I'm glad to see you hold up your head so bravely. So you did fancy being a Viscountess, did you! but it is not a heartbreaking matter either, my girl!'

This was too much for Mary, and when her father would have kissed her, she laid her head on his shoulder and wept silently but bitterly.

'Ha! what's all this? Why, you don't pretend to care for a young mercenary scamp like that?'

'He is the noblest, most generous, most disinterested man I ever knew!' said Mary, standing apart, and speaking clearly. 'I give him up because—you command me, father, but I will not hear him spoken of unjustly.'

'Ha! ha! so long as you give him up, we won't quarrel. He shall be all that, and more too, if you like; and we'll never fight over the matter again, since I have you safe back, my child.'

'I do not mean to mention him again,' said Mary; 'I wish to obey you.'

'Then there's an end of the matter. You'll get over it, my girl, and we'll find some honest man worth two of your niggardly, proud-spirited earls. There, I know you are a reasonable girl that can be silent, and not go on teasing. So, Mary, you may have a cup of tea for me to-morrow in the sala, like old times. Goodnight, my dear.'

Waiting upon himself! That was the reward that Mr. Ponsonby held out to his daughter for crushing her first love!

But it was a reward. Anything that drew her father nearer to her was received with gratitude by Mary, and the words of kindness in some degree softened the blow. She had never had much hope, though now she found it had been more than she had been willing to believe; and even now she could not absolutely cease to entertain some hopes of the results of Oliver's return, nor silence one lingering fancy that Louis might yet wait unbound; although she told herself of his vacillation between herself and Isabel, of his father's influence, and of the certainty that he would see many more worthy of his love than herself. Not any one who could love him so well—oh no!

But when Mary found her thoughts taking this turn, she rose up as she lay, clasped her hands together, and repeated half aloud again and again, 'Be Thou my all!'

And by the morning, though Mary's cheek was very white, and her eyes sunken for want of sleep, she had a cheerful word for her father, and a smile, the very sight of which would have gone to the heart of any one of those from whom he had cut her off.

Then she wrote her letters. It was not so hard to make this final severance as it had been to watch Louis's face, and think of the pain she had to inflict. Many a time had she weighed each phrase she set down, so that it might offend neither against sincerity nor resignation, and yet be soothing and consoling. Some would have thought her letter stiff and laboured, but she had learned to believe that a grave and careful style befitted a serious occasion, and would have thought incoherency childish or affected.

She released him entirely from his engagement, entreating him not to rebel against the decision, but to join her in thankfulness that no shade need be cast over the remembrance of the happy hours spent together; and begging him not to grieve, since she had, after the first pain, been able to acquiesce in the belief that the separation might conduce to his happiness; and she should always regard him as one of those most near and dear to her, and rejoice in whatever was for his welfare, glad that his heart was still young enough to form new ties. 'Forgive me for speaking thus,' she added; 'I know that it may wound you now, but there may come a time when it may make you feel more at ease and unfettered; and I could not endure to imagine that the affection which you brought yourself to lavish on one so unworthy, should stand in the way of your happiness for life.' She desired him to make no answer, but to consider this as the final dissolution: and she concluded by all that she thought would prove most consoling, as to the present state of affairs with her; and with a few affectionate words, to show that he was still a great deal to her, though everything he might not be.

This done, Mary faced her life in the New World. She had to form her habits for herself, for her importance in the house was gone; but she went to work resolutely, and, lonely as she was, she had far more resources than if she had never been at Ormersfield. She had many hours to herself, and she unpacked her books, and set herself courses of study, to which Louis had opened the door. She unveiled her eyes to natural history, and did not find flower or butterfly unsoothing. She undertook the not very hopeful task of teaching a tiny negro imp, who answered the purpose of a bell, to read and work; and she was persevering in her efforts to get Xavier and Dolores to make her father comfortable.

Her father was decidedly glad of her company. He liked conversation, and enjoyed the morning meeting, to which Mr. Ward was often a welcome addition, delighting in anything so English, and finding Miss Ponsonby much improved by her introduction to English society. Sometimes Mary wrote for her father, and now and then was consulted; and she was always grateful for whatever made her feel herself of use. She was on kind and friendly terms with Rosita, but they did not become more intimate than at first. The Senora was swinging in a hammock half-asleep, with a cigarette between her lips, all the morning; and when she emerged from this torpid state, in a splendid toilette, she had too many more congenial friends often to need her step-daughter in her visits, her expeditions to lotteries, and her calls on her old friends the nuns. On a fast-day, or any other occasion that kept her at home, she either arranged her jewels, discussed her dresses, or had some lively chatter, which she called learning English. She coaxed, fondled, and domineered prettily over Mr. Ponsonby; and he looked on amused, gratified her caprices, caressed her, and seemed to regard her as a pretty pet and plaything.

CHAPTER VI
THE TWO PENDRAGONS

> The red dragon and the white,
> Hard together gan they smite,
> With mouth, paw, and tail,
> Between hem was full hard batail.
>   *The History of Merlin.*

SPRING was on the borders of summer, when one afternoon, as Clara sat writing a note in the drawing-room, she heard a tap at the door of the little sitting-room, and springing to open it, she beheld a welcome sight.

'Louis! How glad I am! Where do you come from?'

'Last from the station,' said Louis.

'What makes you knock at that door, now the drawing-room is alive?'

'I could not venture on an unceremonious invasion of Mrs. James Frost's territory.'

'You'll find no distinction of territory here,' laughed Clara. 'It was a fiction that we were to live in separate rooms, like naughty children. Does not the drawing-room look nice?'

'As much improved as the inhabitant. Where are the other natives?'

'Granny and Isabel are walking, and will end by picking up Jem coming out of school. We used to wait for him so often, that at last he said we should be laughed at, so there's a law against it which no one dares to transgress but granny.'

'So I conclude that you are a happy family.'

'After all, it was worth spending two years at school to enjoy properly the having it over.'

'I give Jem credit for having secured a first-rate governess for you.'

'That she is! Why, with her I really do like reading and drawing all the morning! I almost believe that some day I shall wake up and find myself an accomplished young lady! And, Louis, have you read the last Western Magazine?'

'I have read very little for sport lately.'

'Then I must tell you. Jem was bemoaning himself about having nothing to give to the new Blind Asylum, and the next evening Isabel brought out the prettiest little manuscript book, tied with blue ribbon, and told him to do as he pleased with it. It was a charming account of her expedition to the Hebrides, written out for her sisters, without a notion of anything further; but Jem sent it to this Magazine, and it is accepted, and the first part is out. She will have quite a sum for it, and all is to go to the Blind Asylum!'

'Capital!—Let me take it home to night, Clara, and I will stand an examination on it to-morrow.'

'We ask her whether she projects a sketch of the Paris Revolution,' said Clara, laughing. 'She has a famous heap of manuscripts in her desk, and one long story about a Sir Roland, who had his name before she knew Jem, but it is all unfinished, she tore out a great many pages, and has to make a new finish; and I am afraid the poor knight is going to die of a mortal wound at his lady's feet. Isabel likes sad things best;—but oh! here they come, and I'm talking dreadful treason.'

Three more joyous-looking people could hardly have been found than those who entered the room, welcoming Louis with delight, and asking what good wind had brought him.

'Partly that Inglewood is crying out for the master's eye,' said Louis; 'and partly that my father fancied I looked fagged, and kindly let me run down for a holiday.'

'I am of his mind,' said Mrs. Frost, tenderly; 'there is an M.P. expression gathering on your brows, Louis.'

'For you to dispel, Aunt Kitty. I told him you were the best dissipation, and Virginia was of the same mind. Isabel, she says Dynevor Terrace is the only place she ever wishes to see again.'

'Do you often see Virginia?' asked Isabel.

'Not unless I go early, and beg for her; and then she generally has some master. That last onset of accomplishments is serious!'

'Yes,' said Isabel, 'the sense of leisure and tranquillity here is marvellous!'

'Not leisure in the sense of idleness,' said James.

'No,' said Isabel; 'but formerly idle requirements thronged my time, and for nothing worth doing could I find leisure.'

'There is nothing more exacting than idle requirements,' said James. 'Pray is Clara accepting that invitation? Come to dinner, Louis, and give us an excuse.'

'No, he won't,' said Mrs. Frost, 'he will take my side. These young people want to cast off all their neighbours.'

'Now, granny,' exclaimed James, 'have we not dutifully dined all round? Did not Isabel conduct Clara to that ball? Is it not hard to reproach us with sighing at an evening immolated at the shrine of the Richardsons?'

'Well, my dears, you must judge.'

'I am ready to do whatever you think right; I leave you to settle it,' said Isabel, moving out of the room, that Louis might be free for a more intimate conversation.

'Now,' cried James, 'is it in the nature of things that she should live in such society as Mrs. Walby's and Mrs. Richardson's? People who call her Mrs. James!'

'Such a queen as she looks among them!' said Clara.

'One comfort is, they don't like that,' said James. 'Even Mrs. Calcott is not flattered by her precedence. I hope we shall soon be dropped out of their parties. As long as I do my duty by their sons, what right have they to impose the penance of their society on my wife? All the irksomeness of what she has left, and none of the compensations!'

'Blissful solitude' said Louis, 'thereto I leave you.'

'You are not going yet! You mean to dine here?' was the cry.

'My dear friends,' he said, holding up his hands, 'if you only knew how I long to have no one to speak to!'

'You crying out for silence!' exclaimed James.

'I am panting for what I have not had these five months—space for my thoughts to turn round.'

'Surely you are at liberty to form your own habits!' said James.

'I am told so whenever my father sees me receive a note,' said Louis, wearily; 'but I see that, habituated as he is to living alone, he is never really at ease unless I am in the way; so I make our hours agree as far as our respective treadmills permit; and though we do not speak much, I can never think in company.'

'Don't you have your rides to yourself?'

'Why, no. My father will never ride enough to do him good, unless he wants to do me good. People are all surprised to see him looking so well; the country lanes make him quite blooming.'

'But not you, my poor boy,' said his aunt; 'I am afraid it is a sad strain.'

'There now, Aunt Kitty, I am gone. I must have the pleasure of looking natural sometimes, without causing any vituperation of any one beyond seas.'

'You shall look just as you please if you will only stay. We are just going to dinner.'

'Thank you, let me come to-morrow. I shall be better company when I have had my sulk out.'

His aunt followed him to the stairs, and he turned to her, saying, anxiously, 'No letter?' She shook her head. 'It would be barely possible,' he said, 'but if it would only come while I am at home in peace!'

'Ah! this is sadly trying!' said she, parting his hair on his brow as he stood some steps below her, and winning a sweet smile from him.

'All for the best,' he said. 'One thing may mitigate another. That political whirlpool might suck me in, if I had any heart or hopes for it. And, on the other hand, it would be very unwholesome to be left to my own inertness—to be as good for nothing as I feel.'

'My poor dear boy, you are very good about it. I wish you could have been spared.'

'I did not come to make you sad, Aunt Kitty,' he replied, smiling; 'no; I get some energy back when I remember that this may be a probation. Her mother would not have thought me man enough, and that is what I have to work for. Whether this end well or not, she is the leading star of my life.' And, with the renewal of spirit with which he had spoken, he pressed his aunt's hand, and ran down stairs.

When he rode to Northwold, the following afternoon, having spent the morning in walking over his fields, he overtook a most comfortable couple—James and Isabel, returning from their holiday stroll, and Louis, leaving his horse at the inn, and joining them, began to hear all their school affairs. James had thrown his whole heart into his work, had been making various reforms, introducing new studies, making a point of religious instruction, and meditating on a course of lectures on history, to be given in the evenings, the attendance to be voluntary, but a prize held out for proficiency. Louis took up the subject eagerly, and Isabel entered into the discussion with all her soul, and the grammar-school did indeed seem to be in a way to become something very superior in tone to anything Northwold had formerly seen, engrossing as it did all the powers of a man of such ability, in the full vigour of youth.

Talking earnestly, the trio had reached the Terrace, and James was unlatching the iron gate, when he interrupted himself in the midst of detailing his views on modern languages to say, 'No, I have nothing for you.'

'Sir, I beg your pardon!' was the quick reply from a withered, small, but not ill-dressed old man, 'I only asked—'

'Let the lady pass,' said James, peremptorily, wishing to save his wife from annoyance, 'it is of no use, I never look at petitions.'

'Surely he is not a beggar!' said Isabel, as he drew her on.

'You may be easy about him, my dear,' said James. 'He has laid hold of Louis, who would swallow the whole Spanish legion of impostors. He will be after us directly with a piteous story.'

Louis was after him, with a face more than half arch fun—'Jem, Jem, it is your uncle!'

'Nonsense! How can you be so taken in! Don't go and disappoint granny—I'll settle him.'

'Take care, Jem—it is Oliver, and no mistake! Why, he is as like you as Pendragon blood can make him! Go and beg his pardon.'

James hastened down stairs, as Louis bounded up—sought Mrs. Frost in the sitting-rooms, and, without ceremony, rushed up and knocked at the bed-room door. Jane opened it.

'He is come!' cried Louis—'Oliver is come.'

Old Jane gave a shriek, and ran back wildly, clapping her hands. Her mistress started forward—'Come!—where?'

'Here!—in the hall with Jem.'

He feared that he had been too precipitate, for she hid her face in her hands; but it was the intensity of thanksgiving; and though her whole frame was in a tremor, she flew rather than ran forward, never even seeing Louis's proffered arm. He had only reached the landing-place, when beneath he heard the greeting—'Mother, I can take you home—Cheveleigh is yours.' But to her the words were drowned in her own breathless cry—'My boy! my boy!' She saw, knew, heard nothing, save that the son, missed and mourned for thirty-four years, was safe within her arms, the longing void filled up.

She saw not that the stripling had become a worn and elderly man,—she recked not how he came. He was Oliver, and she had him again! What was the rest to her?

Those words? They might be out of taste, but Fitzjocelyn guessed that to speak them at the first meeting had been the vision of Oliver's life—the object to which he had sacrificed everything. And yet how chill and unheeded they fell!

Louis could have stood moralizing, but his heart had begun to throb at the chance that Oliver brought tidings of Mary. He felt himself an intrusive spectator, and hastened into the drawing-room, when Clara nearly ran against him, but stood still. 'I beg your pardon, but what is Isabel telling me? Is it really?'

'Really! Kindred blood signally failed to speak.'

Clara took a turn up and down the room. 'I say, Louis, ought I to go down?'

'No; leave him and granny to their happiness,' said Louis; and James, at the same moment running up, threw himself into a chair, with an emphatic 'There!'

'Dear grandmamma!' said Isabel; 'I hope it is not too much for her.'

James made no answer.

'Are you disappointed in him, dear James?' she continued.

'I could not be disappointed,' he answered, shortly.

'Poor man—he has a poor welcome among you,' said Louis.

'Welcome is not to be bought,' said James. 'I could not stand hearing him reply to poor granny's heartfelt rapture with his riches and his Cheveleigh, as if that were all she could prize.'

Steps were mounting the stairs, and the alert, sharp tones of Oliver were heard—'Married then? Should have waited—done it in style.'

James and Isabel glanced at each other in amused indignation; and Mrs. Frost entered, tremulous with joy, and her bright hazel eyes lustrous with tears, as she leant on the arm of her recovered son. He was a little, spare, shrivelled man, drolly like his nephew, but with all the youthfulness dried out of him, the freckles multiplied by scores, and the keen black eyes sunken, sharpened, and surrounded with innumerable shrewd puckers. The movements were even more brisk, as if time were money; and in speech, the small change of particles was omitted, and every word seemed bitten off short at the end; the whole man, in gesture, manner, and voice, an almost grotesque caricature of all James's peculiarities.

'Mrs. Roland Dynevor, I presume? said Oliver, as Isabel came forward to meet him.

'Never so known hitherto,' returned her husband. 'My wife is Mrs. James Frost, if you please.'

'That is over now,' said Oliver, consequentially; and as his mother presented to him 'poor Henry's little Clara,' he kissed her affectionately, saying, 'Well-grown young lady, upon my word! Like her father—that's right.'

'Here is almost another grandchild,' said Mrs. Frost—'Louis Fitzjocelyn—not much like the Fitzjocelyn you remember, but a new M.P. as he was then.'

'Humph!' said Oliver, with a dry sound, apparently expressing, 'So that is what our Parliament is made of. Father well?' he asked.

'Quite well, thank you, sir.'

Oliver levelled his keen eyes on him, as though noting down observations, while he was burning for tidings of Mary, yet held back by reserve and sense of the uncongeniality of the man. His aunt, however, in the midst of her own joy, marked his restless eye, and put the question, whether Mary Ponsonby had arrived?

'Ha! you let her go, did you?' said Oliver, turning on Louis. 'I told her father you'd be no such fool. He was in a proper rage at your letter, but it would have blown over if you had stuck by her, and he is worth enough to set you all on your legs.'

Louis could not bring himself to make any answer, and his mother interrupted by a question as to Dona Rosita.

'Like all the rest. Eyes and feet, that's all. Foolish business! But what possessed Ormersfield to make such a blunder? I never saw Ponsonby in such a tantrum, and his are no trifles.'

'It was all the fault of your clerk, Robson,' said James; 'he would not refute the story.'

'Sharp fellow, Robson,' chuckled Oliver; 'couldn't refute it. No; as he told me, he knew the way Ponsonby had gone on ever since his wife went home, and of late he had sent him to Guayaquil, about the Equatorial Navigation—so he had seen nothing;—and, says he to me, he had no notion of bringing out poor Miss Ponsonby—did not know whether her father would thank him; and yet the best of it is, that he pacifies Ponsonby with talking of difficulty of dealing with preconceived notions. Knows how to get hold of him. Marriage would never have been if he had been there, but it was the less damage. Mary would have had more reason to have turned about, if she had not found him married.'

'But, Oliver,' said his mother, 'I thought this Robson was an honest man, in whom you had entire confidence!'

'Ha! ha! D'ye think I'd put that in *any* man? No, no; he knows how far to go with me. I've plenty of checks on him. Can't get business done but by a wide-awake chap like that.'

'Is Madison under him?' asked Louis, feeling as if he had been apprenticing the boy to a chief of banditti.

'The lad you sent out? Ay. Left him up at the mines. Sharp fellow, but too raw for the office yet.'

'Too scrupulous!' said James, in an undertone, while his uncle was explaining to his mother that he could not have come away without leaving Robson to manage his affairs, and Mr. Ponsonby, and telling exultingly some stories of the favourite clerk's sharp practice.

The party went down together in a not very congenial state.

Next to Mrs. Frost's unalloyed gladness, the most pleasant spectacle was old Jane, who volunteered her services in helping to wait, that she might have the delight of hovering about Master Oliver, to whom she attended exclusively, and would not let Charlotte so much as offer him the potatoes. And Charlotte was in rather an excited state at the presence of a Peruvian production, and the flutter of expecting a letter which would make her repent of the smiles and blushes she had expended over an elaborate Valentine, admired as an original production, and valued the more, alas! because poor Marianne had received none. Charlotte was just beginning to repent of her ungenerous triumph, and agitation made her waiting less deft and pretty than usual; but this mattered the less, since to Oliver any attendance by women-servants was a shock, as were the small table and plain fare; and he looked round uneasily.

'Here is an old friend, Oliver,' said his mother, taking up a curious old soup-ladle.

'I see. It will take some time to get up the stock of plate. I shall give an order as I pass through London. To be engraved with the Dynevor crest as before, or would you prefer the lozenge, ma'am?'

'Oh, my dear, don't talk of it now! I am only sorry this is nothing but mutton-broth; but that's what comes of sudden arrivals, Oliver.'

'It shall be remedied at home,' said Oliver, as if he considered mutton-broth as one degree from famine.

'I know you had it for me,' said Louis. 'If Jane excels in one art before all others, it is in mutton-broth.'

Oliver darted a glance as if he imagined this compliment to be mere derision of his mother and Jane.

Things went on in this style all the evening. Oliver had two ideas—Cheveleigh, and the Equatorial Steam Navigation Company—and on these he rang the changes.

There was something striking in his devotion of a lifetime to redeem his mother's fortunes, but the grandeur was not easily visible in the detail. He came down on Dynevor Terrace as a consequential, moneyed man, contemptuous of the poverty which he might have alleviated, and obtruding tardy and oppressive patronage. He rubbed against the new generation in too many places for charity or gratitude to be easy. He was utterly at variance with taste, and openly broached unworthy sentiments and opinions, and his kindness and his displeasure were equally irksome. If such repugnance to him were felt even by Louis, the least personally affected, and the best able to sympathize with his aunt; it was far stronger in James, abhorring patronage, sensible that, happen what might, his present perfect felicity must be disturbed, and devoid of any sentiment for Cheveleigh that could make the restoration compensate for the obligation so unpleasantly enforced; and Isabel's fastidious taste made her willing to hold aloof as far as might be without vexing the old lady.

There was no amalgamation. Fitzjocelyn and Isabel were near the window, talking over her former home and her sisters, and all the particulars of the society which she had left, and he had entered; highly interesting to themselves and to the listening Clara, but to the uninitiated sounding rather like 'taste, Shakspeare, and the musical glasses.'

Oliver and his mother, sitting close together, were living in an old world; asking and answering many a melancholy question on friends, dead or lost sight of, and yet these last they always made sure that they should find when they went home to Cheveleigh—that home to which the son reverted with unbroken allegiance; while the whole was interspersed with accounts of his plans, and explanations of his vast designs for the renovation of the old place.

James hovered on the outskirts of both parties, too little at ease to attach himself to either; fretted by his wife's interest in a world to which he was a stranger, impatient of his uncle's plans, and trebly angered by observing the shrewd curious glances which the old man cast from time to time towards the pair by the window. Fortunately, Mrs. Frost was still too absolutely wrapt in maternal transport to mark the clouds that were gathering over her peace. To look at her son, wait on him, and hear his voice, so fully satisfied her, that as yet it made little difference what that voice said, and it never entered her mind to suppose that all her dear ones were not sharing her bliss.

'You were the first to tell me,' she said, as she bade Louis good night with fondness additional to her messenger of good news; but, as he pressed her dear old trembling hand, his heart misgave him whether her joy might not be turned to pain; and when he congratulated Jane, and heard her call it a blessed day, he longed to be certain that it would prove so.

And, before he could sleep that night, he wrote a letter to Tom Madison, warning him to let no temptation nor bad example lead him aside from strict justice and fair dealing; and advising him rather to come home, and give up all prospects of rising, than not preserve his integrity.

James and Isabel were not merciful to their uncle when they could speak of him without restraint; and began to conjecture his intentions with regard to them.

'You don't wish to become an appendage to Cheveleigh?' said James, fondly.

'I! who never knew happiness till I came here!'

'I do not know what my uncle may propose,' said James, 'but I know you coincide in my determination that he shall never interfere with the duties of my office.'

'You do not imagine that he wishes it?'

'I know he wishes I were not in Holy Orders. I knew he disliked it at the time of my ordination; but if he wished me to act according to his views, he should have given himself the right to dictate.'

'By not neglecting you all your youth.'

'Not that I regret or resent what concerns myself; but it was his leaving me a burden on my grandmother that drove me to become a clergyman, and a consistent one I will be, not an idle heir-apparent to this estate, receiving it as his gift, not my own birthright.'

'An idle clergyman! Never! never!' cried Isabel. 'I should not believe it was you! And the school—you could not leave it just as your plans are working, and the boys improving?'

'Certainly not; it would be fatal to abandon it to that stick, Powell. Ah! Isabel,' as he looked at her beautiful countenance, 'how I pity the man who has not a high-minded wife! Suppose you came begging and imploring me not to give any umbrage to the man, because you so doted upon diamonds.'

'The less merit when one has learnt that they are very cold hard stones,' said Isabel, smiling.

Isabel was a high-minded wife, but she would have been a still better one if her loving admiration had allowed her to soften James, or to question whether pride and rancour did not lurk unperceived in the midst of the really high and sound motives that prompted him.

While their grandmother could only see Oliver on the best side, James and Isabel could only see him on the worst, and lost the greatness of the design in the mercenary habits that exclusive perseverance in it had produced. It had been a false greatness, but they could not grant the elevation of mind that had originally conceived it.

The following day was Sunday, and nothing worse took place than little skirmishes, in which the uncle and nephew's retort and rejoinder were so drolly similar, that Clara found herself thinking of Miss Faithfull's two sandy cats over a mouse; but she kept her simile to herself, finding that Isabel regarded the faintest, gentlest comparison of the two gentlemen almost as an affront. All actual debate was staved off by Mrs. Frost's entreaty that business discussion should be deferred. 'Humph!' said Oliver, 'you reign here, ma'am, but that's not the way we get on at Lima.'

'I dare say,' said James.

Mrs. Frost's joy was still undimmed. It was almost a trance of gladness, trembling in her smile, and overflowing in her eye, at every congratulation and squeeze of the hand from her friends.

'Dear Jemmy,' said she, taking his arm as they went home in the evening, 'did not that psalm seem meant for us?—"If riches increase, set not your heart upon them."'

James had been thinking it meant for some one; but, as he said, 'certainly not for you, dear granny.'

'Ah! snares of wealth were set far enough from me for a time! I never felt so covetous as when there was a report that there was to be an opposition school. But now your dear uncle is bringing prosperity back, I must take care not to set my heart even on what he has gained for me.'

'I defy riches to hurt you,' said James, smiling.

'Ah! Jemmy, you didn't know me as a county grandee,' she said, with a bright sad look, 'when your poor grandpapa used to dress me up. I'm an old woman now, past vanities, but I never could sit as loose to them as your own dear wife does. I never tried. Well, it will be changed enough; but I shall be glad to see poor old Cheveleigh. It does me good to hear poor Oliver call it home. If only we had your dear father!'

'To me Dynevor Terrace is home,' said James.

'A happy home it has been,' said the old lady.

''Goodness and mercy have followed me all the days of my life!' And now, Oliver, whom I never thought to see again—oh! what can I do to be thankful enough! I knew what he was doing! I knew he was not what you all thought him! And roughing it has been no harm to you or Clara, and it is all over now! And the dear old place comes back to the old name. Oh, James, I can sometimes hardly contain myself—that my poor boy has done it, and all for me, and his brother's children!'

James could scarcely find it in his heart to say a single word to damp her joy, and all his resolution enabled him to do was to say gently, 'You know, dear granny, we must not forget that I am a clergyman.'

'I know. I have been telling your uncle so; but we can do something. You might take the curacy, and do a great deal of good. There used to be wild places sadly neglected in my time. I hope that, since it has been given back to us, we may feel it more as a stewardship than I did when it was mine.'

James sighed, and looked softened and thoughtful.

'Your uncle means to purchase an annuity for Jane,' she added; 'and if we could only think what to do for the Faithfulls! I wonder whether they would come and stay with us. At least they can never vex themselves again at not paying rent!'

After a pause—'Jem, my dear, could you manage to give your uncle the true account of your marriage? He admires Isabel very much, I can tell you, and is pleased at the connexion. But I fancy, though he will not say so, that Mr. Ponsonby has desired him to find out all he can about Louis; and unluckily they have persuaded themselves that poor Louis courted Isabel, supposing that she was to have Beauchastel, and, finding his error, betook himself to Mary.'

'Turning Isabel over to me! Extremely flattering.'

'Now, Jem, don't be angry. It is only foolish talk! But unluckily I can't persuade your uncle not to think the real story all my partiality; and you might do much more, if it be not too unpleasant to you.'

'Thank you, granny, it is out of the question. If it were as he does us the honour to imagine, I should be the last person to confess it. My evidence could be of no service to Fitzjocelyn, when my uncle's maxim is to place confidence in no one. The sole refutation in my power is the terms on which we meet.'

'Now, I have vexed you. I wish I had said nothing about it; but when dear Louis's happiness may depend on his report—'

'If I were base enough to have acted as he supposes, I should be base enough to deny it. There is not enough to be hoped to make me speak with unreserve on such a subject.'

He saved himself from saying—to such a man; but the shrewd, suspicious old bachelor was not an inviting confidant for the vicissitudes of delicate and tender feelings of such recent date, and Mrs. Frost reproached herself with asking too much of her proud, sensitive grandson.

The black gown and trencher cap by no means gratified Oliver, when James set off to school on Monday morning; but he consoled himself with observing, 'We shall soon put an end to that.'

'James is quite devoted to the school,' said Isabel, and she was answered by the dry growl.

'It will be a hard thing to transplant our young people,' said Mrs. Frost, 'they have managed to be very happy here.'

'So hard of transplantation that I doubt the possibility,' said Isabel. 'You have made us take very deep root here.'

'Have you ever seen Cheveleigh, Mrs. Dynevor?'

'Never.'

'Poor Oliver! you and I think no place equal to our birthplace,' said Mrs. Frost.

'I should think Mrs. Roland Dynevor would find it compensation. How many beds did we make up, mother, the year my father was sheriff?'

'You must go to Jane for that,' said his mother, laughing. 'I'm sure I never knew.'

'I believe it was twenty-seven,' said Oliver, gravely. 'I know there were one hundred and eighty-five persons at the ball, and that the room was hung with blue brocade, mother; and you opened the ball with Lord Francis. I remember you had violet satin and white blonde.'

'My dear, how can you remember such things! You were a little bit of a schoolboy!'

'I was sixteen' said Oliver. 'It was the year '13. I will have the drawing-room hung with blue brocade, and I think Mrs. Roland Dynevor will own that nothing can exceed it.'

'Very likely,' said Isabel, indifferently; and she escaped, beckoning with her Clara, who was rather entertained with the reminiscences over which granny and Uncle Oliver seemed ready to linger for ever; and yet she was rather ashamed of her own amusement and interest, when she heard her sister-in-law say, 'If he did but know how weary I am of that hateful thing, a great house!'

'I hope Cheveleigh is not grander than Ormersfield,' said Clara, in an odd sort of voice.

The ladies, for the first time, did not sit together this morning. Clara practised, and Isabel took the Chapel in the Valley out of her desk, and began a process of turning the Sir Roland into Sir Hubert.

Oliver and his mother were in the sitting-room, and, on James's return from school in the middle of the day, he was summoned thither. Mrs. Frost was sitting by the fire, rather tearful and nervous, and her son stood full in the front, as dignified and magnanimous as size and features would permit, and the same demeanour was instantly and unconsciously assumed by his nephew, who was beyond measure chafed by the attempt at a grand coup.

'I have requested your presence,' began Oliver, 'as the eldest son of my elder brother, and thus, after my mother, the head of our family. You are aware that when unfortunate circumstances involved my mother's property, it was my determination to restore the inheritance to her, and to my dear brother Henry. For this object, I have worked for the last thirty-four years, and a fortunate accident having brought our family estate into the market, I have been enabled to secure it. I am now ready to make it over to my mother, with entail to yourself and your heirs, as representatives of my brother Henry, and settling five thousand pounds on your sister, as the portion to which the younger children of our family have always been entitled. If you are willing to reside at our family seat with my mother, I will assure you of a suitable allowance during her lifetime, and—'

Nothing was more intolerable to a man like James than a shower of obligations; and his spirit, angered at the very length of the address, caught at the first opening for avoiding gratitude, and beheld in the last proposal an absolute bribe to make him sacrifice his sacred ministry, and he burst forth, 'Sir, I am much obliged to you, but no offers shall induce me to forsake the duties of my calling.'

'You mistake, if you think I want anything unclerical. No occasion to hunt—Mr. Tresham used in my day—no one thought the worse of him—unlucky your taking Orders.'

'There is no use in entering on that point,' said James. 'No other course was left open to me, and my profession cannot be taken up nor laid down as a matter of convenience.'

'Young men are taught to think more seriously than they were in our day,' said Mrs. Frost. 'I told you that you must not try to make him turn squire.'

'Well! well! good living may be had perhaps. Move to Cheveleigh, and look out for it at leisure, if nothing else will content him. But we'll have this drudgery given up. I'll not go home and show my nephew, heir of the Dynevors, keeping a third-rate grammar-school,' said Oliver, with his one remaining Eton quality of contempt for provincial schools.

The Northwold scholar and master were both roused to arms in James.

'Sir,' he said, 'you should have thought of that when you left this heir of the Dynevors to be educated by the charity of this third-rate grammar-school.'

'Is this your gratitude, sir!' passionately exclaimed Oliver; 'I, who have toiled my whole life for your benefit, might look for another return.'

'It was not for me,' said James. 'It was for family pride. Had it been from the affection that claims gratitude, you would not have left your mother in her old age, to labour unaided for the support of your brother's orphans. For ourselves, I thank you; the habits nurtured by poverty are the best education; but I cannot let you suppose that a grand theatrical restoration can atone to me for thirty years' neglect of my grandmother, or that my gratitude can be extorted by benefactions at the expense of her past suffering.'

'Jem! dear Jem! what are you saying!' cried Mrs. Frost. 'Don't you know how kindly your uncle meant? Don't you know how happy we have been?'

'You may forgive. You are his mother, and you were injured, but I can never forget what I have seen you undergo.'

'You foolish boy, to forget all our happiness—'

'Nor,' proceeded James, 'can I consent to forego the career of usefulness that has been opened to me.'

'But, Jem, you could be so useful in the parish! and your uncle could not wish you to do anything unhandsome by the trustees—'

'I wish him to do nothing, ma'am,' said Oliver. 'If he is too high and mighty to accept a favour, it is his own loss. We can do without him, if he prefers the Fitzjocelyn patronage. Much good may it do him!'

James deigned no answer, looked at his watch, and found it time to return to the school.

Oliver broke out into angry exclamations, and his mother did her utmost to soothe him. He had no turn for being a country-gentleman, he was fit for nothing but his counting-house, and he intended to return thither as soon as he had installed his mother at Cheveleigh; and so entirely did all his plans hinge upon his nephew, that even now he was persuaded to hold out his forgiveness, on condition that James would apologize, resign the school, and call himself Dynevor.

Mrs. Frost hoped that Isabel would prevail on her husband to listen favourably; but Isabel gloried in his impracticability, and would have regarded any attempt at mediation as an unworthy effort to turn him aside from the path of duty. She replied, that she would never say a word to change his notions of right, and she treated poor Oliver with all the lofty reserve that she had formerly practised upon possible suitors.

When Fitzjocelyn came in the afternoon to take leave, before his return to London, Mrs. Frost begged him to use his influence with James. 'Who would have thought it would have so turned out?' she said. 'My poor Oliver! to be so met after all his generous plans! and yet Jem does want to do right!'

Unfortunately, Louis felt that, to own Oliver's generosity, it was necessary to be out of sight of him; and finding that there was silence and constraint in the drawing-room, he asked Isabel to walk with him to meet James.

'One breathes freely!' said she, as they left the house. 'Was there ever a more intolerable man?'

'Never was a man who made a more unlucky error in judgment.'

'And that is all you call it?'

'The spurious object warped the mind aside,' said Louis. 'The grand idea was too exclusive, and now he suffers for the exclusiveness. It is melancholy to see the cinder of a burnt-offering to Mammon, especially when the offering was meant for better things.'

In this strain he chose to talk, without coming to particulars, till, near the corner of the old square, they met the shouting throng of boys, and presently James himself, descending the steps of the grim old grey building.

'I thought you would forgive me for coming to meet you under such an escort,' said Isabel, 'especially as it was to escape from our Peruvian relative.'

'Poor man! it was a great pity he did not come last year!' said Louis.

'I am glad I have no temptation to bend to his will,' returned James.

'Ha! I like the true core of the quarrel to display itself.'

'Fitzjocelyn, you do not mean that you do not fully approve of the course I have taken!'

'Extremely magnanimous, but not quite unprecedented. Witness St. Ronan's Well, where the younger Scrogie abjures the name of Mowbray.'

'Pshaw! Louis, can't you understand? Frost is a glorious name to me, recording my grandmother's noble exertions on our behalf, but I can imagine it to be hateful to him, recalling the neglect that made her slaving necessary.'

'For which amiable reason you insist on obtruding it. Pray, are the houses henceforth to be Frost Terrace or Arctic Row?'

'Are you come to laugh or to remonstrate?' exclaimed James, stopping.

'Oh! you want to put on your armour! Certainly, I should never tell if I were come to remonstrate, nor should I venture in such a case—'

'Then you are come to approve,' said Isabel. I knew it!'

'Little you two care—each of you sure of an admiring double.'

'I care for your opinion as much as ever I did,' said James.

'Exactly so,' said Louis, laughing.

'I desire to have your judgment in this matter.'

'If I could judge, I would,' said Louis. 'I see you right in principle, but are you right in spirit? I own my heart bleeds for Aunt Kitty, regaining her son to battle with her grandson.'

'I am very sorry for her,' said James; 'but it can't be helped. I cannot resign my duties here for the sake of living dependent on a suitable allowance.'

'Ah! Jem! Jem! Oliver little knew the damage his neglect did you.'

'What damage?'

'The fostering an ugly little imp of independence.'

'Aye! you grandees have naturally a distaste for independence, and make common cause against it.'

'Especially when in a rabid state. Take care, Jem. Independence never was a Christian duty yet—'

'Then, you want me to go and live on the hoards for the sake of which my grandmother was left to toil. You would like to see me loitering about, pensioned to swell the vanity of Cheveleigh, neglecting my vows, forsaking my duties—'

'You unreasonable man! Is there no way in this whole world for you to do your duty as a clergyman, but hearing Northwold boys the Latin grammar?'

'Then, what do you want me to do?'

'I don't want you to do anything. You are the man to know what is right; only, Isabel, don't help him to hate people more than can possibly be avoided; and don't break dear Aunt Kitty's heart amongst you. That's what I care most about!'

When Louis bade his aunt farewell, he threw his arm round her neck, looked fondly at her, and said, 'Dear aunt, you won't let them tease you?'

'No, my dear, I am getting past being teased,' she said. 'Vexations don't hurt me as much as love does me good, and they'll not forget their affection. It is all goodness in Jem, and poor Oliver will understand it when I have got him into our home ways again; but he has been so long away from home, poor fellow!'

'That's right. I won't be uneasy for you. Squabble as they will, they won't hurt you. But, oh! Dynevor Terrace without you!'

'Ah! you must come to me at *home*!'

'Home! I'm like Jem, jealous for this old house.'

'It is odd how little I feel these things,' said his aunt. 'If any one had told me, when I tore myself away from Cheveleigh, that I should have it back, how little I should have thought that I could take it so easily! I wonder at myself when I wake in the morning that I am not more moved by it, nor by leaving this dear old place. I suppose it is because I have not long to stay anywhere. I can keep nothing in my head, but that I have got my Oliver!'

'I believe it is the peace that is not of this world!' said Louis.

CHAPTER VII
ROLAND AND OLIVER

'Twas old ancestral pride,
'Twas hope to raise a fallen house
From penury's disgrace,
To purchase back from usurers
The birthright of his race.
The Lump of Gold—C. MACKAY.

Mary's letter arrived not long after Louis's return to London; and her calm, serious, beautifully-expressed farewell came upon him at last like a blow which had been long impending, but of which preparation had failed to lessen the weight.

'Ah!' said the Earl, when the chief part had been read to him, 'she is admirable and excellent as ever. It is a great disappointment that she is unattainable, but I am glad she writes so sensibly, and sees that it is right you should think no more about her. After all, the connexion with that fellow Ponsonby might have been very troublesome, and it is well, as she says, that it was all over while you are so young.'

'Young or old, there is no other Mary in the world,' said Louis, sadly.

'We will say no more about it now. I understand you, but you will think differently by-and-by.'

Louis did not answer. He knew that others might have been deceived by the tardiness and uncertainty of his attachment, but that it had taken such deep root, that he believed he could no more detach himself from Mary than if she were his wife. His heart fainted as he thought of years without the strength and soothing which her very letter breathed forth; as he pictured to himself alternations between his chill and stately home and the weary maze of London, foresaw persuasions from his father to induce him to form some new attachment, and dreaded to think of the facility with which, perhaps, he might still be led out of his own convictions. Yet he still believed that patience and perseverance would win the day, and tried to derive encouragement and energy from the thought that this might be a trial sent for the very purpose of training him in steadfastness.

A strong impulse drew him to Bryanston Square, where Miss Ponsonby was very kind and warm, the more so because she had discovered how much easier it had been to say than to unsay, and strongly regretted the injustice she had done him. He had the satisfaction of talking for a good hour about Mary, and of sending a message, that he did not write because he wished to be guided by her in everything, and that he was striving to work so as to please her. The conversation ended with some good auguries as to the effect of Oliver's return to Peru; and Louis went away cheered, bearing the final dismissal better than his father had expected. Lord Ormersfield attributed his tranquillity to having his mind settled; and so it was, though not quite as his lordship imagined.

Meantime, there was a lull at Dynevor Terrace. Oliver was gone to take possession and furnish the mansion, and Mrs. Frost's great object was to keep the subject from irritating her grandson, so as to save him from binding himself by any rash vows. Cheveleigh was treated in the domestic circle with judicious silence, Oliver's letters were read by his mother in private, and their contents communicated to Jane alone, whose happiness was surpassing, and her contempt for Dynevor Terrace quite provoking to poor Mrs. Martha.

'Really,' said Charlotte one day, 'I don't think a catastrophe is half so pretty as it ought to be. Mr. Oliver is but a poor little puny man, and I never knew Mr. James so hard to please.'

Charlotte and Marianne had begun to merge their rivalry in honest friendship, cemented by Marianne's increasing weakness, and difficulty in getting through even the light work her mistress required. Jane petted her now still more than Charlotte, and was always promising her the delightful air and the luxuries of Cheveleigh.

'See here, Charlotte,' said Marianne, one afternoon when they sat down together to their sewing; Marianne's eyes were brighter, and her cheeks pinker, than for many days—'See here; it is for your good I show it you, that you mayn't build on no false expectations. It was marked private; but I think it but fair you should see.'

'Mine was marked private too,' said Charlotte, slowly, as she fixed her eyes on the envelope Marianne held out to her, and putting her hand into her pocket, pulled out a similar one, directed to Miss Arnold.

Marianne scarcely suppressed a shriek, gasped, and turned pale. Each lady then proceeded to unfold a pink sheet of note-paper, containing an original copy of verses, each labelled, 'On a hair of — —.' Then came a scented shining note, requesting to be informed whether the right construction had been put on some words that had dropped from the Miss Conways, and if it were true that the reverend and respected Mr. F. Dynevor had come into a large fortune. In that case, Mr. Delaford, mercenary considerations apart, would take the earliest opportunity of resigning his present position, and entering the family which contained his charmer.

The Merry Wives were parodied by the hysterical maids. Charlotte might afford to laugh, but Marianne's heart was more in the matter, and they struck up such a chorus that Jane broke upon them, declaring that they would frighten Mrs. James Frost out of her senses. When Charlotte told her what was the matter, her comment was, 'And a very good thing, too, that you should find him out in time! A pair of silly girls you! I always was thankful I never could write, to be deluded with nonsense by the post; and I am more so than ever now! Come, leave off crying, Marianne; he ain't worth it.'

'But how shall we answer him, Mrs. Beckett?' said Charlotte.

'Never demean yourself to answer him,' said Jane; 'let him never hear nought about you—that's the best for the like of him. I can tell him he need not be in no hurry about giving warning to Lady Conway. At Cheveleigh we'll have a solemn, steady butler, with no nonsense, nor verses, nor guitars—forty years old—and a married man.'

Charlotte took the advice, and acted with dignified contempt and silence, relieved to imagine that Tom had never been in danger from such a rival. Marianne did not divulge the tender and melancholy letter of reproach that she posted privately; but she grew paler, and coughed more, all that bright summer.

Mrs. Frost had refused to let any cause remove her from Northwold, until after an event which it was hoped would render James less disdainful of his inheritance. But—'Was there ever anything more *contrary*?' exclaimed Jane, as she prepared to set out the table for a grand tea. 'There's Master James as pleased and proud of that there little brown girl, as if she was as fine a boy as Master Henry himself. I do believe, upon my word, it is all to spite poor dear Master Oliver.'

Poor Jane, she was almost growing tart in her partizanship of Oliver.

The little brown girl was no dove of peace. Her father decidedly triumphed in the mortification that her sex was to others of the family; and though he averred that the birth of a son would not have made him change his mind, he was well satisfied to be spared the attack which would have ensued. Oliver, like Jane, appeared to regard the poor child as a wilful offence, and revenged himself by a letter announcing that Clara would be his heiress, information which Mrs. Frost kindly withheld from her granddaughter, in the hope of a reconciliation.

Lord Ormersfield took James in hand, undertaking to make him hear common sense; but the sense was unfortunately too common, and the authoritative manner was irritating, above all when a stately warning was given that no Church-preferment was to be expected from his influence; whereupon James considered himself insulted, and they parted very stiff and grand, the Earl afterwards pronouncing that nothing was so wrongheaded as a conscientious man. But they were too much accustomed to be on respectfully quarrelsome terms to alter their regard for one retort more or less; and after all, there were very few men whom Lord Ormersfield liked or esteemed half so much as the fearless and uncompromising James Frost—James Frost—as he curtly signed himself, in spite of all Louis's wit on Rolands and Olivers—and yet those soft satirical speeches did more than all direct attacks to shake his confidence in his own magnanimity; more especially because Fitzjocelyn always declared himself incompetent to judge, and never failed to uphold that he was so far right, that his ministry must stand above all worldly considerations.

The breach had become so wide, that Oliver would not have accepted the terms he had formerly offered. His object seemed to be to pique his nephew and niece, by showing them what they had lost. He wrote the most magnificent descriptions of Cheveleigh, and insisted that his mother and Clara should come and take possession on the eightieth birthday of the former, the 14th of September; and Isabel was recovering so rapidly, that there was nothing to oppose to his project, although the new Catharine would be scarcely three weeks old by that time.

Thereupon came down, addressed to Clara, a case of Peruvian jewels, newly set in London—intended doubtless to excite great jealousy in her sister-in-law. Poor Oliver! could he but have known that Isabel only glanced at them to tell Clara the names of the ornaments, and to relieve her mind by assurances that the whole of a set need not be worn at once! Next arrived an exceedingly smart French milliner, who, by the help of Jane and Marianne, got Clara into her toils, and pinned and measured her for a whole mortal morning; and even grandmamma ordered a black velvet gown and accompaniments.

Lastly, there descended on Clara's devoted head a cheque for a sum which terrified her imagination, and orders to equip herself suitably as Miss Dynevor of Cheveleigh, who was to enjoy the same allowance half-yearly. Her first idea was what delightful presents could be made to every one; but as she was devising showers of gifts for her niece, James cut her short,—'I am sorry to give you pain, Clara, but it must be understood that neither directly nor indirectly can I nor mine receive anything bought with my uncle's money.'

'That was the only thing to make me not hate it.'

'It is best you should hate it.'

'I do! Why did he come home to bother us? Oh, Jem, can't I still live here, and only visit there?'

'No, Clara. The care of granny is your first duty; and during her life, so long as you are single, her home must be yours.'

The edict was given in stern self-abnegation; but James was very kind to her, treating her as a victim, and spending his leisure in walking about with her, that she might take leave of every favourite haunt. He was indulgent enough even to make no objection to going with her to Ormersfield, where she wandered about the park, visited old scenes with Louis, and went over all his improvements. His cottages had as yet the sole fault of looking too new, and one of his tenants would not shut up his pigs; but otherwise all was going on well, and Inglewood was in the excitement of Louis's first harvest. He walked about with ears of wheat in his hand, talked knowingly of loads and acres, and had almost taught his father to watch the barometer. It added to Clara's regrets that she should miss the harvest-supper, for which he and Mr. Holdsworth had wonderful designs; but it was not to take place until Fitzjocelyn's return from Cheveleigh. Oliver had invited him and his father to conduct Mrs. Frost thither, and add eclat to her reception; and this, as Clara said, 'was the only comfort in the business.'

James had effectually destroyed all pleasure on her part, and had made the change appear an unmitigated misfortune, even though she did not know what she would have thought the worst. Congratulations were dreadful to her, and it was all that Isabel could do to persuade her to repress her dislike so as not to distress her grandmother.

To Mrs. Frost it was pain to leave what she owned, with thankful tears, to have been a happy, peaceful refuge for her widowhood and poverty; she grieved over each parting, clung to the Faithfulls, reiterated fond counsels to Isabel, and could hardly bear to detach herself from the great-grandchild. But still it was her own son, and her own home, and Oliver and Cheveleigh were more to her than even James and Dynevor Terrace; so that, though she was sorry, it was not with a melancholy sorrow, and she could still hope against hope, that uncle and nephew might be brought together at last, and that a son of James would yet reign in the dear old place.

Besides, she had not time to be unhappy. She was fully employed nursing Isabel, doing honour to the little one, answering Oliver's letters, superintending Clara's wardrobe; choosing parting gifts for innumerable friends, high and low; and making arrangements for the inexperienced household.

Jane's place was to be—not exactly supplied, but occupied by a cook. Miss Dynevor was to have 'a personal attendant;' and Mrs. Beckett begged that Marianne might be chosen, since she could not bear to see the poor thing sent away, when in so much need of care. The diamonds, the French millinery, and Jane's motherly care, came in strong contrast to the miserable lodging, or the consumptive hospital, which poor Marianne had begun to anticipate; and weeping with gratitude, she declared that she had never seen nor thought of such kindness since her mother died.

Isabel seldom roused herself to understand anything about her servants; but she liked Marianne, and was glad Clara should have her, since she was not strong enough to undertake nursery cares. She believed it had not agreed with her to sit up late. Compunction for having been the cause had never dawned on Isabel's mind.

Charlotte was to remain at Dynevor Terrace; James and Isabel wished to keep her, and Mrs. Beckett thought her sufficiently indoctrinated with her ways to have some chance of going on well. 'Besides,' as Jane said, 'I can't be accountable for taking her into that large family, until I see what company there may be. She's a well-behaved girl enough, but she's too pretty and too simple-like for me to have her among the common run of servants. I'll see what I can do for her, when I see what sort of a housekeeper it is.'

And Jane gave Charlotte infinite injunctions, varying from due care of the 'chaney images' to reserve with mankind. 'Because you see, Charlotte' she said, 'you'll be terribly forsaken. Mrs. James, poor dear!—she would not know if the furniture weren't rubbed once in ten years; but you must make it a pride to yourself to be faithful.'

'I am faithful!' cried Charlotte. 'I never cared for that traitor, Delaford, and his guitar; but I could not get rid of him. And I'll tell you what—I'll seal up his fine red book, and all his verses; and you shall leave them in London as you go through, with my compliments. I think that will be proper and scornful.'

'Hoity-toity! That's what she's at! The best thing you can do too, Charlotte; and I'm glad that you've too much spirit to pine like poor Marianne. I'd take my affidavit that if the crowner could sit upon her when she dies—and die she will—that there fine gentleman and his guitar will be found at the bottom of her chest. But don't go off about that now—though 'tis the reason I won't part from the poor thing till I can help—the better luck for you that you'd got more in your head than vanities and furbelows. What I meant was not being faithful to him out in Peru—that's your own affair, but the being faithful to your duty to your mistress, whether she's after you or not. You know what a good servant is, and you've got to show it ain't all eye-service.'

Charlotte cried heartily. No one else was allowed that privilege when the 13th came, excepting Mrs. Frost herself. James, afraid that a scene would hurt his wife, severely forbade Clara to give way; and the poor girl, mute and white, did as she was told, and ventured not a word of farewell, though her embraces were convulsive, and when she went down stairs she could not help kissing Charlotte.

James handed his grandmother to her seat in the carriage which was to take her to the station.

'Good-bye, my dear,' she said; 'I know the day will come when all this will be made up. You know how I have loved you both.'

'I wish my uncle all good.'

'I see it now,' she said, holding his hand between both of hers. 'It is my fault. I fostered our family pride. May God take away the sin from us both!'

The words were hardly articulate through tears, and perhaps James did not hear. He hurried Clara down the garden and into the carriage, and she had her last nod from Miss Faithfull at the open window. Miss Mercy was at the station, whither school-hours had hindered James from accompanying them, but where they found Lord Ormersfield and Louis.

The warm-hearted little woman was all tears and smiles. 'Oh! dear Mrs. Frost, I am so sorry, and yet it is selfish. I am so happy! but where shall we find such another neighbour?'

'Come and see us. You know you are to persuade your sister.'

'Ah!' She shook her head. 'Salome is hard to move. But you—you are such a traveller—you will come to see Mr. James?'

'I'm eighty to-morrow: I little expect to make any more journeys except one, Mercy. I never look to see poor Northwold more; but it has been a place of blessings to me, and you have been one of them. Don't think I'm too glad to go away, but I cannot but be thankful that my dear boy is bringing me home to lay me down where my father and his father lie.'

It was said with that peculiar cheerfulness with which happy old age can contemplate the end of the pilgrimage, and she looked at Louis with a sunny smile.

CHAPTER VIII
THE RESTORATION

> When silent time, wi' lightly foot,
>   Had trod on thirty years,
> I sought again my native land
>   Wi' mony hopes and fears.
> As I drew near my ancient pile,
>   My heart beat a' the way;
> The place I passed seemed yet to speak
>   Of some dear former day.
> Some pensy chiels, a new-sprung race,
>   Wad next their welcome pay;
>
> But sair on ilka well-kenned face
>   I missed the youthful bloom.
>   Miss Blamire

Oliver had sent orders to his mother to sleep in London, and proceed the next morning by a train which would arrive at about two o'clock.

On that eventful morning, Clara was the prey of Mrs. Beckett, Marianne, and the French milliner, and in such a flounced glace silk, such a lace mantle, and such a flowery bonnet was she arrayed, that Lord Ormersfield bowed to her as a stranger, and Louis talked of the transformations of the Giraffe. 'Is it not humiliating,' she said, 'to be so altered by finery? You might dress Isabel for ever, and her nobleness would surmount it all.'

'If you are not the rose, at least you have lived near the rose,' said Louis. 'You don't fall quite short of the character of Miss Dynevor.'

'I wish I were going to school,' said Clara, as they passed along familiar streets; 'then, at least, some one would pity me.'

After two hours spent on the railroad, the train entered a district with the bleakness, but not the beauty, of the neighbourhood of mountains; the fresh September breeze was laden with smoke, and stations stood thick upon the line. As the train dashed up to one of these, a flag was seen waving, and the shout of 'Cheveleigh, Cheveleigh road!' greeted them.

On the platform stood a tall footman, in the most crimson of coats, powdered hair, and a stupendous crimson and white shoulder-knot, auch as Clara had only seen going to St. James's. She would never have imagined that she had any concern with such splendour; but her grandmother asked him if the carriage were there, as a mere matter of course, and Jane devolved on him all luggage cares, as coolly as if she had been ruling over him all his life.

As they issued from the station, a thin, uncertain, boyish cheer rang out, and before them stood a handsome open carriage and four chestnut horses, with crimson postillions, and huge crimson-and-white satin rosettes.

'Wont they all turn to rats and pumpkins?' whispered Clara to Louis.

'Bless the poor boy!' cried Mrs. Frost, between laughing and crying, 'what has he been about? Does he think I am the Sheriff's lady still?'

The party entered the carriage, and the crowd of little boys and girls, flymen and porters, got up another 'hurrah!' as the four horses went thundering off, with Mrs. Frost apologizing—'Poor Oliver's notions were on such a grand scale!—He had been so long absent, that he did not know how much these things have been disused.' But no one could look at her bright tearful eyes, and quivering mouth, without seeing that she exulted in her son's affection and his victory; and after all it was natural to her, and a resumption of old habits.

They drove through two miles of brown flat heath, with far-away mountain outlines, which she greeted as dear friends. Here and there the engine-house of a mine rose up among shabby buildings, and by-and-by was seen a square church-tower, with lofty pinnacles, among which floated forth a flag. The old lady caught hold convulsively of Clara's hand—'The old church!—My old church!—See, Clara, that is where your dear grandfather lies!—My last home!'

With brimming eyes Mrs. Frost gazed on it as it came forth more distinctly, and Clara looked with a sense of awe; but rending her away from grave thoughts, shouts burst upon her ears, and above them the pealing crash of all the bells, as they dashed under a splendid triumphal arch, all evergreens and dahlias, forming the word 'Welcome!' and were met by a party on horseback waving their hats, while a great hurrah burst out from the numbers who lined the street. Mrs. Frost bowed her thanks and waved her hand. 'But oh!' she said, almost sobbing, 'where am I? This is not Cheveleigh.'

Lord Ormersfield showed her a few old houses that they both recognised, looking antiquated in the midst of a modern growth of narrow, conceited new tenements. The shouting crowd had, to Fitzjocelyn's eyes, more the aspect of a rabble than of a genuine rejoicing peasantry. What men there were looked beer-attracted rather than reputable, and the main body were whooping boys, women, nurse-girls, and babies. The suspicion crossed him that it was a new generation, without memories of forty years since, wondering rather than welcoming, in spite of arches, bells, and shouts.

After another half-mile, a gate swung wide beneath another arch, all over C. D., the F. studiously omitted; and the carriage wheeled in amid a shower of tight little nosegays from a squadron of school-children. They drove up the long approach, through fir plantations, which drew from Mrs. Frost a cry of friendly recognition—for her husband had planted them; but they had not taken kindly to the soil, and fifty years had produced but a starveling growth. Beyond lay an expanse of parched brown turf, here and there an enclosure of unprosperous trees, and full in front stood the wide space of stuccoed wall, with a great Gothic window full in the midst, and battlements in the castellated style of the early years of the nineteenth century.

No one spoke. After the first glance, Mrs. Frost shut her eyes to restrain the hot tears that arose at the thought of the wintry morning, when ice-drops hung hoary on the fir-trees, as she had driven away from the portal, whence music was now pealing forth a greeting, and where Oliver was standing on the very spot where, with clenched hand, he had vowed that all should be restored.

Alas! how much was in his power to restore?

Gaily-dressed people surrounded the entrance, and, amid triumphant strains from the band, the carriage stopped, and Oliver held out his hand, saying, 'Welcome home, mother!'

She leant forward, kissed his brow, and suffered him to lead her up the steps to the hall-door, Lord Ormersfield conducting Clara. At the door Mrs. Frost paused, to turn, curtsey, and sign her thanks to the throng who had followed. Her noble aspect and demeanour, so full of dignity and feeling, obtained a fresh and more genuine acclamation; but throughout there was a strange sense of unreality; she seemed like one performing a part to gratify her son. Clara asked her cousin if it were not like acting a play; and it was plain to him that the spectators beheld it with more curiosity than sympathy.

They were a new race. Property had changed hands rapidly in a region of trade and manufacture, and the old Dynevor name had been forgotten past recall, amid the very population who were thriving upon the identical speculations which had swamped Mr. Frost's fortune. If the crowd without looked like a mob, the assembly within had a parvenu appearance; and as Oliver handed his mother across the hall, he muttered something, as if he were disappointed both in the number and consequence of his guests.

He led her into a magnificent apartment, all gilding, blue brocade, and mirrors, as far as might be after the model of the days of the Shrievalty; but the bare splendour could ill recall the grace and elegance that had then reigned there without effort. Peru had not taught Oliver taste either of the eye or of the mind, and his indefatigable introductions—'My mother, Mrs. Dynevor, my niece, Miss Dynevor, Lord Ormersfield, Lord Fitzjocelyn,' came so repeatedly as quite to jingle in their ears.

Sir Andrew Britton, a burly cotton lord, with a wife in all the colours of the rainbow, seemed to be the grand guest. His lady seated herself beside Mrs. Frost, and began to tell her, with a tone of patronage, how good a neighbourhood it was, and how much pleasure she should have in introducing Miss Dynevor.

In vain did Mrs. Frost look for a face she knew, and inquire from her new acquaintance after familiar old names of places and people. The places were either become factories, or some charming new family lived there; and for the people, it seemed as if she might as well ask for antediluvians; Lady Britton had seldom heard their names, or if any trace survived, they had never been on her visiting list.

At last Oliver came up to her, saying, 'Here, ma'am, Mr. Henderson claims an early acquaintance with you.'

'Mr. Henderson!' and she eagerly started up, but looked baffled.

'Little George Henderson,' said the grey-headed gentleman—for once a real gentleman—'I assure you I have not forgotten the happy days I have spent here.'

'Little George!' as she took him by both hands—'who would have thought it! You were little George with the apple cheeks. And are no more of you here?'

He shook his head sadly. 'They would have been even more glad than I am to welcome you home; they were older, and knew you better.'

'Ah! I must learn to ask no questions. And yet, that dear sister Fanny of yours—'

'Gone many years since, ma'am. She died in India. I hope my daughter Fanny may put you a little mind of her.'

'Is she not here?'

'Why, no. I wished to bring her, but she is but fifteen, and mamma will not trust her out without herself. We are quiet people, and the world is growing too gay for us.'

'Clara and I must come to find you out. Can you believe this tall creature is poor dear Henry's daughter?' as Clara hastened to greet her father's playfellow, with an alacrity which piqued Lady Britton into a supercilious aside to Lord Fitzjocelyn that the Hendersons were in poor circumstances, and no one visited them.

'And is no one here whom I know? Not one of the old set, George?' asked the old lady, mournfully.

'I fear there is hardly any one,' said Mr. Henderson. 'All seem even to me new people. Stay, do you recollect old Mrs. Golding?'

After a little confusion, Mr. Henderson's old Mrs. Golding proved to be Mrs. Frost's young Mrs. Golding; and, on the eager inquiry whether she were present, ensued the melancholy answer that she was deaf and infirm, only just able to smile with pleasure at the tidings of her old friend's restoration; and the daughter, whom she could only just believe to be grown up, was a worn, elderly woman. Not even the one heartfelt greeting was without sadness; and Clara likewise met with one solitary satisfaction, and that a very mixed one. Mr. Danvers, the young curate, whom Oliver had not thought worth presenting, was hailed by Fitzjocelyn as if their slight Oxford acquaintance had been an intimacy, and was by him introduced to Clara as belonging to James's college. She frankly held out her hand, but was discomfited by his inquiry for her brother, whom he had hoped to meet. Louis said something about not expecting the schoolmaster abroad in the half-year, and Clara was not at all grateful to him for relieving her from the embarrassment, but regarded the reply as a shabby prevarication, and was much inclined to speak out; but Louis was drawing the curate into conversation about the population, and hearing but a desponding history. It was interrupted when Oliver, after waiting in vain for more distinguished company, began to marshal his guests to the grand hall, paved with black and white marble, and with a vast extent of wall and window, decked with evergreens, flags, and mottoes. Here a cold collation was prepared, with a band in a music-gallery above, and all the et ceteras dear to county papers. Oliver himself handed in Lady Britton, his mother fell to the lot of the Earl, and Fitzjocelyn received orders to conduct a handsome, young, giggling Mrs. Smithers, who, never having been in contact with a live Lord, wanted to make the most of him, and, before she had arrived at her place, was declaring that it was a most interesting occasion, just like a scene at the Opera.

Louis glanced back to see what became of Clara, and, finding her following with Sir Andrew Britton, contrived to sit immediately opposite to her, at the long, narrow table, with nothing between them but a couple of cold chickens and a tongue garnished with transfixed crayfish. His eyes were, perhaps, a greater support to her than even conversation, for she gathered a little philosophy and charity from their cheering smile and arch twinkling, and she managed to listen civilly to her neighbour, while she saw that her cousin was being very polite to Mrs. Smithers. She was a great way from all other friends, for the table had been spread for a more numerous assembly, and the company sat in little clusters, with dreary gaps between, where moulds of jelly quaked in vain, and lobster-salads wasted their sweetness on the desert air. Her uncle could just be seen in the far perspective at the head of the table, and, between him and the Earl, Louis descried his Aunt Catharine, looking bright, with a little embellishing flush on her withered cheek.

Sir Andrew was not a lady's man; and, after he had heard how far Miss Dynevor had come to-day, that she had never ridden, and had not seen the Menai tubular bridge, he discontinued the difficult task; and she, finding that he had not even seen the cathedral, which she had passed only fifteen miles off, gave him up, and occupied herself with watching the infinite variety of affectations which Mrs. Smithers was playing off, and the grave diversion with which Louis received them. The lady was evidently trying to discover what had been the intermediate history of Mrs. and Miss Dynevor; and Louis was taking pleasure in baffling her, with cool, quiet answers, especially when she came to the question whether Miss Dynevor had not a brother, and why he was not present. It appeared that Oliver had made almost as if his mother had been buried and dug up again; involving the thirty-four years of her exile in such utter mystery, that people had begun to make all sorts of wild stories to account for her proceedings; and Lord Fitzjocelyn's explanation that she had lived in her own house in Northwold, and taught him the Latin grammar, seemed quite a disappointment from the simplicity and want of romance.

The weary banquet had arrived at ices, and Clara hoped the end was near, when the worse trial of speeches began. Mr. Henderson was declaring how strongly he felt the honour which had been devolved on him, of expressing the universal joy in having so excellent and much-beloved a neighbour restored by the noble exertions of her son. He said all that the rest of the world ought to have felt, and so heartily and sincerely as to make every one imagine the whole the general sentiment, and the welcoming hurrah was cordial and joyous. Mrs. Frost was deeply touched and gratified, and Lord Ormersfield congratulated himself on having instigated Oliver to give this toast to Mr. Henderson. If Clara could have driven James from her mind, she would have been delighted, but there could be no triumph for her where he was excluded.

The Earl returned thanks on behalf of his aunt, and said a great deal that could have come from the mouth of no one 'unaccustomed to public speaking,' ending by proposing the health of 'Mr. Oliver Frost Dynevor.' In the midst of 'the fine old English gentleman,' while Louis was suppressing a smile at the incongruity, a note was brought to him, which he tossed to Clara, purporting that he was to return thanks for her. She bent over the table to say, 'You will say nothing I cannot bear to hear,' folded her hands, and shut her eyes, as if she had been going to stand fire.

Oliver's clear, harsh tones, incapable of slowness or solemnity, began to return thanks for himself, and pronounce this to be the happy day to which he had been looking throughout his life—the day of restoring the family inheritance to his mother, and the child of his elder brother; he faltered—he never could calmly speak of Henry. Failing the presence of one so dear, he rejoiced, however, to be able to introduce to them his only daughter, and he begged that his friends would drink the health of the heiress of Cheveleigh, Miss Dynevor.

Never did toast apparently conduce so little to the health of the subject. Unprepared as Clara was for such a declaration, it was to her as if she had been publicly denounced as the supplanter of her brother. She became deadly white, and sat bolt upright, stiff and motionless, barely stifling a scream, and her eyes fixed between command and entreaty on her cousin without seeing, far less acknowledging, the bows levelled at her. Louis, alarmed by her looks, saw that no time was to be lost; and rising hastily before any one was ready, perilled his fame for eloquence by rapidly assuring the gentlemen and ladies that Miss Dynevor was truly sensible of the kindness of their welcome, and their manner of receiving the toast. Then pushing back his chair, with 'never mind,' to Mrs. Smithers and her scent-bottle, he was at the back of Clara's chair almost before her confused eyes had missed him in her gasps for breath, and impulse to do something desperate; and so she might, if his voice had not been in her ear, his hand grasping hers, both to console and raise her. 'Clara, come, take care.' She obeyed, but trembling so much that he was obliged to support her. Others would have risen in alarm, but he silenced them by signs, and entreaties that no one would frighten her grandmother. There was a large glass door standing open under the Gothic window, and through it he led her out upon a wide green lawn. She drew her breath in sobs, but could not speak. Louis asked her to untie her bonnet, and touched the string, which was merely a streamer. This brought a kind of laugh, but she unfastened the bonnet herself, and the first use she made of her breath was fiercely to exclaim—'How could you! Why did you not tell them I never will—'

'Sit down,' said Louis, gently. 'Let me fetch some water.'

'No—no—let me get away from this place!' and she almost dragged him along, as fresh cheers and peals of music broke out, till they had entered a lonely walk in a sort of wilderness of shrubs. Still she hurried on, till they came out on a quiet little garden, where the tinkling of a little fountain was the only sound; the water looked clear and fresh with the gold-fish darting in it, and the sun shone calmly on the bright flowers and wavy ferns adorning the rockwork.

'What are you doing, Clara? You must rest here,' said he, drawing her down on a rustic bench, intended to represent a crocodile.

'I can't rest here! I must go home! I'm going home to Jem!' she exclaimed, obeying, however, because, though she could run, she could not stand.

'Dear Clara,' he said, affectionately, 'it was much worse than I expected. I never believed he could have committed himself to such an open declaration, especially without warning.'

'I'll not stay!' cried Clara, with all the vehemence of her Dynevor nature. 'I'll go straight home to Northwold to-morrow morning—to-night if I could. Yes, I will! I never came here for this!'

'And what is to become of my poor Aunt Kitty?'

'She has her Oliver! She would not have me put Jem out of his birthright.'

'James will not be put into it.'

She wrenched away her hand, and looked at him with all her brother's fierceness. 'And you!' she cried, 'why could not you speak up like a man, and tell them that I thank none of them, and will have nothing to say to any of them; and that if this is to belong to any one, it must be to my noble, my glorious, generous brother; and, if he hasn't it, it may go to the Queen, for what I care! I'll never have one stone of it. Why could you not say so, instead of all that humbug'!'

'I thought the family had afforded quite spectacles enough for one day,' said Louis; 'and besides, I had some pity upon your grandmother, and on your uncle too.'

'Jem told me grandmamma claimed my first duty; but he never knew of this wicked plan.'

'Yes, he did.'

'Knew that I was to supplant him!'

'Yes; we all knew it was a threat of your uncle; but we spared you the knowledge, thinking that all might yet be accommodated, and never expecting it would come on you in this sudden way.'

'Then I think I have been unfairly used,' cried Clara; 'I have been brought here on false pretences. As if I would have come near the place if I had known it!'

'A very false pretence that your grandmother must not be left alone at eighty, by the child whom she brought up.'

'Oh, Louis! you want to tear me to pieces!'

'I have pity on my aunt; I have far more pity on your uncle.' Clara stared at him. 'Here is a man who started with a grand heroic purpose to redeem the estate, not for himself, but for her and his brother; he exiles himself, he perseveres, till this one pursuit, for which he denies himself home, kindred, wife or child, absorbs and withers him up. He returns to find his brother dead; and the children, for whom he sacrificed all, set against him, and rejecting his favours.'

This was quite a new point of view to Clara. 'It is his own fault,' she said.

'That a misfortune is by our own fault is no comfort,' said Louis. 'His apparent neglect, after all, arose from his absorption in the one object.'

'Yes; but how shameful to wish James to forget his Ordination.'

'A strong way of putting it. He asked too much: but he would have been, and may yet be, contented with concessions involving nothing wrong. His way of life can hardly have taught him to appreciate James's scruples, as we do; and even if right and wrong were more neatly partitioned between them than I think they are, it would still be hard on him to find this destined heir spurning his benefits.'

'What are you coming to, Louis! You think James right?

'I would give the world to think so, Clara. One motive is too high for praise, the other—No, I will say nothing of it. But I could wish I had not precipitated matters last year.'

'What, would you have robbed us of our few happy months?'

'It was your uncle whom I robbed; he would otherwise have come home like a good genius; but he found you all happy without him, and with no gratitude to spare for him. And there he sits at the head of that long melancholy table, trying to bring back days that have gone too far ever to be recalled, and only raising their spectres in this mocking finery; scarcely one man present, whose welcome comes from his heart; his mother past the days of heeding the display, except for his sake; his nephew rejecting him; you indignant and miserable. Oh, Clara! I never saw more plainly money given for that which is not bread, and labour for that which satisfieth not. Empty and hollow as the pageant was, I could better bear to take my part in it, so far as truth would let me, than tell that poor man that the last of his brother's children rejects him and his benefits.'

'At this rate, you will make a hero of Uncle Oliver.'

'It is because he is one of this world's heroes that he is distasteful to you.'

'I don't understand.'

'Exclusive devotion to one object, grand though it was, has made him the man he appears to us. Think what the spirit must have been that conceived and carried out such a design! Depend upon it there is a greatness in him, which may show, when, as dear granny says, she has cured him of all he learnt away from home. I think that must be the work for which you are all brought together here.'

'But I can't thrust out Jem. I won't stay here on those terms. I shall protest—'

'It is not graceful to make an uproar about your own magnanimity, nor to talk of what is to happen after a man's death. You don't come here to be heiress, but to take care of your grandmother. There is no need to disturb the future, unless, to be sure, you were obliged to explain your expectations.'

'Ah! to be sure, any way I could restore it all to James.'

'Or, better still, you may yet be able to draw the uncle and nephew together, and bring back peace and union.'

'Then I must stay and bear all this, you think?'

'As a mere matter of obedience, certainly.'

Clara's countenance fell.

'That may deprive it of the brilliance of a voluntary sacrifice; but, after all, it is what makes your course safe and plain.'

'And very dismal, just because no one will believe so.'

'So the safer for humility,' said Louis. 'Perhaps the dear old Terrace did not offer training and trial enough. I try to believe something of the kind in my own case. If choice had been mine, I should hardly have been exactly what I am; and you know how my chief happiness has been put far from me; but I can imagine that to be at the summit of my wishes might foster my sluggishness, and that I might rest too much on better judgment than my own, if it were beside me. Probation maybe safer than joy; and you may do more good to yourself and others than even under Isabel's wing. Only think of the means in your hands, and all the wretched population round! There will be some hope of help for the curate now—besides, I shall know where to come for subscriptions next time I run crazy about any wonderful charity.'

Clara smiled. 'I suppose I must bear it,' she said.

'For shame, Clara! With Aunt Kitty, who would make a palace of a dungeon, in the glorious glow of such a sunset, turning each cloud to red and purple radiance by the very force of love and faith, who could regret the being beside her? My own dear and precious aunt, to see her so happy, with bliss and peace so undisturbed, so far above these toys, and these distresses, gives me a sort of fear—'

'Oh, don't, Louis—'

They were interrupted by approaching voices. Clara hastily started up, as her uncle and Lady Britton appeared in the green alley.

'Oh, must I go back to them all! My head does ache!'

Louis gave her his arm, pursued the path in the opposite direction, and emerged at the lower end of the bowling-green, with the battlemented front of the house rising before them. Presently, he met his father searching for him. 'Poor Clara has been overcome,' he said, in explanation. 'The speechifying has been too much for her.'

It was the first time that Clara had appeared to the Earl in any light but that of an idle school-girl, and he said, kindly, 'It must have been very trying. There should have been more preparation. Your uncle would have shown better taste in sparing your grandmamma so obtrusive a reception, and I was much pained both for her and for you during some of the speeches.'

Sympathy from Lord Ormersfield nearly overthrew Clara again, and she involuntarily squeezed Louis's arm. He asked for his aunt, and was told, 'She is in the house, entertaining these people. They do not know when to go away. How could Oliver inflict such a party on her and such a style of people!'

'I must go and help her,' said Louis.

Clara was in no condition to appear, but Louis caused Mrs. Beckett to be summoned, and committed her to her care. Her transport was one of the few pleasant things of that day. 'Oh, Miss Clara! Oh, my Lord! Was there ever the like? Isn't Master Oliver the most blessed boy? Missus in her own home again! Eight men, and a French man-cook! If ever I thought to see the day! Her old room just as it was, only grander! Oh, if poor Mr. James was but here!'

'Ay, Jane, and here's Clara thinking herself ill about Mr. James. Take her up and give her some tea, and make her fit to behave prettily by-and-by, that granny may not be vexed.'

Having seen her safe under Jane's fondling care and infectious exultation, he betook himself to the drawing-room, relieved his aunt's anxiety by a whisper, and won golden opinions from the whole company, before they were fairly got rid of; and Oliver begged to conduct his mother to her apartment. 'Yes, my dear, I must go to poor little Clara.'

'I've no fears for Clara,' said Oliver, as he led her upstairs. 'Knowing young fellow to wait for my announcement! I can give her near double what Ponsonby could. I'd not object—old Dynevor blood—'

'My poor Oliver, you have so learnt to think of money, that you can't believe others live for anything else. You'll learn your mistake.'

'You think the young chap meant nothing? I shall look sharp after him, then. I look on Clara as my own. I'll have no trifling.'

'You may save yourself the trouble,' said his mother. 'They understand each other—they have always been like brother and sister, and I cannot have the children teased, or things put into their heads.'

Oliver laughed his scornful chuckle, and said he did not understand that sort of brother and sister, but happily he became absorbed in showing his mother the fittings of her splendid bedroom.

Clara had the comfort of clinging round her grandmother's neck, and being told that it was all nonsense. Jem should have his rights, and Uncle Oliver would learn to love and honour him at last; and she was a good child, and ought to have been prepared, if granny could have guessed he would do it so publicly and suddenly, but she must forgive him, for he was beside himself at having got them home again, and he could not make enough of her because she was poor Henry's child. So she saw granny must not be grieved, and she let herself be dressed for a constrained dinner in the vast dining-room, where the servants outnumbered the diners, and the silver covers bore the Dynevor dragon as a handle, looking as spiteful as some of the race could do.

Oliver was obliged to conclude that no offer had passed between the two young people; but on the way home next morning the Earl observed, 'Clara Frost has a fine figure, and is much improved by dress. She shows excellent feeling, and does credit to her education.'

'The Pendragon blood never had a finer development,' said Louis.

'Even supposing justice done to poor James, she will have a handsome portion. Oliver will have far more to dispose of than the five thousand pounds guaranteed to her.'

'Poor child!' said Louis.

'Yes, I pity her for being exposed to his parading. He forgot the gentleman in his merchant's office. If you should ever have any thoughts of rescuing her from him, my approval would not be wanting, and it would be the easiest way of restoring her brother.'

'My dear father, if Clara and I were always sister and brother when she was poor, we certainly shall be no more now.'

Lord Ormersfield mentally execrated Mr. Ponsonby, and felt that he had spoken too soon.

Jane's felicity was complete when, a few days after, she received, addressed in Lord Fitzjocelyn's handwriting, an Illustrated News, with a whole page containing 'the reception of Mrs. Dynevor of Cheveleigh,' with grand portraits of all the flounces and veils, many gratuitous moustaches, something passing for Oliver standing up with a wine-glass in his hand, a puppy that would have perfectly justified Mr. Ponsonby's aversion representing Lord Fitzjocelyn, and no gaps at the banquet-table.

That picture Mrs. Beckett caused to be framed and glazed, kept it as her treasure for life, and put it into her will as a legacy to Charlotte Arnold.

CHAPTER IX
THE GIANT OF THE WESTERN STAR

> Come, let us range the subterranean vast,
> Dark catacombs of ages, twilight dells,
> And footmarks of the centuries long past,
> Which look on us from their sepulchral cells.
>
> Then glad emerge we to the cheering day,
> Some sun-ranged height, or Alpine snowy crown,
> Or Chimborazo towering far away
> O'er the great Andes chain, and, looking down,
> On flaming Cordilleras, mountain thrown
> O'er mountain, vast new realms.
> The Creation—REV. I. WILLIAMS.

The same impression of the Illustrated London News which delighted Jane Beckett's simple heart in England, caused no small sensation at Lima.

Dona Rosita cast one glance at El Visconde there portrayed, and then became absorbed in Clara's bonnet; Mr. Robson pronounced Lord Ormersfield as good a likeness as Mr. Dynevor, Mr. Ponsonby cast a scornful look and smile at the unlucky figure representing Fitzjocelyn; and not a critical voice was heard, excepting Tom Madison's, who indignantly declared that they had made the young Lord look as if he had stood behind a counter all his life.

The juxtaposition of Lord Fitzjocelyn and Mr. Dynevor's niece, was not by any means forgotten. It looked very like a graceful conclusion to Oliver's exertions that he should crown their union, and the county paper, which had likewise been forwarded, very nearly hinted as much. Mr. Ponsonby took care that the paragraph should be laid in his daughter's way, and he offered her the sight of Oliver Dynevor's own letter.

Mary suspected that he regarded it as something conclusive, and took care to read it when there were no eyes to mark her emotions. 'Ormersfield and his son were there,' wrote Oliver. 'The young man is not so soft as he looks. They tell me he is going to work sensibly at the estate, and he has a sharp eye for the main chance. I hear he played fast and loose till he found your daughter had better prospects than Miss Conway, whom my fool of a nephew chose to marry, and now he is making up to my niece. My mother dotes on him, and I shall make no objection—no extravagance that I can see, and he will take care of the property. You will take no offence, since you refuse the tender altogether.'

Of this Mary believed two sentences—namely, that Aunt Catharine doted on Fitzjocelyn, and that he was not so soft as he looked, which she took as an admission that he was not comporting himself foolishly. She was quite aware that the friendship between him and Clara might deceive an uninitiated spectator; and, though she commanded herself to think that an attachment between them would be equally natural and desirable, she could not but look with great satisfaction at the easy unsuspicious tone of Mrs. Frost's letter, which, after mentioning with much affection and gratitude all Oliver's attempts to make her happy, in spite of the many sad changes around, ended by saying that poor Clara felt the separation from her brother so much, that without dear Louis she did not know how she would have gone through the festivities. 'You can guess how he is everything to us all,' said Aunt Kitty, 'and I brightened up his looks with giving him your last letter to read. I dare say, Miss Mary, you would like to scold me.'

Aunt Kitty! Aunt Kitty! you dearly loved a little kindly mischief! Let that be as it might, Mr. Ponsonby thought that Mr. Dynevor's letter had certainly not had much effect, for Mary was more lively and cheerful than he had seen her since her first arrival. Mary's cheerfulness was becoming the more necessary to him, since he was beginning a little to weary of the childish charms of his young Limenian wife. Rosita had neither education nor conversation; and when all her pretty ways had been tried on him in succession, they began to grow tedious. Moreover, the playful submission which she had brought from her convent was beginning to turn into wilfulness. Her extravagances in dress were appalling. She refused to wear the same dresses twice, and cried, stamped her graceful foot, and pouted when he remonstrated. She managed to spend every evening in amusement, either at the Opera, or at evening parties, where her splendid eyes, and scraps of broken English, made great havoc among young lieutenants and midshipmen visiting Lima. Mr. Ponsonby was growing tired of these constant gaieties, and generally remained at home, sending Mary in his stead, as a sort of guard over her; and Mary, always the same in her white muslin, followed Rosita through all the salas of Lima—listened to the confidences of Limenian beauties—talked of England to little naval cadets, more homesick than they would have chosen to avow—and felt sure of some pleasure and interest for the evening, when Mr. Ward came to stand by her chair.

One afternoon, as Mary sat in her window reading, a gay voice exclaimed, 'Beso las manos a Usted;' and looking up, she saw one of the prettiest figures imaginable. A full dark purple satin skirt just revealed the point of a dainty white satin shoe. It was plaited low on the hips, and girded loosely with a brightly striped scarf. The head and upper part of the person were shrouded in a close hood of elastic black silk webbing, fastened behind at the waist, and held over the face by the hand, which just allowed one be-ringed finger and one glancing dark eye to appear, while the other hand held a fan and a laced pocket-handkerchief. So perfectly did the costume suit the air and shape of the lady, that, as she stood among Mary's orange trees, it was like an illusion, of the fancy, but consternation took away all the charm from Mary's eyes. 'Tapada, she cried; 'you surely are not going out, tapada?'

'Ah, you have found me out,' cried Rosita. 'Yes, indeed I am! and I have the like saya y manto ready for you. Come, we will be on the Alameda; Xavier waits to attend us. Your Senor Ouard will be at his evening walk.'

But Mary drew back. This pretty disguise was a freak, such as only the most gay ladies permitted themselves; and she had little doubt that her father would be extremely displeased at his wife and daughter so appearing, although danger there was none; since, though any one might accost a female thus veiled, not the slightest impertinence was ever allowed. Mary implored Bosita to wait till Mr. Ponsonby's views should be known; but she was only laughed at for her English precision, and the pretty creature danced away to her stolen pleasure.

She came in, all glory and delight at the perplexity in which she had involved the English officers, the guesses and courtesies of her own countrymen, and her mystification of Mr. Robson, who had evidently recognised her, though pretending to treat her as a charming stranger.

The triumph was of short duration. For the first time, she had aroused one of Mr. Ponsonby's gusts of passion; she quailed under it, wept bitterly, and made innumerable promises, and then she put on her black mantilla, and, with Xavier behind her, went to her convent chapel, and returned, half crying over the amount of repetitions of her rosary by which her penance was to be performed, and thereby all sense of the fault put away. Responsibility and reflection never seemed to be impressed on that childish mind.

Mary had come in for some of the anger, for not having prevented Rosita's expedition; but they were both speedily forgiven, and Mary never was informed again of her using the saya y manto.

Their minds were diverted by the eager desire of one of the young officers to visit the silver mines. It had been an old promise to Mary from her father to take her to see them; but in her former residence in Peru, it had never been fulfilled. He now wished to inspect matters himself, in order to answer the numerous questions sent by Oliver; and Rosita, eagerly catching at any proposal which promised a variety, a party was made up for ascending to the San Benito mines, some days' journey from Lima. Mary and Rosita were the only ladies; but there were several gentlemen, three naval officers, and Mr. Ward, who was delighted to have an opportunity of visiting the wonders which had been, for many years, within his reach without his rousing himself from his business to see them. Tents, bedding, and provisions were to be carried with them, and Mary had full occupation in stimulating Dolores to bring together the requisite preparations; while Mr. Ward and Robson collected guides, muleteers, and litters.

It was a merry party, seated on the gaily-trapped mules, with an idle young midshipman to make mischief, and all in spirits to enjoy his nonsense, in the exhilaration of the mountain air blowing freshly from the snowy summits which seemed to rise like walls before them. The steaming, misty, relaxing atmosphere of Lima was left behind, and with it many a care and vexation. Mr. Ponsonby brought his mule to the side of his wife's litter, and exchanged many a joke in Anglo-Spanish with her and the lieutenant; and Mr. Ward, his brow unfurrowed from counting-house cares, walked beside Mary's mule, gathered each new flower for her, and listened to her narrative of some of the causes for which she was glad, with her own eyes, to see Tom Madison in his scene of action.

The first day of adventure they slept at a hacienda, surrounded with fields where numerous llamas were pasturing. The next began the real mountain work; the rock looked like a wall before them, and the white summits were sharply defined against the blue sky. The sharper air made Rosita shiver; but the English travellers congratulated themselves on something like a breeze, consoling them for the glow with which the sunbeams beat upon the rocks. The palms and huge ferns had given place to pines, and these were growing more scanty. Once or twice they met a brown Indian, robed in a coloured blanket, with a huge straw hat, from beneath which he gazed with curious, though gentle eyes, upon the cavalcade. By-and-by, looking like a string of ants descending a perpendicular wall, Mary beheld a row of black specks slowly moving. She was told that these were the mules bringing down the metal in panniers—the only means of communication, until, as the lieutenant promised, a perpendicular railroad should be invented. The electricity of the atmosphere made jokes easily pass current. The mountain was 'only' one of the spurs of the Andes, a mere infant among the giants; but, had it been set down in Europe, Mont Blanc must have hid his diminished head; and the view was better than on some of the more enormous neighbours, which were both further inland, and of such height, that to gaze from them was 'like looking from an air-balloon into vacancy.' Whereas here Mary had but to turn her head, as her mule steadily crept round the causeway—a legacy of the Incas—to behold the expanse of the Pacific, a sheet of glittering light in the sunshine, the horizon line raised so high, that the first moment it gave her a sense of there being something wrong with her eye, before the feeling of infinity rushed upon her.

They were turning the flank of the mountain, and losing the sunshine. The evening air was almost chill, and the clearness such that they already saw the ragged height whither they were bound rising in craggy shattered grandeur, every flat space or gentler declivity covered with sheds and huts for the work-people, and cavernous mouths opening on the cliff-side. Dark figures could be distinctly seen moving about; and as to the descending mules, they seemed to be close on the other side of a narrow ravine. Rosita, who, now it came to the point, was not without fears of sleeping on the bare mountain-side, wanted to push on; she was sure they could arrive before night, but she was told that she knew nothing of mountain atmosphere; and she was not discontented with the bright fire and comfortable arrangements on which they suddenly came, after turning round a great shoulder of rock. Mr. Robson and the sumpter-mules had quietly preceded them, and the gipsying on the Andes was likely to be not much less luxurious than an English pic-nic. The negro cook had done his best; Mary made her father's coffee, and Rosita was waited on to her satisfaction. And when darkness came on, too early for English associations with warm days, the lights of the village at the mine glittered merrily, and, apparently, close at hand; and the stars above shone as Mary had never seen them, so marvellously large and bright, and the Magellan clouds so white and mysterious. Mr. Ward came and told her some of the observations made on them by distinguished travellers; and after an earnest conversation, she sought her matted bed, with a pleasant feeling on her mind, as if she had been unusually near Louis's world.

Clear, sharp, and cold was the air next day; the snow-fields glistened gloriously in the rising sun, and a rose-coloured mist seemed to rise from them. Rosita was shown the unusual spectacle of hoar frost, and shiveringly profited by Mary's ample provision of wraps. The hill-sides were beyond conception desolate and bare. Birds were an almost unknown race in Peru; and here even green things had departed, scarcely a tuft of blossom looking out on the face of the red and purple rock; and the exceeding stillness so awful, that even the boy-sailor scarce dared to speak above his breath. Rosita began to repent of having come near so horrible a place; and when she put her head out of her litter, and beheld herself winding along a ledge projecting from the face of a sheer precipice, she would have begged to go back instantly; but her husband spoke in a voice of authority which subdued her; she drew in her head into her basket-work contrivance, and had recourse to vows to Sta Rosa of Lima of a chaplet of diamond roses, if she ever came safely down again.

Mary had made up her mind that they should not have been taken thither if there were any real danger; and so, though she could have preferred her mule taking the inner side of the ledge, and was not too happy when it climbed like a cat, she smiled, and answered all inquiries that she did not think she ought to be frightened. The region was in general more stern than beautiful, the clefts between the hills looking so deep, that it seemed as if an overthrown mountain could hardly fill them; but now and then came sudden peeps of that wonderful ocean; or almost under her feet, as if she could throw a stone into it, there would lie an intensely green valley, shut in with feathering pines, and the hacienda and grazing llamas dwindled, so that they could have been taken for a Swiss farm and flocks of sheep.

Not till the middle of the day did they meet the line of mules, and not until the sunset did they find themselves close before the wonderful perforated San Benito summit. It was, unlike many other metalliferous hills, an isolated, sharply-defined mass of rock, breaking into sudden pinnacles and points, traversed with veins of silver. These veins had been worked with galleries, which, even before the Spanish conquest, had honeycombed the solid rock, and had been thought to have exhausted its riches; but it had been part of Oliver Dynevor's bold speculations to bring modern science to profit by the leavings of the Peruvians and their destroyers. It was a marvellous work, but it might still be a question whether the profit would bear out the expense.

However, that was not the present consideration. No one could feel anything but admiring astonishment at the fantastic craggy height of peaks and spires, rising against the darkening sky, like the very stronghold of the Giant of the Western Star; and, with the black openings of the galleries, here and there showing the lights of the workmen within. Mary remembered the tales, in which Louis used vainly to try to interest her, of metal-working Dwarfs within the mountains; and would have been glad to tell him that, after all, reality was quite as strange as his legends.

The miners, Indians and negroes, might truly have been Trolls, as, with their brown and black countenances, and wild bright attire, they came thronging out of their rude houses, built of piled stones on every tolerably level spot. Three or four stout, hearty Cornish miners, with picks on their shoulders, made the contrast stranger; and among them stood a young man, whose ruddy open face carried Mary home to Ormersfield in one moment; and she could not but blush almost as if it had been Louis, when she bent her head in acknowledgment of his bow.

He started towards her as if to help her off her mule; but Mr. Ponsonby was detaining him by questions, and Mr. Ward, as usual, was at her rein. In a wonderfully brief time, as it seemed to her, all the animals were led off to their quarters; and Robson, coming up, explained that Madison's hut, the only habitable place, had been prepared for the ladies—the gentlemen must be content to sleep in their tent.

'The hut was at least clean,' said Robson, as he ushered them in; and Mary felt as if it were a great deal more. It was rudely built, and only the part near the hearth was lined with matting; the table and the few stools and chairs were rough carpentry, chiefly made out of boxes; but upon the wall hung a beautiful print from Raffaelle, of which she knew the giver as surely as if his name had been written on it; and the small bookcase suspended near contained, compressed together, an epitome of Louis's tastes—the choicest of all his favourites, in each class of book. Mary stood by it, reading the names, and trying to perceive Louis's principle of selection in each case. It jarred upon her when, as the gentlemen loitered about, waiting for the evening meal, they came and looked at the titles, with careless remarks that the superintendent was a youth of taste, and a laugh at the odd medley— Spenser, Shakspeare, 'Don Quixote,' Calderon, Fouque, and selections from Jeremy Taylor, &c.

Mary would hear no more comments. She went to the fire, and tried to persuade Rosita they would come safe down again; and then, on the apology for a mantelshelf, she saw some fossils and some dried grasses, looking almost as if Fitzjocelyn had put them there.

She did not see Madison that night; but the next morning he presented himself to act as their guide through the wonders of the extraordinary region where his lot had been cast. She found that this was only the first floor of the wondrous castle. Above and above, rose galleries, whence the ore was lowered down to the buildings here placed, where it underwent the first process of separation. The paths above were fit for none, save a chamois, or a barefooted Indian, or a sailor—for the midshipman was climbing aloft in such places, that Tom's chief work was to summon him back, in horror lest he should involve himself in endless galleries, excavated before the days of Atahualpa.

Much of the desperate scrambling which Madison recommended as plain-sailing, was beyond Mr. Ponsonby; but where he went, Mary went; and when he stopped, she, though she had not drawn since the master at her school had resigned her, as a hopeless case, applied herself to the perpetration of an outline of the rocks, that, as she said, 'her aunts might see what sort of place it was.' Her steady head, and firm, enterprizing hand and foot, enabled her to see the crowning wonder of the mountain, one of the ventanillas or windows. Mr. Ward, having visited it, came back bent on taking her thither; there was no danger, if she were not afraid. So, between him and Tom Madison, she was dragged up a steep path, and conducted into a gallery cut out in the living rock, growing gloomier and gloomier, till suddenly there was a spot of light on the sparkling floor, and Mary found herself beneath an opening through the mountain crown, right up into the sky, which, through the wild opening, looked of the deepest, most ultra-marine, almost purple blue, utterly beyond conception in the glory of intense colour, bringing only to her mind those most expressive, yet most inexpressive words, 'the body of heaven in His clearness.' She felt, what she had often heard said, that to all mountain tops is given somewhat of the glory that dwelt on Sinai. That ineffable blue was more dazzling than even the fields beyond fields of marvellous white that met her eye on emerging from the dark gallery.

'I never wish so much that Lord Fitzjocelyn should see anything as that,' said Tom Madison, when Mary, in her gratitude, was trying to say something adequate to the trouble she had given, though the beauty was beyond any word of admiration.

'He would—' she began to answer, but the rest died away, only answered by Tom with an emphatic 'He *would*!' and then began the difficulties of getting down.

But Mary had the pleasure at the next pause of hearing Mr. Ward say, 'That is a very fine intelligent young fellow, worthy of his library. I think your father has a prize in him!'

Mary's eyes thanked Mr. Ward, with all her heart in them. It was worth going up the Andes for such a sentence to put into a letter that Aunt Kitty would show to Louis.

Robson seemed anxious to monopolize the attention of the gentlemen, to the exclusion of Madison; and while Tom was thus thrust aside, Mary succeeded in having a conversation with him, such as she felt was a sort of duty to Louis. She asked him the names of the various mountain-peaks in sight, whose bare crags, too steep to support the snow, here and there stood out dark in salient contrast to the white scenery, and as he gave them to her, mentioning the few facts that he had been able to gather respecting them, she was able to ask him whether he was in the habit of seeing anything approaching to society. He smiled, saying that his nearest neighbours were many miles off—an engineer conducting some far more extensive mining operations, whom he sometimes met on business, and an old Spanish gentleman, who lived in a valley far down the mountain side, with whom he sometimes smoked his cigar on a Sunday, if he felt inclined for a perpendicular promenade on a Peruvian causeway for nearly four miles. Mary asked whether he often did feel inclined. No, he thought not often; he had generally worked hard enough in the week to make his book the best company; but he liked now and then to see something green for a change after these bare mountains and rocks, and the old Don Manrique was very civil and agreeable. Then, after a few minutes' conversation of this kind, something of the old conscious abruptness of tone seemed to come over the young man, and looking down, he said bluntly, 'Miss Ponsonby, do you think there would be any objection to my coming into Lima just for Christmas?'

'I suppose not; I cannot tell.'

Tom explained that all the miners would be making holiday, and the senior Cornishman might safely be left in charge of the works, while he only wished to spend Christmas-day itself in the city, and would be a very short time absent. He blushed a little as he spoke, and Mary ventured to reply to what she gathered of his thought, 'No other day would suit you as well?'

'No, ma'am, it hardly would,' he answered, gravely.

'I will try what can be done,' said Mary, 'unless you would speak to Mr. Ponsonby yourself.'

He looked inquiringly at Mr. Ponsonby's figure some paces distant, and shook his head.

'I will try,' repeated Mary; and then she added, 'These grand hill-tops and blue sky almost make a church—'

'Yes, ma'am,' said Tom, his black eyes lighting at the thought; 'I've felt so sometimes, but 'tis a mighty lonely one after a time. I've taken my book, and got out of earshot of the noise the blacks make; and I do assure you, Miss Ponsonby, the stillness was enough to drive one wild, with nothing but savage rocks to look at either! Not a green plant, nor a voice to answer, unless one got to the mountain echoes, and they are worse—'

'But surely you have the Cornishmen! What do they do on a Sunday?'

'They lie about, and smoke and sleep, or go down to the valley,' said Tom. 'I never thought of them.'

'I think you should,' said Mary, gravely. 'If you are in any authority over them, it must give you a charge over their souls. I think you should, at least, give them the choice of reading the service with you.'

'I'll think about it,' said Madison, gruffly.

'I will send up some books for them to make an opening,' said Mary. 'I should not like to think of men living in such scenes, without being the better for them.'

Robson was here obliged to call Madison to refer some question to him; but Mary had another talk with him, when he begged to know if there were likely soon to be an opportunity of sending to England. He had some fossils which he wished to send to Lord Fitzjocelyn; and he fetched them, and explained his theories with regard to them as if he had almost forgotten that she was not his young Lord. She carried his request to her father, and was answered that of course he might take a holiday if he could leave the works with safety; he had better spend a few days in the town when he did come. With this answer she made him happy; and they set off, to the extreme joy of Rosita, who had engrossed much less attention than she had expected, and declared she would never have come into these horrible places if she could have imagined what they were like. Certainly, no one wished to have her company there again.

When Mr. Ponsonby mentioned the permission which he had accorded to Madison, Robson coughed and looked annoyed. Mary could not help suspecting that this was because the request had not been preferred through himself. 'So the young fellow wants to be coming down, does he? I thought his ardour was too hot to last long.'

'Very natural that the poor lad should want a holiday,' said Mr. Ponsonby. 'It must take a tolerable flow of spirits to stand long, being so many feet above the level of the sea, in caves fit for a robber's den at the theatre.'

'Oh, I am making no objection, sir,' returned Robson; 'the young man may take his pleasure for what I care, so he can be trusted not to neglect his business.'

Here the path narrowed, and Mary had to fall back out of hearing; but she had an unpleasant suspicion that Robson was telling her father something to Tom's disadvantage, and she had to consider how to avoid rousing a jealousy, which she knew might be dangerous.

Mr. Ward, however, came up to interrupt her thoughts and watch the steps of her mule. The worst difficulties of the descent had precluded all conversation; and the party were just beginning to breathe freely, think of terra firma as not far off, and gaze with easier minds on the marvellous ocean. Mary went on in very comfortable discussion of the wonders they had seen, and of Madison's remark that the performances of the Incas made one quite ashamed of the achievements of modern science—a saying in which Mr. Ward perfectly agreed; and then he began to say something rather long, and a little disconnected, and Mary's mind took an excursion to Aunt Kitty, and the reading of the letter that she was going to write, when suddenly something in Mr. Ward's voice startled her, and recalling her attention, she discovered, to her dismay, that he was actually making her an offer! An offer! She would as soon have expected one from her father! And oh! how well expressed—how entirely what it ought to be! How unlike every one of those three of her past experience!

In great distress she exclaimed, 'Oh, Mr. Ward, pray do not—indeed, I cannot!'

'I feared that I was but too likely to meet with such an answer,' said Mr. Ward; 'and yet your father encouraged me to hope, that in course of time—'

'Then papa has told you what he thinks?' said Mary.

'I applied to him before I could venture to join this party. Mary, I am aware that I can bring none of the advantages which have'—his voice faltered—'which have forestalled me; but the most true and earnest affection is already yours.'

'I am very sorry for it, Mr. Ward,' said Mary, gravely, though much touched. 'It is very kind of you, but it is only fair and candid to tell you that papa has probably led you into a mistake. He thinks that the—the object was weak and unworthy, and that my feelings could be easily overcome. He does not know—'

'He assured me that all was at an end—'

'It is,' said Mary; 'but I am certain that I shall never feel for any one else the same as'—and the tears were coming last. 'You are very kind, Mr. Ward, but it is of no use to think that this can ever be.'

'Forgive me for having harassed you,' said Mr. Ward, and they went on so long in silence that Mary hoped it was over, and yet he did not go away from her. She was sorry to see the grieved, dejected expression on his good, sensible, though somewhat worn countenance; and she esteemed him highly; but who could have thought of so unlucky a fancy coming into his head? When, at length, he spoke again, it was to say that he begged that she would forget what was past, and allow him to continue on his former footing. Mary was glad to have something grateful to say, and answered that she should have been very sorry to lose him as a friend; whereupon his face cheered up, he thanked her, and fell back from her rein. In spite of her past trials of the futility of the attempt to live with a rejected suitor as if nothing had happened, she had hopes of the possibility when her own heart was untouched, and the gentleman nearly doubled her years; but when she talked to her father, she gathered that it was considered by both gentlemen that the proposal had been premature, and that her final detachment from Louis was reckoned on as so certain that Mr. Ward was willing to wait, as if it were only a matter of time. He was so wealthy and prosperous, and a connexion with him would have been so useful to the firm, that Mary was grateful to her father for forbearing to press her on what he evidently wished so earnestly. Mr. Ward had exactly the excellent, well-balanced character, which seemed made to suit her, and she could have imagined being very happy with him, if—No, no—Mr. Ward could not be thought of at the same moment.

Yet, whatever she might say, no one would believe her; so she held her peace, and wrote her history of the silver mines; and Mr. Ward haunted the house, and was most kindly forbearing and patient, and Mary found at every turn, how good a man he was, and how cruel and mistaken his sister thought her.

And Christmas came, when the churches were perfect orange-groves, and the scene of the wanderers of Bethlehem was acted from house to house in the twilight. The scanty English congregation met in the room that served as a chapel in the Consul's house—poor Mary alone of all her household there to keep the feast; and Mr. Ward was there, and Madison had come down from his mountain. There were hearts at home that would rejoice to hear that.

Mary saw him afterwards, and he thanked her for her suggestion respecting the miners. Two had been only as shy as Tom himself; they had been reading alone, and were glad to join company, a third was beginning to come, and it had led to a more friendly intercourse. Mary sent him away, very happy with some books for them, some new Spanish reading for himself, an astronomical book, and her little celestial globe—for the whole firmament of stars had been by no means lost on him. That interview was her Christmas treat. Well for her that she did not hear Robson say, 'That young man knows how to come over the ladies. I shall keep a sharper look-out after him. I know no harm of him, but if there's one man I trust less than another, it is one that tries the serious dodge.'

CHAPTER X
THE WRONG WOMAN IN THE WRONG PLACE

> Give me again my hollow tree,
> My crust of bread, and liberty.
> The Town Mouse and the Country Mouse—POPE.

The new cook's first compliment to Charlotte was, 'Upon my word, you are a genteel young woman, I dare say you have a lot of sweethearts.'

The indignant denial of the Lady of Eschalott was construed into her being 'sly,' and Mrs. Cook promised herself to find her out.

Those were not happy days with the little maiden. The nurse looked down on her, and the cook filled the kitchen with idlers, whose looks and speeches were abhorrent to her. Sometimes the woman took offence at her for being high; at others, she forced on her advice upon her dress, or tried to draw out confidences either on lovers or the affairs of the family. Charlotte was sadly forlorn, and shut herself up in her pantry, or in her own little attic with Jane's verbenas which cook had banished from the kitchen, and lost her sorrows in books hired at the library. She read, and dreamt, created leisure for reading, lived in a trance, and awoke from it to see her work neglected, reproach herself, and strain her powers to make up for what was left undone. Then, finding her efforts failing, she would be distressed and melancholy, until a fresh novel engrossed her for a time, and the whole scene was enacted over again.

Still, it was not all idleness nor lost ground. The sense of responsibility was doing her good, she withstood the cook's follies, and magnanimously returned unopened a shining envelope of Mr. Delaford's. At Christmas, when Mr. and Mrs. Frost went to pay a visit at Beauchastel, and the cook enjoyed a course of gaieties, the only use she made of her liberty was to drink tea once with Mrs. Martha, and to walk over to Marksedge to see old Madison, who was fast breaking, and who dictated to her his last messages to his grandson.

James and Isabel spent a pleasant lively Christmas with their hospitable old friends, and James returned full of fresh vigour and new projects. His first was to offer his assistance to the Vicar, so as to have a third service on the Sunday; but there were differences of opinion between them, and his proposal was received so ungraciously, that a coolness arose, which cut him off from many openings for usefulness.

However, he had enough to occupy him in his own department, the school. He was astonished at his boys' deficiency in religious instruction, and started a plan for collecting them for some teaching for an hour before morning service. Mr. Calcott agreed with him that nothing could be more desirable, but doubted whether the parents would compel their sons to attend, and advised James to count the cost, doubting whether, in the long run, he would be able to dispense with one day of entire rest. This was the more to be considered, since James expended a wonderful amount of energy in his teaching, did his utmost to force the boys on, in class and in private, drilled his usher, joined in the games, and gave evening lectures on subjects of general information.

Some responded to his training, and these he strenuously encouraged, asking them to dinner and taking them to walk; and these were enthusiastically fond of him, and regarded his beautiful wife as a being of a superior order. Fitzjocelyn and James used to agree that intercourse with her was a very important element in their training, and the invitations were made as impartial as possible, including the intelligent and well-conducted, irrespective of station. Isabel's favourite guest was a good, well-mannered lad, son to Mr. Ramsbotham's follower, the butcher, but, unluckily, Mrs. Richardson and her friends did not esteem it a compliment when their sons were asked to meet him, and, on the other hand, James did not always distinguish real merit from mere responsiveness to his own mind. Dull boys, or such as had a half sullen, half conservative dislike to change, did not gain notice of an agreeable kind, and while intending to show strict justice, he did not know how far he was affected by his prepossessions.

His lectures had emancipated him from evening parties; and, after Mrs. Frost's departure, visiting gave Isabel little trouble. The calm, lofty manners that had been admired in Miss Conway, were thought pride in Mrs. James Frost, and none of the ladies of Northwold even wished to do more than exchange morning calls with her, and talk among themselves of her fine-ladyism. She recked nothing of their keeping aloof; her book and her pen were far pleasanter companions on her alternate evenings of solitude, and in them she tried to lose her wishes for the merry days spent with granny and Clara, and her occasional perceptions that all was not as in their time. James would sometimes bring this fact more palpably before her.

The separation of the families had not diminished the income of the household, but the difference in comfort was great. Isabel knew nothing of management, and did not care to learn. She had been willing to live on a small scale, but she did not understand personal superintendence, she was careless of display, and perfectly happy as long as she was the guest of the grandmother, but she had no comprehension of petty tidinesses or small economies. Now James, brought up on a very different scale, knew in detail how the household ought to live, and made it a duty not to exceed a fixed sum. He had the eye for neatness that she wanted; he could not believe it a hardship to go without indulgences to which his grandmother and sister had not been accustomed. Thus, he protested against unnecessary fires; Isabel shivered and wore shawls; he was hurt at seeming to misuse her, resigned his study fire, and still found the coals ever requiring to be renewed, insisted that his wife should speak to the cook, and mystified her by talking about the regulation of the draught of the kitchen fire; and when Isabel understood, she forgot the lecture.

He was a devoted and admiring husband, but he could not coolly discover innumerable petty neglects and wasteful habits. Impatient words broke out, and Isabel always received them so meekly that he repented and apologized; and in the reconciliation the subject was forgotten, but only to be revived another time. Isabel was always ready to give warm aid and sympathy in all his higher cares and purposes, and her mild tranquillity was repose and soothing to him, but she was like one in a dream. She had married a vision of perfection, and entered on a romance of happy poverty, and she had no desire to awaken; so she never exerted her mind upon the world around her, when it seemed oppressive; and kept the visionary James Frost before her, in company with Adeline and the transformed Sir Hubert. It was much easier to line his tent with a tapestry of Maltese crosses, than to consider whether the hall should be covered with cocoanut matting.

How Christmas passed with Clara, may be seen in the following letter:—

'Cheveleigh, Jan. 1851.

'Dearest Jem,—I can write a long letter to-night, for a fortunate cold has spared me from one of Sir Andrew's dinner-parties. It is a reminiscence of the last ball, partly brought on by compunction at having dragged poor granny thither, in consideration of my unguarded declaration of intense dislike to be chaperoned by Lady Britton. Granny looks glorious in black velvet and diamonds, and I do trust that her universal goodwill rendered the ball more tolerable to her than it was to me. She, at least, is all she seems; whereas I am so infested with civilities, that I long to proclaim myself little Clara Frost, bred up for a governess, and the laughing-stock of her school. Oh! for that first ball where no one danced with me but Mr. Richardson, and I was not a mere peg for the display of Uncle Oliver's Peruvian jewels! I have all the trouble in the world to be allowed to go about fit to be seen, and only by means of great fighting and coaxing did I prevail to have my dress only from London instead of Paris.

'And no wonder I shivered all the way to the ball. Fancy Jane insisting on my going to display my dress to that poor dying Marianne; I was shocked at the notion of carrying my frivolities into such a scene, but Jane said her mind ran on it, and it was 'anything to take off her thoughts from that man.' So I went into her room, and oh! if you could have seen the poor thing, with her short breath and racking cough, her cheeks burning and her eyes glistening at that flimsy trumpery. One bunch of the silver flowers on my skirt was wrong; she spied it, and they would not thwart her, so she would have the needle, and the skeleton trembling fingers set them right. They said she would sleep the easier for it, and she thanked me as if it had really set her more at rest; but how sad, how strange it seems, when she knows that she is sinking fast, and has had Mr. Danvers with her every day. He thinks all is well with her; but it was a melancholy, blank, untaught mind, to begin to work on. Louis would call her life a mournful picture of our civilization. She has told it all to Jane: she was of the mechanic class, just above the rank that goes to Sunday-schools; she went to a genteel weekly school, and was taken out pleasuring on Sunday—no ground-work at all. An orphan at fifteen, she never again knew tenderness. Then came dressmaking till her health failed, and she tried service. She says, Isabel's soft tones made a paradise for her; but late hours, which she did not feel at the time, wore her out, and Delaford trifled with her. Always when alone he pretended devotion to her, then flirted with any other who came in his way, and worry and fretting put the finish to her failing health. She had no spirit to break entirely with him, and even now is pining for one kind word, which he seems to be too hard and selfish to send to her, in answer to a letter of forgiveness that she wrote a fortnight back. What a wretch he must be! Jane says, he tried flirting with poor little Charlotte, and that she was a little 'took up' with his guitar and his verses; but then, Jane says, 'Charlotte has somewhat at the bottom, and knows better than to heed a man as wasn't real religious.' I suppose that is the true difference between Charlotte and Marianne, and even if we looked into Delaford's history, most likely we should find him another nineteenth-century victim to an artificial life. At least, I trust that Jane has been the greatest blessing, Marianne herself speaks of her as more than a mother to her; and I believe I told you of the poor girl's overpowering gratitude, when she found we would not turn her out to die homeless. We read, and we talk, and Mr. Danvers comes; but I believe dear old Jane does more for her than all.

'Poor Jane! when her task of nursing is over, I do not know what she will turn to. The grand servants only keep terms with her because Uncle Oliver gave notice that no one should stay in the house who did not show respect to his *friend* Mrs. Beckett. It takes all her love for Missus and Master Oliver to make her bear it; and her chief solace is in putting me to bed, and in airing Master Oliver's shirt and slippers. You would laugh to hear her compassionating the home minced-pies! and she tells me she would give fifty pounds rather than bring Charlotte here. My uncle wished grandmamma to manage the house, and she did so at first, but she and the servants did not get on well together; and she said, what I never knew her say before, that she is too old, and so we have an awful dame who rules with a high hand.

'You ask whether the dear granny is happy. You know she is all elasticity, and things are pleasanter here to her than to me, but I do not think she enjoys life as she did at home. It is hard to have her whole mission reduced to airing those four horses. We have tormented my uncle out of making us use more than two at a time, by begging for six and the Lord Mayor's coach; but aired alternately they must be, and we must do it, and by no road but what the coachman chooses; and this does not seem to me to agree with her like trotting about the town on her errands. There is no walking here, excepting in the pleasure-ground, where all my grandfather's landscape-gardening has been cut up so as to be a mere vexation to her. The people round are said to be savage and disaffected, and the quarter of a mile between the park and the village is subject to miners going home. They did once holloa at me, and orders were issued that I should walk no more. I believe that if they saw me fearless, and coming among them for friendly purposes, they would leave off hooting; but the notion frightens granny, so I am a prisoner. They are the people to think it a mockery to be visited by a lady bedizened as I am, and stuck up in a carriage; so we can do very little except through Mr. Danvers, and my uncle is always discontented at the sight of him, and fancies he is always begging. A little sauciness on my part has the best effect when anything is wanted, for my uncle is very kind to me in his own fashion, which is not mine.

'We have made something of a nest in the last of the suite of rooms, the only one habitably small; but it is wonderful where all the time in the day goes. My uncle likes me to ride with him in the morning, and I have to help granny air the horses in the afternoon; and in the evening, when we are lucky enough to dine alone, I play them both asleep, unless they go to backgammon. Think of granny reduced to that! We should be very happy when he is detained in his study, but that granny thinks it is bad for him. Dear granny!

I see the object of her life is to win him back to serious thoughts. She seems to think of him like a schoolboy who must be lured to find home pleasanter than idle ways; and she begs me quite sadly to bear with him, and make him happy, to prevent him from longing after his counting-house at Lima. She tried to make him promise never to go back, but he has only promised never to go while she lives, and she seems to think it would be fatal, and to charge all his disregard of religious matters upon herself for having sent him out. If you could see her pleased smile when we extort a subscription, or when she gets him to church; but when those South American mails come in on Sundays—alas! Those accounts are his real element, and his moments of bliss are over the 'Money-market and City intelligence,' or in discussing railway shares with Sir Andrew. All the rest is an obstinate and dismal allegiance to the days of Shrievalty, about as easy to recall as the days when the Pendragons wore golden collars and armlets. Imitated hospitality turns into ostentation; and the people who seek after silver covers and French cookery are no more to my taste than they are, in good earnest, to Uncle Oliver's. The nice people, if there are any, won't come in our way, except Mr. Henderson; and when we do pluck up courage to disgust Mr. Coachman by calling on Mrs. Henderson, we are very happy. But she is a wise woman, and will not bring her pretty Fanny into our world; and when I press her, behold! I remember what I used to think of patronage.

'But Louis has promised to come at Easter, and he will teach me a little more charity, I hope; and, what is better (no, I don't mean that), will tell me about the dear, dear, trebly dear Terrace and all the doings. I hope you will begin your Sunday scheme; but granny fears the bad set will not care, and the good will prefer having their families together. It is worse than I expected even of Mr. Purvis to refuse the afternoon service, when you offered to take all the trouble off his hands; granny hopes you will take care what you are about with him. Tell Louis we have a famous letter from Mary to show him if he will bring us all news of every one, and especially of his godchild. Contrary to custom, you tell us more about her than her mamma does.

'Your most affectionate Sister,
    'CLARA.'

Before Easter, Charlotte's poor rival was lying at rest in Cheveleigh churchyard, and Jane's task of love was at an end.

CHAPTER XI
AUNT CATHARINE'S HOME

> The lady sleeps—O may her sleep,
> As it is lasting, so be deep!
> Heaven have her in its sacred keep!
> This bed being changed for one more holy,
> This room for one more melancholy,
> Some tomb, that oft hath flung its black
> And wing-like panels fluttering back,
> Triumphant o'er the fluttering palls
> Of her grand family funerals.
> E. A. POE.

The summer was nearly over, when, one morning at breakfast, Louis surprised his father by a sound, half consternation, half amusement, and handed him a note, containing these words:—

> 'DEAR F.,—There were three of us last night; there are five this morning. Isabel and the twins are doing well. Heaven knows what is to become of us!
> 'Yours,
>   J. F.'

'What would you have?' said Lord Ormersfield, calmly. 'The poorer people are, the more children they have!'

He went on with his own letters, while Louis laughed at the enunciation of this inverse ratio; and then took up the note again, to wonder at the tone of anxiety and distress, so unlike James. He went to call on Lady Conway, and was better satisfied to find that James had written in a lively strain to her, as if proud of his little daughters, and resolved not to be pitied. Of this he was in no danger from his sisters-in-law, who looked upon twin-girls as the only blessing needed to complete Isabel's felicity, had devised three dozen names for them, and longed to be invited to Northwold to see them.

Nothing was heard of James for more than a week, and, as London grew hotter, dustier, and drearier than ever, Fitzjocelyn longed, more than he thought wholesome to confess, after Ormersfield turf, the deep ravines, and rushing brooks. The sun shone almost through the blind of the open window on the large library table, where sat Louis at his own end, writing to his Inglewood bailiff, and now and then solacing himself by lifting with the feather of his pen one of the bells of a delicate lily in a glass before him—a new spectacle on the Earl's writing-table; and so was a strip of vellum, with illuminations rich and rare—Louis's indulgence when he felt he had earned an hour's leisure. There was a ring at the door, a step on the stairs, and before the father and son stood James, his little black bag in his hand, like himself, all dust, and his face worn, heated, and tired.

'Then you have not heard from Cheveleigh?' he said, in answer to their astonished greetings, producing a note, which was eagerly read:—

> 'Dearest Jem,—My uncle says I may write to you, in case you can leave Isabel, that he will be glad to see you. I told you that dear grandmamma had a cold, and so we would not let her come to Isabel; but I little guessed what was coming. It only seemed a feverish cold, and Jane and I almost laughed at my uncle for choosing to send for a doctor. He was not alarmed at first, but yesterday she was inert and sleepy, and he asked for more advice. Dr. Hastings came to-day, and oh! Jem, he calls it a breaking up of the constitution, and does not think she will rally. She knows us, but she is almost always drowsy, and very hard to rouse. If you can come without hurting Isabel, I know you will. We want you all the more, because my uncle will not let me send for Mr. Danvers. Poor Uncle Oliver is dreadfully troubled.
> 'Your most affectionate CLARA.'

'Transplantation has killed her—I knew it would!' said James, as Louis stood, with the note in his hand, as if not yet understanding the blow.

'Nay,' said the Earl, 'it is an age at which we could hardly hope she would long be spared. You could leave Mrs. James Frost with comfort?'

'Yes, Miss Mercy undertakes her—she is doing well—she would not hear of my staying. I must go on, the train starts at two,' he added, hastily, looking at the time-piece.

'We will send you,' said Lord Ormersfield. 'Take time to rest. You look very ill! You should have some luncheon.'

'No, thank you!' said James, at first with the instinct of resistance; but yielding and confessing, 'Charlotte went into hysterics, and I had nothing to eat before I came away.'

Louis came forward from the window where he had been standing as in a dream, he laid his hand on James's shoulder, and said, 'I will go!' His voice was hardly audible, but, clearing it, and striving to recall his thoughts, he added, 'Father, I can be spared. The division is not coming on to-night, or you could get me a pair.'

The Earl looked doubtfully at James.

'Yes, let me go,' said Louis. 'I must see her again. It has been mother and son between us.' And, hiding his face in his hands, he hurried out of the room.

'Let him come,' said James. 'If duty and affection claim a right, none have such as he.'

'I hesitate only as to acting unceremoniously by your uncle.'

'This is no moment for ceremony—no time to deprive her of whatever she loves best.'

'Be it so, then. His own feelings are his best passport, and well has she deserved all that he can ever feel! And, James, if she should express any desire to see me, if I can be of any use in settling matters, or could promote any better understanding with your uncle, I am ready at a moment's notice. I would come at once, but that many might be burdensome to your uncle and sister.'

The two cousins were quickly on their way. James took a second-class ticket, the first time he had ever done so in travelling with his cousin. Fitzjocelyn placed himself beside him without remark.

James dozed as well as the narrow seat would permit, and only woke to chafe at each halt, and Louis mused over the associations of those scenes, and last year's triumphant return. Had the change of habits truly hastened the decay of her powers? had her son's toil and success been merely to bring her home to the grave of her fathers, at the expense of so many heartburnings, separations, and dissensions? At least, he trusted that her last hours might be crowned by the peacemaker's joy, and that she might see strife and bitterness laid aside between Oliver, and Henry's only surviving son.

Alas! it was not to be. The shutters and blinds were closed, and Clara met them at the door, her pale face and streaming eyes forestalling the tidings. The frame, hitherto so vigorous and active, had been spared long or weary decay; and tranquil torpor had mildly conducted the happy, gentle spirit to full repose. She had slumbered away without revival or suffering, as one who did 'rest from her labours,' and her eyes had been closed on the previous night.

Clara wept as she spoke, but she had been alone with her sorrow long enough to face it, and endure calmly.

Not so her brother. It was anguish to have come too late, and to have missed the last word and look; and he strode madly up and down the room, almost raving at the separation and removal which he declared had killed her.

'Oh, speak to him, Louis!' cried Clara. 'Oh, what shall I do?'

As she spoke, the door was opened, and Mr. Dynevor came in, with a grief-stricken look and quieter manner, but his entrance instantly silenced all James's demonstrations, and changed them into a haughty, compressed bitterness, as though he actually looked on him in the light of his grandmother's destroyer.

'Ah! James,' began his uncle, gently, 'I wish you had been here earlier!'

'I left home by the first train after hearing. I ought to have heard sooner.'

'I could not suppose you would choose to come here without serious reason,' said Oliver, with more dignity than usual. 'However, I would willingly forget, and you will remain here for the present.'

'I must apologize for having thrust myself on you, sir,' said Louis, 'but, indeed, I could not stay away. After what she has been to me, ever since I can remember her—' and tears cut him short.

'Sir, it does you honour!' returned Oliver. 'She was attached to you. I hope you will not leave us as yet.'

Louis felt as if he could not leave the house where what was mortal of his dear old aunt yet remained, and he likewise had a perception that he might be a support and assistance to Clara in keeping the peace between her brother and uncle; so he gratefully accepted the invitation.

Mr. Dynevor presently explained that he intended the funeral to take place at the end of the week.

'I can not be so long from home,' said James, in a quick, low voice.

Clara ran up to her uncle, laid her hand on his arm, and drew him into a window, whence he presently turned, saying, 'Your sister tells me that you cannot be so long absent in the present state of your family. If possible, the day shall be hastened.'

James was obliged to say, 'Thank you!' but any concession seemed to affect him like an injury.

Grievous work was it to remain at Cheveleigh, under the constant dread of some unbecoming outbreak between uncle and nephew. Fortunately, Oliver had too much on his hands to have much time to spend with the others; but when they were together, there was scarcely a safe subject, not even the intended names of the twins. James made hasty answer that they had already received their names, Mercy and Salome. Louis and Clara both cried out incredulously.

'Yes,' said James. 'We don't like family names.'

'But such as those!'

'I wish nothing better for them than to be such another pair of faithful sisters. May they only do as well, poor children!'

The end was softer than the beginning, and there was a tight short sigh, that seemed to burst upward from a whole world of suppressed anxiety and despondence.

It was not easy to understand him, he would not talk of home, was brief about his little Catharine; and when Clara said something of Isabel's writings, formerly his great pride, and feared that she would have no more time for them, his blunt answer was, 'She ought not.'

These comparatively indifferent topics were the only resource; for he treated allusions to his grandmother as if they were rending open a wound, and it was only in his absence that Louis and Clara could hold the conversations respecting her, which were their chief comfort and relief. If they were certain that Oliver was busy, and James writing letters, they would walk up and down the sheltered alley, where Louis had last year comforted Clara. The green twilight and chequered shade well accorded with the state of their minds, darkened, indeed, by one of the severest losses that could ever befall either of them, and yet it was a sorrow full of thankfulness and blessed hope.

Louis spoke of his regret that scenes of uncongenial gaiety should have been forced upon her last year.

'I believe it made very little difference to her,' said Clara. 'She did just what Uncle Oliver wished, but only as she used to play with us, no more; nay, rather less for her own amusement than as she would play at battledore, or at thread-paper verses.'

'And she was not teased nor harassed?'

'I think not. She was grieved if I were set against Uncle Oliver's plans, and really hurt if she could not make him think as she did about right and wrong, but otherwise she was always bright. She never found people tiresome; she could find something kind to say to and for the silliest; and when my uncle's display was most provoking, she would only laugh at 'poor Oliver's' odd notions of doing her honour. I used to be quite ashamed of the fuss I would make when I thought a thing vulgar; when I saw that sort of vanity by the side of her real indifference, springing from unworldliness.'

'And then her mornings were quiet?'

'More quiet than at home. While we were riding, she used to sit with her dear old big Bible, and the two or three old books she was so fond of. You remember her Sutton and her Bishop Home, and often she would show me some passage that had struck her as prettier than ever, well as she had always known it. Once she said she was very thankful for the leisure time, free from household cares, and even from friendly gossip; for she said first she had been gay, then she had been busy, and had never had time to meditate quietly.'

'So she made a cloister of this grand house. Ah! I trusted she was past being hurt by external things. That grand old age was like a pure glad air where worldly fumes could not mount up. My only fear would have been this unlucky estrangement making her unhappy.'

'I think I may tell you how she felt it,' said Clara; 'I am trying to tell James, but I don't know whether I can. She said she had come to perceive that she had confounded pride with independence. She blamed herself, so that I could not bear to hear it, for the grand fine things in her life. She said pride had made her stand alone, and unkindly spurn much that was kindly meant. I don't mean that she repented of the actions, but of the motives; she said the glory of being beholden to no one had run through everything; and had been very hurtful even to Uncle Oliver. She never let him know all her straits, and was too proud, she said, to ask, when she was hurt at his not offering help, and so she made him seem more hard-hearted, and let us become set against him. She said she had fostered the same temper in poor Jem, who had it strongly enough by inheritance, and that she had never known the evil, nor understood it as pride, till she saw the effects.'

'Did they make her unhappy?'

'She cried when she spoke of it, and I have seen her in tears at church, and found her eyes red when she had been alone, but I don't think it was a hard, cruel sorrow; I think the sunshine of her nature managed to beam through it.'

'The sunshine was surely love,' said Louis, 'making the rainbow of hope on the tears of repentance. Perhaps it is a blessing vouchsafed to the true of heart to become aware of such a hidden constitutional infirmity in time to wash it out with blessed tears like those.'

'Hidden,' said Clara, 'yes, indeed it was, even from herself, because it never showed in manner, like my pride; she was gracious and affable to all the world. I heard the weeding-women saying, 'she had not one bit of pride,' and when I told her of it, she shook her head, and laughed sadly, and said that was the kind of thing which had taken her in.'

'Common parlance is a deceitful thing,' said Louis, sighing; 'people can't even be sincere without doing harm! Well, I had looked to see her made happy by harmony between those two!'

'She gave up the hope of seeing it,' said Clara, 'but she looked to it all the same. She said meekly one day that it might be her penalty to see them at variance in her own lifetime, but over her grave perhaps they would be reconciled, and her prayers be answered. How she did love Uncle Oliver! Do you know, Louis, what she was to him showed me what the mother's love must be, which we never missed, because—because we had her!'

'Don't talk of it, Clara,' said Louis, hastily; 'we cannot dwell on ourselves, and bear it patiently!'

It was truly the loss of a most tender mother to them both; bringing for the first time the sense of orphanhood on the girl, left between the uncongenial though doting uncle, and the irritable though affectionate brother; and Louis, though his home was not broken up, suffered scarcely less. His aunt's playful sweetness had peculiarly accorded with his disposition, and the affection and confidence of his fond, clinging nature had fastened themselves upon her, all the more in the absence of his own Mary. Each loss seemed to make the other more painful. Aunt Kitty's correspondence was another link cut away between him and Peru, and he had never known such a sense of dreariness in his whole life. Clara was going patiently and quietly through those trying days, with womanly considerateness; believing herself supported by her brother, and being so in fact by the mere sisterly gratification of his presence, though she was far more really sustained and assisted by Fitzjocelyn. How much happier was the sorrow of Louis and

Clara than that of James or Oliver! Tempers such as those in which the uncle and nephew but too closely resembled each other were soured, not softened by grief, and every arrangement raised discussions which did not tend to bring them nearer together.

Oliver designed a stately funeral. Nothing was too much for him to lavish on his mother, and he was profuse in orders for hangings, velvet, blazonry, mutes, and hired mourners, greedy of offers of the dreary state of empty carriages, demanding that of Lord Ormersfield, and wanting James to write to Lady Conway for the same purpose.

Nothing could be more adverse to the feelings of the grandchildren; but Clara had been schooled into letting her uncle have his way, and knew that dear granny would have said Oliver might do as he pleased with her in death as in life, owning the affection so unpleasantly manifested; James, on the other hand, could see no affection, nothing but disgusting parade, as abhorrent to his grandmother's taste as to his own. He thought he had a right to be consulted, for he by no means believed himself to have abdicated his headship of the family; and he made his voice heard entirely without effect, except the indignation of his uncle, and the absence of the Conway carriage; although Lord Ormersfield wrote that he should bring Sir Walter in his own person, thus leaving James divided between satisfaction in any real token of respect to his grandmother, and dislike to gratifying Oliver's ostentation by the production of his baronet kin.

Sydney Calcott wrote to him in the name of various former scholars of Mrs. Frost, anxious to do her the last honours by attending the funeral. Homage to her days of gallant exertion in poverty was most welcome and touching to the young people; but their uncle, without taste to understand it, wishing to forget her labours, and fancying them discreditable to a daughter of the Dynevors, received the proposal like an indignity; and but for Fitzjocelyn's mediation and expostulations, it would have been most unsuitably rejected. He was obliged to take the answer into his own hands, since Oliver insisted that his mother was to be regarded in no light save that of Mrs. Dynevor, of Cheveleigh; and James was equally resolved that she should be only Mrs. Frost, of Dynevor Terrace.

It was heart-sickening to see these bickerings over the grave of one so loving and so beloved; and very trying to be always on the alert to obviate the snappings that might at any time become a sharp dissension; but nothing very distressing actually arose until the last day before the funeral, when the three cousins were sitting together in the morning-room; James writing letters.

'I am asking Lady Conway to give you a bed to-morrow night, Clara,' he said. 'We shall be at home by three o'clock.'

'Oh, Jem!' said Clara, clasping her hands to keep them from trembling; 'I never thought of that.'

'You are not ready! That is unlucky, for I cannot come to fetch you; but I suppose you can travel down with Jane. Only I should have thought it easier to do the thing at once.'

'But, Jem! has my uncle said anything? Does he wish me to go?'

James laid down his pen, and stood upright, as if he did not understand her words.

Clara came up to him, saying, 'I believe I ought to do what he may wish.'

'I told you,' said James, as if her words were not worth considering, 'that you need only remain here on her account, who no longer needs you.'

Louis would have left them to themselves, but Clara's glance sued for his protection, and, as he settled himself in his chair, she spoke with more decision.—'Dear James, nothing would make me so happy as to go to dear home; but I do not think grandmamma would like me to leave Uncle Oliver.'

'Oh, very well,' said James, sitting down to his writing, as if he had done with her; 'I understand.'

'Dear James! O tell me you are not angry with me! Tell me you think I am right!' cried Clara, alarmed by his manner.

'Quite right in one point of view,' he said, with acrimony.

'James,' said Louis, very low, but so as to make them both start, 'that is not the way to treat your sister!'

'We will renew the discussion another time, if you wish it, Clara,' said James.

'No,' said Clara, 'I wish Louis to be here. He will judge for me,' and she spoke clearly, her face colouring. 'It was grandmamma's great wish that I should love my uncle. She used to beg me to be patient with him, and rejoiced to see us together. She often said he must not be left with no one to make a home for him, and to go out to Lima again.'

'Did she ever desire you to remain here?'

'No,' said Clara, 'she never did; but I am convinced that if she had known how soon she was to leave us, she would have done so. I feel as much bound as if she had. I have heard her call him my charge. And not only so, but my uncle has never varied in his kindness to me, and when he worked all his life for grandmamma, and my father, it would be wicked and cruel in me—if he does care for me—to forsake him, now he has lost them all, and is growing old.'

'You need not scruple on that score,' said James. 'He has attained his object, and made the most of it. He is free now, and he will soon find a Rosita, if his mines are not sufficient for him.'

'James, you should not say wrong things,' said Clara.

'I am not likely to think it wrong, whatever you may. I have no expectations. Do not rise up in arms against me, Fitzjocelyn, I do not accuse her. I might have foreseen it. She meant well at first, but the Terrace cannot bear competition with a place like this. Where two so-called duties clash, she is at perfect liberty to make her choice. It would not be easy to come down to what I have to offer. I understand. The world will call it a wise choice. Say no more, Clara, I feel no anger.'

She attempted no words; she clasped her hands over her face, and ran out of the room.

'James,' said Louis, rising, indignation rendering his voice more low and clearly distinct than ever, 'I little thought to hear you insult that orphan sister of yours in her grief. No! I shall not defend her, I shall go to give her what comfort I can. Heaven help her, poor lonely child!'

He was gone. James paced about in desperation, raving against Louis for maintaining what he thought Clara's self-deception; and, in the blindness of anger, imagining that their ultra-generosity would conduct them to the repair of Ormersfield with the revenues of Cheveleigh; and, disdainful as he was, it seemed another cruel outrage that his rightful inheritance should be in the hands of another, and his children portionless. He was far too wrathful to have any consistency or discrimination in his anger, and he was cruelly wounded at finding that his sister deserted him, as he thought, for her uncle's riches, and that his own closest friend was ready to share the spoil.

In the stillness of the house, the sound of a door had revealed to Louis where to seek his cousin. It was in the grand saloon, where the closed shutters availed not to exclude the solid beams of slanting sunlight falling through the crevices, and glancing on the gilding, velvet, and blazonry upon the costly coffin, that shut her out from the dear tender hands and lips that had never failed to caress away her childish griefs. At first, the strange broad lines of shadowy light in the gloom were all he could see, but one ray tinged with paly light a plaited tress, which could only be Clara's flaxen hair.

She had flung herself, crouching in a heap, on the floor, never stirring, so that he almost feared she had fainted; and, kneeling on one knee beside her, spoke soothingly: 'My poor little dear Clary, this is the worst of all, but you know it was not Jem who spoke. It was only prejudice and temper. He is not himself.'

The dim light seemed to encourage Clara to lift her head to listen to the kind words. 'Was I so very wrong?' she murmured; 'you know I never thought of that! Will he forgive me, and let me come home? But, oh, granny! and what is to become of my uncle?' she ended, with a sound of misery.

'Not here, not now, Clara—' said Louis; 'She is in perfect peace; unhurt by our unhappy dissensions; she is with Him who looks at hearts, who can take away all variance.'

There was a short space of silence, as the two cousins knelt in the darkened room, in the sunbeams, which seemed as if they could not yet forsake her who had lived in the light of love.

Presently Louis gave Clara his hand to raise her, and led her into the adjoining room, also dim, but full of sweet fragrant breezes from the garden. He seated her on a low couch, and stood by, anxiously watching her.

'If he had only told me I was wrong!' she sighed.

'He could not tell you so, Clara, for it is not wrong, and he knows it is not. He will thank you by-and-by for not attending to him, now that he does not know what he says. He is fairly distracted with this grief coming upon his home cares.'

'Cares at dear, dear happy home!' cried Clara. 'Never!'

'Ah, Clara! I fear that much comfort went away with dear granny. I think he is overtasking himself at the school; and three children within a year may well make a man anxious and oppressed.'

'And I have vexed and disappointed him more!' exclaimed she. 'No wonder he was angry, and ready to impute anything! But he will believe me, he will forgive me, he will take me home.'

'It is my belief,' said Fitzjocelyn, in his peculiar way, 'that the worst injury you could do to James would be to give way to the spirit that has possessed him.'

'But, Louis,' cried Clara, wildly astonished, 'I must go; I can't have Jem saying these things of me.'

'His saying them does not make them true.'

'He is my brother. He has the only right to me. If I must choose between him and my uncle, he must be mine—mine.'

'You have not to choose between him and your uncle. You have to choose between right and wrong, between his frenzy and his true good.'

'My brother! my brother! I go with my brother!' was still her vehement cry. Without listening to her cousin's last words, she made a gesture to put him aside, and rose to hurry to her brother.

But Louis stood before her, and spoke gravely. 'Very well. Yield yourself to his management. Go back to be another burden upon a household, poor enough already to sour him with cares. Let him tell your uncle that both his brother's children loathe the fruit of the self-sacrifice of a lifetime. Transgress your grandmother's wishes; condemn that poor man to a desolate, objectless, covetous old age; make the breach irreconcilable for ever; and will James be the better or the happier for your allowing his evil temper the full swing?'

Clara wrung her hands. 'My uncle! Yes, what shall I do with my uncle? If I could only have them both?'

'This way you would have neither. Keep the straight path, and you may end in having both.'

'Straight—I don't know what straight is! It must be right to cling to my own brother in his noble poverty. Oh! that he should imagine me caring for this horrid, horrid state and grandeur!'

Louis recurred to the old argument, that James did not know what he was saying, and recalled her to the remembrance of what she had felt to be the right course before James's ebullition. She owned it most reluctantly; but oh! she said, would James still forgive her, and not believe such dreadful things, but trust and be patient with her, and perhaps Uncle Oliver might after all be set on going to Peru, and beyond remonstrance. Then it would all come right—no, not right, for granny had dreaded his going. Confused and distressed by the conflicting claims, Clara was thankful for the present respite given to her by Louis's promise that his father should sound her uncle as to his wishes and intentions. Lord Ormersfield's upright, unimpassioned judgment appeared like a sort of refuge from the conflict of the various claims, and he was besides in a degree, her guardian, being the sole executor of the only will which Mrs. Frost had ever made, soon after the orphans came under her charge, giving the Terrace to James, and dividing the money in the Funds between the two.

Weeping, but not unhopeful—convinced, though not acknowledging it—only praying for strength and patience, and hungering for one kind word from James—Clara quitted that almost brother, in whose counsel he had constrained her to seek relief, and went to her own chamber, there to throw herself on the guidance of that Friend, who sticketh closer than a brother.

The remaining part of the day passed quietly. James did not consciously make any difference in his manner, meaning to be still affectionate, though disappointed, and pitying her mistake, both as to her present happiness and future good.

Lord Ormersfield and Walter arrived in the evening, and James applied himself to finding occupation for his brother-in-law, whom he kept out of the way in the garden very satisfactorily. The Earl was so softened and sorrowful, that Clara hardly knew him. He deeply felt the loss of the kind, gentle aunt, whose sympathy had been more to him than he had known at the time; the last remnant of the previous generation, the last link with his youth, and he was even more grieved for the blank she left with Louis than for himself. By Louis's desire, he inquired into Oliver's intentions. 'Must stay here,' was the answer. 'Can't leave that child alone with the property. I can look to the Equatorial Company here—must do without me out there. No, no, I can't leave the girl to her brother; he'd teach her his own nasty, spiteful temper, and waste the property on all those brats. No, I'm fixed here; I must look after Henry's child, fine girl, good-tempered girl; takes after Henry, don't you think so?'

That Clara took after her father in anything but being tall and fair, would hardly have been granted by any one who knew her better than the Earl, but he readily allowed it, and Oliver proceeded:—'As long as she does not marry, here I am; but I trust some one will soon take the care of her off my hands—man who would look after the property well. She's a good girl too, and the finest figure in the whole county; lucky him who gets her. I shall be sorry to part with the child, too, but I shall be working for her, and there's nothing left that cares a rush for me now, so I might as well be out of the way of the young things. I know the old place at Lima, and the place knows me; and what do I care for this now my mother is gone? If I could only see Clara safe settled here, then I should care as little what became of me as I suppose she would.'

The Earl was touched by the dreary, desponding tone of the reply, and reported it to Louis and Clara with such terms, that Clara's decision was made at once, namely, that it would be wrong and cruel to cast away her uncle, and be swayed by James's prejudice; and Lord Ormersfield told her with grave approval that she was quite right, and that he hoped that James would recover from his unreasonable folly.

'Make Jem forgive me,' said Clara, faintly, as her announcement of her purpose, when she finally sought her room, obliged to be thought meanly of, rather than do ill, denying her fondest affections, cutting herself off from all she loved, and, with but this consolation, that she was doing as grandmamma would have bidden her. Oh, how her heart yearned after home!

On the morrow, Clara sorrowed in her solitary chamber alone with faithful Jane, who, amid her bursts of tears, felt the one satisfaction, that her dear mistress had lived to be buried like the stock she came of, and who counted the carriages and numbered the scarfs, like so many additional tributes from the affection of her dear Master Oliver.

Once on that day James was visibly startled from his heavy, stern mood of compressed, indignant sorrow. It was as he advanced to the entrance of the vault, and his eye was struck by a new and very handsome tablet on the wall. It was to the father, mother, and young brother and sisters, whose graves had been hastily made far away in the time of the pestilence, the only Dynevors who did not lie in the tombs of their fathers. For one moment James moved nearer to his uncle. Could he have spoken then, what might not have followed? but it was impossible, and the impulse passed away.

But he was kind when he hurried upstairs for a last embrace to Clara. He still felt fondly, brotherly, and compassionate; and all the more, because she had proved more weak against temptation than he had expected. His farewell was, 'Good-bye, my poor Clara, God bless you.'

'Oh, thank you!' cried Clara, from the bottom of her heart. 'You forgive me, James?'

'I forgive; I am sorry for you, my poor child. Mind, Dynevor Terrace is still your home, if you do not find the happiness you expect in your chosen lot.'

'Happiness!' but he had no time to hear. He was gone, while she sobbed out her message of love for Isabel, and Louis ran up, pale with repressed suffering, and speaking with difficulty, as he wrung her hand, and murmured, 'Oh, Clara! may we but abide patiently.'

After his good-bye, he turned back again to say, 'I'm selfish; but let me put you in mind not to let the Lima correspondence drop.'

'Oh, no, no; you know I won't.'

'Thank you! And let me leave you Mary's keynote of comfort, 'Commit thy way unto the Lord, and He will bring it to pass.''

'Thank you,' said Clara, in her turn, and she was left alone.

CHAPTER XII
THE FROST HOUSEHOLD

> The wind of late breathed gently forth,
> Now shifted east, and east by north,
> Bare trees and shrubs but ill, you know,
> Could shelter them from rain or snow,
> Stepping into their nests they paddled,
> Themselves were chilled, their eggs were addled,
> Soon every father bird and mother
> Grew quarrelsome, and pecked each other.
>   Pairing Time Anticipated—COWPER.

Three weeks longer did the session drag on, but on the joyful day when release was given, Lord Ormersfield was surprised to find Mr. Dynevor's card upon his table, with an address at Farrance's hotel.

Louis alone was at leisure to repair thither. He found Clara alone, looking as if her grief were still very fresh, and, though striving to speak gaily, the tears very near the surface.

'We are going abroad,' she said; 'Uncle Oliver thinks it a part of my education, and declares he will not have me behind the Miss Brittons. We are bound straight for Switzerland.'

'Lucky girl,' said Louis.

'I'm sure I don't care for it,' said Clara; 'mountains and pictures are not a bit in my line, unless I had Isabel and you, Louis, to make me care.'

'Learn, then,' said Louis; 'it shows that your education is defective. Yes, I see,' he continued, as Clara signed heavily, 'but you don't know the good it will do you to have your mind forcibly turned aside.'

'If I could only sit quiet in a corner,' said Clara.

'So you will, in many a corner of a railway carriage.'

She smiled a little. 'The truth is,' she said, 'that poor Uncle Oliver cannot be quiet. I can't see what pleasure Italy will be to him, but he is too miserable at home. I never saw such restless unhappiness!' and her eyes filled with tears. 'Oh, Louis! I am glad you would not let me say anything about leaving him. Sometimes when he bids me good night, he puts his arm round me, and says so pitifully that I do not care for him. Do you know, I think mine is the little spar of love that he tries to cling to in the great ship wreck; and I feel quite sorry and hypocritical that it is such a poor, miserable shred.'

'It will grow,' said Louis, smiling.

'I don't know; he is terribly provoking sometimes—and without dear granny to hinder the rubs. O, Louis! it is true that there is no bearing to stay at home in those great empty rooms!'

'And Jane?'

'Oh, she goes,' said Clara, recovering a smile; 'she is firmly persuaded that we shall run into another revolution, and as she could not frighten us by the description of your wounds, she decides to come and dress ours when we get any. Dear old Jenny, I am glad she goes; she is the only creature I can talk to; but, Louis, before my uncle comes in, I have something to give you.'

It was the letters that Mary had written to her aunt since the parting, and the Spanish books which she had left in her charge.

'It is very kind in you, Clara,' said Louis, fervently.

They talked of Mary, and a little of James, from whom Clara had once heard; but it had been a stiff letter, as if a barrier were between them, and then Mr. Dynevor came in, and seemed pleased to find Louis there; even asking him whether he could not join them on their tour, and help Clara to speak French.

'No, thank you, sir,' said Louis, 'I am afraid my company brought no good luck last time.'

'Never mind that—manage better now—ha, Clara.'

'It would be very nice; but he has a great deal too much to do at home,' said Clara.

Oliver would not be persuaded that Fitzjocelyn would not meet them abroad, and began magniloquently talking of his courier, and his route, and while he was looking for the map, the two cousins smiled, and Clara said,— 'Lucky you to have work at home, and to stay with it.'

'Only I say, Clara, when you break down anywhere, send me a telegraph.'

'No such good luck,' sighed Clara.

'So he won't come,' said her uncle, when he was gone; 'but we shall have him following us yet—Ha! ha! Never mind, Clara.'

Clara laughed. She knew what her uncle meant, but the notion was to her too impossible and ridiculous even to need a blush. She did not think the world contained Louis's equal; but she had always known that his love was disposed of, and she no more thought of wishing for it than for any other impossible thing. His affection for Mary gave her no more pain than did that of James for Isabel; and she would have treated with scorn and anger anything that impeached his constancy. The pleasure with which he received Mary's letters was the single satisfaction that she carried away with her.

And so she was borne away, and her sad heart could not choose but be somewhat enlivened by change and novelty, while her uncle made it his business to show her everything as rapidly as it could be seen, apparently with no relish himself for aught but perpetual movement.

So passed the autumn with Clara. It was not much brighter at Dynevor Terrace. Clara, being still under age, had it not in her power to resign her half of her grandmother's income, even if her brother would have accepted it; and 70 pounds made a difference in such an income as James's, more especially as his innovations did not tend to fill the school.

Murmurs were going about that Mr. Frost was severe, or that he was partial. Some censured his old opinions, others his new studies; one had been affronted by being almost told his boy was a dunce, another hated all this new-fangled nonsense. The ladies were all, to a woman, up against his wife, her airs, her poverty, her twins, and her housekeeping; and seldom spoke of her save to contrast her with good old Mrs. Frost. And then it was plain that something was wrong between him and his uncle, and no one could believe but that his temper had been the cause. The good Miss Faithfulls struggled in vain to silence scandal, and keep it from 'coming round;' and luckily Isabel was the last person likely either to hear or resent.

The boys met with decreased numbers after the holidays; and James received them with undiminished energy, but with failing patience, and a temper not improved by the late transactions at Cheveleigh, and fretted, as Louis had divined, by home cares.

Of all living women, Isabel was one of the least formed by habits or education to be an economical housewife and the mother of twins. Maternal love did not develop into unwearied delight in infant companionship, nor exclusive interest in baby smiles; and while she had great visions for the future education of her little maidens, she was not desirous to prolong the time spent in their society, but in general preferred peace and Sir Hubert.

On the other hand, James was an unusually caressing father. After hours among rough inattentive boys, nothing rested him so much as to fondle those tender creatures; his eldest girl knew him, and was in ecstasy whenever he approached; and the little pair of babies, by their mere soft helplessness, gave him an indescribable sense of fondness and refreshment. His little ones were all the world to him, and he could not see how a pattern mother should ever be so happy as with them around her. He forgot the difference between the pastime of an hour and the employment of a day. The need of such care on her part was the greater since the nursery establishment was deficient. The grand nurse had almost abdicated on the double addition to her charge, and had only been bribed to stay by an ill-spared increase in wages, and a share in an underling, who was also to help Charlotte in her housemaid's department. Nevertheless, the nurse was always complaining; the children, though healthy, always crying, and their father always certain it was somebody's fault. Nor did the family expenses diminish, retrench his own indulgences as he might. It was the mistress's eye that was wanting, and Isabel did not know how to use it. The few domestic cares that she perceived to be her duty were gone through as weary tasks, and her mind continued involved in her own romantic world, where she was oblivious of all that was troublesome or vexatious. Now and then she was aware of a sluggish dulness that seemed to be creeping over her higher aspirations—a want of glow and feeling on religious subjects, even in the most sacred moments; and she wondered and grieved at a condition, such as she had never experienced in what she had thought far more untoward circumstances. She did not see the difference between doing her best when her will was thwarted, and her present life of neglect and indulgence. Nothing roused her; she did not perceive omissions that would have fretted women of housewifely instincts, and her soft dignity and smooth temper felt few annoyances; and though James could sometimes be petulant, he was always withheld from reproving her both by his enthusiastic fondness, and his sense that for him she had quitted her natural station of ease and prosperity.

On a dark hazy November afternoon, when the boys had been unusually obtuse and mischievous, and James, worn-out, wearied, and uncertain whether his cuts had alighted on the most guilty heads, strode home with his arm full of Latin exercises, launched them into the study, and was running up to the drawing-room, when he almost fell over Charlotte, who was scouring the stairs.

She gave a little start and scream, and stood up to let him pass. He was about to rebuke her for doing such work at such an hour; but he saw her flushed, panting, and evidently very tired, and his wrath was averted.

Hurrying on to the drawing-room, he found Isabel eagerly writing. She looked up with a pretty smile of greeting; but he only ran his hand through his already disordered hair, and exclaimed—

'Our stairs are like the Captain of Knockdunder's. You never know they are cleaned, except by tumbling over the bucket and the maid.'

'Are they being done?' said Isabel, quietly. 'I suppose the maids were busy this morning.'

'And Charlotte, too! She looks half dead. I thought Ellen was to do such work, and ought to have done it in proper time.'

'Little Catharine is so fretful, that Ellen cannot be spared from the nursery.'

'I suppose she might be, if you were not absorbed in that writing.'

'I had the children with me, while the servants were at dinner; but Kitty was so troublesome, that I could not keep her. I am particularly anxious to finish this.'

'Some people would think a sick child more engrossing than that—' He had very nearly said trash, but he broke off short.

'There is nothing really the matter with her,' began Isabel, composedly; but James did not wait to listen, and muttering, 'That girl will be killed if she goes on,' he ran up to the nursery, whence he already heard a sound of low fretting.

The child was sitting on the nurse's lap, with a hot red spot on one cheek, teased and disturbed by the noises that the lesser ones were constantly making, as one lay in her cot, and the other was carried about by the girl. As he entered, she shrieked joyously, and stretched out her arms, and Kitty was at once clinging, hugging round his neck. Sending Ellen down to finish the stairs, he carried off the little girl, fondling and talking to her, and happy in her perfect content. But he did not go to the drawing-room. 'No, no, mamma must not be interrupted,' he bitterly thought, as he carried her down to the fireless study, hung his plaid round himself and her, and walked up and down the room with her, amusing her till she fell into a slumber on his shoulder.

Isabel could not at once resume her pen. Her even temper was for once ruffled, and her bosom swelled at the thought that his reproach was unjust; she was willing to do what was fitting, and he ought not to expect her to be an absolute nursery-maid. Women must keep up the tone of their own minds, and she might be being useful to the world as well as to her own family. If he wanted a mere household drudge, why had he not looked elsewhere? Up went her queenly head, as she believed her powers were meant for other things; but her heart gave a painful throb at the recollection that poverty had been her voluntary choice, and had seemed perfect felicity with James. Alas! she loved, honoured, and admired him, as her upright, unselfish, uncompromising husband, but worries, and rebukes, and tart answers, had made many a rent in the veil in which her fancy had enfolded him. Sir Roland had disappeared, and James and Sir Hubert were falling farther and farther asunder.

And Isabel sighed, partly at the memory of the imaginary being for whom she had taken James, and partly at the future prospect, the narrow sphere, the choice between solitude and dull society, the homely toils that must increase, worn-out garments, perpetual alphabets, children always whining, and James always irritated, thinking her remiss, and coming in with that furrow on his forehead, and his hair standing up wildly. She shrank from the contemplation, took her letter-case on her knee, moved close to the fire to profit by the light, stirred up a clear flame, and proceeded with the benevolent hermit, who came to the rescue when Sir Hubert was at the last gasp, and Adeline had received his beautiful resigned words. The hermit had transported him into his hut, and comforted Adeline, and was beginning a consolatory harangue, making revelations that were to set everything right, when just as he had gone as far as 'My son, know that I did not always wear this amice,' there was a tap at the door, and she saw Fitzjocelyn, who had been at Oakstead for the last few weeks, attending to some matters connected with his constituency.

'Ah! is it you?' she said, her lap too full of papers for her to rise. 'I did not know you were come home.'

'I came yesterday; and what company do you think I had in the train as far as Estminster?'

'Ah, I can guess! How does Louisa look?'

'Rather languid; but Estminster is to work wonders. She declares that Northwold is her best cure, and I am speculating whether she will prevail. I think Lady Conway dreads your example.'

'Mamma does not allow for the force of imagination,' said Isabel, not exactly knowing what prompted either the words or the sigh.

'I am come to ask if you will kindly give me a dinner. My father is gone to the book-club meeting, so I thought we would try to revive old times,' he said, smiling, but sadly, for the present scene was little like the No. 5 of old times.

'We shall be delighted,' said Isabel, with alacrity, relieved at avoiding a tete-it-tete with her husband at present, and refreshed by the sight of one belonging to her former life, and external to her present round of monotonous detail. 'Fortunately, it is not a lecture night and James will be very glad.'

I suppose he is not come in from school?'

'Yea, he is. I think he is in the study. I will let him know,' she said, with her hand on the bell.

'I will go to him,' said Louis, departing out of consideration that she might wish for space to attend to dinner, room, and dress. The two last were scarcely in such a state as he had been used to see at No. 5: books were on the sofa, the table-cover hung awry; the Dresden Shepherd's hat was grimed, and his damsel's sprigged gown hemmed with dust; there were no flowers in the vases, which his aunt had never left unsupplied; and Isabel, though she could not be otherwise than handsome and refined, had her crape rumpled, and the heavy folds of her dark hair looking quite ready for the evening toilette; and, as she sat on her low seat by the fire, the whole had an indescribable air of comfort passing into listless indulgence.

Fitzjocelyn politely apologized to Ellen for a second time stepping over her soapy deluge, and, as he opened the study door with a preliminary knock, a voice, as sharp and petulant as it was low, called out, 'Hollo! Be quiet there, can't you! You've no business here yet, and I have no time to waste on your idleness.'

'I am sorry to hear it,' said Louis, advancing into the dim light of the single bed-room candle, which only served to make visible the dusky, unshuttered windows, and the black gulf of empty grate. James was sitting by the table, with his child wrapped in the plaid, asleep on his breast, and his disengaged hand employed in correcting exercises. Without moving, he held it out, purple and chilled, exclaiming, 'Ha! Fitzjocelyn, I took you for that lout of a Garett.'

'Is this an average specimen of your reception of your scholars?'

'I was afraid of his waking the child. She has been unwell all day, and I have scarcely persuaded her to go to sleep.'

'Emulating Hooker.'

'As little in patience as in judgment,' sighed James.

'And which of them is it who is lulled by the strains of 'As in proesenti?''

'Which?' said James, somewhat affronted. 'Can't you tell sixteen months from five?'

'I beg her pardon; but I can't construct a whole child from an inch of mottled leg—as Professor Owen would a megalosaurus from a tooth. Does she walk?'

'Poor child, she *must*!' said James. 'She thinks it very hard to have two sisters so little younger than herself,' and he peeped under the plaid at the little brown head, and drew it closer round, with a look of almost melancholy tenderness, guarding carefully against touching her with his cold hands.

'She will think it all the better by-and-by,' said Louis.

'You had better not stay here in the cold. I'll come when I have heard that boy's imposition and looked over these exercises.' And he ran his hand through his hair again.

'Don't! You look like enough to a lion looking out of a bush to frighten ten boys already,' said Louis. 'I'll do the exercises,' pulling the copy-books away.

'What, you don't trust me?' as James detained them.

'No, I don't,' said James, his cousin's brightness awakening his livelier manner. 'It needs an apprenticeship to be up to their blunders.'

'Let me read them to you. I gave notice to Isabel that I am come to dinner, and no doubt she had rather I were disposed of.'

James objected no farther, and the dry labour was illuminated by the discursive remarks and moralizings which Louis allowed to flow in their natural idle course, both to divert his dispirited cousin, and to conceal from himself how much cause there was for depression. When the victim of the imposition approached, Louis prevented the dreaded clumsy entrance, seized on a Virgil, and himself heard the fifty lines, scarcely making them serve their purpose as a punishment, but sending the culprit away in an unusually amiable temper.

Services from Louis were too natural to James to be requited with thanks; but he was not uncivil in his notice of a wrong tense that had been allowed to pass, and the question was argued with an eagerness which showed that he was much enlivened. On the principle that Louis must care for all that was his, as he rose to take the still-sleeping child upstairs, he insisted that his cousin should come with him, if only for the curiosity of looking at the other two little animals, and learning the difference between them and Kitty, at whom he still looked as if her godfather had insulted her.

It was pretty to see his tenderness, as he detached the little girl from her hold, and laid her in the cot, making a little murmuring sound; and boasted how she would have shown off if awake, and laughed over her droll little jealousies of his even touching the twins. As she was asleep, he might venture; and it was comical to hear him declaring that no one need mistake them for each other, and to see him trying to lay them side by side on his knees to be compared, when they would roll over, and interlace their little scratching fingers; and Louis stood by teasing him, and making him defend their beauty in terms that became extravagant. He was really happy here; the careworn look smoothed away, the sharpness left his tones, and there was nothing but joyous exultation and fondness in his whole manner.

The smile did not last long, for Louis was well-nigh thrown downstairs by a dustpan in a dark corner, and James was heard muttering that nothing in that house was ever in its right place; and while Louis was suggesting that it was only himself who was not in the right place, they entered the drawing-room, which, like the lady, was in the same condition as that in which he had left it. Since Isabel had lost Marianne and other appliances, she had thought it not worth while to dress for dinner; so nothing had happened, except that the hermit had proved to be Adeline's great uncle, and had begun to clear up the affair of the sacrilege.

He was reluctant to leave off when the gentlemen appeared; but Isabel shut him up, and quietly held out the portfolio to James, who put it on the side-table, and began to clear the books away and restore some sort of order; but it was a task beyond his efforts.

Dinner was announced by Charlotte, as usual, all neat grace and simplicity, in her black dress and white apron, but flushed and heated by exertions beyond her strength. All that depended on her had been well done; but it would not seem to have occurred to her mistress that three people ate more than two; and to Louis, who had been too busy to take any luncheon, the two dishes seemed alarmingly small. One was of haricot mutton, the other of potatoes; and Charlotte might be seen to blush as she carried Lord Fitzjocelyn the plate containing a chop resembling Indian rubber, decorated with grease and with two balls of nearly raw carrot, and followed it up with potatoes apparently all bruises.

Louis talked vigorously of Virginia and Louisa—secretly marvelling how his hosts had brought themselves down to such fare. Isabel was dining without apparently seeing anything amiss, and James attempted nothing but a despairing toss of his chin, as he pronounced the carrots underdone. After the first course there was a long interval, during which Isabel and Louis composedly talked about the public meeting which he had been attending, and James fidgetted in the nervousness of hardly-restrained displeasure; but suddenly a frightful shrieking arose, and he indignantly cried, 'That girl!'

'Poor Charlotte in her hysterics again,' said Isabel, moving off, quickly for her, with the purple scent-bottle at her chatelaine.

'Isabel makes her twice as bad,' exclaimed James; 'to pet her with eau-de-Cologne is mere nonsense. Some day I shall throw a bucket of cold water over her.'

Isabel had left the door open, and they heard her softly comforting Charlotte with 'Never mind,' and 'Lord Fitzjocelyn would not care,' till the storm lulled. Charlotte crept off to her room, and Isabel returned to the dinner-table.

'Well, what's the matter now?' said James.

'Poor Charlotte!' said Isabel, smiling; 'it seems that she trusted to making a grand appearance with the remains of yesterday's pudding, and that she was quite overset by the discovery that Ellen and Miss Catharine had been marauding on them.'

'You don't mean that Kitty has been eating that heavy pudding at this time of night?' cried James.

'Kitty eats everything,' was the placid answer, 'and I do not think we can blame Ellen, for she often comes down after our dinner to find something for the nursery supper.'

'Things go on in the most extraordinary manner,' muttered James.

'I suppose Charlotte misses Jane,' said Louis. 'She looks ill.'

'No wonder,' said James, 'she is not strong enough for such work. She has no method, and yet she is the only person who ever thinks of doing a thing properly. I wish your friend Madison would come home and take her off our hands, for she is always alternating between fits of novel-reading and of remorse, in which she nearly works herself to death with running after lost time.'

'I should be sorry to part with her,' said Isabel; 'she is so quiet, and so fond of the children.'

'She will break down some day,' said James; 'if not before, certainly when she hears that Madison has a Peruvian wife.'

'There is no more to come,' said Isabel, rising; 'shall we come upstairs?'

James took up the candles, and Louis followed, considerably hungry, and for once provoked by Isabel's serene certainty that nobody cared whether there were anything to eat. However, he had forgotten all by the time he came upstairs, and began to deliver a message from Lady Conway, that she was going to write in a day or two to beg for a visit from Isabel during her sojourn at Estminster, a watering-place about thirty miles distant. Isabel's face lighted with pleasure. 'I could go?' she said, eagerly turning towards James.

'Oh, yes, if you wish it,' he answered, gruffly, as if vexed at her gratification.

'I mean, of course, if you can spare me,' she said, with an air of more reserve.

'If you wish it, go by all means. I hope you will.'

'The Christmas holidays are so near, that we may both go,' said Isabel; but James still had not recovered his equanimity, and Louis thought it best to begin talking of other things; and, turning to James, launched into the results of his Inglewood crops, and the grand draining plan which was to afford Marksedge work for the winter, and in which his father had become much interested. But he did not find that ready heed to all that occupied him of which he used to be certain at the Terrace. Isabel cared not at all for farming, and took no part in 'mere country squire's talk;' and James was too much overburthened with troubles and anxieties to enter warmly into those of others. Of those to whom Louis's concerns had been as their own, one had been taken from him, the other two were far away; and the cold 'yes,' 'very good,' fell coldly on his ear.

The conversation reverted to the school; and here it appeared that two years' experience had taken away the freshness of novelty, and the cycle of disappointment had begun. More boys were quitting the school than the new-comers could balance; and James spoke with acute vexation of the impracticability of the boys, and the folly of the parents. The attendance at his evening lectures had fallen off; and he declared that there was a spirit of opposition to whatever he did. The boys disobeyed, knowing that they should be favoured at home, and if they were punished, the parents talked of complaints to the trustees. The Sunday teaching was treated as especially obnoxious: the genteel mothers talked ridiculously about its resembling a charity-school, the fathers did not care whether their sons went or not, and he had scarcely five boys who appeared there regularly, and of them one was the butcher's son, who came rather in spite of his parents than with their consent. Attendance at church was more slack than ever; and when he lectured the defaulters, and gave them additional tasks in the week, it was resented as an injustice. To crown all, Mr. Ramsbotham had called, and had been extremely insolent about a boy whose ears had been boxed for reading Pickwick in school, under cover of his Latin grammar, and Isabel was almost indignant with Miss Faithfull for having ventured to hint to her that she wished Mr. Frost would be a little more gentle with the boys.

Isabel was fully alive now, and almost as vehement as her husband, in her complaints against his many foes. There was no lack of sympathy here, indeed, there might be rather too much, for she did not afford the softening influence that James had hitherto found at home.

'Well, Jem,' said Louis, at last, 'I think you should keep your hands off the boys.'

'You are not bitten with the nonsense about personal dignity and corporal punishment?' said James.

'By no means. I have an infinite respect for the great institution of flogging; but a solemn execution is one thing, a random stroke another.'

'Theories are very good things till you come to manage two score dunces without sense or honour. There is only one sort of appeal to their feelings that tells.'

'Maybe so, but I have my doubts whether you are the man to make it.'

Louis was sorry he had so spoken, for a flush of pain came up in James's face at the remembrance of what Fitzjocelyn had long ago forgotten—a passionate blow given to deter him from a piece of wilful mischief, in which he was persisting for the mere amusement of provoking. It stood out among all other varieties of cuff, stroke, and knock, by the traces it had left, by Mrs. Frost's grief at it, and the forgiveness from the Earl, and it had been the most humiliating distress of James's childhood. It humbled him even now, and he answered—

'You may be right, Louis; I may be not sufficiently altered since I was a boy. I have struck harder than I intended more than once, and I have told the boys so.'

'I am sure, if they had any generosity, they would have been touched with your amends,' cried Isabel.

'After all, a schoolmaster's life does not tend to mend the temper,' concluded James, sighing, and passing his hand over his forehead.

'No,' thought Louis, 'nor does Isabel's mutton!'

CHAPTER XIII
THE CONWAY HOUSEHOLD

> And ye shall walk in silk attire,
> And siller hae to spare,
> Gin ye'll consent to be his bride,
> Nor think of Donald mair.
> Miss BLAMIRE.

What makes you so lame to-day?' asked Lord Ormersfield, as Louis crossed the library, on returning from an interview to which he had been summoned in another room.

'I only stumbled over an obstruction on the Frost staircase yesterday,' said Louis. 'Poor Jem chose to have me up to the nursery; and to see him in the paternal character is the funniest as well as the pleasantest spectacle the house affords.'

'Ah! it is not what it was,' said the Earl. 'I suppose I must call there before the holidays, though,' he added, reluctantly. 'But what did that man, Ramsbotham, want with you?'

'To ask our interest for that appointment for his friend Grant.'

'Indeed! what could bring him here?'

'Why, unluckily, he fancied he had some claim on me, on the score of Jem Frost's election. I was too innocent then to know what those things go for.'

'You may say so!' ejaculated the Earl. 'So he was insolent enough to bring that up, was he?'

'Worse,' said Fitzjocelyn; 'he wanted to threaten that, unless I would oblige him now, there were matters which it was his duty to lay before the trustees. I told him he would do, of course, whatever was his duty; whereupon he thought my Lordship was interested in Mr. Frost.'

'Intolerably impertinent! I hope you set him down!'

'I told him that neither Mr. Frost nor I should wish him to pretermit his duty on any consideration whatever. Then he harked back to what he did for us at the election; and I was forced to tell him that if he considered that he had thereby established a claim on me, I must own myself in his debt; but as to reciprocating it, by putting in a person like Grant, that was against my conscience. He flew into a passion, informed me that Mr. Frost would take the consequences, mounted the British Lion, and I bowed him out upon that majestic quadruped, talking grandly of illiberal prejudices and the rising generation.'

'You acknowledged that he had a claim on you?'

'As things go in this world, I suppose it is true.'

'Louis! you will never know how to deal with those people.'

'I am afraid not. I could not, either boldly or diplomatically, get rid of the charge; so there was nothing for it but to confess. That's not the worst of it. I am afraid he really will be able to take revenge on poor Jem, and I'm sure he can't afford to lose any more scholars.'

'Such a fellow as that will not have much in his power against James,' said Lord Ormersfield. 'What I am afraid of is, that you have cut the ground from under your feet. I cannot see how you are ever to stand for Northwold.'

'Nor I,' said Louis. 'In fact, father, I have always thought it most wonderfully kind forbearance that you never reproached me more for my doings on that occasion. I believe we were all too happy,' he presently added, with a sigh, which was re-echoed by his father, at the same time trying to say something about youthfulness, to which Louis, who had been leaning thoughtfully on the mantelpiece, presently answered—'How much wiser old people are than young! An original axiom, is not it? but it is the last which one learns!'

'You would hardly act in the same way now?' said his father.

'I wonder when it ever answers to interfere with the natural course of events!' responded Louis, musingly. 'There were two things that Mr. Calcott told me once upon a time.' Those two things he left unuttered. They were—that the gentleman would be wasted on the school, and that the lady was not made for a poor man's wife. No wonder they made him sigh, but he concluded by exclaiming aloud—

'Well, I hope they will both go to Estminster, and come back with fresh life!'

The Estminster invitation was already on the road; but, unfortunately, Lady Conway had been unable to secure lodgings large enough to receive the children. She was urgent, however, that Isabel should come as soon as possible, since Louisa had been more unwell than usual, and was pining for her eldest sister; and she hoped that James would join her there as soon as the holidays should set him free.

James was hurt to find Isabel so much delighted to go, but resolved that she should not be deprived of the pleasure, and petulantly denied the offers, which became even entreaties, that she might wait till he could accompany her. He arranged, therefore, that he should follow her in a fortnight's time, the Miss Faithfulls undertaking the charge of their small namesakes; and Lady Conway wrote to fix a day when Delaford should come to take care of Isabel on her journey.

James and Isabel laughed at this measure. Mrs. James Frost was certainly not in circumstances to carry such a hero of the buttery in her suite; and Lady Conway herself had more sense than to have proposed it, but for Delaford's own representations. In fact, there was a pretty face at Dynevor Terrace, and he had been piqued enough by the return of his letters to be resolved on re-establishing his influence. Therefore did he demonstrate to my Lady that the only appropriate trains would bring him to Northwold at seven in the evening, and take him and Mrs. James Frost Dynevor away at eleven next morning; and therefore did Isabel look up in a sudden fit of recollection, as the breakfast was being removed, and say, 'Charlotte, Delaford is coming on Tuesday to fetch me to Estminster, and will sleep here that night.'

Isabel little guessed that in the days when she viewed the fantastic Viscount as her greatest enemy, the announcement of his approach would have been far less appalling to her.

'The wretch! the traitor! the vile deceiver!' thought Charlotte, not chary of her epithets, and almost ready to wreak her vengeance on the silver spoons. 'He has gone and broken poor Marianne's heart, and now he wants to treat me the same, and make me faithless to poor Tom, that is up in the mountain-tops and trusts to me! O me, what shall I do? Mrs. Beckett is gone, and there's no one to give me an advice! If I speak to him or scorn him, he'll take his advantage all alike—and his words are so fine and so soft, that do what I will to hate him when I'm away, he is sure to wind round me when he's there; and I can't get away, and I'm a poor, lonely, fatherless and motherless orphan, and a vain girl, that has listened already to his treacherous suit more than poor Tom would think for.'

Charlotte worked on in much grief and perplexity for some minutes, revolving the vanity that had led to her follies, and humbling herself in her own eyes. Suddenly, a flash of thought crossed her, and woke a smile upon her face, almost a look of mischief. She tied on a clean apron, and running upstairs, opened the drawing-room door, and said, 'If you please, ma'am, might I ask Miss Faithfull's Martha to tea on Tuesday night?'

'Oh yes, if you like,' said Isabel, never raising her eyes from the rebuilding of the ruined chapel in the valley.

Away skipped Charlotte, and in two minutes was at the back door of the House Beautiful. Mrs. Martha had been grimly kind to her ever since she had been afflicted with the cook for a fellow-servant, and received her only with a reproof for coming gadding out, when she ought to be hard at work; but when she heard the invitation, she became wrathful—she had rather go ten miles out of her way than even look at 'that there Ford.'

But Charlotte explained her purpose, and implored, and put her in mind that Mrs. Beckett was gone, and she had no protector; and Martha relented, told her that if she had minded her she would never have been in the scrape at all, but agreed, not without satisfaction, to afford Mr. Delaford the society of his old acquaintance.

And so when Mr. Delaford, with his whiskers freshly curled and his boots in a state of fascinating polish, walked up Dynevor Terrace, the door was opened by Ellen, and the red-faced cook and the upright Mrs. Martha sat on either side the fire. Daintily did he greet them, and stand warming himself before the fire, adapting his conversation to them for the next ten minutes, before he ventured to ask whether Miss Arnold were still an inmate. 'Taking out dinner—taking in tea,' gruffly replied Martha.

Mr. Delaford waited, but Ellen only ran in for one moment to fetch the kettle, and Martha discoursed as usual on the gold mines in Peru. By-and-by, when the parlour tea could by no possibility be supposed to be farther prolonged, there swept into the kitchen the stately nurse. Charlotte had run up to the nursery, and begged as a favour that she might be left to watch the children, while Mrs. Nurse entertained Mr. Delaford below-stairs; and in pity to so grand a gentleman, constrained to mix with such 'low servants,' the nurse had yielded, and Charlotte sat safe and sound by the nursery fire, smiling at his discomfiture, and reading over Tom's letters with an easier conscience than for many a day.

Mr. Delaford was too much of a gentleman to be uncivil to the three dames by the kitchen fire, but he watched every step and every creaking door. He even went the length of coming up to family prayers, in hopes of there meeting Charlotte; but she only joined the procession at the parlour door, and had flown upstairs, like a little bird, before he was out again.

The gentleman was affronted, and resolved to make her feel it. They could not but meet at the kitchen breakfast, and he barely acknowledged her. This was the most trying stroke of all, for it set her, in the eyes of the cook and nurse, on a level with the inferior servants, to whom he would not have deigned a look, and it was not easy to resist showing that she was on more familiar terms with him than all. But the instinct of self-protection and the wisdom of sincerity came to her aid. She abstained from raising her eyes to his face, from one conscious word or glance; she locked herself into her pantry when she took down the breakfast-things, and avoided every encounter, even when she had begun to feel that it would have been more flattering had he made more efforts. At last, dire necessity obliged her to accept his aid in carrying her mistress's box down the stairs. He walked backwards, she forwards. She would not meet his eye, and he was too well-bred for one word on the stairs; but in the garden he exclaimed, 'Miss Arnold, what have I done?'

'I never ought to have listened to you,' said Charlotte. 'It was not right by neither of us; so please say no more.'

'If you could understand—'

'I don't want to understand nothing.'

Charlotte drove him on with the box till they were close to the fly, and then, leaving him and the man to adjust the packing, flew back to announce that all was ready for her mistress. The last kisses were given to the children, and a message left with Charlotte for her master, who was in school; then she stood with Miss Catharine in her arms, and saw the fly drive off.

'Well,' said Mrs. Cook, 'that butler thinks himself a great beau, no doubt! I asked him whether he thought you pretty, Charlotte, and he said you hadn't no air nor no complexion. It's as I tells you—nobody will never take no notice of you while you goes about so dowdy.'

Charlotte did not know whether she was glad that the cook could not tease her about Delaford, or mortified to be supposed beneath his notice. No air, forsooth! She who had often heard it said that she looked like any lady!

'But oh,' said Charlotte to herself, as she spent her daily five minutes at noonday in quiet thought, 'am I not a poor silly thing not to be thankful that care has been round me this time, and that I have not been let to do nothing giddy nor false by Tom, whatever I may have thought!'

Meanwhile, Isabel had found it much harder to part with her babies for three weeks than it had seemed at the first proposal; and there were tears in her eyes as she gazed at the peaked, red-tiled roof of the old grammar-school, and reckoned the days and hours before her husband would join her.

Other associations revived when she found herself at Estminster, and was received with shrieks of joy, caresses, and exclamations too fond and foolish to bear repetition; and then the pale Louisa rested against her, stroking her hand, and Lady Conway fondled her, and Virginia, looking formed and handsome, retreated a little way to study her and declare that she was the same Isabel, neither altered nor grown older—it was all a dream that she had ever left them.

She almost felt it so herself, so entirely did she fit into the old habits, the little quiet dinner (only it seemed unusually good), the subsequent closing round the fire with the addition of Miss King and Louisa, the easy desultory chat, the books with Mudie's stamp lying about, the music which must be practised. It was very like being Miss Conway still; and when she awoke the next morning to find it late, and to the impulse of hurrying up, or *not* hurrying, expecting to find James making breakfast himself, and cross at being made late for school, she turned on her pillow, half doubting whether she had dreamt these two years in one long night, and remembering that captive mermaid, who had but to resume her maritime headgear and return to her native element, to forget the very existence of her fisherman husband and children. No! Isabel was not come to that! but she was almost ashamed to enjoy her extra hour's repose; and then the leisurely breakfast—nay, even the hot rolls and clear coffee were appreciated; and she sighed as she called up the image of the breakfast over an hour ago, the grim kettle, the bad butter, the worse fire, and James, cold and hurried, with Kitty on his knee gnawing a lump of crust. It was a contrast to Lady Conway reading her letters and discussing engagements with comfortable complacency, and Virginia making suggestions, and Louisa's grave bright eyes consulting hers, and Miss King quietly putting in a remark, and the anticipation of Walter's return, as if he were the only person wanting.

The sisters always resented their mother's habit of talking of 'poor Isabel,' regarding her as the happiest of women; and they were confirmed in their belief by seeing her looking exceedingly well and handsome, with perhaps a little more dignity and a sweeter smile. Virginia loved to snatch private interviews with Miss King, to express her confidence in dear Isabel's felicity, in the infallibility and other perfections of James, and in the surpassing cleverness of little Catharine; and Louisa was always sighing to behold the twins. But, to the delight of the school-room, the chapel in the valley was produced in a complete form, and a very pretty romance it was; but the hermit and the brilliant denouement were quite a shock to the young ladies, just when their tears were prepared, and Virginia was almost angry.

'Oh, my dear, there is trouble enough in the world!' said Isabel; 'Hubert and Adeline have been my companions so long, that at least I must leave them happy.'

'Indeed,' said Miss King, 'I am almost surprised that you have been able to finish them at all, with so much re-writing.'

To her surprise, Isabel blushed, and her answer partook of self-defence. 'James is so busy, and the children so young, that this has been my great resource. When my little girls are older, I must begin educating in earnest. I want to talk over Madame Neckar's book with you, Miss King.'

'All systems begin alike from infant obedience, I believe,' said the governess.

'Yes,' said Isabel, 'little Catharine is obedience itself with us. It is curious to see how well she knows the difference between us and the nurses. There are great tempests upstairs, and her papa takes them very much to heart. He always has her downstairs when he is at home; and he has accustomed her to so much attention, that there is no doing anything while she is by, or I would have her more with me.'

The self-justifying tone rather puzzled Miss King. She noted likewise that Isabel was backward in entering into details of her home life, and that she never said a word to encourage her sister's wishes to visit her at Northwold. Knowing Isabel as the governess did, she was sure that she would not merely talk of things on the surface, if her spirit were fully content. Only once did she go any deeper, and that was as she took up a little book of religious poetry of which she had been very fond. 'Ah!' she said, 'I don't feel these things as I used. I think practical life dulls one.'

'I should have said, practical life made things real,' said Miss King.

Isabel had not found out that having duties and not doing them was less practical than having no particular task.

Another cloud of mystery was over the relations with Mr. Dynevor and Clara. Isabel baffled all Lady Conway's inquiries and advice by entering into no particulars, but adhering to her own version of the matter, 'that Mr. Dynevor had required of James conditions incompatible with his duty,' and not deigning to explain either duty or conditions, as beyond the capacity of her hearer.

Of Clara no account was vouchsafed, except that Isabel believed she was abroad; 'they had been very much disappointed in her,' and Isabel was afraid that she was a good deal altered; and the subject seemed so painful, that Virginia did not venture to push her inquiries any farther.

The great subject of interest in the Conway family was that Virginia and Louisa were going to lose their maid; and the suggestion somehow arose that Charlotte should be her successor. It was agreed on all hands that nature had formed her for a lady's-maid, and a few lessons from a hairdresser would make her perfection; and she would be invaluable in reading to Louisa when restless and unable to sleep.

Isabel gave herself credit for the most notable arrangement she had ever made—promoting the little maiden, whom she really liked, and relieving herself from the constant annoyance about sparing Ellen from the nursery by obtaining a stronger housemaid. She had only a few scruples, or rather she knew that James would have some, as to exposing Charlotte to Delaford's attentions after what she had heard in Clara's letter; but the least hint on this score led to a panegyric upon Delaford's perfections—his steadiness, his prudence, his cleverness on journeys, his usefulness in taking care of Walter. 'I know that Walter is safe when he is with Delaford,' said Lady Conway. And even the sensible Miss King observed, smiling, 'that there always *would* be nonsense between men and maidservants; and there were many more dangerous places than the present. She would watch over Charlotte, and Fanshawe was quite to be trusted.'

The Conway family knew rather less about their own servants' hall than they did of feudal establishments five hundred years ago.

Still, Isabel, in her superior prudence, resolved to consult Fanshawe on the true state of affairs. Fanshawe was a comfortable portly personage, chiefly absorbed in her caps and her good cheer, and faring smoothly through life, on the principle of always saying what was expected of her, and never seeing anything to anybody's disadvantage.

She assured Mrs. James Frost that she did not think Delaford to blame; many girls would be foolish about a man with personal advantages, but she could not see it was his fault. Poor Marianne had been always weakly, and, 'After all, ma'am, some young women will put constructions upon anything,' said Mrs. Fanshawe, deciding that at least she should make no mischief by sacrificing poor Marianne.

Isabel did not like to come to more individual inquiries, lest she should prepare discomfort for Charlotte; but she easily satisfied herself that all was as right as convenient, and having occasion to write some orders to Charlotte, communicated the proposal, saying that all should be settled on her return.

There was wild work in the brain of the poor little Lady of Eschalott. No more stairs to scrub! No more mats to shake! No more hurrying after lost time, and an uneasy remembrance of undone duties! No more hardening of fingers, no more short-sleeved lilac, no more vulgarities from the cook! Ladylike dress, high wages, work among flowers and gauzes, reading to Miss Louisa, housekeeper's-room society, rank as 'Arnold' or 'Miss Arnold!' How much more suitable to the betrothed of the Superintendent at San Benito! To be sure, she was aware that a serpent lurked among the flowers; but she had shown him a bit of her mind once, and she found she could take care of herself, and keep him at a distance.

With her eyes shut, she already beheld Jane Beckett meeting her, when seated at the back of a carriage, with a veil and a parasol, addressing her as a grand lady, and kissing and praising her when she found her little Charlotte after all.

CHAPTER XIV
THE TRUSTEES' MEETING

> Know you not, master, to some kind of men
> Their graces serve them but as enemies?
> As You Like It.

'My Lord,' said Frampton, entering the library late one evening, in visible perturbation, and addressing himself to Fitzjocelyn, 'there is a person wishing to see you.'

'What person at this time of night?' said Louis.

'In fact, my Lord,' said the butler, hesitating, 'it is the young person at Mr. Frost's.'

'Something must be the matter!' cried Louis, starting up.

'She would explain nothing to me, she insisted on seeing your lordship; and—in fact—she was in such a state of agitation that I left her with Mrs. Bowles.'

Louis lost no time in hurrying into the hall. Charlotte must have followed Frampton without his knowledge, for she was already there; and, springing with clasped hands towards Fitzjocelyn, she cried, sobbing, 'My Lord, my Lord, come to master!'

'Is he ill? or the children?'

'No, no! but he'll be off, he'll be off like poor Tom!' exclaimed Charlotte, between her gasps; 'but I've locked it!' and she waved a door-key, and seemed about to laugh hysterically.

'Sit down, Charlotte,' said Louis, authoritatively, bringing a chair. 'If you do not explain yourself reasonably at once, I shall call Mrs. Bowles, and desire her to put you to bed.'

She made an imploring gesture, sank trembling into the chair, and, after a few incoherent efforts, managed to speak—'If you would but come to master, my Lord—I know it is something bad.'

Louis thought it wisest to despatch Frampton at once to order the carriage to be brought out immediately; and this so far pacified Charlotte, that she could speak comprehensibly on the cause of her alarm. 'He is in such a way!' she began. 'He went out to the school-examination, I believe, in his cap and gown, this morning; he was gone all day, but just at dusk I heard him slam-to the front door, fit to shake the house down, like he does when he is put out. I'd a thought nothing of that; but by-and-by I heard him stamping up and down the study, like one in a frenzy, and I found his cap and gown lying all of a heap in a corner of the hall. Then, Mr. Calcott came to call; and when I went into the study, master had his head down on the table, and wouldn't see no one; he fairly stamped to me to be gone, and bring him no more messages. Mr. Calcott, he looked so sorry and concerned, and sent in again. I was to say that he hoped some arrangement might be made, if Mr. Frost would only see him; but master had locked the door, and hallooed out that I was to say he was obliged, but couldn't see nobody. So Mr. Calcott was forced to go; and there was poor master. Not one morsel of dinner has he had. I knocked, but he would not open, only said he did not want for nothing. No, not even when 'twas time for Miss Catharine to come down. She thumped at the door, and called 'Papa' so pretty; but he never heeded, except to call out, 'Take her away!' Charlotte was crying so much that she could hardly proceed. 'Then I knew it must be something very melancholy indeed. But by-and-by he opens the door with a great jerk, and runs right up to the lumber-room. I saw his face, and 'twas like a corpse, my Lord; and he brings down his portmanteau into his dressing-room, and I hears him pulling out all his drawers. 'He'll be gone!' I thinks, 'he'll be off to America, too! And my poor mistress!' So I went up quietly, and in secret, unbeknown to them all, and got my bonnet; and I've run every step of the way—for you are the only one, my Lord, as can soothe his wounded spirit; and I've locked both the doors, and here's the key, so he can't be gone till you come.'

'Locked the doors!' cried Louis. 'What have you done? Suppose your mistress or Miss Clara were ill?'

'Oh, no—no, it is not that,' said Charlotte; 'or why should he flee from the face of his children? Why, I took Miss Salome up to the top of the stairs, when she was screaming and crying with all her might, and you would not have thought he was within a mile of her. No, my Lord, no one can't do nothing but you.'

'I'll come at once,' said Louis. 'You did quite right to fetch me; but it was a frightful thing to lock the door.'

Sending Charlotte to the housekeeper, he went to communicate her strange intelligence to his father, who shared his dismay so much as almost to wish to come with him to Northwold; but Louis felt he could deal better alone with James. His fears took the direction of the Italian travellers, knowing that any misfortune to them must recoil on James with double agony after such a parting.

In very brief space the carriage was at Northwold, and desiring that it should wait at the corner of the Terrace, Louis followed Charlotte, who had jumped down from the box, and hastened forward to unlock the door; and he was in time to hear the angry, though suppressed, greeting that received her. 'Pretty doings, ma'am! So I have caught you out at last, though you did think to lock me in! He shan't come in! I wonder at your impudence! The very front door!'

'Oh, cook, don't!' The poor breathless voice managed at last to be heard. 'This is Lord Fitzjocelyn.'

Cook had vanished out of sight or hearing before Louis's foot was within the threshold. The study-door was open, the fire expiring, the books and papers pushed back; and James's fierce, restless tread was heard pacing vehemently about his own room. Louis ran hastily up, and entered at once. His cousin stood staring with wild eyes, his hair was tossed and tangled, his face lividly pale, and the table was strewn with fragments of letters, begun and torn up again; his clothes lay tumbled in disorder on the floor, where his portmanteau lay open and partly packed. All Louis's worst alarm seemed fulfilled at once. 'What has happened?' he cried, catching hold of both James's hands, as if to help him to speak. 'Who is ill?—not Clara?'

'No—no one is ill,' said James, withdrawing his hands, and kneeling down by his box, with an air of feigned indifference; 'I am only going to London.'

'To London?'

'Aye, to see what is to be done,—ship—chaplaincy, curacy, literature, selling sermons at five shillings each,—what not. I am no longer master of Northwold school!' He strove to speak carelessly, but bending over his packing, thrust down the clothes with desperate blows.

Louis sat down, too much dismayed to utter a word.

'One morning's work in the conclave,' said James, with the same assumed ease. 'Here's their polite reprimand, which they expected me to put up with,—censuring all my labour, forbidding Sunday-classes, accusing me of partiality and cruelty, with a lot of nonsense about corporal punishment and dignity. I made answer, that if I were master at all, I must be at liberty to follow my own views, otherwise I would resign; and, would you believe it, they snapped at the offer—they thought it highly desirable! There's an end of it.'

'Impossible!' cried Louis, casting his eye over the reprimand, and finding that the expressions scarcely warranted James's abstract of them. 'You must have mistaken!'

'Do you doubt *that*?' and James threw to him a sheet where, in Richardson's clerkly handwriting, the trustees of King Edward's Northwold Grammar School formally accepted the resignation of the Reverend James Roland Frost Dynevor.

'They cannot be so hasty! Did not Mr. Calcott call to gee you?'

'An old humbug!'

'I'll go and see him this instant. Something may be done.'

'No,' said James, holding him down by the shoulder, 'I will not be degraded by vain solicitations.'

'This must be that wretched Ramsbotham!' exclaimed Louis. 'Oh, Jem! I little thought he had so much power to injure you.'

'It is as well you did not,' said James. 'It would have made no difference, except in the pain it would have cost you; and the only gratification in this business is, that I suffer because neither you nor I would deny our principles. I thank you, Fitzjocelyn!' and he straightened himself in the satisfaction of persecuted rectitude.

'You have very little to thank me for,' said Louis, wringing his hand, and turning aside, as if unable yet to face the full extent of the evil.

'Never fear for us,' continued James, boldly; 'we shall struggle on. Mens conscia,—you see I can't forget to be a schoolmaster.'

'But what are you about? Where are you going?'

'To London. You spoke to a publisher about my lectures on history; they will serve for introduction. He may make me his hack—a willing one, while I advertise—apply for anything. I must be gone!'

'You do not look fit for a night journey. You would be too early at Estminster to see Isabel.'

'Don't name her!' cried James, starting round as if the word were a dart. 'Thank Heaven that she is away! I must write to her. Maybe, Lady Conway will keep her till I am settled—till I have found some lodging in London where no one will know us.'

'And where you may run up a comfortable doctor's bill.'

With a gesture—half passion, half despair—James reiterated, 'There's no staying here. I must be gone. I must be among strangers.'

'Your mens conscia would better prove that it has no cause for shame by staying here, instead of rushing out of sight into the human wilderness, and sacrificing those poor little—'

James struck his foot on the floor, as though to intercept the word; but Louis continued, apparently unmoved by his anger—'Those poor little children. If misfortune and injury be no disgrace to the injured, I call it cowardly pride to fly off by night to hide oneself, instead of living in your own house, like an honest man.'

'Live!—pray what am I to live on?' cried James, laughing hoarsely.

'You will not find out by whirling to London in your present state.'

In fact, Louis's most immediate care was to detain him for that one night. There was a look of coming illness about him, and his desperate, maddened state of mind might obscure his judgment, and urge him into some precipitate measure, such as he might afterwards rue bitterly for the sake of the wife and children, the bare thought of whom seemed at present to sting him so intolerably. Moreover, Louis had a vague hope that so harsh a proceeding would be abandoned by the trustees; his father would remonstrate, and James might be able to think and to apologize. He was hardly a rational being to-night, and probably would have driven away any other companion; but long habit, and external coolness, enabled Louis to stand his ground, and to protract matters till the clock, striking eleven, relieved him, as much as it exasperated James, by proving it so late that the last train would have already past.

He persisted in declaring that he should go by the first in the morning, and Louis persuaded him to go to bed, after Charlotte had brought them some tea, which, he said, choked him. Deciding on sleeping at No. 5, Louis sent home the carriage, with a note to his father; and Charlotte pressed her hands together in a transport of gratitude when she found that he was not going to abandon her master. She did her best to make the forlorn house comfortable; but it was but cold comfort, with all the fires gone out, and he was too sad and anxious to heed it.

She was at his door early the next morning, with a summons more alarming than surprising. She was sure that master was very ill.

There was James lying across his bed, half-dressed, turned away from the dim morning light, and more frightfully pale than ever. He started angrily at Louis's entrance, and sprang up, but fell back, insisting with all his might that nothing ailed him but a common headache, which needed only to be left quiet for an hour or two. He said it venomously.

'A very uncommon headache,' thought Louis. 'My belief is, that it is little short of brain fever! If I could only feel his pulse! But it would be very like taking a mad dog's hand. There's nothing for it but to fetch old Walby. He may have some experience of refractory patients.'

'Go home, Louis,' reiterated James, savagely, on opening his eyes and finding him not gone. 'I tell you I want nobody. I shall be in London before night.'

And starting up, he tried to draw the curtain at his feet, to shut out the tardy dawn; but too giddy to persevere, he sank back after one noisy pull.

Louis drew it completely, shaded the window, and would have settled the pillows, but was not allowed; and obtaining an impatient grunt by way of dismissal, he ran down stairs, caught up hat and stick, and set off to summon Mr. Walby from his comfortable family breakfast-table. The good old doctor was more concerned than amazed. He could hardly surmount the shock to his trustee conscience, on hearing of the consequence of yesterday's proceedings.

'I was much grieved at the time,' he said, as they walked to the Terrace together. 'You will believe me that I was no willing party, my Lord.'

'I could never believe that you would do anything hard towards any one, Mr. Walby,' said Louis, kindly; and a few more like assurances led the old man to volunteer the history of the case in confidence.

Ramsbotham had brought before the meeting of the trustees a serious mass of charges, on which he founded a motion that Mr. Frost should be requested to resign. Every one rejected such a measure, and the complaints were sifted. Some were palpably false, others exaggerated, others related to matters of principle; but deducting these, it still was proved that the Sunday attendance and evening lectures were too visibly the test of his favour, and that the boys were sometimes treated with undue severity, savouring of violent temper. 'I must confess, my Lord,' said Mr. Walby, sinking his voice, 'I am afraid Mr. Frost is too prompt with his hand. A man does not know how hard he hits, when he knocks a boy over the ears with a book. Mrs. Barker's little boy really had a gathering under the ear in consequence;—I saw it myself.'

Louis was confounded; he had nothing to say to this; he knew the force that irritation gave to James's hand too well to refuse his credence, and he could only feel shame and dismay, as if himself guilty by his misjudged patronage.

Mr. Walby proceeded to say that, under the circumstances, the trustees had decided on remonstrating by letter, after the examination; and it was easy to perceive that the reprimand, which might have been wise and moderate from the Squire, had gained a colour from every one concerned, so as to censure what was right and aggravate what was wrong. Mr. Frost's reply had been utterly unexpected; Ramsbotham and the bookseller had caught at the resignation, and so did the butcher, who hated the schoolmaster for having instilled inconveniently high principles into his son. Richardson abstained from voting; Mr. Calcott fought hard for Mr. Frost, but the grocer was ill, and only poor old Mr. Walby supported him, and even they felt that their letter had not deserved such treatment. Alas! had not Fitzjocelyn himself taught Northwold that the Squire was not a dictator? Even then, Mr. Calcott, still hoping that an apology might retrieve the day, had set forth to argue the matter with James Frost, whom he could not suppose serious in his intentions, but thought he meant to threaten the trustees into acquiescence. The doors had been closed against him, and Mr. Walby feared that now the step was known, it was too late to retract it. 'The ladies would never allow it,' he declared; 'there was no saying how virulent they were against Mr. Frost; and as to consideration for his family, that rather inflamed their dislike. They had rich relations enough! It would be only too good for so fine a lady to be brought down.' Every one had some story of her pride, neglect, or bad housewifery. 'And I can tell you,' said Mr. Walby, 'that I am not in their good books for declaring that I never saw anything from her but very pretty, affable manners.'

With these words they reached the house; and with sighs and murmurs of 'Ah! poor young man!' Mr. Walby followed Louis to the landing-place, where they both paused, looking at each other in doubt how to effect an entrance, Louis suddenly remembering that no presence would be more intolerable to the patient than that of a trustee. However, there was nothing for it but to walk in, and announce, as a matter of course, that he had thought it right to call in Mr. Walby.

The extremity of displeasure brought James to his feet, and out into the passage, saying, with grave formality, that he was much obliged, and glad to see Mr. Walby as a friend, but Lord Fitzjocelyn was mistaken in thinking him in need of his advice. Many thanks, he would trouble him no further; and affecting a laugh, he said that Fitzjocelyn seemed never to have heard of a bad headache.

'Acting does not mend matters, Jem,' said Louis. 'You had much better confess how really ill you are.'

Excessive giddiness made James stagger against his cousin, and Louis, throwing his arms round him, looked in great alarm to the doctor for help, but was answered by something very like a smile. 'Aye, aye, sir, there's nothing for it but to go to bed. If his lordship there had seen as many cases of jaundice as I have, he would not look so frightened. Very wholesome disorder! Yes, lie down, and I'll send you a thing or two to take.'

So saying, Mr. Walby helped Louis to lay their unwilling invalid on the bed without much resistance or reply, and presently departed, so infinitely relieved that he could not help indulging in a little chuckle at the young Viscount's mistake. As soon as he was gone, James revived enough to protest that it was all nonsense, doctors must needs give a name to everything; if they would only let him alone, he should be himself and off to London in two hours; and that it was Fitzjocelyn himself who was looking excessively ill, and as yellow as a guinea. He would not hear of undressing and going absolutely to bed, and fairly scolded every one out of sight. Good Miss Mercy, who had trotted in at the tidings of illness, stood at the nursery-door, telegraphing signs of commiseration in answer to Louis's looks of perplexity.

'At least,' she said, 'you had better come to breakfast with us, and hear what my sister says—Salome always knows what is best.'

He soon found himself in the snug parlour, where the small round breakfast-table, drawn close to Miss Faithfull's fireside chair, had a sort of doll's-house air of cheerful comfort, with the tiny plates, tea-cups, and the miniature loaf, and the complicated spider-legs, among which it was not easy to dispose of his own length of limb.

The meal passed in anxious consultation. There might be no danger, but the disorder was severe and increasing. James's health had long been suffering from harass of mind, want of exercise, and unwholesome diet; and the blow of the previous day had brought things to a crisis. There he lay, perfectly unmanageable, permitting neither aid nor consolation, unable to endure the sight of any one, and too much stupefied by illness to perceive the impracticability of his wild scheme of seeking employment in London.

Miss Faithfull pronounced that either Mercy or Lord Fitzjocelyn must go and fetch Mrs. James Frost home.

'I was only thinking how long we could keep her away,' said Louis. 'Pray don't be shocked, dear Miss Mercy, but I thought I could nurse poor Jem much better alone than with another dead weight on our hands.'

'They would neither of them thank you,' said Miss Faithfull, laughing. 'Depend upon it, she will know best how to deal with him.'

'Well, you see more of their household than I do, but I have never dared to think of her! Do you remember the words, 'if thou hast run with the footmen and they have wearied thee—"

'There are some people who can run with the horsemen better than with the footmen,' said Miss Salome. 'You know we are very fond of young Mrs. Frost. We cannot forget her sweetness when she lived in this house, and she has always been most kind and friendly. I do believe that to display the most admirable qualities, she only needs to be roused.'

'To live in the house with Jem, and Jem's three babies, and yet want rousing!'

'I have thought,' said Salome, diffidently, 'that he was only too gentle with her.'

'Do you know how very severe you are growing, Miss Faithfull?' said Louis, looking her in the face, in the gravity of amusement.

'I mean,' said Miss Faithfull, blushing, 'though of course I do not know, that I have fancied it might be better for both if he could have gone to the root of the matter, and set fairly before her the prime duties requisite in the mistress of such a family. He may have done so.'

'I think not,' said Louis; 'it would be awkward when a woman fancied she embraced poverty voluntarily for his sake. Poverty! It was riches compared with their present condition. Isabel on 150 pounds a-year! It may well make poor Jem ill to think about it! I only wonder it is not a brain-fever!'

'Lord Fitzjocelyn regrets that brain-fever,' said Miss Faithfull.

'Probably my ideas on the subject are derived from the prevalence of the complaint in light literature,' said Louis, smiling. 'It would be more dignified, and suit Isabel better. Poor Isabel! I hope I have done her injustice. She behaved gloriously at the barricades, and has a great soul after all; but I had begun to think heroines not calculated for moderate circumstances. May they do better in no circumstances at all! Heighho! how a heavy heart makes one talk nonsense! So I am to fetch the poor thing home, Miss Faithfull.'

This was determined on, whether with or without James's consent; Miss Mercy undertaking that she and Martha would help Charlotte, and dispose of the children in the House Beautiful; and she went back with Louis to fetch them, when little Catharine was found peeping through the bars of her prison-gate at the top of the nursery-stairs, shouting lustily for papa. She graciously accepted her godfather as a substitute, and was carried by him to her kind neighbour's house, already a supplementary home. As to her father, Louis found him more refractory than ever. His only greeting was, 'Why are not you gone home?' He scorned Mr. Walby's prescriptions, and made such confident assertions that he should be off to London in the evening, that Fitzjocelyn almost reverted to the brain-fever theory, and did not venture to hint his intention to any one but Charlotte, telling her that he should now almost think her justified in locking the doors.

Sending information to his father, he started for Estminster, very disconsolate, and full of self-reproach for the hasty proceedings which had borne such bitter fruits. The man and the situation had been an injustice to each other; a sensitive irritable person was the very last to be fit for a position requiring unusual judgment and temper, where his energy had preyed upon itself. His being placed there had been the work of Louis's own impetuous scorn of the wisdom of elder and graver heads. Such regrets derived additional poignancy from the impossibility of conferring direct assistance upon James, and from the degree of justice in the hard measure which had been dealt to him, would make it for ever difficult to recommend him, and yet the devising future schemes for his welfare was the refuge which Louis's mind most willingly sought from the present perplexity of the communication in store for poor Isabel.

As he put out his head at the Estminster station, a familiar voice shouted, 'Hollo! Fitzjocelyn, how jolly! Have you got James there? I told Isabel it would be no use; but when she did not get a letter this morning, she would have it that he was coming, and got me to walk up with her.'

'Where is she?' asked Louis, as he jumped out and shook hands with Walter.

'Walking up and down the esplanade. She would not come into the station, so I said I would run up to satisfy her. I don't know what she will say to you for not being Frost.'

'Do you mean that she is anxious!'

'It is the correct thing, isn't it, when wives get away from their husbands, and have not the fragment of a letter for twenty-four whole hours? But what do you mean, Fitzjocelyn?' asked the boy, suddenly sobering. 'Is anything really the matter?'

'Yes, Walter,' said Louis; 'we must tell your sister as best we can. James is ill, and I am come for her.'

Walter was silent for a few minutes, then drew a sigh, saying, 'Poor Isabel, I wish it had not been! These were the only comfortable holidays I have had since she chose to marry.'

Isabel here came in sight, quickening her pace as she first saw that her brother had a companion, but slackening in disappointment when she perceived that it was not her husband; then, the next moment hurrying on, and as she met them, exclaiming, 'Tell me at once! What is it?'

'Nothing serious,' said Louis. 'The children are all well, but I left James very uncomfortable, though with nothing worse than a fit of jaundice.'

The inexperienced Isabel hardly knew whether this were not as formidable as even the cherished brain-fever, and becoming very pale, she said, 'I am ready at once—Walter will let mamma know.'

'There will be no train for two hours,' said Louis. 'You will have plenty of time to prepare.'

'You should have telegraphed,' said Isabel, 'I could have come by the first train.'

Trembling, she grasped Walter's arm, and began hastening home, impatient to be doing something. 'I knew something was wrong,' she exclaimed; 'I ought to have gone home yesterday, when there was no letter.'

'Indeed, there—was nothing the matter yesterday, at least, with his health,' said Louis. 'You are alarming yourself far too much—'

'To be sure, Isabel,' chimed in Walter. 'A fellow at my tutor's had it, and did nothing but wind silkworm's silk all the time. We shall have James yet to spend Christmas with us. Everybody laughs at the jaundice, though Fitzjocelyn does look so lugubrious that he had almost frightened *me*.'

'Is this true?' said Isabel, looking from one to the other, as if she had been frightened in vain.

'Quite true, Isabel,' said Walter. 'Never mind Fitzjocelyn's long face; I wouldn't go if I were you! Don't spoil the holidays.'

'I must go, Walter dear,' said Isabel, 'but I do not think Lord Fitzjocelyn would play with my fears. Either he is very ill, or something else is wrong.'

'You have guessed it, Isabel,' said Louis. 'This illness is partly the effect of distress of mind.'

'That horrid meeting of trustees!' cried Isabel. 'I am sure they have been impertinent.'

'They objected to some of his doings; he answered by threatening to resign, and I am sorry to say that the opposition set prevailed to have his resignation accepted.'

'A very good thing too,' cried Sir Walter. 'I always thought that school a shabby concern. To be under a lot of butchers and bakers, and nothing but cads among the boys! He ought to be heartily glad to be rid of the crew.'

Isabel's indignation was checked by a sort of melancholy amusement at her brother's view, but Louis doubted whether she realized the weight of her own words as she answered—'Unfortunately, Walter, it is nearly all we have to live upon.'

'So much the better,' continued Walter. 'I'll tell you—you shall all go to Thornton Conway, and I'll come and spend my holidays there, instead of kicking my heels at these stupid places. I shan't mind your babies a bit, and Frost may call himself my tutor if he likes. I don't care if you take me away from Eton.'

'A kind scheme, Walter,' said Isabel, 'but wanting in two important points, mamma's consent and James's.'

'Oh, I'll take care of mamma!'

'I'm afraid I can't promise the same as to James.'

'Ah! I see. Delaford was quite right when he said Mr. Frost was a gentleman who never knew what was for his own advantage.'

As they arrived at the house, Isabel desired to know how soon she must be ready, and went upstairs. Walter detained his cousin—'I say, Fitzjocelyn, have they really got nothing to live on?'

'No more than will keep them from absolute want.'

'I shall take them home,' said Walter, with much satisfaction. 'I shall write to tell James that there is nothing else to be done. I cannot do without Isabel, and I'll make my mother consent.'

Fitzjocelyn was glad to be freed from the boy on any terms, and to see him go off to write his letter.

Walter was at least sincere and warm-hearted in his selfishness, and so more agreeable than his mother, whom Louis found much distressed, under the secret conviction that something might be expected of her. 'Poor Isabel! I wish she could come to me; but so many of them—and we without a settled home. If there were no children—but London houses are so small; and, indeed, it would be no true kindness to let them live in our style for a little while. They must run to expenses in dress; it would be much more economical at home, and I could send Walter to them if he is very troublesome.'

'Thank you,' said Louis. 'I think James will be able to ride out the storm independently.'

'I know that would be his wish. And I think I heard that Mr. Dynevor objected to the school. That might be one obstacle removed.'

Lady Conway comforted herself by flourishing on into predictions that all would now be right, and that poor dear Isabel would soon be a much richer woman than herself; while Louis listened to the castle-building, not thinking it worth while to make useless counter-prophecies.

The sisters were upstairs, assisting Isabel, and they all came down together. The girls were crying; but Isabel's dark, soft eyes, and noble head, had an air of calm, resolute elevation, which drove all Louis's misgivings away, and which seemed quite beyond and above the region of Lady Conway's caresses and affectionate speeches. Walter and Virginia came up to the station, and parted with their sister with fondness that was much mure refreshing, Walter reiterating that his was the only plan.

'Now, Fitzjocelyn,' said Isabel, when they were shut into a coupe, 'tell me what you said about distress of mind. It has haunted me whether you used those words.'

'Could you doubt his distress at such a state of affairs?'

'I thought there could be no distress of mind where the suffering is for the truth.'

'Ah! if he could quite feel it so!'

'What do you mean? There has been a cabal against James from the first to make him lay aside his principles, and I cannot regret his refusal to submit to improper dictation, at whatever cost to myself.'

'I am afraid he better knows than you do what that cost is likely to be.'

'Does he think I cannot bear poverty?' exclaimed Isabel.

'He had not said so—' began Louis; 'but—'

'You both think me a poor, helpless creature,' said Isabel, her eyes kindling as they had done in the midst of danger. 'I can do better than you think. I may be able myself to do something towards our maintenance.'

He could not help answering, in the tone that gave courtesy to almost any words, 'I am afraid it does not answer for the wife to be the breadwinner.'

'Then you doubt my writing being worth anything?' she asked, in a hurt tone of humility. 'Tell me candidly, for it would be the greatest kindness;'

and her eye unconsciously sought the bag where lay Sir Hubert, whom all this time her imagination was exalting, as the hero who would free them from their distresses.

'Worth much pleasure to me, to the world at large,' said Louis; 'but—you told me to speak plainly—to your home, would any remuneration be worth your own personal care?'

Isabel coloured, but did not speak.

Louis ventured another sentence—'It is a delicate subject, but you must know better than I how far James would be likely to bear that another, even you, should work for his livelihood.'

When Isabel spoke again, it was to ask further particulars; and when he had told all, she found solace in exclaiming at the folly and injustice of James's enemies, until the sense of fairness obliged him to say, 'I wish the right and the wrong ever were fairly divided in this world; and yet perhaps it is best as it is: the grain of right on either side may save the sin from being a presumptuous one.'

'It would be hard to find the one grain of right on the part of the Ramsbotham cabal.'

'Perhaps you would not think so, if you were a boy's mother.'

'Oh!' cried Isabel, with tears in her eyes, 'if he thought he had been too hasty, he always made such reparation that only cowards could help being touched. I'm sure they deserved it, and much more.'

'No doubt,' said Louis; 'but, alas! if all had their deserts—'

'Then you really think he was too severe?'

'I think his constitutional character was hardly fit for so trying a post, and that his family and school troubles reacted upon each other.'

'You mean Clara's conduct; and dear grandmamma—oh! if she could but have stayed with us! If you could have seen how haggard and grieved he came home from Cheveleigh! I do not think he has been quite the same ever since.'

'And No. 5 has never been the same,' said Louis.

'Tell me,' said Isabel, suddenly, 'are we very poor indeed?'

'I fear so, Isabel. Till James can find some employment, I fear there is a stern struggle with poverty before you.'

'Does that mean living as the Faithfulls do?'

'Yes, I think your means will be nearly the same as theirs.'

'Fitzjocelyn,' said Isabel, after a long pause, 'I see what you have been implying all this time, and I have been feeling it too. I have been absorbed in my own pursuits, and not paid attention enough to details of management, and so I have helped to fret and vex my husband. You all think my habits an additional evil in this trial.'

'James has never said a word of the kind,' cried Louis.

'I know he has not; but I ought to have opened my eyes to it long ago, and I thank you for helping me. There—will you take that manuscript, and keep it out of my way? It has been a great tempter to me. It is finished now, and it might bring in something. But I can have only one thought now—how to make James happier and more at ease.'

'Then, Isabel, I don't think your misfortunes will be misfortunes.'

'To suffer for right principles should give strength for anything,' said Isabel. 'Think what many better women than I have had to endure, when they have had to be ashamed of their husband, not proud of him! Now, I do hope and trust that God will help us, and carry us and the children through with it!'

Louis felt that in this frame she was truly fit to cheer and sustain James. How she might endure the actual struggle with penury, he dared not imagine; at present he could only be carried along by her lofty composure.

James still lay on his tossed, uncomfortable bed in the evening twilight. The long, lonely hours, when he imagined Louis to have taken him at his word and gone home, had given him a miserable sense of desertion, and as increasing sensations of illness took from him the hopes of moving on that day, he became distracted at the thought of the anxiety his silence would cause Isabel, and, after vainly attempting to write, had been lying with the door open, watching for some approaching step.

There was the familiar sound of a soft, gliding step on the stairs, then a pause, and the sweet soft voice, 'My poor James, how sadly uncomfortable you are!'

'My dear!' he cried, hastily raising himself, 'who has been frightening you?'

'No one, Fitzjocelyn was so kind as to come for me.'

'Ah! I wished you to have been spared this unpleasant business.'

'Do you think I could bear to stay away! Oh, James! have I been too useless and helpless for you even to be glad to see me?'

'It was for your own sake,' he murmured, pressing her hand. 'Has Fitzjocelyn told you?'

'Yes,' said Isabel, looking up, as she sat beside him. 'Never mind, James. It is better to suffer wrong than to do it. I do not fear but that, if we strive to do our duty, God will help us, and make it turn out for the best for our children and ourselves.'

He grasped her hand in intense emotion.

'I know you are anxious about me,' added Isabel. 'My ways have been too self-indulgent for you to think I can bear hardness. I made too many professions at first; I will make no more now, but only tell you that I trust to do my utmost, and not shrink from my duties. And now, not a word more about it till you are better.'

CHAPTER XV
SWEET USES OF ADVERSITY

> One furnace many times the good and bad will hold;
> But what consumes the chaff will only cleanse the gold.
> R. C. TRENCH.

During the succeeding days, James had little will or power to consider his affairs; and Isabel, while attending on him, had time to think over her plans. Happily, they had not a debt. Mrs. Frost had so entirely impressed her grandson's mind with her own invariable rule of paying her way, that it had been one of his grounds for pride that he had never owed anything to any man.

They were thus free to choose their own course, but Lord Ormersfield urged their remaining at Northwold for the present. He saw Mr. Calcott, who had been exceedingly concerned at the turn affairs had taken, and very far from wishing to depose James, though thinking that he needed an exhortation to take heed to his ways. It had been an improper reprimand, improperly received; but the Earl and the Squire agreed that nothing but morbid fancy could conjure up disgrace, such as need prevent James Frost from remaining in his own house until he could obtain employment, provided he and his wife had the resolution to contract their style of living under the eye of their neighbours.

This gave neither of them a moment's uneasiness. It was not the direction of their pride; and even before James's aching head was troubled with deliberation, Isabel had discussed her plan with the Miss Faithfulls. She would imagine herself in a colony, and be troubled with no more scruples about the conventional tasks of a lady than if she were in the back-woods.

They would shut up some of the rooms, take one servant of all-work, and Isabel would be nursery-maid herself. 'We may do quite as well as the carpenter's wife,' she said; 'she has more children and less income, and yet always seems to me the richest person whom I know.'

James groaned, and turned his face away. He could not forbid it, for even Isabel's exertion must be permitted rather than the dishonour of living beyond their means; and he consoled himself with thinking that when the deadening inertness of his illness should leave him, he should see some means of finding employment for himself, which would save her from toil and exertion, and, in the meantime, with all his keen self-reproach, it was a blessed thing to have been brought back to his enthusiastic admiration for her, all discontents and drawbacks utterly forgotten in her assiduous affection and gallant cheerfulness.

Lord Ormersfield had readily acceded to his son's wish to bring the party to spend Christmas at Ormersfield, as soon as James could be moved. During their visit the changes were to be made, and before setting out Isabel had to speak to the servants. Charlotte's alacrity and usefulness had made her doubly esteemed during her master's illness; and when he heard how she was to be disposed of, he seemed much vexed. He said that she was a legacy from his grandmother, and too innocent and pretty to be cast about among strange servants in all the places where the Conways visited; and that he would not have consented to the transfer, but that, under their present circumstances, it was impossible to keep her. If any evil came to her, it would be another miserable effect of his own temper.

Isabel thought he exaggerated the dangers, and she spoke brightly to Charlotte about fixing the day of her going to Estminster, so as to be put into the ways of the place before her predecessor departed. The tears at once came into Charlotte's eyes, and she answered, 'If you please, ma'am, I should be very sorry to leave, unless I did not give satisfaction.'

'That is far from being the reason, Charlotte; but we cannot keep so good a servant—Mr. Frost has given up—'

'I have been put out of the school,' said James, from his sofa, in his stern sense of truth. 'We must live on as little as possible, and therefore must part with you, Charlotte, though from no fault of yours. You must look on us as your friends, and in any difficulty apply to us; for, as Mrs. Frost says, we look on you as a charge from my grandmother.'

Charlotte escaped to hide her tears; and when, a few minutes after, the Ormersfield carriage arrived, and nurses and babies were packed in, and her master walked feebly and languidly down stairs, and her mistress turned round to say, kindly, 'You will let me know, Charlotte?' she just articulated, 'Thank you, ma'am, I will write.'

Mr. Frost's words had not been news to Charlotte. His affairs had been already pretty well understood and discussed, and the hard, rude, grasping comments of the vulgar cook—nay, even of the genteel nurse—had been so many wounds to the little maiden, bred up by Jane in the simplicity of feudal reverence and affection for all that bore the name of Frost Dynevor.

Her mistress left to the tender mercies of some servant such as these, some one who might only care for her own ease and profit, and not once think of who and what she had been! The little children knocked about by some careless girl! Never, never! All the doubts and scruples about putting her own weak head and vain heart in the way of being made faithless to Tom revived, reinforced by her strong and generous affection. A romantic purpose suddenly occurred to her, flushing her cheek and brightening her eye. In that one impulse, scrubbing, washing dishes, short lilac sleeves were either forgotten, or acquired a positive glory, and while the cook was issuing her invitations for a jollification and gossip at the expense of Mr. and Mrs. Frost, Charlotte sat in her attic, amid Jane's verbenas, which she had cherished there ever since their expulsion from the kitchen, and wrote and cried, and left off, to read over, and feel satisfied at, the felicity of her phrases, and the sentiment of her project.

> 'Dear and Honoured Madam,—Pardon the liberty I am taking but I am sure that you and my reverend and redoubted master would not willingly have inflicted so much pain as yesterday on a poor young female which was brought up from an orphan child by my dear late lamented mistress and owes everything to her and would never realize the touching lines of the sublime poet
> Deserted in his utmost need
> By those his former bounty fed.
> As to higher wages and a situation offering superior advantages such as might prove attractive to other minds it has none to me. My turn is for fidelity in obscurity and dear and honoured lady I am a poor unprotected girl which has read in many volumes of the dangers of going forth into the snares of a wealthy and powerful family and begs you not to deprive her of the shelter of the peaceful roof which has been her haven and has been the seen of the joys and sorrows of her career. Dear lady pardon the liberty that I have taken but it would brake my heart to leave you and master and the dear children espeshilly in the present winter of adversity which I have hands to help in to the best of my poor abilities. Dear and honoured lady I have often been idle but I will be so no more I love the dear little ladies with all

my heart and I can cook and act in any capacity and wages is no object I will not take none nor beer neither—and the parlour tea-leaves will be sufficient. Dear and honoured master and mistress forgive the liberty a poor girl has taken and lend a favourable ear to my request for if you persist in parting with me I know I shall not survive it.

'Your humble and faithful Servant,
   'CHARLOTTE ARNOLD.'

Isabel received this letter while she was at breakfast with Lord Ormersfield and Louis, and it was, of course, impossible to keep it to herself. 'Talking of no wages!' said the Earl. 'Send her off at once.'

'You will despise me,' said Isabel, with tears in her eyes; 'but there is something very touching in it, in spite of the affectation. I believe she really means it.'

'Affectation is only matter of taste,' said Louis. 'Half the simplicity of our day is only fashion; and Charlotte's letter, with a few stops, and signed Chloe, would have figured handsomely in Mrs. Radcliffe's time.'

'It does not depend on me,' said Isabel; 'James could not bear her going before, and I am sure he will not now.'

'I think he ought not,' said Louis. 'Poor girl! I do believe the snares of wealthy families and fidelity in obscurity, really mean with her the pomps and vanities versus duty and affection.'

'I am sure I would not drive her back to them,' said Isabel; 'but I am only afraid the work will be too much for her strength.'

'The willing heart goes all the way,' said Louis; 'and maybe it will be more wholesome than London, and sitting up.'

Isabel coloured and sighed; but added, that it would be infinite relief on the children's account to keep some one so gentle-handed, and so entirely to be trusted.

James's decision was immediate. He called the letter a farrago, but his laugh was mixed with tears at the faithful affection it displayed. 'It was mere folly,' he said, 'to think of keeping her without wages; but, if she would accept such as could be afforded after taking a rough village girl for her food to do the hard work, the experiment should be made, in the hope that the present straits would only endure for a short time.

This little event seemed to have done him much good, and put him more at peace with the world. He was grateful for Lord Ormersfield's kindness and forbearance, and the enforced rest from work was refreshing him; while Isabel had never been so cheerful and lively in her life as now, when braced manfully for her work, full of energy, and feeling that she must show herself happy and courageous to support his depressed spirits. She was making a beginning—she was practising herself in her nursery duties, and, to her surprise, finding them quite charming; and little Kitty so delighted with all she did for her, that all the hitherto unsounded depths of the motherly heart were stirred up, and she could not think why she had never found out her true happiness. She looked so bright and so beautiful, that even Lord Ormersfield remarked it, pitying her for trials which he thought she little realized; but Louis augured better, believing that it was not ignorance but resolution which gave animation and brilliancy to her dark eye and cheerfulness to her smile.

Fitzjocelyn took her to Dynevor Terrace in the afternoon to settle the matter with Charlotte; and, on the way, he took the opportunity of telling her that he had been reading Sir Hubert, and admired him very much, discussing him and Adeline with the same vivid interest as her own sisters showed in them as persons, not mere personages. Isabel said they already seemed to her to belong to a world much farther back than the last fortnight.

'There is some puzzle in the middle,' said Louis. 'I can't make out the hero whose addresses were so inconvenient to Adeline, and who ran away from the pirates. He began as a crabbed old troubadour, who made bad verses; and then he went on as a fantastic young Viscount, skipping and talking nonsense.'

'Oh!' cried Isabel, much discomposed. 'Did I leave that piece there? I took it to Estminster by mistake, and they told me of it. I should have taken it out.'

'That would have been a pity,' said Louis, 'for the Viscount is a much more living man than the old troubadour. When he had so many plans of poems for the golden violet that he made none at all, I was quite taken with him. I began to think I was going to have a lesson.'

Isabel blushed and tried to laugh, but it was so unsuccessful that Louis exclaimed in high glee—'There! I do believe I was the fantastic Viscount! Oh! Isabel, it was too bad! I can fairly acquit myself of skipping ever since I had the honour of your acquaintance.'

'Or of running away from the pirates,' said Isabel. 'No, it was a great deal too bad, and very wrong indeed. It was when you did not run away that I was so much ashamed, that I thought I had torn out every atom. I never told any one—not even Virginia!'

Louis had a very hearty laugh, and, when Isabel gaw him so excessively amused, she ventured to laugh too at her ancient prejudice, and the strange chance which had made the fantastic Viscount, Sir Roland's critic.

'You must restore him,' said Louis, returning to business. 'That old troubadour is the one inconsistency in the story, evidently not fitting into the original plot. I shall be delighted to sit for the portrait.'

'I don't think you could now,' said Isabel. 'I think the motley must have been in the spectacles with which I looked at you.'

'Ah! it is a true poem,' said Louis, 'it must have been a great relief to your feelings! Shall I give it back to you?'

'Oh! I can't touch it now!' cried Isabel. 'You may give it to me, and if ever I have time to think again of it, I may touch it up, but certainly not now.'

'And when you do, pray don't omit the Viscount. I can't lose my chance of going down to posterity.'

He went his way, while Isabel repaired to the Terrace, and found Charlotte awaiting her answer in much trepidation.

The low wages, instead of none at all, were a great disappointment, doing away with all the honour and sentiment, and merely degrading her in the eyes of her companions; but her attachment conquered this objection, and face to face with her mistress, the affectation departed, and left remaining such honest and sincere faithfulness and affection, that Isabel felt as if a valuable and noble-hearted friend had suddenly been made known to her. It was a silly little fanciful heart, but it was sound to the core; and when Isabel said, 'There will be very hard work, Charlotte, but we will try to do our best for Mr. Frost and the children, and we will help each other,' Charlotte felt as if no task could be too hard if it were to be met with such a look and smile.

'Is it settled?' asked Lord Fitzjocelyn, as Charlotte opened the door for him.

'Oh, yes, thank you, my Lord—'

'But, Charlotte, one thing is decided. Mrs. Frost can afford no more eau de Cologne. The first hysterics and you go!'

He passed upstairs, and found Isabel beginning to dismantle the drawing-room—'Which you arranged for us!' she said.

A long, deep sigh was the answer, and Louis mused for some moments ere he said—'It is hard work to say good-bye to trifles with which departed happiness seems connected.'

'Oh, no!' cried Isabel, eagerly. 'With such a home, the happiness cannot be departed.'

'No, not with such a home!' said Louis, with a melancholy smile; 'but I was selfish enough to be thinking who hung that picture—'

'I don't think you were the selfish person,' said Isabel.

'Patience and work!' said Louis, rousing himself. 'Some sort of good time *must* come,'—and he quickly put his hand to assist in putting the Dresden shepherd and shepherdess into retirement, observing that they seemed the genii of the place, and he set his mind on their restoration.

'I do not think,' said Isabel, as she afterwards narrated this scene to her husband, 'that I ever realized his being so much attached to Mary Ponsonby; I thought it was a convenient suitable thing in which he followed his father's wishes, and I imagined he had quite recovered it.'

'He did not look interesting enough? Yes! he was slow in knowing his own mind; but his heart once given there is no recalling it, whatever his father may wish.'

'Or my mother,' said Isabel, smiling.

'Ah! I have never asked you what your party say of him in the London world.'

'They say he quite provokes them by being such a diligent member, and that people debate as to whether he will distinguish himself. Some say he does not care enough, and others, that he has too many crotchets.'

'Just so! Public men are not made of that soft, scrupulous stuff, which only hardens and toughens when principle is clear before him. Well, as to society—'

'Virginia says he is hardly ever to be had; he is either at the House, or he has something to do for his father; he slips out of parties, and they never catch him unless they are in great want of a gentleman to take them somewhere, and then no one is so useful. Mamma has been setting innumerable little traps for him, but he marches straight through them all, and only a little tone of irony betrays that he sees through them. Every one likes him, and the only complaint is, that he is so seldom to be seen, keeping almost entirely to his father's set, always with his father—'

'Ay! I can bear to watch his submission better than formerly. His attentions are in such perfect good taste that they are quite beautiful; and his lordship has quite ceased snubbing, and begins to have a glimmering that when Louis says something never dreamt of in his philosophy, the defect may be in his understanding, and not in Fitzjocelyn's.'

'I could excuse him for not always understanding Fitzjocelyn! But there never were two kinder people in the world; and I could not have imagined that I should ever like Lord Ormersfield half so much.'

'He is improved. Louis's exclusive devotion has not been lost on him. Holdsworth has been sitting with me, and talking of the great change in the parish. He told me that at his first arrival here, seven years ago, when he was very young, he found himself quite disheartened and disgusted by the respectability of the place. Every one was cold, distant, correct, and self-esteeming; so perfectly contented with themselves and the routine, that he felt all his ardour thrown away, and it seemed to him that he was pastor to a steam-engine—a mere item in the proprieties of Ormersfield. He was almost ready to exchange, out of weariness and impatience, when Fitzjocelyn came home, and awoke fresh life and interest by his absurdities, his wonderful philanthropies, and extraordinary schemes. His sympathy and earnestness were the first refreshment and encouragement; and Holdsworth declares that no one can guess the benefit that he was to him even when he was most ridiculous. Since that, he says, the change has been striking, though so gradual. Louis has all the same freshness and energy, but without the fluctuation and impetuosity. And his example of humility and sincerity has worked, not only in reclaiming the wild outlying people, but even awakening the comfortable dependents from their self-satisfaction. Even Frampton is far from the impenetrable person he used to be.'

'And I suppose they have done infinite good to the wild Marksedge people!'

'Some are better, some are worse. I believe that people always are worse when they reject good. I am glad to find, too, that the improvements answer in a pecuniary point of view. His Lordship is amazed at his son's sagacity, and they have never been so much at ease in money matters.'

'Indeed! Well, I must own that I have always been struck with the very small scale on which things are done here. Just the mere margin of what is required by their station, barely an indulgence!'

'I fancy you must look into subscriptions for Fitzjocelyn's means,' said James; 'and for the rest, they have no heart for new furniture till he marries.'

'Well! I wonder if Mary is worth so much heart! It might be the best thing for him if she would find some worthy merchant. He is very young still, and looks younger. I should like him to begin the world again.'

'Ha! Isabel, you want to cook up a romance of your own for him.'

James was recovering cheerfulness. He thought he was bracing himself to bear bravely with an unmerited wrong. The injustice of his sentence hid from him the degree of justice; and with regard to his own temper, he knew better what he restrained than what he expressed, and habitually gave himself credit for what he did not say or do. There was much that was really good in his present spirit, and it was on the way to be better; but his was not the character to be materially altered by the first brunt of a sudden shock. It was a step that he had brought himself to forgive the trustees. He did not yet see that he had any need to be forgiven.

At the end of three weeks James and Isabel returned to their home, and to their new way of life; and Fitzjocelyn had only time to see that they were beginning their struggle with good courage, before the meeting of Parliament summoned him to London.

Isabel fully justified Miss Faithfull's prediction. She was too truly high-minded to think any task beneath her; and with her heart in, not out of her immediate work, she could not fail to be a happier woman. Success gave as much pleasure in a household duty as in an accomplishment—nay, far more when it was a victory over herself, and an increase to the comfort of her husband. Her strength was much tried, and the children often fatigued and harassed her; but there was unspeakable compensation in their fondness and dependence on her, and even in the actual services themselves. The only wonder began to be how she could have ever trusted them in any hands but her own. Her husband's affection and consideration were sources of joy ever renewed; and though natural irritability and pressing anxieties might now and then betray him into a hasty word, his penitence so far surpassed the momentary pain it might have cost her, that she was obliged to do her utmost to comfort him. She sometimes found herself awkward or ignorant, and sometimes flagged from over-exertion; yet throughout, James's approval, and her own sense that she was striving to do her best, kept her mind at rest. Above all, the secret of her happiness was, that the shock of adversity had awakened her from her previous deadness and sluggishness of soul, and made her alive to a feeling of trust and support, a frame of mind ever repenting, ever striving onwards. Thus she went bravely through the very class of trials that she would once have thought merely lowering, inglorious, and devoid of poetry. What would have been in itself sordid, gained a sweetness from the light of love and duty, and never in all her dreamy ease had she been as cheerful and lighthearted as in the midst of hardship and rigid economy. Her equable temper and calm composure came to her aid; and where a more nervous and excitable woman would have preyed upon herself, and sunk under imaginary troubles, she was always ready to soothe and sustain the anxious and sensitive nature of her husband. After all, hers was the lightest share of the trial. To her, the call was to act, and to undergo misfortunes occasioned by no fault of hers; to him, the call was the one most galling to an active and eager man—namely, to endure, and worse, to see endured, the penalty of his own errors. In vain did he seek for employment. A curacy, without a fair emolument, would have been greater poverty than their present condition, as long as the house was unlet; and, though he answered advertisements and made applications, the only eligible situations failed; and he knew, among so many candidates, the last to be chosen would be a person of violent temper, unable to bear rebuke. Disappointment came upon disappointment, and the literary work, with which, through Louis's exertions, he had been supplied, was not likely to bring in any speedy return.

All that he could do was to take more than his part in domestic trifles, such as most men would have scorned, and to relieve his wife as far as possible of the children, often at the cost of his writing. He bore the brunt of many a trial of which she was scarcely aware—slights from the harsh vulgar, and compassion from the kind vulgar; and the proud self-assertion was gone which had hardened him to all such stings. To his lot fell the misery of weighing and balancing what comforts could best be cut off without positive injury to his wife and little ones. To consider whether an empty house should be repaired for a doubtful tenant, to make the venture, and have it rejected, was a severe vexation, when the expense trenched on absolute necessaries, and hardly less trying was it to be forced to accept the rent of the House Beautiful, knowing how ill it could be spared; and yet, that without it he must lapse into the hopeless abyss of debt. Moreover, there was

>The terrible heart thrill
>To have no power of giving

to some of the poor who had learnt to look to the Terrace in his grandmother's time, and meals were curtailed, that those in greater need might not be left quite unaided.

Nor was this the only cause for which James underwent actual stern privation. The reign of bad cookery was over. Charlotte, if unmethodical, was delicately neat; and though she kept them waiting for their dinner, always served it up with the precision of past prosperity. Cheap cookery and cottage economy were the study, and the results were pronounced admirable; but the master was the dispenser; and when a modicum of meat was to make nourishing a mountain of rice, or an ocean of broth, it would occur to him, as he helped Isabel, that the piece de resistance would hardly hold out for the kitchen devourers. He would take the recipe at its word, and dine on the surrounding structure; and in spite of the cottage economy, he was nearly as hungry after dinner as before it, and people began to say that he had never recovered his looks since his illness. These daily petty acts of self-denial and self-restraint had begun to tame his spirit and open his eyes in a manner that neither precept nor example had yet effected.

Charlotte had imbibed to the full the spirit of patient exertion which pervaded the house. Mrs. Martha had told her she was a foolish girl, and would be tired of the place in a fortnight; but when she did not see her tired, she would often rush in after her two mistresses were shut up for the evening, scold Charlotte for her want of method, and finish all that was left undone, while Charlotte went up to the nursery to release her mistress. As to novels and sentiment, they had gone after Sir Hubert; and though Charlotte was what Martha expressively called 'fairly run off her feet,' she had never looked better nor happier. Her mistress treated her like a friend; she doted on the children, and the cook was out of the kitchen; Delaford was off her mind, and neither stairs nor even knife-cleaning could hurt her feelings. To be sure, her subordinate, a raw girl from Marksgedge, devoured all that was set before her, and what was not eatable, she broke; but as she had been sent from home with no injunctions but to 'look sharp and get stout,' so she was only fulfilling her vocation, and on some question of beer, her mother came and raved at Charlotte, and would have raved at Mrs. Frost, if her dignified presence had not overawed her. So she only took the girl away in offence, and Charlotte was much happier with an occasional charwoman to share her labours.

There was much happiness in No. 5, notwithstanding that the spring and summer of 1851 were very hard times; and perhaps felt the more, because the sunny presence of Louis Fitzjocelyn did not shine there as usual.

He was detained in London all the Easter recess by his father's illness. Lord Ormersfield was bound hand and foot by a severe attack of rheumatism, caught almost immediately after his going to London. It seemed to have taken a strong hold of his constitution, and lingered on for weeks, so that he could barely move from his armchair by the fire, and began to give himself up as henceforth to be a crippled old man—a view out of which Louis and Sir Miles Oakstead tried by turns to laugh him; indeed, Sir Miles accused him of wanting to continue his monopoly of his son—and of that doubly-devoted attention by which Louis enlivened his convalescence.

Society had very little chance with Fitzjocelyn now, unless he was fairly hunted out by the Earl, who was always haunted by ungrounded alarms for his health and spirits, and never allowed him to fail in the morning rides, which were in fact his great refreshment, as much from the quiet and the change of scene, as from the mere air and exercise.

'Father,' said he, coming in one day a little after Easter, 'you are a very wise man!'

'Eh!' said the Earl, looking up in wonder and expectation excited by this prelude, hoping for the fulfilment of some political prediction.

'He is a wise man,' proceeded Louis, 'who does not put faith in treasures, especially butlers; also, who does not bring a schoolboy to London with nothing to do!'

'What now?' said the Earl. 'Is young Conway in a scrape?'

'I am,' said Fitzjocelyn; 'I have made a discovery, and I don't exactly see what to do with it. You see I have been taking the boy out riding with me, as the only thing I could well do for him these holidays. You must know he is very good and patronizing; I believe he thinks he could put me up to a few things in time. Well, to-day, as we passed a questionable-looking individual, Walter bowed, as if highly elated by the honour of his acquaintance, and explained to me that he was the celebrated—I forget who, but that's owing to my defective education. The fact is, that this Delaford, to whom my aunt implicitly trusts, has been introducing this unlucky boy to a practical course of Bell's Life—things that I went through Eton, and never even heard of.' And he detailed some of them.

'No more than she might have expected,' said Lord Ormersfield.

'And what is to be done?'

'I should say, never interfere between people and their servants, still less between them and their sons. You will do no good.'

'I cannot see this go on!' cried Louis. 'The boy told me all, by way of showing me his superiority. I believe he wants to introduce me to some of his distinguished friends. They flatter him, and make him a great man; and as to any scruples about his mother, Delaford has disposed of her objections as delicate weaknesses. When I began to look grave, the poor boy set it down to my neglected training, always spending my holidays in the country, and not knowing what fast men are up to.'

'And so he goes to destruction—just the sort of boy that does,' said the Earl, with due acquiescence in the course of the world.

'He need not,' exclaimed Louis. 'He is a nice boy, a very nice boy, if only he cared for his mother, or knew right from wrong.'

Lord Ormersfield smiled at these slight exceptions.

'He is heartily fond of Isabel,' said Louis. 'If I thought Jem could do any good, I would send for him; but he has made my aunt so much afraid of unworldliness just now, that I only wonder she lets Miss King stay on.'

'You had better leave it alone,' said the Earl, 'unless you can do anything with the boy. I am glad that I am not his guardian!'

'I wish I was,' sighed Louis.

'I suppose you will grow older some day,' said Lord Ormersfield. 'However, I see you will not be contented without going your own way to work.'

'When the Earl saw his son the next day, Louis looked radiant at having taken one step. He had seen his aunt, and she had endured the revelation with more equanimity than he could have supposed possible. 'It was a house where they took things easily,' as he said; a house where nothing was more feared than a scene; and Lady Conway had thanked her nephew greatly for his communication; promised what he did not ask, that he should not be betrayed to Walter; assured him that the butler should be dismissed, without giving any reason, before the summer holidays; and for the few remaining days before Walter returned to Eton, she thought she might reckon on her dear Fitzjocelyn for keeping his eye upon him: no doubt all would be right when Delaford was once gone.

It was the old want of a high standard—the love of ease rather than the love of right. The Earl laughed at her short-sighted policy, and resented her saddling Louis with the care of her son; while Louis philosophized upon good-nature, and its use and abuse.

Whether Mr. Delaford learnt that Sir Walter had betrayed him to Lord Fitzjocelyn, or whether he took alarm from the young gentleman being kept under surveillance, he scented danger; and took the initiative, by announcing to my Lady that he intended to retire from his situation into private life at the month's end.

Lady Conway rejoiced in being spared the fabrication by which she had intended to dismiss her paragon without hurting his feelings, thanked Fitzjocelyn more than ever, and was sure that dear Walter would do very well.

But no sooner had Delaford departed than a series of discoveries began to be made. Lady Conway's bills reached back to dates far beyond those of the cheques which she had put into Delaford's hands to pay them, and a tissue of peculation began to reveal itself, so alarming and bewildering to her, that she implored her nephew to investigate it for her.

Louis, rather against the will of his father, who was jealous of any additional tasks thrown on him, entered into the matter with the head of an accountant, and the zeal of a pursuer of justice; and stirred up a frightful mass of petty and unblushing fraud, long practised as a mere matter of course upon the mistress, who had set the example of easy-going, insincere self-seeking. It involved the whole household so completely, that there was no alternative but a clearance of every servant, whether innocent or guilty, and a fresh beginning. Indeed, so great had been the debts which had accumulated, that there was no doubt that the treacherous butler must have been gambling to a great extent with his mistress's money; and the loss was so heavy that Lady Conway found she should be obliged to retrench, 'just when she should have been so glad to have helped poor dear Isabel!' She must even give up a season in London, but dear Virginia was far too good and sensible to repine.

Lord Ormersfield, who had become much interested in the investigation, and assisted much by his advice, wanted her to go to Thornton Conway; and Louis urged the step warmly as the best hope for Walter. But she could not live there, she said, without far too heavy an expenditure; and she would make visits for the present, and find some cheap place abroad, where the girls could have masters.

And so her establishment was broken up, and Louis wrote warm congratulations to James that poor little Charlotte had not been tempted into the robber's den. Isabel could not help reading the whole history to Charlotte, who turned white at the notion of such wickedness, and could hardly utter a word; though afterwards, as she sat rocking little Mercy to sleep, she bestowed a great deal of good advice on her, 'never to mind what nobody said to her, above all, when they talked like a book, for there were a great many snakes and vipers in the grass, and 'twas best to know good friends when one had them.' And coupled with her moralizing, there was no small degree of humble thankfulness for the impulse that had directed her away from the evil. How could she ever have met Tom again if she had shared in the stigma on the dishonest household? Simple-hearted loyalty had been a guard against more perils than she had even imagined!

CHAPTER XVI
THE VALLEY OF HUMILIATION

This Valley is that from whence also the King will give to His their Vineyards; and they that go through it shall sing, as Christian did, for all he met with Apollyon.—Pilgrim's Progress.

The close of the session still found Lord Ormersfield so stiff, bent, and suffering, that Louis with some difficulty persuaded him into trying the experiment of foreign baths, and in a few weeks' time they were both established at the Hotel du Grand Monarque at Aix-la-Chapelle.

The removing his son to a dull watering-place, when he had so many avocations at home, had been a great vexation to the Earl; but he was delighted at the versatile spirits which made a holiday and delight of the whole, and found an endless fund of interest and occupation even in his attendance on the wearisome routine of health-seeking. German books, natural history, the associations of the place, and the ever-fresh study of the inhabitants and the visitors, were food enough for his lively conversation; and the Earl, inspirited by improving health, thought he had never enjoyed his son so much.

They were already old inhabitants of their hotel, when one afternoon they were much amused by finding a consequential courier gesticulating vehemently to the whole establishment on the apartments he was to secure for a superb Milord Anglais, who seemed to require half the hotel. Their sitting-room, overlooking the court, was especially coveted, and the landlord even followed them upstairs with many excuses to ask if they could exchange it for another for only two days. Lord Ormersfield's negative had all the exceeding politeness of offended dignity; and Louis was much amused at the surmises, with which he consoled himself, that this was nothing but some trumpery speculator, most likely a successful quack doctor—no one else went about in such a style.

In a grave, grand way, he was not a little curious, and took care to place himself where he could command a view of the court; while Louis, making no secret of his own amusement, worked up an excitement to entertain his father, and stood watching at the window.

'Crack! crack! there are the postilion's whips! Now for the Grand Monarque himself—thundering under the archway! Why, there are only two of them, after all!—a lady and a little yellow old man! Father, you are right after all—he is the very pattern of a successful quack! How tall the lady is! Halloo!' and he stood transfixed for a moment, then sprang to the door, replying to his father's astonished question—'Clara! Clara Dynevor!'

The party were in course of proceeding up the principal staircase—the tall figure of a young lady in mourning moving on with so stately, so quiet, and almost weary a manner, that Louis for a moment drew back, doubting whether the remarkable height had not deceived him. Her head was turned away, and she was following the host, scarcely exerting herself to gaze round, when she came close to the open door, where Louis moved slightly forwards. There was a little ecstatic shriek, and both her hands were clasped in his, while her face was glowing with animation and delight.

'I don't know how to believe it!' she said; 'can you be here?'

'We are curing my father. Had you not heard of his illness?'

'I hear nothing,' said Clara, sadly, as she held out her hand to Lord Ormersfield, who had also come to meet her; and her uncle, who followed close behind, was full of cordial rejoicings on the encounter.

There was Jane Beckett also, whom Louis next intercepted on her way to the bedrooms, laden with bags, and smiling most joyously to see him. 'To be sure, my young Lord! And your papa here too, my Lord! Well! who'll be coming abroad next, I wonder?'

'I wonder at nothing since I have met you here, Jane.'

'And I am right glad of it, my Lord. You'll cheer up poor Miss Clara a bit, I hope—for—Bless me! wont those Frenchmen never learn to carry that box right side up?'

And off rushed Jane to a never-ending war of many tongues in defence of Clara's finery; while Louis, following into the sitting-room, found Mr. Dynevor inviting his father to the private dinner which he had ordered for greater dignity.

The proposal was accepted for the sake of spending the evening together, but little was thus gained; for, excepting for that one little scream, Louis would hardly have felt himself in the company of his Giraffe. She had become a very fine-looking person, not quite handsome, but not many degrees from it, and set off by profuse hair, and every advantage of figure and dress; while her manner was self-possessed and formal, indifferent towards ordinary people, but warm and coaxing towards her uncle. Blunt—almost morose to others—he was fondling and affectionate towards her; continually looking at the others as if to claim admiration of her, appealing to her every moment, and even when talking himself, his keen eye still seeming to watch every word or gesture.

The talk was all Switzerland and Italy—routes and pictures, mountains and cathedrals—all by rote, and with no spirit nor heart in the discussion—not a single word coming near home, nothing to show that Dynevor Terrace had any existence. Louis bade Clara good-night, mortified at the absence of all token of feeling for her brother, and more than half repenting his advice to remain with her uncle. How could the warm-hearted girl have become this cold, haughty being, speaking by mechanism? He scarcely felt inclined to see her again; but early the next morning, as he was at breakfast with his father, there was a knock at the door, and a voice said, 'May I come in?' and as Louis opened, there stood the true Clara, all blushes and abruptness. 'I beg your pardon if it is wrong,' she said, 'but I could not help it. I must hear of him—of James.'

Lord Ormersfield welcomed her in an almost fatherly manner, and made her sit down, telling her that she had come at a good moment, since Louis had just received a letter; but he feared that it was not a very good account of Isabel.

'Isabel! Is anything the matter?'

'You are behindhand. Had you not heard of the arrival of number four?'

'I never hear anything,' said Clara, her eyes overflowing.

'Ha! not since we last met?' asked the Earl.

'They wrote once or twice; but you know they thought me wrong, and it has all died away since I went abroad. The last letter I had was dated in November.'

'You know nothing since that time!'

'No; I often thought of writing to Miss Faithfull, but I could not bear to show how it was, since they would not answer me. So I made bold to come to you, for I cannot ask before my uncle. He is quite passionate at the very name.'

'He is kind to you?' asked Lord Ormersfield, hastily.

'Most kind, except for that, the only thing I care about. But you have a letter! Oh! I am famishing to hear of them!'

She did not even know of the loss of the school; and her distress was extreme as she heard of their straits. 'It must be killing Isabel,' she said; 'if I could but be at home to work for her!'

'Isabel has come out beyond all praise,' said Louis. 'I am afraid there is much for them to undergo; but I do believe they are much happier in the midst of it.'

'Everybody must be happy in Dynevor Terrace,' said Clara.

Louis shook his head and smiled, adding, 'But, Clara, I do believe, if it were to come over again, Jem would hardly act in the same way.'

'Do you think he has forgiven me?'

'Judge for yourself.'

Her hand trembling, she caught at the well-known handwriting that to her seemed as if it could hardly be the property of any one else; and it was well for her that Louis had partly prepared her for the tone of depression, and the heavy trials it revealed, when she had been figuring to herself the writer enjoying all the felicity from which she was banished.

'No. 5, Dynevor Terrace, Sept. 14th, 1851.

'Dear Fitzjocelyn,—I ought to have written yesterday; but I took the whole duty at Ormersfield on Sunday, and was too lazy the next day to do more than keep the children out of the way, and look after Isabel; for, though I am told not to be uneasy, she does not regain strength as she has done before. Over-exertion, or bad nursing, one or both, tell upon her; and I wish we may not have too dear a bargain in the nurse whom she chose for cheapness' sake. My lectures were to have paid the expenses, but the author's need is not always the first consideration; the money will not be forthcoming till Christmas, and meantime we cannot launch out. However, Ormersfield partridges are excellent fare for Isabel, and I could return thanks for the abundant supply that would almost seem disproportionate; but you can guess the value as substantial comforts. A box of uneatable grouse from Beauchastel, carriage twelve shillings, was a cruel subject of gratitude; but those good people mean more kindly than I deserve; and when Isabel is well again, we shall rub on. This little one promises more resemblance to her than the others. We propose to call her Frances, after my poor mother and sister. Do you remember the thrill of meeting their names in Cheveleigh church? That memorial was well done of my uncle. If these children were to be left as we were, you would, I know, be their best friend; but I have a certain desire to see your own assurance to that effect. Don't fancy this any foreboding, but four daughters bind a man to life, and I sometimes feel as if I hardly deserved to see good days. If I am spared to bring up these children, I hope to make them understand the difference between independence and pride.

'I have been looking back on my life; I have had plenty of time during these months of inaction, which I begin to see were fit discipline. Till Holdsworth left his parish under my charge the other day for six weeks, I have exercised no office of my ministry, as you know that Mr. Purvis's tone with me cut me off from anything that could seem like meddling with him. I never felt more grateful to any man than I did when Holdsworth made the proposal. It was as if my penance were accepted for the spirit against which you too justly warned me before my Ordination. Sunday was something between a very sorrowful and a very happy day.

'I did not see the whole truth at first. I was only aware of my unhappy temper, which had provoked the immediate punishment; but the effort (generally a failure) to prevent my irritability from adding to the distresses I had brought on my poor wife, opened my eyes to much that I had never understood. Yet I had presumed to become an instructor—I deemed myself irreproachable!

'I believe the origin of the whole was, that I never distinguished a fierce spirit of self-exaltation from my grandmother's noble resolution to be independent. It was a demon which took the semblance of good, and left no room for demons of a baser sort. Even as a boy at the Grammar-school, I kept out of evil from the pride of proving myself gentlemanly under any circumstances; the motive was not a bit better than that which made me bully you. I can never remember being without an angry and injured feeling that my uncle's neglect left my grandmother burdened, and obliged me to receive an inferior education; and with this, a certain hope that he would never put himself in the right, nor lay me under obligations. You saw how this motive actuated me, when I never discerned it. I trust that I was not insincere, though presumptuous and self-deceiving I was to an extent which I can only remember with horror. If it approached to sacrilege, may the wilful blindness be forgiven! At least, I knew it not; and with all my heart I meant to fulfil the vows I had taken on me. Thus, when my uncle actually returned, there was a species of revengeful satisfaction in making my profession interfere with his views, when he had made it the only one eligible for me. How ill I behaved—how obstinately I set myself against all mediation—how I wrapped myself in self-approval—you know better than I do. My conceit, and absurdity, and thanklessness, have risen up before me; and I remember offers that would have involved no sacrifice of my clerical obligations—offers that I would not even consider— classing them all as 'mere truckling with my conscience.' What did I take for a conscience?

'Ever since, things have gone from bad to worse, grieving my dear grandmother's last year, and estranging me from my poor little sister because she would not follow my dictation. At last my sins brought down the penalty, and I would not grieve except for the innocent who suffer with me. Perhaps, but for them, I should never have felt it. Nor do I feel tempted to murmur; for there is a strange peace with us throughout, in spite of a sad heart and too many explosions of my miserable temper, and the sight of the hardships so bravely met by my dear wife. But for all this, I should never have known what she is! She whispered to me last evening, when she saw me looking tired and depressed, that she had no fears for the future, for this had been the happiest year of her life. Nothing can make her forget to soothe me!

'I have written a long rigmarole all about myself; but an outpouring is sometimes a relief, and you have borne with me often enough to do so now. My poor Clara's pardon, and some kind of clerical duty, are my chief wishes; but my failures in the early part of the year have taught me how unworthy I am to stir a step in soliciting anything of the kind. Did I tell you how some ten of the boys continue to touch their hats to me? and Smith, the butcher's son, often comes to borrow a book, and consult me on some of the difficulties that his father throws in his way. He is a fine fellow, and at least I hope that my two years at the school did him no harm. I was much impressed with the orderliness at Ormersfield Sunday-school. I wish I could have got half as much religious knowledge into my poor boys. I walked through your turnips in the South field, and thought they wanted rain. Frampton tells me the Inglewood harvest is in very good condition; but I will see the bailiff, and give you more particulars, when I can be better spared from home for a few hours. Kitty's assistance in writing has discomposed these last few lines.

'Yours ever,
    'J.R.F.D.'

Clara turned away and groaned aloud several times as she read; but all she said, as she gave it back to Louis, was, 'What is to be done? You must talk to my uncle.'

'Ah, Clara! young gentlemen of the nineteenth century make but a bad hand of the part of benevolent fairy.'

'I don't think my speaking would be of any use,' said Clara. 'Oh, if this only would have been a boy!'

Lord Ormersfield undertook to sound Mr. Dynevor, and found an early opportunity of asking whether he had heard of poor James's misfortune. Yes, he had known it long ago. No wonder, with such a temper. Kept it from the child, though. Would not have her always hankering after them.

Was he aware of his great distress and difficulties? Ha, ha! thought so! Fine lady wife! No end of children—served him right!—to bring down his pride.

Lord Ormersfield hazarded a hint that James had seen his errors, and the school was no longer in the way.

'No, no!' said Oliver. 'Too late now. Drink as he has brewed. He should have thought twice before he broke my poor mother's heart with his cantankerous ways. Cheveleigh beneath him, forsooth! I'm not going to have it cut up for a lot of trumpery girls! I've settled the property and whatever other pickings there may be upon my little Clara—grateful, and worthy of it! Her husband shall take Dynevor name and arms—unless, to be sure, he had a title of his own. The girl was much admired at Rome last winter, had a fair offer or two, but not a word will she say to any of them. I can't tell what's in her head, not I!'

And he looked knowingly at Lord Ormersfield, and willingly extended his stay at Aix-la-Chapelle, letting Fitzjocelyn organize expeditions from thence to Liege and other places in the neighbourhood.

The two cousins were so glad to be together, and the Earl so much pleased that Louis should have anything which gave him so much delight as this meeting with his old playfellow, that he did all in his power to facilitate and prolong their intercourse. He often sacrificed himself to Oliver's prosings on the Equatorial navigation, that the two young people might be at liberty; and he invited Clara to their early breakfast and walk before her uncle wanted her in the morning. These were Clara's times of greatest happiness, except that it gave her a new and strange sensation to be talked to by his lordship like a grown-up—nay, a sensible woman. Once she said to herself, laughing, 'He really treats me almost as if I were poor Mary herself.' And then came another flash: 'Perhaps he would even like me on the same terms!' And then she laughed again, and shook her head: 'No, no, my Lord, your son is much too good for that! Uncle Oliver would not have looked so benignant at us when we were sitting in the gardens last night, if he had known that I was giving Louis all my Lima letters. I wish they were more worth having! It was very stupid of me not to know Mary better, so that we write like two old almanacs. However, my letter from hence will be worth its journey to Peru.'

Clara's heart was several degrees lighter, both from the pleasure of the meeting and a suggestion of the Earl's, upon which she had at once acted, and which seemed, even as she laid pen to paper, to bring her somewhat nearer to her brother.

Her letter arrived at No. 5, on the next Monday morning at breakfast-time. It did not at first attract the attention of James. The Sunday exertions had again left a mental and physical lassitude, showing how much care and privation had told upon his strength; and Isabel's still tardy convalescence weighed him down with anxiety for the future, and almost with despair, as he thought of the comforts for want of which she suffered, though so patiently and silently dispensing with them. To his further vexation, he had, on the previous Saturday, seen Charlotte receiving at the back-door an amount of meat beyond her orders; and, having checked himself because too angry and too much grieved to speak at once, had reserved the reproof for the Monday, when Charlotte brought in her book of petty disbursements.

Failing to detect the obnoxious item, he said, 'Where's the account of the meat that came in on Saturday?'

'There, sir!' said Charlotte, indicating the legitimate amount, but blushing violently.

'That was not all?' he said, with a look of stern, interrogation.

'Oh! if you please, sir, that was nothing!'

'This will not do, Charlotte! I can have nothing taken into my house without being paid for. I insist on knowing what you could mean?'

'Oh, sir!' tearfully exclaimed the girl, 'it is paid for—I'll show you the account, if you will—with my own money. I'd not have had you hear of it for the world; but I could not bear that nurse's insinuations about her meat five times a-day—she that never nursed nothing like a real lady before! But I meant no harm, sir; and I hope you'll excuse the liberty, for I did not mean to take none; and I'm sure I'm quite contented for my own part, nor never meant to complain.'

'I know you did not, Charlotte! You are only too patient and kind—' But his voice broke down, and he was forced silently to sign to her to leave him.

'Can humiliation go farther!' he thought. 'My boasted independence ending in this poor, faithful servant being stung, by the sneers of this hired woman, into eking out her scanty meals with her own insufficient wages!'

Little Catharine, who had been gazing with dilated black eyes, came scrambling on his knee to caress him, perceiving that he was grieved.

'Ah! Kitty, Kitty!' he said, 'it is well that you are too young to feel these troubles!'

'Papa! letter!' cried Kitty, waving the unregarded letter in the triumph of discovery.

'The Reverend James Frost.' It was the writing formed by his own copies, which he could not see without a sharp pang of self-reproach for cruel injustice and unkindness.

Kitty slid down with the empty envelope to act reading to the twins, whom she caught by turns as they crawled away, and set up straight before her. Her operations and their remonstrances, though as loud as they were inarticulate, passed utterly unheard and unheeded by their father, as he read:—

> 'Hotel du Grand Monarque. Aix-la-Chapelle,
> Sept. 18th.
>
> 'My Dearest James,—As a mere matter of honesty and justice, I may venture to write to you. You always accepted

from dear grandmamma the income from the money in the Stocks. I did not know that half of it has since come to me, till Lord Ormersfield paid me this last year's dividend; and if you will not have his enclosed cheque for it, put it in the fire, for I will never have it in any form. It is not my uncle's, but my own; and if you would make me very happy, write to me here. You must not suppose that I am trying to buy a letter; but I look on this as yours, and I thought you had it till Lord Ormersfield told me about it. We met him and Louis quite unexpectedly—the best thing that has happened to me for years, though they told me much that grieves me exceedingly—but I cannot write about it till I know that I may. Tell me of dear Isabel and the babes. My heart yearns after them! it would leap up at the sight of a stone from the Terrace!

'Your ever affectionate
    'Clara.'

His first impulse was, as though he feared to repent, to turn to his desk, the tears of feeling still in his eyes, and dash off these words:—

'Your bounty, my dearest sister, is scarcely less welcome than the forgiving spirit which prompted it. I will not conceal that I was sorely in need of means to supply Isabel with the comforts that she requires. That your affection can survive my treatment last year, makes me equally grateful to you and ashamed of what then took place.'

He scarcely dared to look upon those phrases. Great as were his needs, and kindly as the proffer was made, it was new and painful to him to be under any such obligation, and he could hardly bend his spirit to know that never again should he be able to feel that he had never been beholden for money to a living creature. And while he felt it due to his sister to own the full extent of the benefit, he weighed his words as he wrote on, lest the simplest facts should look like a craving for further assistance.

Charlotte came up to remove the breakfast, and he looked up to give an order for some nourishing dainty for her mistress, adding, 'What did that mutton come to? No, I am not displeased with you, but Miss Clara has sent me some money.'

His assurance was needed, for Charlotte went down thinking she had never seen master look so stern. He had spoken from a sense that the truth was due to the generous girl, but each word had been intense pain. He wrote on, often interrupted by little riots among the children, and finally by a sharp contention, the twins having possessed themselves of a paper-knife, which Kitty, with precocious notions of discipline, considered as forbidden; and little Mercy was rapped over the fingers in the struggle. The roar brought down interference, and Kitty fell into disgrace; but when, after long persuasion, she was induced to yield the paper-cutter, kiss and make friends, Mercy, instead of embracing, locked her fingers into her dark curls, and tugged at them in a way so opposite to her name, that all Kitty's offence was forgotten in her merit for stopping her scream half-way at the sight of her father's uplifted finger, and his whisper of 'Poor mamma!'

That life of worry and baby squabbles, the reflection of his own faults, was hard to bear; and with a feeling of seeking a refuge, when the two little ones had fallen into their noonday sleep, and were left with their mother to the care of good Miss Mercy, he set out for some parish work at Ormersfield, still taking with him little Kitty, whose quicksilver nature would never relieve her elders by a siesta.

He was afraid to speak to Isabel until he should have composed himself, and, harassed and weary in spirits and in frame, he walked slowly, very sore at the domestic discovery, and scarcely feeling the diminution of the immediate pressure in the new sense of degradation. He could own that it was merited, and was arguing with himself that patience and gratitude were the needful proofs that the evil temper had been expelled. He called back his thankfulness for his wife's safety, his children's health, the constancy of his kind friends, and the undeserved ardour of his young sister's affection, as well as poor little Charlotte's unselfishness. The hard exasperated feeling that once envenomed every favour, and barbed every dart that wounded him, was gone; he could own the loving kindness bestowed on him, both from Heaven and by man, and began to find peace and repose in culling the low fragrant blossoms which cheered even the Valley of Humiliation.

He turned down the shady lane, overhung by the beech-trees of Mr. Calcott's park, and as he lifted Kitty in his arms to allow her the robin-redbreast, he did not feel out of tune with the bird's sweet autumnal notes, nor with the child's merry little voice, but each refreshed his worn and contrite spirit.

The sound of hoofs approaching made him turn his head; and while Kitty announced 'horse!' and 'man!' he recognised Mr. Calcott, and felt abashed, and willing to find a retreat from the meeting; but there was no avoiding it, and he expected, as usual, to be passed with a bow; but the Squire slackened his pace as he overtook him, and called out, good-humouredly, 'Ha, Mr. Frost, good morning' (once it would have been Jem).

'I always know you by the little lady on your shoulder. I was intending to call on you this afternoon on a little business; but if you will step up to the house with me, I shall be much obliged.'

James's heart beat thick with undefined hope; but, after all, it might be only to witness some paper. After what had occurred, and Mrs. Calcott considering herself affronted by Isabel, bare civility was forgiveness; and he walked up the drive with the Squire, who had dismounted, and was inquiring with cordial kindness for Mrs. Frost, yet with a little awkwardness, as if uncertain on what terms they stood, more as if he himself were to blame than the young clergyman.

Arriving at the house, James answered for his little girl's absence of shyness, and she was turned over to the Miss Calcotts, while the Squire conducted him to the study, and began with hesitation and something of apology—'It had struck him—it was not worth much—he hardly liked to propose it, and yet till something better should turn up—anything was better than doing nothing.' To which poor James heartily agreed. The board of guardians, where Mr. Calcott presided, were about to elect a chaplain to the union workhouse; the salary would be only fifty pounds, but if Mr. Frost would be willing to offer himself, it would be a great blessing to the inmates, and there would be no opposition.

Mr. Calcott, making the proposal from sincere goodwill, but with some dread how the Pendragon blood would receive it, was absolutely astounded by the effect.

Fifty pounds additional per annum was a boon only to be appreciated after such a pinching year as the past; the gratitude for the old Squire's kind pardon was so strong, and the blessing of re-admission to pastoral work touched him so deeply, that, in his weakened and dejected state, he could not restrain his tears, nor for some moments utter a word. At last he said, 'Oh, Mr. Calcott, I have not deserved this at your hands.'

'There, there,' said the Squire, trying to laugh it off, though he too became husky, 'say no more about it. It is a poor thing, and can't be made better; but it will be a real kindness to us to look after the place.'

'Let me say thus much,' said James, 'for I cannot be at peace till I have done so—I am aware that I acted unjustifiably in that whole affair, both when elected and dismissed.'

'No, no, don't let's go over that again!' said Mr. Calcott, in dread of a scene. 'An over-ardent friend may be a misfortune, and you were very young. Not that I would have taken your resignation if it had been left to me, but the world is grown mighty tender. I dare say you never flogged a boy like what I underwent fifty years ago, and was the better for it,' and he launched into some frightful old-world stories of the like inflictions, hoping to lead away from personalities, but James was resolved to say what was on his mind. 'It was not severity,' he said, 'it was temper. I richly deserved some portion of the rebuke, and it would have been well for me if that same temper had allowed me to listen to you, sir, or to reason.'

'Well,' said Mr. Calcott, kindly, 'you think very rightly about the matter, and a man of six-and-twenty has time to be wiser, as I tell Mrs. Calcott, when Sydney treats us to some of his theories. And now you have said your say, you must let me say mine, and that is, that there are very few young couples—aye, or old ones—who would have had the sense to go on as you are doing, fighting it out in your own neighbourhood without nonsense or false shame. I honour you and Mrs. Frost for it, both of you!'

James coloured deeply. He could have found commendation an impertinence, but the old Squire was a sort of patriarch in the county, and appreciation of Isabel's conduct must give him pleasure. He stammered something about her having held up wonderfully, and the salary being an immense relief, and then took refuge in matter-of-fact inquiries on his intended functions.

This lasted till nearly half-past one, and Mr. Calcott insisted on his staying to luncheon. He found the ladies greatly amused with their little guest—a very small, but extremely forward and spirited child, not at all pretty, with her brown skin and womanly eyes, but looking most thoroughly a lady, even in her little brown holland frock, and white sun-bonnet, her mamma's great achievement. Neither shy nor sociable, she had allowed no one to touch her, but had entrenched herself in a corner behind a chair, through the back of which she answered all civilities, with more self-possession than distinctness, and convulsed the party with laughing, when they asked if she could play at bo-peep, by replying that 'the children did.' She sprang from her place of refuge to his knee as soon as he entered, and occupied that post all luncheon time, comporting herself with great discretion. There was something touching in the sight of the tenderness of the young father, taking off her bonnet, and settling her straggling curls with no unaccustomed hands; and Mrs. Calcott's heart was moved, as she remarked his worn, almost hollow cheeks, his eyes still quick, but sunk and softened, his figure spare and thin, and even his dress not without signs of poverty; and she began making kind volunteers of calling on Mrs. Frost, nor were these received as once they would have been.

'He is the only young man,' said Mr. Calcott, standing before the fire, with his hands behind him, as soon as the guest had departed, 'except his cousin at Ormersfield, whom I ever knew to confess that he had been mistaken. That's the difference between them and the rest, not excepting your son Sydney, Mrs. Calcott.'

Mamma and sisters cried in chorus, that Sydney had no occasion for such confessions.

The Squire gave his short, dry laugh, and repeated that 'Jem Frost and young Fitzjocelyn differed from other youths, not in being right but in being wrong.'

On which topic Mrs. Calcott enlarged, compassionating poor Mr. Frost with a double quantity of pity for his helpless beauty of a fine lady-wife; charitably owning, however, that she really seemed improved by her troubles. She should have thought better of her if she had not kept that smart housemaid, who looked so much above her station, and whom the housekeeper had met running about the lanes in the dark, the very night when Mr. Frost was so ill.

'Pshaw! my dear,' said her husband, 'cannot you let people be judges of their own affairs?'

It was what he had said on the like occasions for the last thirty years; but Mrs. Calcott was as wise as ever in other folks' matters.

The fine lady-wife had meanwhile been arranging a little surprise for her husband. She was too composed to harass herself at his not returning at midday, she knew him and Kitty to be quite capable of taking care of each other, and could imagine him detained by parish work, and disposing of the little maiden with Betty Gervas, or some other Ormersfield friend, but she had thought him looking fagged and worried, she feared his being as tired as he had been on the Sunday, and she could not bear that he should drink tea uncomfortably in the study, tormented by the children. So she had repaired to the parlour, and Miss Mercy, after many remonstrances, had settled her there; and when the good little lady had gone home to her sister's tea, Isabel lay on the sofa, wrapped in her large soft shawl, languidly attempting a little work, and feeling the room dreary, and herself very weak, and forlorn, and desponding, as she thought of James's haggard face, and the fresh anxieties that would be entailed on him if she should become sickly and ailing. The tear gathered on her eyelash as she said to herself, 'I would not exert myself when I could; perhaps now I cannot, when I would give worlds to lighten one of his cares!' And then she saw one little bit of furniture standing awry, in the manner that used so often to worry his fastidious eye; and, in the spirit of doing anything to please him, she moved across the room to rectify it, and then sat down in the large easy chair, wearied by the slight exertion, and becoming even more depressed and hopeless; 'though,' as she told herself, 'all is sure to be ordered well. The past struggle has been good—the future will be good if we can but treat it rightly.'

Just as the last gleams were fading on the tops of the Ormersfield coppices, she heard the hall-door, and James's footstep; and it was more than the ordinary music of his 'coming up the stair;' there was a spring and life in it that thrilled into her heart, and glanced in her eye, as she sat up in her chair, to welcome him with no forced smile.

And as he came in with a pleased exclamation, his voice had no longer the thin, worn sound, as if only resolute resignation prevented peevishness; there was a cheerfulness and solidity in the tone, as he came fondly to her side, regretted having missed her first appearance, and feared she had been long alone.

'Oh, no; but I was afraid you would be so tired! Carrying Kitty all the way, too! But you look so much brighter.'

'I am brighter,' said James. 'Two things have happened for which I ought to be very thankful. My dear, can you bear to be wife to the chaplain of the Union at fifty pounds a-year!'

'Oh! have you something to do? cried Isabel; 'I am so glad! Now we shall be a little more off your mind. And you will do so much good! I have heard Miss Mercy say how much she wished there were some one to put those poor people in the right way.'

'Yes; I hope that concentrated earnestness of attention may do something to make up for my deficiency in almost every other qualification,' said James. 'At least, I feel some of the importance of the charge, and never was anything more welcome.'

'And how did it happen?'

'People are more forgiving than I could have hoped. Mr. Calcott has offered me this, in the kindest way; and as if that were not enough, see what poor little Clara says.'

'Poor little Clara!' said Isabel, reading the letter; 'you don't mean to disappoint her!'

'I should be a brute if I did. No; I wrote to her this morning to thank her for her pardoning spirit.'

'You should have told me; I should like to send her my love. I am glad she has not quite forgotten us, though she mistook the way to her own happiness.'

'Isabel! unless I were to transport you to Cheveleigh a year ago, nothing would persuade you of my utter wrong-headedness.'

'Nor that, perhaps,' said Isabel, with a calm smile.

'Not my having brought you to be grateful for the Union chaplaincy?'

'Not if you had brought me to the Union literally,' said Isabel, smiling. 'Indeed, dear James, I think we have both been so much the better and happier for this last year, that I would not have been without it for any consideration; and if any mistakes on your part led to it, they were mistakes on the right side. Don't shake your head, for you know they were what only a good man could have made.'

'That may be all very well for a wife to believe!'

And the rest of the little dispute was concluded, as Charlotte came smiling up with the tea.

CHAPTER XVII
'BIDE A WEE.'

> Come unto these yellow sands,
> And then take hands!
>
> Tempest

The Ponsonby family were spending the hot season at Chorillos, the Peruvian watering-place, an irregular assembly of cane-built, mud-besmeared ranches, close on the shore of the Pacific, with the mountains seeming to rise immediately in the rear.

They had gone for Mr. Ponsonby's health, and Rosita's amusement; and in the latter object they had completely succeeded. In her bathing-dress, full trousers, and a beautifully-embroidered blouse, belted at the waist, a broad-brimmed straw hat, and her raven hair braided in two long tresses, she wandered on the shore with many another fair Limenian, or entered the sea under the protection of a brown Indian; and, supported by mates or gourds, would float for hours together among her companions, splashing about, and playing all sorts of frolics, like so many mermaids.

In the evening she returned to more terrestrial joys, and arraying herself in some of her infinite varieties of ball-dresses, with flowers and jewels in her hair, a tiny Panama hat cocked jauntily on the top of her head, and a rich shawl with one end thrown over the shoulder, she would step daintily out in her black satin shoes, with old Xavier in attendance, or sometimes with Robson as her cavalier, to meet her friends on the beach, or make a call in the lamp-lit corridor of some other rancho. There were innumerable balls, dances, and pic-nics to the rich and fertile villages and haciendas around, and fetes of every description almost every evening; visits to the tombs of the old Peruvians, whose graves were often rudely and lightly searched for the sake of their curious images and golden ornaments. The Senora declared it was the most lovely summer she had ever spent, and that nothing should induce her to return to Lima while her friends remained there.

The other object, of re-invigorating Mr. Ponsonby, had not been attained. He had been ailing for some time past, and, instead of deriving benefit from the sea-breezes, only missed the comforts of home. He was so testy and exacting that Mary would have seldom liked to leave him to himself, even if she had been disposed to lead the life of a fish; and she was seldom away from him, unless Robson came down from Lima to transact business with him.

Mary dreaded these interviews, for her father always emerged from them doubly irritable and dispirited; and when Rosita claimed the Senor Robson as her knight for her evening promenade, and the father and daughter were left alone together, he would blame the one lady for going, the other for staying—then draw out his papers again, and attempt to go over them, with a head already aching and confused—be angry at Mary's entreaties that he would lay them aside, or allow her to help him—and presently be obliged with a sigh to desist, and lie back in his chair, while she fanned him, or cooled his forehead with iced water. Yet he was always eager and excited for Robson to come; and a delay of a day would put his temper in such a state that his wife kept out of his sight, leaving Mary to soothe him as she might.

'Mary,' said her father one evening, when she was standing at the window of the corridor, refreshing her eye with gazing at the glorious sunset in the midst of a pile of crimson and purple clouds, reflected in the ocean—'Mary, Ward is going to Mew York next week.'

'So soon?' said Mary.

'Aye, and he is coming here to-morrow to see you.'

Mary still looked out with a sort of interest to see a little gold flake change its form as it traversed a grand violet tower.

'I hope you will make him a more reasonable answer than you did last time,' said her father; 'it is too bad to keep the poor man dangling on at this rate! And such a man!'

'I am very sorry for it, but I cannot help it,' said Mary; 'no one can be kinder or more forbearing than he has been, but I wish he would look elsewhere.'

'So you have not got that nonsense out of your head!' exclaimed Mr. Ponsonby, with muttered words that Mary would not hear. 'All my fault for ever sending you among that crew! Coming between you and the best match in Lima—the best fellow in the world—strict enough to content Melicent or your mother either! What have you to say against him, Mary? I desire to know that.'

'Nothing, papa,' said Mary, 'except that I wish he could make a better choice.'

'I tell you, you and he were made for each other. It is the most provoking thing in the world, that you will go on in this obstinate way! I can't even ask the man to do me a kindness, with having an eye to these abominable affairs, that are all going to the dogs. There's old Dynevor left his senses behind him when he went off to play the great man in England, writing every post for remittances, when he knows what an outlay we've been at for machinery; and there's the Equatorial Company cutting its own throat at Guayaquil, and that young fellow up at the San Benito not half to be trusted—Robson can't make out his accounts; and here am I such a wretch that I can hardly tell what two and two make; and here's Ward, the very fellow to come in and set all straight in the nick of time; and I can't ask him so much as to look at a paper for me, because I'm not to lay myself under an obligation.'

'But, papa, if our affairs are not prosperous, it would not be fair to connect Mr. Ward or any one with them.'

'Never you trouble yourself about that! You'll come in for a pretty fortune of your own, whatever happens to that abominable cheat of a Company; and that might be saved if only I was the man I was, or Dynevor was here. If Ward would give us a loan, and turn his mind to it, we should be on our legs in an instant. It is touch and go just now!—I declare, Mary,' he broke out again after an interval, 'I never saw anything so selfish as you are! Lingering and pining on about this foolish young man, who has never taken any notice of you since you have been out here, and whom you hear is in love with another woman—married to her very likely by this time—or, maybe, only wishing you were married and out of his way.'

'I do not believe so,' answered Mary, stoutly.

'What! you did not see Oliver's letter from that German place?'

'Yes, I did,' said Mary; 'but I know his manner to Clara.'

'You do? You take things coolly, upon my word!'

'No,' said Mary. 'I know they are like brother and sister, and Clara could never have written to me as she has done, had there been any such notion. But that is not the point, papa. What I know is, that while my feelings are what they are at present, it would not be right of me to accept any one; and so I shall tell Mr. Ward, if he is still determined to see me. Pray forgive me, dear papa. I do admire and honour him very much, but I cannot do any more; and I am sorry I have seemed pining or discontented, for I tried not to be so.'

A grim grunt was all the answer that Mr. Ponsonby vouchsafed. His conscience, though not his lips, acquitted poor Mary of discontent or pining, as indeed it was the uniform cheerfulness of her demeanour that had misled him into thinking the unfortunate affair forgotten.

He showed no symptoms of speaking again; and Mary, leaning back in her chair, had leisure to recover herself after the many severe strokes that had been made at her. There was one which she had rebutted valiantly at the moment, but which proved to have been a poisoned dart—that suggestion that it might be selfish in her not to set Louis even more free, by her own marriage!

She revolved the probabilities: Clara, formed, guided, supported by himself, the companion of his earlier youth, preferred to all others, and by this time, no doubt, developed into all that was admirable. What would be more probable than their mutual love? And when Mary went over all the circumstances of her own strange courtship, she could not but recur to her mother's original impression, that Louis had not known what he was doing. Those last weeks had made her feel rather than believe otherwise, but they were far in the distance now, and he had been so young! It was not unlikely that even yet, while believing himself faithful to her, his heart was in Clara's keeping, and that the news of her marriage would reveal to them both, in one rush of happiness, that they were destined for each other from the first.

Mary felt intense pain, and yet a strange thrill of joy, to think that Louis might at last be happy.

She drew Clara's last letter out of her basket, and re-read it, in hopes of some contradiction. Clara's letters had all hitherto been stiff. She had not been acknowledged to be in the secret of Mary's engagement while it subsisted, and this occasioned a delicacy in writing to her on any subject connected with it; and so the mention of the meeting at the 'Grand Monarque' came in tamely, and went off quickly into Lord Ormersfield's rheumatism and Charlemagne's tomb. But the remarkable thing in the letter was the unusual perfume of happiness that pervaded it; the conventional itinerary was abandoned, and there was a tendency to droll sayings—nay, some shafts from a quiver at which Mary could guess. She had set all down as the exhilaration of Louis's presence, but perhaps that exhilaration, was to a degree in which she alone could sympathize.

Mary was no day-dreamer; and yet, ere Rosita's satin shoe was on the threshold, she had indulged in the melancholy fabric of a castle at Ormersfield, in which she had no share, except the consciousness that it had been her self-sacrifice that had given Louis at last the felicity for which he was so well fitted.

But at night, in her strange little room, lying in her hammock, and looking up through her one unglazed window, high up in the roof, to the stars that slowly travelled across the space, she came back to a more collected opinion. She had no right to sacrifice Mr. Ward as well as herself. Louis could not be more free than she had made him already, and it would be doing evil that good might come, to accept the addresses of one man while she could not detach her heart from another. 'Have I ever really tried yet? she thought. 'Perhaps I am punishing him and poor Mr. Ward, because, as papa says, I have languished, and have never tried in earnest to wean my thoughts from him. He was the one precious memory, besides my dear mother, and she never thought it would come to good. He will turn out to have been constant to Clara all the time, though he did not know it.'

Even if Mr. Ponsonby had been in full health, he would have had no inclination to spare Mary the conversation with Mr. Ward, who took his hot nine miles' ride from Lima in the early morning, before the shadow of the mountains had been drawn up from the arid barren slope leading to Chorillos.

He came in time for the late breakfast, when the table was loaded with various beautiful tropical fruits, tempting after his ride, and in his state of suspense. He talked of his journey, and of his intended absence, and his regret, in a manner half mechanical, half dreamy, which made Mary quite sorry for him; it was melancholy for a man of his age to have fixed so many fond hopes where disappointment was in store for him. She wished to deal as kindly with him as she could, and did not shrink away when her father left them, muttering something about a letter, and Rosita went to take her siesta.

With anxious diffidence he ventured to ask whether she remembered what had passed between them on the San Benito mountain.

'Yes, Mr. Ward, but I am afraid I do not think differently now, in spite of all your kindness.'

Poor Mr. Ward's countenance underwent a change, as if he had hoped more. 'Your father had given me reason to trust,' he said, 'that you had recovered your spirits; otherwise I should hardly have presumed to intrude on you. And yet, before so long an absence, you cannot wonder that I longed to hear something decisive.'

'Indeed I wished what I said before to be decisive. I am very sorry to give pain to one so much kinder than I deserve, and to whom I look up so much, but you see, Mr. Ward, I cannot say what is untrue.'

'Miss Ponsonby,' said Mr. Ward, 'I think you may be acting on a most noble but mistaken view. I can well believe that what you have once experienced you can never feel again. That would be more than I should dare to ask. My own feeling for you is such that I believe I should be able to rejoice in hearing of the fulfilment of your happiness, in your own way; but since there seems no such probability, cannot you grant me what you can still give, which would be enough to cause me the greatest joy to which I have ever aspired; and if my most devoted affection could be any sufficient return, you know that it is yours already.'

The grave earnestness with which he spoke went to Mary's heart, and the tears came into her eyes. She felt it almost wrong to withstand a man of so much weight and worth; but she spoke steadily—'This is very kind—very kind indeed; but I do not feel as if it would be right.'

'Will you not let me be the judge of what will satisfy me?'

'You cannot judge of my feelings, Mr. Ward. You must believe me that, with all my esteem and gratitude, I do not yet feel as if I should be acting rightly by you or by any one else, under my present sentiments.'

'You do not *yet* feel?'

Mary felt that the word was a mistake. 'I do not think I ever shall,' she added.

'You will not call it persecution, if I answer that perhaps I may make the venture once more,' he said. 'I shall live on that word 'yet' while I am at New York. I will tease you no more now; but remember that, though I am too old to expect to be a young lady's first choice, I never saw the woman whom I could love, or of whom I could feel so sure that she would bring a blessing with her; and I do believe that, if you would trust me, I could make you happy. There! I ask no answer. I only shall think of my return next year, and not reckon on that. I know you will tell me whatever is true.' He pressed her hand, and would fain have smiled reassuringly.

He took leave much more kindly than Mary thought she deserved, and did not appear to be in low spirits. She feared that ahe had raised unwarrantable hopes, but the truth was, that Mr. Ponsonby had privately assured him that, though she could not yet believe it, poor girl! the young man in England would be married before many months were over to old Dynevor's niece. There would be no more difficulty by the time he came back, for she liked him heartily already, and was a sensible girl.

So Mr. Ward departed, and Mary was relieved, although she missed his honest manly homage, and sound wise tone of thought, where she had so few to love or lean on. She thought that she ought to try to put herself out of the way of her cousins at home as much as possible, and so she did not try to make time to write to Clara, and time did not come unsought, for her father's health did not improve; and when they returned to Lima, he engrossed her care almost entirely, while his young wife continued her gaieties, and Mary had reason to think the saya y manto disguise was frequently donned; but it was so much the custom of ladies of the same degree, that Mary thought it neither desirable nor likely to be effectual to inform her father, and incite him to interfere. She devoted herself to his comfort, and endeavoured to think as little as she heard of English cousins.

There was not much to hear. After returning home quite well, Lord Ormersfield was laid up again by the first cold winds, and another summer of German brunnens was in store for him and Louis. Lady Conway had taken a cottage in the Isle of Wight, where Walter, having found the Christmas holidays very dull, and shown that he could get into mischief as well without Delaford as with him, she sent him off in a sort of honourable captivity to James and Isabel, expecting that he would find it a great punishment. Instead of this, the change from luxury to their hard life seemed to him a sort of pic-nic. He enjoyed the 'fun' of the waiting on themselves, had the freedom of Ormersfield park for sport; and at home, his sister, whom he had always loved and respected more than any one else. James had time to attend to him, and to promote all his better tastes and feelings; and above all, he lost his heart to his twin nieces. It was exceedingly droll to see the half quarrelsome coquetries between the three, and to hear Walter's grand views for the two little maidens as soon as he should be of age. James and Louis agreed that there could not be much harm in him, while he could conform so happily to such a way of life. Everything is comparative, and the small increase to James's income had been sufficient to relieve him from present pinching and anxiety in the scale of life to which he and Isabel had become habituated. His chaplaincy gave full employment for heart and head to a man so energetic and earnest; he felt himself useful there, and threw himself into it with all his soul; and, what was more wonderful, he had never yet quarrelled with the guardians; and the master told Mr. Calcott that he had heard Mr. Frost was a fiery gentleman, but he had always seen him particularly gentle, especially with the children in school. The old women could never say enough in his praise, and doated on the little brown fairy who often accompanied him.

There was plenty to be done at home—little luxury, and not much rest; but Isabel's strength and spirits seemed a match for all, in her own serene quiet way, and the days passed very happily.

Charlotte had a workhouse girl under her, who neither ate nor broke so vehemently as her predecessor. One night, when Charlotte sat mending and singing in the nursery, the girl came plodding up in her heavy shoes, saying, 'There's one wanting to see ye below.'

'One! Who can it be?' cried Charlotte, her heart bounding at the thought of a denouement to her own romance.

'He looks like a gentleman,' said the girl, 'and he wanted not to see master, but Miss Arnold most particular.' More hopes for Charlotte. She had nearly made one bound downstairs, but waited to lay awful commands on the girl not to leave the children on no account; then flew down, pausing at the foot of the stairs to draw herself up, and remember dignity and maidenliness. Alas for her hopes! It was Delaford! His whiskers still were sleek and curly; he still had a grand air; but his boots were less polished—his hat had lost the gloss—and he looked somewhat the worse for wear.

Poor Charlotte started back as if she had seen a wild beast in her kitchen. She had heard of his dishonesty, and her thoughts flew distractedly to her spoons, murder, and the children. And here he was advancing gracefully to take her hand. She jumped back, and exclaimed, faintly, 'Mr. Delaford, please go away! I can't think what you come here for!'

'Ah! I see, you have listened to the voice of unkind scandal,' said Mr. Delaford. 'I have been unfortunate, Miss Arnold—unfortunate and misunderstood—guilty never. On the brink of quitting for ever an ungrateful country, I could not deny myself the last sad satisfaction of visiting the spot where my brightest hours have been passed;' and he looked so pathetic, that Charlotte felt her better sense melting, and spoke in a hurry—

'Please don't, Mr. Delaford, I've had enough of all that. Please go, and take my best wishes, as long as you don't come here, for I know all about you.'

But the intruder only put his hand upon his heart, and declared that he had been misrepresented; and let a cruel world think of him as it might, there was one breast in which he could not bear that a false opinion, of him should prevail. And therewith he reached a chair, and Charlotte found herself seated and listening to him, neither believing, nor wishing to believe him, longing that he would take himself away, but bewildered by his rhetoric. In the first place, he had been hastily judged; he had perhaps yielded too much to Sir Walter—but youth, &c.; and when Lady Conway's means were in his hands, it had seemed better—he knew now that it had been a weakness, but so he had judged at the time—to supply the young gentleman's little occasions, than to make an eclat. Moreover, if he had not been the most unfortunate wretch in the world, a few lucky hits would have enabled him to restore the whole before Lord Fitzjocelyn hurried on the inquiry; but the young gentleman thought he acted for the best, and Mr. Delaford magnanimously forgave him.

Charlotte could not follow through half the labyrinth; and sat pinching the corner of her apron, with a vague idea that perhaps he was not so bad as was supposed; but what would happen if her master should find him there? She never looked up, nor made any answer, till he began to give her a piteous account of his condition; how he did not know where to turn, nor what to do; and was gradually beginning to sell off his 'little wardrobe to purchase the necessaries of life.' Then the contrast began to tell on her soft heart, and she looked up with a sound of compassion.

In the wreck of his fortunes and hopes, he had thought of her; he knew she had too generous a spirit to crush a wretch trodden down by adversity, who had loved her truly, and who had once had some few hopes of requital. Those were, alas! at an end; yet still he saw that 'woman, lovely woman, in our hours of ease'—And here he stumbled in his quotation, but the fact was, that his hopes being blasted in England, he had decided on trying his fortune in another hemisphere; but, unfortunately, he had not even sufficient means to pay for a passage of the humblest description, and if he could venture to entreat for a—in fact, a loan—it should be most faithfully and gratefully restored the moment the fickle goddess should smile on him.

Charlotte felt a gleam of joy at the prospect of getting rid of him on any terms. She belonged to a class who seldom find the golden mean in money matters, being either exceedingly close and saving, or else lavish either on themselves or other people. Good old Jane had never succeeded in saving; all her halfpence went to the beggars, and all her silver melted into halfpence, or into little presents; and on the receipt of her wages, she always rushed on to the shop like a child with a new shilling. Reading had given Charlotte a few theories on the subject, but her practice had not gone far. She always meant to put into the savings' bank; but hiring books, and daintiness, though not finery, in dress, had prevented her means from ever amounting to a sum, in her opinion, worth securing. The spirit of economy in the household had so far infected her that she had, in spite of her small wages, more in hand than ever before, and when she found what Mr. Delaford wanted, a strange mixture of feelings actuated her. She pitied the change in his fortunes; she could not but be softened by his flattering sayings,—she could not bear that he should not have another chance of retrieving his character—she knew she had trifled unjustifiably with his feelings, if he had any,—and she had a sense of being in fault. And so the little maiden ran upstairs, peeped into her red-leather work-box, pulled out her bead-purse, and extracted therefrom three bright gold sovereigns, and ran downstairs again, trembling at her own venturesomeness, afraid that their voices might be heard. She put the whole before Delaford, saying—

'There—that is all that lays in my power. Don't mention it, pray. Now, please go, and a happy journey to you.'

How she wished his acknowledgments and faithful promises were over! He did hint something about refreshment, bread-and-cheese and beer, fare which he used to despise as 'decidedly low,' but Charlotte was obdurate here, and at last he took his leave. There stood the poor, foolish, generous little thing, raking out the last embers of the kitchen fire, conscious that she had probably done the silliest action of her life, very much ashamed, and afraid of any one knowing it; and yet strangely light of heart, as if she had done something to atone for the past permission that she had granted him to play with her vanity.

'Some day she might tell Tom all about it, and she did not think he would be angry, for he knew what it was to have nowhere to go, and to want to try for one more chance.'

CHAPTER XVIII
THE CRASH

> Late and early at employ;
>   Still on thy golden stores intent;
>   Thy summer in heaping and hoarding is spent,
> What thy winter will never enjoy.
>   SOUTHEY.

'Stitch! stitch!' said James Frost, entering the nursery on a fine August evening, and finding his wife with the last beams of sunshine glistening on her black braids of hair, as she sat singing and working beside the cot where slept, all tossed and rosy, the yearling child. 'Stitch! stitch! If I could but do needlework!'

'Ah!' said Isabel, playfully, lifting up a sweeter face than had ever been admired in Miss Conway, 'if you will make your kittens such little romps, what would you have but mending?'

'Is it my fault? I am very sorry I entailed such a business on you. You were at that frock when I went to evening prayers at the Union, and it is not mended yet.'

'Almost; and see what a perfect performance it is, all the spots joining as if they had never been rent. I never was so proud of anything as of my mending capabilities. Besides, I have not been doing it all the time: this naughty little Fanny was in such a laughing mood, that she would neither sleep herself nor let the rest do so; and Kitty rose up out of her crib, and lectured us all. Now, don't wake them—no, you must not even kiss the twin cherries; for if they have one of papa's riots, they will hardly sleep all night.'

'Then you must take me away; it is like going into a flower-garden, and being told not to gather.'

'Charlotte is almost ready to come to them, and in the meantime here is something for you to criticise,' said she, taking from the recess of her matronly workbasket a paper with a pencilled poem, on the Martyrs of

Carthage, far more terse and expressive than anything she used to write when composition was the object of the day. James read and commented, and was disappointed when they broke off short— 'Ah! there baby woke.'

'Some day I shall give you a subject. Do you know how Sta. Francesca Romana found in letters of gold the verse of the Psalm she had been reading, and from which she had been five times called away to attend to her household duties?'

'I thought you were never to pity me again—'

'Do you call that pitying you?'

'Worse,' said Isabel, smiling.

'Well, then, what I came for was to ask if you can put on your bonnet, and take a walk in the lanes this lovely evening.'

A walk was a rare treat to the busy mother, and, with a look of delight, she consented to leave her mending and her children to Charlotte. There seldom were two happier beings than that pair, as they wandered slowly, arm-in-arm, in the deep green lanes, in the summer twilight, talking sometimes of the present, sometimes of the future, but with the desultory, vague speculation of those who feared little because they knew how little there was to fear.

'It is well they are all girls,' said James, speaking of that constant topic, the children; 'we can manage their education pretty well, I flatter myself, by the help of poor Clara's finishing governess, as Louis used to call you.'

'If the edge of my attainments be not quite rusted off. Meantime, you teach Kitty, and I teach nothing.'

'You don't lose your singing. Your voice never used to be so sweet.'

'It keeps the children good. But you should have seen Kitty chaunting 'Edwin and Angelina' to the twins this morning, and getting up an imitation of crying at 'turn Angelina, ever dear,' because, she said, Charlotte always did.'

'That is worth writing to tell Fitzjocelyn! It will be a great disappointment if they have to stay abroad all this winter; but he seems to think it the only chance of his father getting thoroughly well, so I suppose there is little hope of him. I should like for him to see Kitty as she is now, she is so excessively droll!'

'Yes; and it must be a great deprivation to have to leave all his farm to itself, just as it is looking so well; only he makes himself happy with whatever he is doing.'

'How he would enjoy this evening! I never saw more perfect rest!'

'Yes;—the sounds of the town come through the air in a hush! and the very star seems to twinkle quietly!'

They stood still without speaking to enjoy that sense of stillness and refreshment, looking up through the chestnut boughs that overshadowed the deep dewy lane, where there was not air enough even to waft down the detached petals of the wild rose.

'Such moments as these must be meant to help one on,' said James, 'to hinder daily life from running into drudgery.'

'And it is so delightful to have a holiday given, now and then, instead of having a life all holiday. Ah! there's a glow-worm—look at the wonder of that green lamp!'

'I must show it to Kitty,' said James, taking it up on a cushion of moss.

'Her acquaintance will begin earlier than mine. Do you remember showing me my first glow-worm at Beauchastel? I used to think that the gem of my walks, before I knew better. It is a great treat to have poor Walter here in the holidays, so good and pleasant; but I must say one charm is the pleasure of being alone together afterwards.'

'A pleasure it is well you do not get tired of, my dear, and I am afraid it will soon be over for the present. I do believe that is Richardson behind us! An attorney among the glow-worms is more than I expected.'

'Good evening, sir,' said the attorney, coming up with them; 'is Mrs. Frost braving the dew?' And then, after some moments, 'Have you heard from your sister lately, Mr. Frost?'

'About three weeks ago.'

'She did not mention then,' said Mr. Richardson, hesitating, 'Mr. Dynevor's health?'

'No! Have you heard anything?'

'I thought you might wish to be aware of what I learnt from, I fear, too good authority. It appears that Mr. Dynevor paid only a part of the purchase-money of the estate, giving security for the rest on his property in Peru; and now, owing to the failure of the Equatorial Steam Navigation Company, Mr. Dynevor is, I fear, actually insolvent.'

'Did you say he was ill?'

'I heard mentioned severe illness—paralytic affection; but as you have not heard from Miss Clara, I hope it may be of no importance.'

After a few more inquiries, and additional information being elicited, good-nights were exchanged, and Mr. Richardson passed on. At first neither spoke, till Isabel said—

'And Clara never wrote!'

'She would identify herself too much with her uncle in his misfortune. Poor dear child! what may she not be undergoing!'

'You will go to her?'

'I must. Whether my uncle will forgive me or not, to Clara I must go. Shall I write first?'

'Oh! no; it will only make a delay, and your uncle might say 'don't come.''

'Right; delay would prolong her perplexities. I will go to-morrow, and Mr. Holdsworth will see to the workhouse people.'

His alert air showed how grateful was any excuse that could take him to Clara, the impulse of brotherly love coming uppermost of all his sensations. Then came pity for the poor old man whose cherished design had thus crumbled, and the anxious wonder whether he would forgive, and deign to accept sympathy from his nephew.

'My dear,' said James, doubtfully; 'supposing, what I hardly dare to imagine, that he should consent, what should you say to my bringing him here?

'I believe it would make you happy,' said Isabel. 'Oh! yes, pray do—and then we should have Clara.'

'I should rejoice to offer anything like reparation, though I do not dare to hope it will be granted; and I do not know how to ask you to break up the home comfort we have prized so much.'

'It will be all the better comfort for your mind being fully at ease; and I am sure we should deserve none at all, if we shut our door against him now that he is in distress. You must bring him, poor old man, and I will try with all my might to behave well to him.'

'It is a mere chance; but I am glad to take your consent with me. As to our affording it, I suppose he may have, at the worst, an allowance from the creditors, so you will not have to retrench anything.'

'Don't talk of that, dearest. We never knew how little we could live on till we tried; and if No. 12 is taken, and you are paid for the new edition of the lectures, and Walter's pay besides—'

'And Sir Hubert,' added James.

'Of course we shall get on,' said Isabel. 'I am not in the least afraid that the little girls will suffer, if they do live a little harder for the sake of their old uncle. I only wish you had had your new black coat first, for I am afraid you won't now.'

'You need not reckon on that. I don't expect that I shall be allowed the comfort of doing anything for him. But see about them I must. Oh, may I not be too late!'

Early the next morning James was on his way, travelling through the long bright summer day; and when, after the close, stifling railway carriage, full of rough, loud-voiced passengers, he found himself in the cool of the evening on the bare heath, where the slanting sunbeams cast a red light, he was reminded by every object that met his eye of the harsh and rebellious sensations that he had allowed to reign over him at his last arrival there, which had made him wrangle over the bier of one so loving and beloved, and exaggerate the right till it wore the semblance of the wrong.

By the time he came to the village, the parting light was shining on the lofty church tower, rising above the turmoil and whirl of the darkening world below, almost as sacred old age had lifted his grandmother into perpetual peace and joy, above the fret and vexation of earthly cares and dissensions. The recollection of her confident trust that reconciliation was in store, came to cheer him as he crossed the park, and the aspect of the house assured him that at least he was not again too late.

The servant who answered the bell said that Mr. Dynevor was very ill, and Miss Dynevor could see no one. James sent in his card, and stood in an agony of impatience, imagining all and more than all he deserved, to have taken place—his uncle either dying, or else forcibly withholding his sister from him.

At last there was a hurried step, and the brother and sister were clasping each other in speechless joy.

'O Jem! dear Jem! this is so kind!' cried Clara, as with arms round each other they crossed the hall. 'Now I don't care for anything!'

'My uncle?'

'Much better,' said Clara; 'he speaks quite well again, and his foot is less numb.'

'Was it paralysis?'

'Yes; brought on by trouble and worry of mind. But how did you know, Jem?'

'Richardson told me. Oh, Clara, had I offended too deeply for you to summon me?'

'No, indeed,' said Clara, pressing his arm, 'I knew you would help us as far as you could; but to throw ourselves on you would be robbing the children, so I wanted to have something fixed before you heard.'

'My poor child, what could be fixed?'

'You gave me what is better than house and land,' said Clara. 'I wrote to Miss Brigham; she will give me employment in the school till I can find a place as daily governess, and she is to take lodgings for us.'

'And is this what it has come to, my poor Clara?'

'Oh, don't pity me! my heart has felt like an India-rubber ball ever since the crash. Even poor Uncle Oliver being so ill could not keep me from feeling as if the burthen were off my back, and I were little Clara Frost again. It seemed to take away the bar between us; and so it has! O Jem! this is happiness. Tell me of Isabel and the babies.'

'You will come home to them. Do you think my uncle would consent?'

She answered with an embrace, a look of rapture and of doubt, and then a negative. 'Oh, no, we cannot be a burthen on you. You have quite enough on your hands. And, oh! you have grown so spare and thin. I mean to maintain my uncle, if—' and her spirited bearing softened into thoughtfulness, as if the little word conveyed that she meant not to be self-confident.

'But, Clara, is this actual ruin? I know only what Richardson could tell me.'

'I do not fully understand,' said Clara. 'It had been plain for a long time that something was on Uncle Oliver's mind; he was so restless all the winter at Paris, and at last arranged our coming home very suddenly. I think he was disappointed in London, for he went out at once, and came back very much discomposed. He even scolded me for not having married; and when I tried to coax him out of it, he said it was for my good, and he wanted to see after his business in Peru. I put him in mind how dear granny had begged him to stay at home; but he told me I knew nothing about it, and that he would have gone long ago if I had not been an obstinate girl, and had known how to play my cards. I said something about going home, but that made him more furious than ever. But, after all, it is not fair to tell all about the last few months. Dr. Hastings says his attack had been a long time coming on, and he must have been previously harassed.'

'And you had to bear with it all?'

'He was never unkind. Oh, no; but it was sad to see him so miserable, and not to know why—and so uncertain, too! Sometimes he would insist on giving grand parties, and yet he was angry with the expense of my poor little pony-carriage. I don't think he always quite knew what he was about; and while he hoped to pull through, I suppose he was afraid of any one guessing at his embarrassments. On this day fortnight he was reading his letters at breakfast—I saw there was something amiss, and said something stupid about the hot rolls, because he could not bear me to notice. I think that roused him, for he got up, but he tottered, and by the time I came to him he seemed to slip down into my arms, quite insensible. The surgeon in the village bled him, and he came to himself, but could not speak. I had almost sent for you then, but Dr. Hastings came, and thought he would recover, and I did not venture. Indeed, Jane forbade me; she is a sort of lioness and her whelps. Well, the next day came Mr. Morrison, who is the Mr. Richardson to this concern, and by-and-by he asked to see me. He kept the doctor in the next room. I believe he thought I should faint or make some such performance, for he began about his painful duty, and frightened me lest my poor uncle should be worse, only he was not the right man to tell me. So at last it came out that we were ruined, and I was not an heiress at all, at all! If it had not been for poor Uncle Oliver, I should have cried 'Hurrah!' I did nearly laugh to hear him complimenting my firmness. I believe the history is this:—Hearing that this place was for sale, brought Uncle Oliver home before his affairs could well do without him. He paid half the price, and promised to pay the rest in three years, giving security on the mines and the other property in Peru; but somehow the remittances have never come properly, and he trusted to some great success with the Equatorial Company to set things straight, but it seems that it has totally failed, and that was the news that overthrew him. Then the creditors, who had been put off with hopes, all came down on him together, and there seems to be nothing to be done but to give up everything to them. Poor Uncle Oliver!—I sat watching him that evening, and thinking how Louis would say the sea had swept away his whole sand castle with one wave.'

'Does he know it? Have any steps been taken?'

'Mr. Morrison showed me what my poor uncle had done. He had really executed a deed giving me the whole estate; he would have borne all the disgrace and persecution himself—for you know it would have been a most horrible scrape, as he had given them security on property that was not really secure. Mr. Morrison said the deed would hold, and that he would bring me counsel's opinion if I liked. But, oh, Jem! I was so thankful that my birthday was over, and I was my own woman! I made him draw up a paper, and I signed it, undertaking that they shall have quiet possession provided they will come to an amicable settlement, and not torment my uncle.'

'I hope he is a man of sense, who will make the best terms?'

'You may see to that now. I'm sure he is a man of compliments. He tells me grand things about my disinterestedness, and the creditors and they have promised to let us stay unmolested as long as I please, which will be only till my uncle can move, for I must get rid of all these servants and paraphernalia, and in the meantime they are concocting the amicable adjustment, and Mr. Morrison said he should try to stipulate for a maintenance for my uncle, but he was not sure of it, without giving up what may yet come from Peru. Jane's annuity is safe—that is a comfort! What work I had to make her believe it! and now she wants us all to live upon it.'

'That was a rare and beautiful power by which my grandmother infused such faithful love into all her dependants. But now for the person really to be pitied.'

'It was only three days ago that it was safe to speak of it, but then he had grown so anxious that the doctors said I must begin. So I begged and prayed him to forgive me, and then told what I had done, and he was not so very angry. He only called me a silly child, and said I did not know what I had done in those few days that I had been left to myself. So I told him dear granny had had it, and that was all that signified, and that I never had any right here. Then,' said Clara, tearfully, 'he began to cry like a child, and said at least she had died in her own home, and he called me Henry's child: and then Jane came and turned me out, and wont let me go near him unless I promise to be good and say nothing. But I must soon; for however she pats him, and says, 'Don't, Master Oliver,' I see his mind runs on nothing else, and the doctor says he may soon hear the plans, and be moved.'

'Can you venture to tell him that I am here?'

Before Clara could answer, Jane opened the door—'Miss Clara, your uncle;' and there she stopped, at the unexpected sight of the brother and sister still hand in hand. 'Here, Jane, do you see him?' cried Clara; and James came forward with outstretched hand, but he was not graciously received.

'Now, Master James, you ain't coming here to worrit your poor uncle?'

'No, indeed, Jane. I am come in the hope of being of some use to him.'

'I'd rather by half it had been Lord Fitzjocelyn,' muttered Jane, 'he was always quieter.'

'Now, Jane, you should not be so cross,' cried Clara, 'when it is your own Jemmy, come on purpose to help and comfort us all! You are going to tell Uncle Oliver, and make him glad to see him, as you know you are.'

'I know,' said James, 'that last time I was here, I behaved ill enough to make you dread my presence, Jane; but I have learnt and suffered a good deal since that time, and I wish for nothing so much as for my uncle's pardon.'

Mrs. Beckett would have been more impressed, had she ever ceased to think of Master Jemmy otherwise than as a self-willed but candid boy; and she answered as if he had been throwing himself on her mercy after breaking a window, or knocking down Lord Fitzjocelyn—

'Well, sir, that is all you can say. I'm glad you are sorry. I'll see if I can mention, it to your uncle.'

Off trotted Jane, while Clara's indignation and excited spirits relieved themselves by a burst of merry laughter, as she hung about her brother, and begged to hear of the dear old home.

The old servant, in her simplicity, went straight upstairs, and up to her nursling, as he had again become. 'Master Oliver,' said she, 'he is come. Master Jem is come back, and 'twould do your heart good to see how happy the children are together—just like you and poor Master Henry.'

'Did she ask him here?' said Mr. Dynevor, uneasily.

'No, sir, he came right out of his own head, because he thought she would feel lost.'

Oliver vouchsafed no reply, and Jane pressed no farther. He never alluded to his guest; but when Clara came into the room, his eye dwelt on her countenance of bright content and animation, and the smiles that played round her lips as she sat silent. Her voice was hushed in the sick-room, but he heard it about the house with the blithe, lively ring that had been absent from it since he carried her away from Northwold; and her steps danced upstairs, and along the galleries, with the light, bounding tread unknown to the constrained, dignified Miss Dynevor. Ah the notice he took that night was to say, petulantly, when Clara was sitting with him, 'Don't stay here; you want to be down-stairs.'

'Oh, no, dear uncle, I am come to stay with you. I don't want, in the least, to be anywhere but here.'

He seemed pleased, although he growled; and next morning Jane reported that he had been asking for how long his nephew had come, and saying he was glad that Miss Dynevor had someone to look after her—a sufferance beyond expectation. In his helpless state, Jane had resumed her nursery relations with him; and he talked matters over with her so freely that it was well that the two young people were scarcely less her children, and had almost an equal share of her affection, so that Clara felt that matters might be safely trusted in her hands.

Clara's felicity could hardly be described, with her fond affections satisfied by her brother's presence, and her fears of managing ill, removed by reliance on him; and many as were the remaining cases, and great as was the suspense lest her uncle should still nourish resentment, nothing could overcome the sense of restored joy ever bubbling up, not even the dread that James might not bear patiently with continued rebuffs. But James was so much more gentle and tolerant than she had ever known him, that at first she could not understand missing the retort, the satire, the censure which had seemed an essential part of her brother. She was always instinctively guarding against what never happened, or if some slight demonstration flashed out, he caught himself up, and asked pardon before she had perceived anything, till she began to think marriage had altered him wonderfully, and almost to owe Isabel a grudge for having cowed his spirit. She could hardly believe that he was waiting so patiently in the guise of a suppliant, when she thought him in the right from the first; though she could perceive that the task was easier now that the old man was in adversity, and she saw that he regarded his exclusion from his uncle's room in the light of a just punishment, to be endured with humility.

James, on his side, was highly pleased with his sister. Having only seen her as the wild, untamed Giraffe, he was by no means prepared for the dignity and decision with which Miss Dynevor reigned over the establishment. Her tall figure, and the simple, straightforward ease of her movements and manners, seemed made to grace those large, lofty rooms; and as he watched her playing the part of mistress of the house so naturally in the midst of the state, the servants, the silver covers, and the trappings, he felt that heiress-ship became her so well, that he could hardly believe that her tenure there was over, and unregretted. 'Even Isabel could not do it better,' he said, smiling; and she made a low curtsey for the compliment, and laughed back, 'I'm glad you have come to see my performance. It has been a very long, dull pageant, and here comes Mr. Morrison, I hope with the last act.'

Morrison was evidently much relieved that Miss Dynevor should have some relative to advise with, since he did not like the responsibility of her renunciation, though owning that it was the only thing that could save her uncle from disgraceful ruin, and perhaps from prosecution; whereas now the gratitude and forbearance of the creditors were secured, and he hoped that

Mr. Dynevor might be set free from the numerous English involvements, without sacrificing his remaining property in Peru. The lawyer seemed to have no words to express to James his sense of Miss Dynevor's conduct in the matter, her promptitude and good sense having apparently struck him as much as her generosity, and there was no getting him to believe, as Clara wished, that the sacrifice was no sacrifice at all—nothing, as she said, but 'common honesty and a great riddance.' He promised to take steps in earnest for the final settlement with the creditors; and though still far from the last act, Clara began to consider of hastening her plans. It was exceedingly doubtful whether Oliver would hear of living at Dynevor Terrace, and Clara could not be separated from him; besides which, she was resolved that her brother should not be burthened, and she would give James no promises, conditional or otherwise.

Mr. Dynevor had discovered that Morrison had been in the house, and was obviously restless to know what had taken place. By-and-by he said to Jane, with an air of inquiry, 'Why does not the young man come near me?'

Mrs. Beckett was too happy to report the invitation, telling 'Master Jem' at the same time that 'he was not to rake up nothing gone and past; there was quite troubles enough for one while.' Clara thought the same, and besides was secretly sure that if he admitted that he had been wrong in part, his uncle would imagine him to mean that he had been wrong in the whole. Their instructions and precautions were trying to James, whose chaplaincy had given him more experience of the sick and the feeble than they gave him credit for; but he was patient enough to amaze Clara and pacify Jane, who ushered him into the sick-chamber. There, even in his worst days, he must have laid aside ill-feeling at the aspect of the shrunken, broken figure in the pillowed arm-chair, prematurely aged, his hair thin and white, his face shrivelled, his eyelid drooping, and mouth contracted. He was still some years under sixty; but this was the result of toil and climate—of the labour generously designed, but how conducted, how resulting?

He had not learned to put out his left hand—he only made a sharp nod, as James, with tender and humble respect, approached, feeling that, how his grandmother was gone, this frail old man, his father's brother, was the last who claimed by right his filial love and gratitude. How different from the rancour and animosity with which he had met his former advances!

He ventured gently on kindly hopes that his uncle was better, and they were not ill taken, though not without fretfulness. Presently Oliver said, 'Come to look after your sister? that's right—good girl, good girl!'

'That she is!' exclaimed James, heartily.

'Too hasty! too great hurry,' resumed Oliver; 'she had better have waited, saved the old place,—never mind what became of the old man, one-half dead already.'

'She would not have been a Clara good for much, if she had treated you after that fashion, sir,' said James, smiling.

He gave his accustomed snort. 'The mischief a girl let alone can do in three days, when once she's of age, and one can't stop her! Women ought never to come of age, ain't fit for it, undo all the work of my lifetime with a stroke of her pen!'

'For your sake, sir!'

'Pshaw! Pity but she'd been safe married—tied it up well with settlements then out of her power. Can't think what that young Fitzjocelyn was after—it ain't the old affair. Ponsonby writes me that things are to be settled as soon as Ward comes back.'

'Indeed!'

'Aye, good sort of fellow—no harm to have him in our concerns—I hope he'll look into the accounts, and find what Robson is at. After all, I shall soon be out there myself, and make Master Robson look about him. Mad to allow myself to stay—but I'll wait no longer. Morrison may put the fellows off'—I'll give him a hint; we'll save the place, after all, when I once get out to Lima. If only I knew what to do with that girl!'

James could not look at him without a conviction that he would never recover the use of his hand and foot; but this was no time to discourage his spirits, and the answer was—'My sister's natural home would be with me.'

'Ha! the child would like it, I suppose. I'd make a handsome allowance for her. I shall manage that when my affairs are in my own hands; but I may as well write to the mountains as to Ponsonby. Aye, aye! Clara might go to you. She'll have enough any way to be quite worth young Fitzjocelyn's while, you may tell him. That mine in the San Benito would retrieve all, and I'll not forget. Pray, how many children have you by this time?'

'Four little girls, sir,' said James, restraining the feeling which was rising in the contact with his uncle, revealing that both were still the same men.

'Hm! No time lost, however! Well, we shall see! Any way, an allowance for Clara's board won't hurt. What's your notion?'

James's notion was profound pity for the poor old man. 'Indeed, sir,' he said, 'Clara is sure to be welcome. All we wish is, that you would kindly bring her to us at once. Perhaps you would find the baths of service; we would do our utmost to make you comfortable, and we are not inhabiting half the house, so that there would be ample space to keep the children from inconveniencing you.'

'Clara is set on it, I'll warrant.'

'Clara waits to be guided by your wishes; but my wife and I should esteem it as the greatest favour you could do us.'

'Ha! we'll see what I can manage. I must see Morrison'—and he fell into meditation, presently breaking from it to say fretfully, 'I say, Roland, would you reach me that tumbler?'

Never had James thought to be grateful for that name! He would gladly have been Roland Dynevor for the rest of his days, if he could have left behind him the transgressions of James Frost! But the poor man's shattered thoughts had been too long on the stretch; and, without further ceremony, Jane came in and dismissed his nephew.

Clara hardly trusted her ears when she was told shortly after, by her uncle, that they were to go to Northwold. Roland wished it; and, poor fellow! the board and lodging were a great object to him. He seemed to have come to his senses now it was too late; and if Clara wished it, and did not think it dull, there she might stay while he himself was gone to Lima.

'A great object the other way,' Clara had nearly cried, in her indignation that James could not be supposed disinterested in an invitation to an old man, who probably was destitute.

Brother and uncle appeared to have left her out of the consultation; but she was resolved not to let him be a burthen on those who had so little already, and she called her old friend Jane to take counsel with her, whether it would not be doing them an injury to carry him thither at all. So much of Jane's heart as was not at Cheveleigh was at Dynevor Terrace, and her answer was decided.

'To be sure, Miss Clara, nothing couldn't be more natural.'

'Nothing, indeed, but I can't put them to trouble and expense.'

'I'll warrant,' said Jane, 'that I'll make whatever they have go twice as far as Charlotte ever will. Why, you know I keeps myself; and for the rest, it will be a mere saving to have me in the kitchen! There's no air so good for Master Oliver.'

'I see you mean to go, Jane,' said Clara. 'Now, I have to look out for myself.'

'Bless me, Miss Clara, don't you do nothing in a hurry. Go home quiet and look about you.'

Jane had begun to call Northwold home; and, in spite of her mournings over the old place, Clara thought she had never been so happy there as in her present dominion over Master Oliver, and her prospects of her saucepans and verbenas at No. 5.

Poor Oliver! what a scanty measure of happiness had his lifelong exertions produced! Many a human sacrifice has been made to a grim and hollow idol, failing his devotees in time of extremity. Had it not been thus with Oliver Dynevor's self-devotion to the honour of his family?

CHAPTER XIX
FAREWELL TO GREATNESS

> Soon from the halls my fathers reared
> Their scutcheons must descend.
>   Scott

Mr. Holdsworth contrived to set James at liberty for a fortnight, and he was thus enabled to watch over the negotiation, and expedite matters for the removal. The result was, that the resignation of the estate, furniture, and of Clara's jewels, honourably cleared off the debts contracted in poor Mr. Dynevor's eagerness to reinstate the family in all its pristine grandeur, and left him totally dependent on whatever might be rescued in Peru. He believed this to be considerable, but the brother and sister founded little hopes on the chance; as, whatever there might be, had been entangled in the Equatorial Company, and nothing could be less comprehensible than Mr. Robson's statements.

Clara retained her own seventy pounds per annum, which, thrown into the common stock, would, James assured her, satisfy him, in a pecuniary point of view, that he was doing no wrong to his children; though he added, that even if there had been nothing, he did not believe they would ever be the worse for what might be spent on their infirm old uncle.

Notice was sent to Isabel to prepare, and she made cordial reply that the two rooms on the ground-floor were being made ready for Mr. Dynevor, and Clara's own little room being set in order; Miss Mercy Faithfull helping with all her might, and little Kitty stamping about, thinking her services equally effectual.

Oliver was in haste to leave a place replete with disappointment and failure, and was so helpless and dependent as to wish for his nephew's assistance on the journey; and it was, therefore, fixed for the end of James's second week. No one called to take leave, except the Curate and good Mr. Henderson, who showed Clara much warm, kind feeling, and praised her to her brother.

She begged James to walk with her for a farewell visit to her grandmother's other old friend. Great was her enjoyment of this expedition; she said she had not had a walk worth having since she was at Aix-la-Chapelle, and liberty and companionship compensated for all the heat and dust in the dreary tract, full of uncomfortable shabby-genteel abodes, and an unpromising population.

'One cannot regret such a tenantry,' said Clara.

'Poor creatures!' said James. 'I wonder into whose hands they will fall. Your heart may be free, Clara; you have followed the clear path of duty; but it is a painful thought for me, that to strive to amend these festering evils, caused very likely by my grandfather's speculations, might have been my appointed task. I should not have had far to seek for occupation. When I was talking to the Curate yesterday, my heart smote me to think what I might have done to help him.'

'It would all have been over now.'

'It ought not. Nay, perhaps, my presence might have left my uncle free to attend to his own concerns.'

'I really believe you are going to regret the place!'

'After all, Clara, I was a Dynevor before my uncle came home. It might have been my birthright. But, as Isabel says, what we are now is far more likely to be safe for the children. I was bad enough as I was, but what should I have been as a pampered heir! Let it go.'

'Yes, let it go,' said Clara; 'it has been little but pain to me. We shall teach my poor uncle that home love is better than old family estates. I almost wish he may recover nothing in Peru, that he may learn that you receive him for his own sake.'

'That is more than I can wish,' said James. 'A hundred or two a-year would come in handily. Besides, I am afraid that Mary Ponsonby may be suffering in this crash.'

'She seems to have taken care of herself,' said Clara. 'She does not write to me, and I am almost ready to believe her father at last. I could not have thought it of her!'

'Isabel has always said it was the best thing that could happen to Louis.'

'Isabel never had any notion of Louis. I don't mean any offence, but if she had known what he was made of, she would never have had you.'

'Thank you, Clara! I always thought it an odd predilection, but no one can now esteem Fitzjocelyn more highly than ahe does.'

'Very likely; but if she thinks Louis can stand Mary's deserting him—'

'It will be great pain, no doubt; but once over, he will be free.'

'It never will be over.'

'That is young-ladyism.'

'I never was a young lady, and I know what I mean. Mary may not be all he thinks her, and she may be dull enough to let her affection wear out; but I do not believe he will ever look at any one again, as he did after Mary on your wedding-day.'

'So you forbid him to be ever happy again!'

'Not at all, only in that one way. There are many others of being happy.'

'That one way meaning marriage.'

'I mean that sort of perfect marriage that, according to the saying, is made in heaven. Whether that could have been with Mary, I do not know her well enough to guess; but I am convinced that he will always have the same kind of memory of her that a man has of a first love, or first wife.'

'It may have been a mistake to drive him into the attachment, which Isabel thinks has been favoured by absence, leaving scope for imagination; but I cannot give up the hope that his days of happiness are yet to come.'

'Nor do I give up Mary, yet,' said Clara. 'Till she announces her defection I shall not believe it, for it would be common honesty to inform poor Louis, and in that she never was deficient.'

'It is not a plant that seems to thrive on the Peruvian soil.'

'No; and I am dreadfully afraid for Tom Madison. There were hints about him in Mr. Ponsonby's letters, which make me very anxious; and from what my uncle says, it seems that there is such an atmosphere of gambling and trickery about his office, that he thinks it a matter of course that no one should be really true and honest.'

'That would be a terrible affair indeed! I don't know for which I should be most concerned, Louis or our poor little Charlotte. But after all, Clara, we have known too many falsehoods come across the Atlantic, to concern ourselves about anything without good reason.'

So they talked, enjoying the leisure the walk gave them for conversation, and then paying the painful visit, when Clara tried in vain to make it understood by the poor old lady that she was going away, and that James was her brother. They felt thankful that such decay had been spared their grandmother, and Clara sighed to think that her uncle might be on the brink of a like loss of faculties, and then felt herself more than ever bound to him.

On the way home they went together to the church, and pondered over the tombs of their ancestry,—ranging from the grim, defaced old knight, through the polished brass, the kneeling courtier, and the dishevelled Grief embracing an urn, down to the mural arch enshrining the dear revered name of Catharine, daughter of Roland, and wife of James Frost Dynevor, the last of her line whose bones would rest there. Her grave had truly been the sole possession that her son's labours had secured for her; that grave was the only spot at Cheveleigh that claimed a pang from Clara's heart. She stood beside it with deep, fond, clinging love and reverence, but with no painful recollections to come between her and that fair, bright vision of happy old age. Alas! for the memories that her brother had sown to spring up round him now!

Apart from all these vipers of his own creating, James after all felt more in the cession of Cheveleigh than did his sister. These were days of change and of feudal feeling wearing out; but James, long as he had pretended to scorn 'being sentimental about his forefathers,' was strongly susceptible of such impressions; and he was painfully conscious of being disinherited. He might have felt thus, without any restoration or loss, as the mere effect of visiting his birthright as a stranger; but, as he received all humbly instead of proudly, the feeling did him no harm. It softened him into sympathy with his uncle, and tardy appreciation of his single-minded devotion to the estate, which he had won not for himself, but for others, only to see it first ungratefully rejected, and then snatched away. Then, with a thrill of humiliation at his own unworthiness, came the earnest prayer that it might yet be vouchsafed to him to tend the exhausted body, and train the contracted mind to dwell on that inheritance whence there could be no casting out.

Poor Oliver was fretful and restless, insisting on being brought down to his study to watch over the packing of his papers, and miserable at being unable to arrange them himself. Even the tenderest pity for him could not prevent him from being an exceeding trial; and James could hardly yet have endured it, but for pleasure and interest in watching his sister's lively good-humour, saucy and determined when the old man was unreasonable, and caressing and affectionate, when he was violent in his impotence; never seeming to hear, see, or regard anything unkind or unpleasant; and absolutely pleased and gratified when her uncle, in his petulance, sometimes ungraciously rejected her services in favour of those of 'Roland,' who, he took it for granted, must, as a man, have more sense. It would sometimes cross James, how would Isabel and the children fare with this ill-humour; but he had much confidence in his wife's sweet calm temper, and more in the obvious duty; and, on the whole, he believed it was better not to think about it.

The suffering that the surrender cost Oliver was only shown in this species of petty fractiousness, until the last morning, when his nephew was helping him across the hall, and Clara close at his side, he made them stand still beside one of the pillars, and groaned as he said, 'Here I waited for the carriage last time! Here I promised to get it back again!'

'I wish every one kept promises as you did,' said James, looking about for something cheerful to say.

'I had hope then,' said Oliver; and well might he feel the contrast between the youth, with such hopes, energies, and determination mighty within him, and the broken and disappointed man.

'Hope yet, and better hope!' James could not help saying.

'Not while there's such a rascal in the office at Lima,' cried Oliver, testily.

'Oh! Uncle Oliver, he did not mean that!' exclaimed Clara.

Mr. Dynevor grumbled something about parsons, which neither of them chose to hear; and Clara cut it short by saying, 'After all, Uncle Oliver, you have done it all! Dear grandmamma came back and was happy here, and that was all that signified. You never wanted it for yourself, you know, and my dear father was not here to have it. And for you, what could you have had more than your nephew and niece to—to try to be like your children! And hadn't you rather have them without purchase than with?' And as she saw him smile in answer to her bright caress, she added merrily, 'There's nothing else to pity but the fir trees and gold fish; and as they have done very happily before without the Pendragon reign, I dare any they will again; so I can't be very sorry for them!'

This was Clara's farewell to her greatness, and cheerily she enlivened her uncle all the way to London, and tried to solace him after the interviews that he insisted on with various men of business, and which did not tend to make him stronger in health or spirits through the next day's journey.

The engine whistled its arriving shriek at Northwold. Happy Clara! What was the summer rain to her? Every house, every passenger, were tokens of home; and the damp rain-mottled face of the Terrace, looking like a child that had been crying, was more welcome to her longing eyes than ever had been lake or mountain.

Isabel and little Catharine stood on the step; but as Mr. Dynevor was lifted out, the little girl shrank out of sight with a childish awe of infirmity. The dining-room had been made a very comfortable sitting-room for him, and till he was settled there, nothing else could be attended to; but he was so much fatigued, that it was found best to leave him entirely to Jane; and Clara, after a few moments, followed her brother from the room.

As she shut the door, she stood for some seconds unobserved, and unwilling to interfere with the scene before her. Halfway upstairs, James had been pulled down to sit on the steps, surrounded by his delighted flock. The baby was in his arms, flourishing her hands as he danced her; Kitty, from above, had clasped tightly round his neck, chattering and kissing with breathless velocity; one twin in front was drumming on his knee, and shrieking in accordance with every shout of the baby; and below, leaning on the balusters, stood their mother's graceful figure, looking up at them with a lovely smiling face of perfect gladness. She was the first to perceive Clara; and, with a pretty gesture to be silent, she pointed to the stand of the Wedgewood jar, under which sat the other little maid, her two fat arms clasped tight round her papa's umbrella, and the ivory handle indenting her rosy cheek, as she fondled it in silent transport.

'My little Salome,' whispered Isabel, squeezing Clara's hand, 'our quiet one. She could not sleep for expecting papa, and now she is in a fit of shy delight; she can't shout with the others; she can only nurse his umbrella.'

Just then James made a desperate demonstration, amid peals of laughter from his daughters. 'We are stopping the way! Get out, you unruly monsters! Let go, Kitty—Mercy; I shall kick! Mamma, catch this ball;' making a feint of tossing the crowing Fanny at her.

Assuredly, thought Clara, pity was wasted; there was not one too many. And then began the happy exulting introductions, and a laugh at little Mercy, who stood blank and open-mouthed, gazing up and up her tall aunt, as if there were no coming to the top of her. Clara sat down on the stairs, to bring her face to a level, and struck up a friendship with her on the spot, while James lilted up his little Salome, her joy still too deep and reserved for manifestation; only without a word she nestled close to him, laid her head on his shoulder, and closed her eyes, as if languid with excess of rapture—a pretty contrast to her sister's frantic delight, which presently alarmed James lest it should disturb his uncle, and he called them up-stairs.

But Clara must first run to the House Beautiful, and little Mercy must needs come to show her the way, and trotted up before her, consequentially announcing, 'Aunt Cara.' Miss Faithfull alone was present; and, without speaking, Clara dropped on the ground, laid her head on her dear old friend's lap, and little Mercy exclaimed, in wondering alarm, 'Aunt Cara naughty—Aunt Cara crying!'

'My darling,' said Miss Faithfull, as she kissed Clara's brow and stroked her long flaxen hair, 'you have gone through a great deal. We must try to make you happy in your poor old home.'

'Oh, no! oh, no! It is happiness! Oh! such happiness! but I don't know what to do with it, and I want granny!'

She was almost like little Salome; the flood of bliss in returning home, joined with the missing of the one dearest welcome, had come on her so suddenly that she was almost stifled, till she had been calmed and soothed by the brief interval of quiet with her dear old friend. She returned to No. 5, there to find that her uncle was going to bed, and Charlotte, pink and beautiful with delight, was running about in attendance on Jane. She went up straight to her own little room, which had been set out exactly as in former times, so that she could feel as if she had been not a day absent; and she lost not a moment in adding to it all the other little treasures which made it fully like her own. She looked out at the Ormersfield trees, and smiled to think how well Louis's advice had turned out; and then she sighed, in the fear that it might yet be her duty to leave home. If her uncle could live without her, she must tear herself away, and work for his maintenance.

However, for the present, she might enjoy to the utmost, and she proceeded to the little parlour, which, to her extreme surprise, she found only occupied by the four children—Kitty holding the youngest upon her feet, till, at the new apparition, Fanny suddenly seated herself for the convenience of staring.

'Are you all alone here!' exclaimed Clara.

'I am taking care of the little ones,' replied Kitty, with dignity.

'Where's mamma!'

'She is gone down to get tea. Papa is gone to the Union; but we do not mean to wait for him,' answered the little personage, with an air capable, the more droll because she was on the smallest scale, of much less substance than the round fat twins, and indeed chiefly distinguishable from them by her slender neat shape; for the faces were at first sight all alike, brown, small-featured, with large dark eyes, and dark curly hair—Mercy, with the largest and most impetuous eyes, and Salome with a dreamy look, more like her mother. Fanny was in a different style, and much prettier; but her contemplation ended in alarm and inclination to cry, whereupon Kitty embraced her, and consoled her like a most efficient guardian; then seeing Mercy becoming rather rude in her familiarities with her aunt, held up her small forefinger, and called out gravely, 'Mercy, recollect yourself!'

Wonders would never cease! Here was Isabel coming up with the tea-tray in her own hands!

'My dear, do you always do that?'

'No, only when Charlotte is busy; and,' as she picked up the baby, 'now Kitty may bring the rest.'

So, in various little journeys, the miniature woman's curly head arose above the loaf, and the butter-dish, and even the milk-jug, held without spilling; while Isabel would have set out the tea-things with one hand, if Clara had not done it for her; and the workhouse girl finally appeared with the kettle.

Was this the same Isabel whom Clara last remembered with her baby in her lap, beautiful and almost as inanimate as a statue? There was scarcely more change from the long-frocked infant to the bustling important sprite, than from that fair piece of still life to the active house-mother. Unruffled grace was innate; every movement had a lofty, placid deliberation and simplicity, that made her like a disguised princess; and though her beauty was a little worn, what it had lost in youth was far more than compensated by sweetness and animation. The pensive cast remained, but the dreaminess had sobered into thought and true hope. Her dress was an old handsome silk, frayed and worn, but so becoming to her, that the fading was unnoticed in the delicate neatness of the accompaniments. And the dear old room! It looked like a cheerful habitation; but Clara's almost instant inquiry was for the porcelain Arcadians, and could not think it quite as tidy and orderly as it used to be in old times, when she was the only fairy Disorder. 'However, I'll see to that,' quoth she to herself. And she gave herself up to the happy tea-drinking, when James was welcomed by another tumult, and was pinned down by Kitty and Salome on either side—mamma making tea in spite of Fanny on her lap—Mercy adhering to the new-comer—the eager conversation—Kitty thrusting in her little oar, and being hushed by mamma—the grand final game at romps, ending with Isabel carrying off her little victims, one by one, to bed; and James taking the tea-tray down stairs. Clara followed with other parts of the equipage, and then both stood together warming themselves, and gossiped over the dear old kitchen fire, till Isabel came down and found them there. And then, before any of the grand news was discussed, all the infant marvels of the last fortnight had to be detailed; and the young parents required Clara's opinion whether they were spoiling Kitty.

Next, Clara found her way to the cupboard, brought the shepherd and shepherdess to light, looked them well over, and satisfied herself that there was not one scar or wound on either—nay, it is not absolutely certain that she did not kiss the damsel's delicate pink cheek—set them up on the mantelpiece, promised to keep them in order, and stood gazing at them till James accused her of regarding them as her penates!

'Why, Jem!' she said, turning on him, 'you are a mere recreant if you can feel it like home without them!'

'I have other porcelain figures to depend on for a home!' said James.

'Take care, James!' said his wife, with the fond sadness of one whose cup overflowed with happiness; 'Clara's shepherdess may look fragile, but she has kept her youth and seen many a generation pass by of such as you depend on!'

'She once was turned out of Cheveleigh, too, and has borne it as easily as Clara,' said James, smiling. 'I suspect her worst danger is from Fanny. There's a lady who, I warn you, can never withstand Fanny!'

Isabel took up her own defence, and they laughed on. Poor Uncle Oliver! could he but have known how little all this had to do with Cheveleigh!

CHAPTER XX
WESTERN TIDINGS

O lady! worthy of earth's proudest throne!
Nor less, by excellence of nature, fit
Beside an unambitious hearth to sit
Domestic queen, where grandeur is unknown—
Queen and handmaid lowly.
           WORDSWORTH.

A house in the Terrace was let, and the rent was welcome; and shortly after, Clara had an affectionate letter from her old school-enemy, Miss Salter, begging her to come as governess to her little brother, promising that she should be treated like one of the family, and offering a large salary.

Clara was much afraid that it was her duty to accept the proposal, since her uncle seemed very fairly contented, and was growing very fond of 'Roland,' and the payment would be so great an assistance, but James and Isabel were strongly averse to it; and her conscience was satisfied by Miss Mercy Faithfull's discovery of a family at the Baths in search of a daily governess.

Miss Frost was not a person to be rejected, and in another week she found herself setting out to breakfast with a girl and three boys, infusing Latin, French, and geography all the forenoon, dining with them, sometimes walking with them, and then returning to the merry evening of Dynevor Terrace.

Mr. Dynevor endured the step pretty well. She had ascendancy enough over him always to take her own way, and he was still buoyed up by the hope of recovering enough to rectify his affairs in Peru. He was better, though his right side remained paralysed, and Mr. Walby saw little chance of restoration. Rising late, and breakfasting slowly, the newspaper and visits from James wiled away the morning. He preferred taking his meals alone; and after dinner was wheeled out in a chair on fine days. Clara came to him as soon as her day's work was over; and, when he was well enough to bear it, the whole party were with him from the children's bedtime till his own. Altogether, the invalid-life passed off pretty well. He did not dislike the children, and Kitty liked anything that needed to be waited on. He took Clara's services as a right, but was a little afraid of 'Mrs. Dynevor,' and highly flattered by any attention from her; and with James his moods were exceedingly variable, and often very trying, but, in general, very well endured.

Peruvian mails were anticipated in the family with a feeling most akin to dread. The notice of a vessel coming in was the signal for growlings at everything, from the post-office down to his dinner; and the arrival of letters made things only worse. As Clara said, the galleons were taken by the pirates; the Equatorial Company seemed to be doing the work of Caleb Balderston's thunderstorm, and to be bearing the blame of a deficit such as Oliver could not charge on it. The whole statement was backed by Mr. Ponsonby, whose short notes spoke of indisposition making him more indebted than ever to the exertions of Robson. This last was gone to Guayaquil to attempt to clear up the accounts of the Equatorial Company, leaving the office at Lima in the charge of Madison and the new clerk, Ford; and Mr. Dynevor was promised something decisive and satisfactory on his return. Of Mary there was no mention, except what might be inferred in a postscript:—'Ward is expected in a few weeks.'

Mr. Dynevor was obliged to resign himself; and so exceedingly fractious was he, that Clara had been feeling quite dispirited, when her brother called her to tell her joyously that Lord Ormersfield and Louis were coming home, and would call in on their way the next evening. Those wretched children must not take her for a walk.

Nevertheless, the wretched children did want to walk, and Clara could not get home till half-an-hour after she knew the train must have come in; and she found the visitors in her uncle's room. Louis came forward to the door to meet her, and shook her hand with all his heart, saying, under his breath,

'I congratulate you!'

'Thank you!' she said, in the same hearty tone.

'And now, look at him! look at my father! Have not we made a good piece of work of keeping him abroad all the winter? Does not he look as well as ever he did in his life?'

This was rather strong, for Lord Ormersfield was somewhat grey, and a little bent; but he had resumed all his look of health and vigour, and was a great contrast to his younger, but far older-looking cousin. He welcomed

Clara with his tone of courteous respect, and smiled at his son's exultation, saying, Fitzjocelyn deserved all the credit, for he himself had never thought to be so patched up again, and poor Oliver was evidently deriving as much encouragement as if rheumatism had been paralysis.

'I must look in at the House Beautiful,' said Louis, presently. 'Clara, I can't lose your company. Won't you come with me?'

Of course she came; and she divined why, instead of at once entering the next house, he took a turn along the Terrace, and, after a pause, asked, 'Clara, when did you last hear from Lima?'

'Not for a long time. I suppose she is taken up by her father's illness.'

He paused, collected himself, and asked again, 'Have you heard nothing from your uncle?'

'Yes,' said Clara, sadly, 'but Louis,' she added, with a lively tone, 'what does not come from herself, I would not believe.'

'I do not.'

'That's right, don't be vexed when it may be nothing.'

'No; if she had found any one more worthy of her, she would not hesitate in making me aware of it. I ought to be satisfied, if she does what is best for her own happiness. Miss Ponsonby believes that this is a man of sterling worth, probably suiting her better than I might have done. She was a good deal driven on by circumstances before, and, perhaps, it was all a mistake on her side.' And he tried to smile.

Clara exclaimed that 'Mary could not have been all he had believed, if—'

'No,' he said, 'she is all, and more than all. I comprehend her better now, and could have shown her that I do. She has been the blessing of my life so far, and her influence always will be so. I shall always be grateful to her, be the rest as it may, and I mean to live on hope to the last. Now for the good old ladies. Really, Clara, the old Dynevor Terrace atmosphere has come back, and there seems to be the same sort of rest and cheering in coming into these old iron gates! After all, Isabel is growing almost worthy to be called Mrs. Frost.' And in this manner he talked on, up to the very door of the House Beautiful, as if to cheat himself out of despondency.

'That was a very pretty meeting,' said Isabel to her husband, when no witness was present but little Fanny.

'What, between his lordship and my uncle?'

'You know better.'

'My dear, your mother once tried match-making for Fitzjocelyn. Be warned by her example.'

'I am doing no such thing. I am only observing what every one sees.'

'Don't be so common-place.'

'That's all disdain—you must condescend. I have been hearing from Mr. Dynevor of the excellent offers that Clara refused.'

'Do you think Uncle Oliver and Clara agree as to excellence?'

'Still,' continued Isabel, 'considering how uncomfortable she was, it does not seem improbable that she would have married, unless some attachment had steeled her heart and raised her standard. I know she was unconscious, but it was Fitzjocelyn who formed her.'

'He has been a better brother to her than I have been; but look only at their perfect ease.'

'Now it is my belief that they were made for each other, and can venture to find it out, since she is no longer an heiress, and he is free from his Peruvian entanglement.'

'Fanny, do you hear what a scheming mamma you have? I hope she will have used it all upon Sir Hubert before you come out as the beauty of the Terrace!'

'Well, I mean to sound Clara.'

'You had better leave it alone.'

'Do you forbid me?'

'Why, no, for I don't think you have the face to say anything that would distress her, or disturb the friendship which has been her greatest benefit.'

'Thank you. All I intend is, that if it should be as I suppose, the poor things should not miss coming to an understanding for want—'

'Of a Christmas-tree,' said James, laughing. 'You may have your own way. I have too much confidence in your discretion and in theirs to imagine that you will produce the least effect.'

Isabel's imagination was busily at work, and she was in haste to make use of her husband's permission; but it was so difficult to see Clara alone, that some days passed before the two sisters were left together in the sitting-room, while James was writing a letter for his uncle. Isabel's courage began to waver, but she ventured a commencement.

'Mr. Dynevor entertains me with fine stories of your conquests, Clara.'

Clara laughed, blushed, and answered bluntly, 'What a bother it was!'

'You are very hard-hearted.'

'You ought to remember the troubles of young ladyhood enough not to wonder.'

'I never let things run to that length; but then I had no fortune. But seriously, Clara, were all these people objectionable?'

'Do you think one could marry any man, only because he was not objectionable? There was no harm in one or two; but I was not going to have anything to say to them.'

'Really, Clara, you make me curious. Had you made any resolution?'

'I know only two men whom I could have trusted to fulfil my conditions,' said Clara.

'Conditions?'

'Of course! that if Cheveleigh was to belong to any of us, it should be to the rightful heir.'

'My dear, noble Clara! was that what kept you from thinking of marriage?'

'Wasn't it a fine thing to have such a test? Not that I ever came to trying it. Simple no answered my purpose. I met no one who tempted me to make the experiment.'

'Two men!' said Isabel, 'if you had said one, it would have been marked.'

'Jem and Louis, of course,' said Clara.

'Oh! that is as good as saying one.'

'As good as saying none,' said Clara, with emphasis.

'There may be different opinions on that point,' returned Isabel, not daring to lift her eyes from her work, though longing to study Clara's face, and feeling herself crimsoning.

'Extremely unfounded opinions, and rather—'

'Rather what?'

'Impertinent, I was going to say, begging your pardon, dear Isabel.'

'Nay, I think it is I who should beg yours, Clara.'

'No, no,' said Clara, laughing, but speaking gravely immediately after, 'lookers-on do not always see most of the game. I have always known his mind so well that I could never possibly have fallen into any such nonsense. I respect him far too much.'

Isabel felt as if she must hazard a few words more—'Can you guess what he will do if Mr. Ponsonby's reports prove true?'

'I do not mean to anticipate misfortunes,' said Clara.

Isabel could say no more; and when Clara next spoke, it was to ask for another of James's wristbands to stitch. Then Isabel ventured to peep at her face, and saw it quite calm, and not at all rosy; if it had been, the colour was gone.

Thus it was, and there are happily many such friendships existing as that between Louis and Clara. Many a woman has seen the man whom she might have married, and yet has not been made miserable. If there be neither vanity nor weak self-contemplation on her side, nor trifling on his part, nor unwise suggestions forced on her by spectators, the honest, genuine affection need never become passion. If intimacy is sometimes dangerous, it is because vanity, folly, and mistakes are too frequent; but in spite of all these, where women are truly refined, and exalted into companions and friends, there has been much more happy, frank intercourse and real friendship than either the romantic or the sagacious would readily allow. The spark is never lighted, there is no consciousness, no repining, and all is well.

Fresh despatches from Lima arrived; and after a day, when Oliver had been so busy overlooking the statement from Guayaquil that he would not even take his usual airing, he received Clara with orders to write and secure his passage by the next packet for Callao.

'Dear uncle, you would never dream of it! You could not bear the journey!' she cried, aghast.

'It would do me good. Do not try to cross me, Clara. No one else can deal with this pack of rascals. Your brother has not been bred to it, and is a parson besides, and there's not a soul that I can trust. I'll go. What! d'ye think I can live on him and on you, when there is a competence of my own out there, embezzled among those ragamuffins?'

'I am sure we had much rather—'

'No stuff and nonsense. Here is Roland with four children already—very likely to have a dozen more. If you and he are fools, I'm not, and I won't take the bread out of their mouths. I'll leave my will behind, bequeathing whatever I may get out of the fire evenly between you two, as the only way to content you; and if I never turn up again, why you're rid of the old man.'

'Very well, uncle, I shall take my own passage at the same time.'

'You don't know what you are talking of. You are a silly child, and your brother would be a worse if he let you go.'

'If Jem lets you go, he will let me. He shall let me. Don't you know that you are never to have me off your hands, uncle? No, no, I shall stick to you like a burr. You may go up to the tip-top of Chimborazo if you please, but you'll not shake me off.'

It was her fixed purpose to accompany him, and she was not solicitous to dissuade him from going, for she could be avaricious for James's children, and had a decided wish for justice on the guilty party; and, besides, Clara had a private vision of her own, which made her dance in her little room. Mary had written in her father's stead—there was not a word of Mr. Ward—indeed, Mr. Ponsonby was evidently so ill that his daughter could think of nothing else. Might not Clara come in time to clear up any misunderstanding—convince Mr. Ponsonby—describe Louis's singlehearted constancy during all these five years, and bring Mary home to him in triumph? She could have laughed aloud with delight at the possibility; and when the other alternative occurred to her, she knit her brows with childish vehemence, as she promised Miss Mary that she would never be her bridesmaid.

Presently she heard Fitzjocelyn's voice in the parlour, and, going down, found him in consultation over a letter which Charlotte had brought to her master. It was so well written and expressed, that Louis turned to the signature before he could quite believe that it was from his old pupil. Tom wrote to communicate his perplexity at the detection of the frauds practised on his employers. He had lately been employed in the office at Lima, where much had excited his suspicion; and, finally, from having 'opened a letter addressed by mistake to the firm, but destined for an individual, he had discovered that large sums, supposed to be required by the works, or lost in the Equatorial failure, had been, in fact, invested in America in the name of that party.' The secret was a grievous burthen. Mr. Ponsonby was far too ill to be informed; besides that, he should only bring suspicion on himself; and Miss Ponsonby was so much occupied as to be almost equally inaccessible. Tom had likewise reason to believe that his own movements were watched, and that any attempt to communicate with her or her father would be baffled; and, above all, he could not endure himself to act the spy and informer. He only wished that, if possible, without mentioning names, Charlotte could give a hint that Mr. Dynevor must not implicitly trust to all he heard.

James was inclined to suppress such vague information, which he thought would only render his uncle more restless and wretched in his helplessness, and was only questioning whether secrecy would not amount to deceit.

'The obvious thing is for me to go to Peru,' said Louis.

'My uncle and I were intending to go,' said Clara.

'How many more of you?' exclaimed James.

'I would not change my native land
For rich Peru and all her gold;'

chanted little Kitty from the corner, where she was building houses for the 'little ones.'

'Extremely to the purpose,' said Louis, laughing. 'Follow her example, Clara. Make your uncle appoint me his plenipotentiary, and I will try what I can to find out what these rogues are about.'

'Are you in earnest?'

'Never more so in my life.'

James beckoned him to the window, and showed him a sentence where Tom said that the best chance for the firm was in Miss Ponsonby's marriage with Mr. Ward, but that engagement was not yet declared on account of her father's illness.

'The very reason,' said Louis, 'I cannot go on in this way. I must know the truth.'

'And your father?'

'It would be much better for him that the thing were settled. He will miss me less during the session, when he is in London with all his old friends about him. It would not take long, going by the Isthmus. I'll ride back at once, and see how he bears the notion. Say nothing to Mr. Dynevor till you hear from me; but I think he will consent. He will not endure that she should be left unprotected; her father perhaps dying, left to the mercy of these rascals.'

'And forgive me, Louis, if you found her not needing you!'

'If she be happy, I should honour the man who made her so. At least, I might be of use to you. I should see after poor Madison. I have sent him to the buccaneers indeed! Good-bye! I cannot rest till I see how my father takes it!'

It was long since Louis had been under an excess of impetuosity; but he rode home as fast as he had ridden to Northwold to canvass for James, and had not long been at Ormersfield before his proposition was laid before his father.

It was no small thing to ask of the Earl, necessary as his son had become to him; and the project at first appeared to him senseless. He thought Mary had not shown herself sufficiently sensible of his son's merits to deserve so much trouble; and if she were engaged to Mr. Ward, Fitzjocelyn would find himself in an unpleasant and undignified position. Besides, there was the ensuing session of Parliament! No! Oliver must send out some trustworthy man of business, with full powers.

Louis only answered, that of course it depended entirely on his father's consent; and by-and-by his submission began to work. Lord Ormersfield could not refuse him anything, and took care, on parting for the night, to observe that the point was not settled, only under consideration.

And consideration was more favourable than might have been expected. The Earl was growing anxious to see his son married, and of that there was no hope till his mind should be settled with regard to Mary. It would be more for his peace to extinguish the hope, if it were never to be fulfilled. Moreover, the image of Mary had awakened the Earl's own fatherly fondness for her, and his desire to rescue her from her wretched home. Even Mr. Ponsonby could hardly withstand Louis in person, he thought, and must be touched by so many years of constancy. The rest might be only a misunderstanding which would be cleared up by a personal interview. Added to this, Lord Ormersfield knew that Clara would not let her uncle go alone, and did not think it fit to see her go out alone with an infirm paralytic; James could not leave his wife or his chaplaincy, and the affair was unsuited to his profession; a mere accountant would not carry sufficient authority, nor gain Madison's confidence; in fact, Fitzjocelyn, and no other, was the trustworthy man of business; and so his lordship allowed when Louis ventured to recur to the subject the next morning, and urge some of his arguments.

The bright clearing of Louis's face spoke his thanks, and he began at once to detail his plans for his father's comfort, Lord Ormersfield listening as if pleased by his solicitude, though caring for little until the light of his eyes should return.

'The next point is that you should give me a testimonial that I *am* a trustworthy man of business.'

'I will ride into Northwold with you, and talk it over with Oliver.'

Here lay the knotty point; but the last five years had considerably cultivated Fitzjocelyn's natural aptitude for figures, by his attention to statistics, his own farming-books, and the complicated accounts of the

Ormersfield estate,—so that both his father and Richardson could testify to his being an excellent man of business; and his coolness, and mildness of temper, made him better calculated to deal with a rogue than a more hasty man would have been.

They found, on arriving, that James had been talking to Mr. Walby, who pronounced that the expedition to Lima would be mere madness for Mr. Dynevor, since application to business would assuredly cause another attack, and even the calculations of the previous day had made him very unwell, and so petulant and snappish, that he could be pleased with nothing, and treated as mere insult the proposal that he should entrust his affairs to 'such a lad.'

Even James hesitated to influence him to accept the offer. 'I scruple,' he said, drawing the Earl aside, 'because I thought you had a particular objection to Fitzjocelyn's being thrown in the way of speculations. I thought you dreaded the fascination.'

'Thank you, James; I once did so,' said the Earl. 'I used to believe it a family mania; I only kept it down in myself by strong resolution, in the very sight of the consequences, but I can trust Fitzjocelyn. He is too indifferent to everything apart from duty to be caught by flattering projects, and you may fully confide in his right judgment. I believe it is the absence of selfishness or conceit that makes him so clear-sighted.'

'What a change! what a testimony!' triumphantly thought James. It might be partial, but he was not the man to believe so.

That day was one of defeat; but on the following, a note from James advised Fitzjocelyn to come and try his fortune again; Mr. Dynevor would give no one any rest till he had seen him.

Thereupon Louis was closeted with the old merchant, who watched him keenly, and noted every question or remark he made on the accounts; then twinkled his eyes with satisfaction as he hit more than one of the very blots over which Oliver had already perplexed himself. So clear-headed and accurate did he show himself, that he soon perceived that Mr. Dynevor looked at him as a good clerk thrown away; and he finally obtained from him full powers to act, to bring the villain to condign punishment, and even, if possible, to dispose of his share in the firm.

Miss Ponsonby was much relieved to learn that Lord Fitzjocelyn was going out, though fearing that he might meet with disappointment; but, at least, her brother would be undeceived as to the traitor in whom he was confiding. No letters were to announce Louis's intentions, lest the enemy should take warning; but he carried several with him, to be given or not, according to the state of affairs; and when, on his way through London, he went to receive Miss Ponsonby's commissions, she gave him a large packet, addressed to Mary.

'Am I to give her this at all events!' he asked, faltering.

'It would serve her right.'

'Then I should not give it to her. Pray write another, for she does not deserve to be wounded, however she may have decided.'

'I do not know how I shall ever forgive her,' sighed Aunt Melicent.

'People are never so unforgiving as when they have nothing to forgive.'

'Ah! Lord Fitzjocelyn, that is not your case. This might have been far otherwise, had I not misjudged you at first.'

'Do not believe so. It would have been hard to think me more foolish than I was. This probation has been the best schooling for me; and, let it end as it may, I shall be thankful for what has been.'

And in this spirit did he sail, and many an anxious thought followed him, no heart beating higher than did that of little Charlotte, who founded a great many hopes on the crisis that his coming would produce. Seven years was a terrible time to have been engaged, and the little workhouse girl thought her getting almost as old as Mrs. Beckett. She wondered whether Tom thought so too! She did not want to think about Martha's first cousin, who was engaged for thirty-two years to a journeyman tailor, and when they married at last, they were both so cross that she went out to service again at the end of a month. Charlotte set up all her caps with Tom's favourite colour, and 'turned Angelina' twenty times a-day.

Then came the well-known Peruvian letters, and a thin one for Charlotte. Without recollecting that it must have crossed Lord Fitzjocelyn on the road, she tore it open the instant she had carried in the parlour letters. Alas! poor Charlotte!

> 'I write to you for the last time, lest you should consider yourself any longer bound by the engagements which must long have been distasteful. When I say that Mr. Ford has for some months been my colleague, you will know to what I allude, without my expressing any further. I am already embarked for the U. S. My enemies have succeeded in destroying my character and blighting my hopes. I am at

present a fugitive from the hands of so-called justice; but I could have borne all with a cheerful heart if you had not played me false. You will never hear more of one who loved you faithfully.

'TH. MADISON.'

Poor Charlotte! The wound was a great deal too deep for her usual childish tears, or even for a single word. She stood still, cold, and almost unconscious till she heard a step, then she put the cruel letter away in her bosom, and went about her work as usual.

They thought her looking very pale, and Jane now and then reproached her with eating no more than a sparrow, and told her she was getting into a dwining way; but she made no answer, except that she 'could do her work.' At last, one Sunday evening, when she had been left alone with the children, her mistress found her sitting at the foot of her bed, among the sleeping little ones, weeping bitterly but silently. Isabel's kindness at length opened her heart, and she put the letter into her hand. Poor little thing, it was very meekly borne: 'Please don't tell no one, ma'am,' she said; 'I couldn't hear him blamed!'

'But what does he mean? He must be under some terrible error. Who is this Ford?'

'It is Delaford, ma'am, I make no doubt, though however he could have got there! And, oh dear me! if I had only told poor Tom the whole, that I was a silly girl, and liked his flatteries now and then, but constant in my heart I always was!'

Isabel could not but suppose that Delaford, if it were he, might have exaggerated poor Charlotte's little flirtation; but there was small comfort here, since contradiction was impossible. The U. S., over which the poor child had puzzled in vain, was no field in which to follow him up—he had not even dated his letter; and it was a very, very faint hope that Lord Fitzjocelyn might trace him out, especially as he had evidently fled in disgrace; and poor Charlotte sobbed bitterly over his troubles, as well as her own.

She was better after she had told her mistress, though still she shrank from any other sympathy. Even Jane's pity would have been too much for her, and her tender nature was afraid of the tongues that would have discussed her grief. Perhaps the high-toned nature of Isabel was the very best to be brought into contact with the poor girl's spirit, which was of the same order, and many an evening did Isabel sit in the twilight, beside the children's beds, talking to her, or sometimes reading a few lines to show her how others had suffered in the same way. 'It is my own fault,' said poor Charlotte; 'it all came of my liking to be treated like one above the common, and it serves me right. Yes, ma'am, that was a beautiful text you showed me last night, I thought of it all day, and I'll try to believe that good will come out of it. I am sure you are very good to let me love the children! I'm certain sure Miss Salome knows that I'm in trouble, for she never fails to run and kiss me the minute she comes in sight; and she'll sit so quiet in my lap, the little dear, and look at me as much as to say, 'Charlotte, I wish I could comfort you.' But it was all my own fault, ma'am, and I think I could feel as if I was punished right, so I knew poor Tom was happy.'

'Alas!' thought Isabel, after hearing Charlotte's reminiscences; 'how close I have lived to a world of which I was in utter ignorance! How little did we guess that, by the careless ease and inattention of our household, we were carrying about a firebrand, endangering not only poor Walter, but doing fearful harm wherever we went!'

CHAPTER XXI
STEPPING WESTWARD

On Darien's sands and deadly dew.
Rokeby.

Enterprise and speed both alike directed Fitzjocelyn's course across the Isthmus of Panama, which in 1853 had newly become practicable for adventurous travellers. A canal conducted him as far as Cruces, after which he had to push on through wild forest and swamp, under the escort of the muleteers who took charge of the various travellers who had arrived by the same packet.

It was a very novel and amusing journey, even in the very discomforts and the strange characters with whom he was thrown, and more discontented travellers used to declare that Don Luis, as he told the muleteers to call him, always seemed to have the best success with the surly hotel-keepers, though when he resigned his acquisitions to any resolute grumbler, it used to be discovered that he had been putting up with the worst share.

A place called Guallaval seemed to be the most squalid and forlorn of all the stations—outside, an atmosphere of mosquitoes; inside, an atmosphere of brandy and smoke, the master an ague-stricken Yankee, who sat with his bare feet high against the wall, and only deigned to jerk with his head to show in what quarter was the drink and food, and to 'guess that strangers must sleep on the ground, for first-comers had all the beds'—hammocks slung up in a barn, or unwholesome cupboards in the wall.

At the dirty board sat several of the party first arrived, washing down tough, stringy beef with brandy. Louis was about to take his place near a very black-bearded young man, who appeared more civilized than the rest, and who surprised him by at once making room for him, leaving the table with an air of courtesy; and when, in his halting Spanish, he begged 'his Grace' not to disturb himself, he was answered, in the same tongue, 'I have finished.'

After the meal, such as it was, he wandered out of the hut, to escape the fumes and the company within; but he was presently accosted by the same stranger, who, touching his slouched Panama hat, made him a speech in Spanish, too long and fluent for his comprehension, at the same time offering him a cigar. He was civilly refusing, when, to his surprise, the man interrupted him in good English. 'These swamps breed fever, to a certainty. A cigar is the only protection; and even then there is nothing more dangerous than to be out at sunset.'

'Thank you, I am much obliged,' said Louis, turning towards the hut. 'Have you been long out here?'

'The first time on the Isthmus; but I know these sort of places. Pray go in, my Lord.'

The title and the accent startled Louis, and he exclaimed, 'You must be from the Northwold country?'

He drew back, and said bluntly, 'Never mind me, only keep out of this pestiferous air.'

But the abrupt surliness completed the recognition, and, seizing his hand, Louis cried, 'Tom! how are you?' You have turned into a thorough Spaniard, and taken me in entirely.'

'Only come in, my Lord; I would never have spoken to you, but that I could not see you catching your death.'

'I am coming: but what's the matter? Why avoid me, when you are the very man I most wished to see?'

'I'm done for,' said Tom. 'The fellows up there have saddled their rogueries on me, and I'm off to the States. I—'

'What do you say? There, I am coming in. Be satisfied, Tom; I am come out with a commission from Mr. Dynevor, to see what can be arranged.'

'That's right,' cried Tom, 'now poor Miss Ponsonby will have one friend.'

'Your letter to Charlotte brought me out—' began Louis; but Madison broke in with an expression of dismay and self-reproach at seeing him walking somewhat lame.

'It is only when I am tired, and not thinking of it,' said Louis; 'do you know that old ash stick, Tom, my constant friend? See, here are the names of all the places I have seen cut out on it.'

'I knew it, and you, the moment you sat down by the table,' said Tom, in a tone of the utmost feeling, as Louis took his arm. 'You are not one to forget.'

'And yet you were going to pass me without making yourself known.'

'A disgraced man has no business to be known,' said Tom, low and hoarsely. 'No, I wish none of them ever to hear my name again; and but for the slip of the tongue that came so naturally, you should not, but I was drawn to you, and could not help it. I am glad I have seen you once more, my Lord—'

He would have left him at the entrance, but Louis held him fast.

'You are the very man I depend on for unravelling the business. A man cannot be disgraced by any one but himself, and that is not the case with you, Tom.'

'No, thank Heaven,' said Tom, fervently; 'I've kept my honesty, if I have lost all the rest.'

Little more was needed to bring Madison to a seat on a wooden bench beside Fitzjocelyn, answering his anxious inquiries. The first tidings were a shock—Mr. Ponsonby was dead. He had long been declining, and the last thing Tom had heard from Lima was, that he was dead; but of the daughter there was no intelligence; Tom had been too much occupied with his own affairs to know anything of her. Robson had returned from Guayaquil some weeks previously, and in the settlement of accounts consequent on Mr. Ponsonby's death, Tom had demurred giving up all the valuable property at the mines under his charge, until he should have direct orders from Mr. Dynevor or Miss Ponsonby. A hot dispute ensued, and Robson became aware that Tom was informed of his nefarious practices, and had threatened him violently; but a few hours after he had returned, affecting to have learnt from the new clerk, Ford, that Madison's peculations required to be winked at with equal forbearance, and giving him the alternative of sharing the spoil, or of being denounced to the authorities. He took a night to consider; and, as Louis started at hearing of any deliberation, he said, sadly, 'You would not believe me, my Lord, but I had almost a mind. They would take away my character, any way; and what advantage was my honesty without that? And as to hurting my employers, they would only take what I did not; and such as that is thought nothing of by very many. I'd got no faith in man nor woman left, and I'd got nothing but suspicion by my honesty; so why should I not give in to the way of the world, and try if it would serve me. But then, my Lord, it struck me that if I had nothing else, I had still my God left.'

Louis grasped his hand.

'Yes, I'm thankful that Miss Ponsonby asked me to read to the Cornish miners,' said Madison. 'One gets soon heathenish in a heathenish place; and but for that I don't believe I should ever have stood it out. But Joseph's words, "How can I do this great wickedness, and sin against God," kept ringing in my ears like a peal of bells, all night, and by morning I sent in a note to Mr. Robson, to say No to what he proposed.'

Every other principle would have cracked in such a conflict, and Louis looked up at Tom with intense admiration, while the young man spoke on, not conscious that it had been noble, but ashamed of owning himself to have been brought to a pass where mere integrity had been an effort.

He had gone back at once to his mines, in some hopes that the threats might yet prove nothing but blustering; but he had scarcely arrived there when an Indian muleteer, to whom he had shown some kindness, brought him intelligence that la justida was in quest of him, but in difficulties how to get up the mountains. The poor Indians guided his escape, conducting him down wonderful paths only known to themselves, hiding him in strange sequestered huts, and finally guiding him safely to Callao, where he had secretly embarked on board an American vessel bound for Panama. Louis asked why he had fled, instead of taking his trial, and confuting Robson; but he smiled, and said, my Lord knew little of foreign justice; besides, Ford was ready to bear any witness that Robson might put into his mouth;—and his face grew dark. Who was this Ford? He could not tell; Mr. Robson had picked him up a few months back, when there was a want of a clerk; like loved like, he supposed, but it was no concern of his. Would it be safe for him to venture back to Peru, under Fitzjocelyn's protection, and assist him in unmasking the treacherous Robson! To this he readily agreed, catching at the hope of establishing his innocence; but declaring that he should then go at once to the States.—'What, not even go home to see Charlotte? I've got a letter for you, when I can get at it.'

Tom made no answer, and Fitzjocelyn feared that, in spite of all his good qualities, his fidelity in love had not equalled his fidelity to his employers. He could not understand his protege during the few days of their journey. He was a great acquisition to his comfort, with his knowledge of the language and people, and his affectionate deference. At home, where all were courtly, he had been almost rude; but here, in the land of ill manners, his attentions were so assiduous that Louis was obliged to beg him to moderate them lest they should both be ridiculous. He had become a fine-looking young man, with a foreign air and dress agreeing well with his dark complexion; and he had acquired much practical ability and information. Mountains, authority, and a good selection of books had been excellent educators; he was a very superior and intelligent person, and, without much polish, had laid aside his peasant rusticities, and developed some of the best qualities of a gentleman. But though open and warm-hearted on many points with his early friend, there was a gloom and moodiness about him, which Louis could only explain by thinking that his unmerited disgrace preyed on him more than was quite manly. To this cause, likewise, Louis at first attributed his never choosing to hear a word about Charlotte; but as the distaste—nay almost sullenness, evoked by any allusion to her, became more apparent, Louis began unwillingly to balance his suspicions between some fresh attachment, or unworthy shame at an engagement to a maidservant.

The poor little damsel's sweet blushing face and shy courtesy, and all her long and steady faithfulness, made him feel indignant at such a suspicion, and he resolved to bring Madison to some explanation; but he did not find the opportunity till after they had embarked at the beautiful little islet of Toboga for Callao. On board, he had time to find in his portmanteau the letter with which she had entrusted him, and, seeking Madison on deck, gave it to him. He held it in his hand without opening it; but the sparkle in his dark eye did not betoken the bashfulness of fondness, and Louis, taking a turn along the deck to watch him unperceived, saw him raise his hand as if to throw the poor letter overboard at once. A few long steps, and Louis was beside him, exclaiming, 'What now, Tom—is that the way you treat your letters?'

'The little hypocrite! I don't want no more of her false words,' muttered Tom, returning, in his emotion, to his peasant's emphatic double negative.

'Hypocrite! Do you know how nobly and generously she has been helping Mr. and Mrs. Frost through their straits? how faithfully—'

'I know better,' said Tom, hoarsely; 'don't excuse her, my Lord; you know little of what passes in your own kitchens.'

'Too true, I fear, in many cases,' said Louis; 'but I have seen this poor child in circumstances that make me feel sure that she is an admirable creature. What misunderstanding can have arisen?'

'No misunderstanding, my Lord. I saw, as plain as I see you, her name and her writing in the book that she gave to Ford—her copying out of his love-poems, my Lord, in the blank pages,—if I had wanted any proof of what he alleged.'

And he had nearly thrown the letter into the Pacific; but Louis caught his arm.

'Did you ever read Cymbeline, Tom?'

'Yes, to be sure I have,' growled Tom, in surprise.

'Then remember Iachimo, and spare that letter. What did he tell you?'

With some difficulty Fitzjocelyn drew from Madison that he had for some time been surprised at Ford's knowledge of Northwold and the neighbourhood; but had indulged in no suspicions till about the epoch of Robson's return from Guayaquil. Chancing to be waiting in his fellow-clerk's room, he had looked at his books, and, always attracted by poetry as the rough fellow was, had lighted on a crimson watered-silk volume, in the first page of which he had, to his horror, found the name of Charlotte Arnold borne aloft by the two doves, and in the blank leaves several extremely flowery poems in her own handwriting.

With ill-suppressed rage he had demanded an explanation, and had been met with provokingly indifferent inuendoes. The book was the gift of a young lady with whom Ford had the pleasure to be acquainted; the little effusions were trifles of his own, inscribed by her own fair hands. Oh, yes! he knew Miss Arnold very well—very pretty, very complaisant! Ah! he was afraid there were some broken hearts at home! Poor little thing! he should never forget how she took leave of him, after forcing upon him her little savings! He was sorry for her, too; but a man cannot have compassion on all the pretty girls he sees.

'And you could be deceived by such shallow coxcombry as this!' said Louis.

'I tell you there was the book,' returned Tom.

'Well, Tom, if Mr. Ford prove to be the Ford I take him to be, I'll undertake that you shall see through him, and be heartily ashamed of yourself. Give me back the letter,—you do not deserve to have it.'

'I don't want it,' said Tom, moodily; 'she has not been as true to me as I've been to her, and if she isn't what I took her for, I do not care to hear of her again. I used to look at the mountain-tops, and think she was as pure as they; and that she should have been making herself the talk of a fellow like that, and writing so sweet to me all the time!—No, my Lord, there's no excusing it; and 'twas her being gone after the rest that made it so bitter hard to me! If she had been true, I would have gone through fire and water to be an honest man worthy of her; but when I found how she had deceived me, it went hard with me to cut myself off from the wild mountain life that I'd got to love, and my poor niggers, that will hardly have so kind a master set over them.'

'You have stood the fiery ordeal well,' said Louis; 'and I verily believe that you will soon find that it was only an ordeal.'

The care of Tom was a wholesome distraction to the suspense that became almost agony as Louis approached Peru, and beheld the gigantic summits of the more northern Andes, which sunset revealed shining out white and fitfully, like the Pilgrim's vision of the Celestial City, although, owing to their extreme distance, even on a bright noonday, nothing was visible but clear deep-blue sky. They seemed to make him realize that the decisive moment was near, when he should tread the same soil with Mary, and yet, as he stood silently watching those glorious heights, human hopes and cares seemed to shrink into nothing before the eternity and Infinite Greatness of which the depth and the height spoke. Yet He remembereth the hairs of our heads, Who weigheth the mountains in the balance, and counteth the isles as a very little thing. Louis took comfort, but nerved himself for resignation; his prayer was more, that he might bear rightly whatever might be in store, than that he should succeed. He could hardly have made the latter petition with that submissiveness and reserve befitting all entreaty for blessings of this passing world.

CHAPTER XXII
RATHER SUDDEN

> O! would you hear of a Spanish lady,
> How she woo'd an Englishman?
> Garments gay, as rich as may be,
> Decked with jewels she had on.
> Old Ballad.

The white buildings of Callao looked out of the palm gardens, and, with throbbing heart, Fitzjocelyn was set on shore, leaving Madison on board until he should hear from him that evening or the next morning.

Hiring a calesa, he drove at once to Lima, to the house of the late Mr. Ponsonby. The heavy folding gates admitted him to the archway, where various negroes were loitering; and as he inquired for the ladies, one of them raised a curtain, and admitted him into the large cool twilight hall, so dark that, with eyes dazzled by the full glare of day, he could hardly discern at the opposite end of the hall, where a little more light was admitted from one of the teatina windows, two figures seated at a table covered with ledgers and papers. As if dreaming, he followed his barefooted guide across the soft India matting, and heard his Spanish announcement, that, might it please her Grace, here was a Senor from England.

Both rose; the one a well-dressed man, the other—it was the well-known action—'Mary!' it was all that he had the power to say; he was hardly visible, but what tone was ever like that low, distinct, earnest voice?

Mary clasped her hands together as if in bewilderment.

'Xavier should not—I will speak,' whispered her companion to her, and beginning, 'Address yourself to me, sir!'

But Mary sprang forward, signing him back with her hand. 'It is my cousin, Lord Fitzjocelyn!' she said, as if breath and effort would serve no more, and she laid her hand in that of Louis.

'Mr. Ward?' said Louis, barely able to frame the question, yet striving for a manner that might leave no thorns behind.

'No; oh, no! Mr. Robson.'

The very sound of the 'No' made his heart bound up again, and his hand closed fast on that which lay within it, while a bow passed between him and Robson.

'And you are come?' as if it were too incredible.

'I told you I should,' he answered.

'I will leave you, Miss Ponsonby,' said Robson; 'we will continue our little business when you are less agreeably engaged.'

He began to gather the papers together, an action which suddenly recalled Louis to the recollection of Tom's cautions as to prudence and alertness, and he forced himself to a prompt tone of business.

'I hope to be able to be of use,' he said, turning to Mary. 'Mr. Dynevor has given me a commission to look into his affairs,' and he put into Robson's hands the letter written by James, and signed by Oliver.

'Thank you, Lord Fitzjocelyn, I shall be very happy to give any explanations you may wish,' said Robson, measuring with his eye his youthful figure and features, and piling up the books.

'I should prefer having these left with me,' said Louis; 'I have but little time before me, and if I could look them over to-night, I should be prepared for you to-morrow.'

'Allow me. You would find it impossible to understand these entries. There is much to be set in order before they would be ready for the honour of your lordship's inspection.'

'I particularly wish to have them at once. You give me authority to act for you, Miss Ponsonby?' he added, looking at her, as she stood holding by the table, as one half awake.

'Oh! yes, I put the whole into your hands,' she answered, mechanically, obeying his eye.

'Allow me, my Lord,' said Robson, as Fitzjocelyn laid the firm hand of detention on the heavy ledgers, and great leathern pocket-book.

'Yes; we had better know exactly what you leave in my charge, Mr. Robson,' said Louis, beginning to suspect that the clerk fancied that the weight and number of the books and bundles of bills might satisfy his unpractised eye, and that the essential was to be found in the pocket-book, on which he therefore retained a special hold; asking, as Robson held out his hand for it, 'is this private property?'

'Why, yes; no, it is and it is not,' said Robson, looking at the lady, as though to judge whether she were attending. 'I only brought it here that Miss Ponsonby might have before her—always a satisfaction to a lady, you know, sir—though Miss Ponsonby's superior talents for business quite enable her to comprehend. But our affairs are not what I could wish. The Equatorial bubble was most unfortunate, and that unfortunate young man, who has absconded after a long course of embezzlement, has carried off much valuable property. I was laying the case before Miss Ponsonby, and showing her what amount had been fortunately secured.'

'What is in the pocket-book?' asked Louis of Mary; and, though she was apparently conscious of nothing around her, he obtained a direct reply.

'The vouchers for the shares.'

'In the Equatorial. Unlucky speculation—so much waste paper,' interrupted Robson. 'Your lordship had better let me clear away the trash, which will only complicate the matter, and distract your understanding.'

'Thank you; as you say there has been fraud, I should be better satisfied to be able to tell Mr. Dynevor that the papers have never been out of my hands. I will call on you early to-morrow.'

Mr. Robson waited to make many inquiries for Mr. Dynevor's health, and to offer every attention to Lord Fitzjocelyn, to introduce him to the Consul, to find apartments for him, &c.; but at last he took leave, and Louis was free to turn to the motionless Mary, who had done nothing all this time but follow him with her eyes.

All his doubts had returned, and, in the crisis of his fate, he stood irresolute, daring neither to speak nor ask, lest feelings should be betrayed which might poison her happiness.

'Is it you?' were her first words, as though slowly awakening.

'It is I, come to be whatever you will let me be,' he answered, as best he could.

'Oh, Louis!' she said, 'this is too much!' And she hid her face in her hands.

'Tell me—one word, Mary, and I shall know what to do, and will not harass nor grieve you.'

'Grieve me! You!' exclaimed Mary, in an inexpressibly incredulous tone.

'Enough! It is as it was before!' and he drew her into his arms, as unresistingly as five years ago, and his voice sank with intense thankfulness, as he said, 'My Mary—my Mary! has He not brought it to pass?'

The tears came dropping from her eyes, and then she could speak.

'Louis, my dear father withdrew his anger. He gave full consent and blessing, if you still—'

'Then nothing is wanting—all is peace!' said Louis. 'You know how you are longed for at home—'

'That you should have come—come all this way! That Lord Ormersfield should have spared you!' exclaimed Mary, breaking out into happy little sentences, as her tears relieved her. 'Oh, how far off all my distress and perplexity seem now! How foolish to have been so unhappy when there you were close by! But you must see Dona Rosita,' cried she, recollecting herself, after an interval, 'I must tell her.'

Mary hurried into another room by a glass door, and Louis heard her speaking Spanish, and a languid reply; then returning, she beckoned to him to advance, whispering, 'Don't be surprised, these are the usual habits. We can talk before her, she never follows English.'

He could at first see no one, but presently was aware of a grass hammock swung from the richly-carved beams, and in it something white; then of a large pair of black eyes gazing full at him with a liquid soft stare. He made his bow, and summoned his best Spanish, and she made an answer which he understood, by the help of Mary, to be a welcome; then she smiled and signed with her head towards him and Mary, and said what Mary only interpreted by colouring, as did Louis, for such looks and smiles were of all languages. Then it was explained that only as a relation did she admit his Excellency el Visconde, before her evening toilette in her duelos was made—Mary would take care of him. And dismissing them with a graceful bend of her head, she returned to her doze and her cigarito.

Mary conducted Louis to the cool, shaded, arched doorway, opening under the rich marble cloister of the court-yard, where a fountain made a delicious bubbling in the centre. She clapped her hands—a little negro girl appeared, to whom she gave an order, and presently two more negroes came in, bringing magnificent oranges and pomegranates, and iced wine and water, on a silver tray, covered with a richly-embroidered napkin. He would have felt himself in the Alhambra, if he could have felt anything but that he was beside Mary.

'Sit down, sit down, you have proved yourself Mary enough already by waiting on me. I want to look at you, and to hear you. You are not altered!' he cried joyfully, as he drew her into the full light. 'You have your own eyes, and that's your very smile! only grown handsomer. That's all!'

She really was. She was a woman to be handsomer at twenty-seven than at twenty-one; and with the glow of unexpected bliss over her fine countenance, it did not need a lover's eye to behold her as something better than beautiful.

And for her! who shall tell the marvel of scarcely-credited joy, every time she heard the music of his softly-dropped distinct words, and looked up at the beloved face, perhaps a little less fair, with rather less of the boyish delicacy of feature, but more noble, more defined—as soft and sweet as ever, but with all the indecision gone; all that expression that had at times seemed like weakness. He was not the mere lad she had loved with a guiding motherly love, but a man to respect and rely on—ready, collected, dealing with easy coolness with the person who had domineered over that house for years. He was all, and more than all, her fondest fancy had framed; and coming to her aid at the moment of her utmost difficulty, brought to her by the love which she had not dared to confide in nor encourage! No wonder that she feared to move, lest she should find herself awakened from a dream too happy to last.

'But oh, Louis,' said she, as if it were almost a pledge of reality to recollect a vexation, 'I must tell you first, for it will grieve you, and we did not take pains enough to keep him out of temptation. That unhappy runaway clerk—'

'Is safe at Callao,' said Louis, 'and is to help me to release you from the meshes they have woven round you. Save for the warning he sent home, I could never have shown cause for coming to you, Mary, while you would not summon me. That was too bad, you know, since you had the consent.'

'That was only just at last,' faltered Mary. 'It was so kind of him, for I had disappointed him so much!'

'What? I know, Mary; his letters kept me in a perpetual fright for the last year; and not one did you write to poor little Clara to comfort us.'

'It was not right in me,' said Mary; 'but I thought it might be so much better for you if you were never put in mind of me. I beg your pardon, Louis.'

'We should have trusted each other better, if people would have let us alone,' said Louis. 'In fact, it was trust after all. It always came back again, if it were scared away for a moment.'

'Till I began to doubt if I were doing what was kind by you,' said Mary. 'Oh, that was the most distressing time of all; I thought if I were out of the way, you might begin to be happy, and I tried to leave off thinking about you.'

'Am I to thank you?'

'I *could* not,—that is the truth of it,' said Mary. 'I was able to keep you out of my mind enough, I hope, for it not to be wrong; but as to putting any one else there—I was forced at last to tell poor papa so, when he wanted to send for Mr. Ward; and then—he said that if you had been as constant, he supposed it must be, and he hoped we should be happy; and he said you had been a pet of my mother, and that Lord Ormersfield had been a real friend to her. It was so kind of him, for I know it would have been the greatest relief to his mind to leave things in Mr. Ward's charge.'

Mary had been so much obliged to be continually mentioning her father, that, though the loss was still very recent, she was habituated to speak of him with firmness; and it was an extreme satisfaction to tell all her sorrows, and all the little softening incidents, to Louis. Mr. Ponsonby had shown much affection and gratitude to her during the few closing days of his illness, and had manifested some tokens of repentance for his past life; but there had been so much pain and torpor, that there had been little space for reflection, and the long previous decline had not been accepted as a warning. Perhaps the intensity of Mary's prayers had been returned into her bosom, in the strong blindness of filial love; for as she dwelt fondly on the few signs of better things, the narration fell mournfully on Louis's ears, as that of an unhopeful deathbed.

An exceeding unwillingness to contemplate death, had prevented Mr. Ponsonby from making a new will. By one made many years back, he had left the whole of his property, without exception, to his daughter, his first wife having been provided for by her marriage settlements, and now, with characteristic indolence and selfishness, he had deferred till too late the securing any provision for his Limenian wife; and only when he found himself dying, had he said to Mary, 'You will take care to provide for poor Rosita!'

So Mary had found herself heiress to a share in the miserably-involved affairs of Dynevor and Ponsonby; and as soon as she could think of the future at all, had formed the design of settling Rosita in a convent with a pension, and going herself to England.

But Rosita was not easily to be induced to give up her gaieties for a convent life; and, moreover, there was absolutely such a want of ready money, that Mary did not see how to get home, though Robson assured her there was quite enough to live upon as they were at present. Nor was it possible to dispose of the mines and other property without Mr. Dynevor's consent, and he might not be in a state to give it.

The next stroke was young Madison's sudden disappearance, and the declaration by Robson that he had carried off a great deal of property—a disappointment to her even greater than the loss. Robson was profuse in compliments and attentions, but continually deferred the statement of affairs that he had promised; and Mary could not bear to accept the help of Mr. Ward, the only person at hand able and willing to assist her. She had at last grown desperate, and, resolved to have something positive to write to Mr. Dynevor, as well as not to go on living without knowing her means, she had insisted on Robson bringing his accounts. She knew just enough to be dissatisfied with his vague statements; and the more he praised her sagacity, the more she saw that he was taking advantage of her ignorance, which he presumed to be far greater than it really was. At the very moment when she was most persuaded of his treachery, and felt the most lonely and desolate—when he was talking fluently, and she was seeking to rally her spirits, and discover the path of right judgment, where the welfare of so many was concerned—it was then that Fitzjocelyn's voice was in her ear.

She had scarcely explained to Louis why his coming was, if possible, doubly and trebly welcome, when the negro admitted another guest, whom Rosita received much as she had done his predecessor, only with less curiosity. Mary rose, blushing deeply, and crossing the room held out her hand, and said simply, but with something of apology, 'Mr. Ward, this is Lord Fitzjocelyn.'

Mr. Ward raised his eyes to her face for one moment. 'I understand,' he said, in a low, not quite steady voice. 'It is well. Will you present me?' he added, as though collecting himself like a brave man after a blow.

'Here is my kindest friend,' she said, as she conducted him to Louis, and they shook hands in the very manner she wished to see, learning mutual esteem from her tone and each other's aspect.

'I am sorry to have intruded,' said Mr. Ward. 'I came in the hope that you might find some means of making me of use to you; and, perhaps, I may yet be of some assistance to Lord Fitzjocelyn.'

He enforced the proposal with so much cordiality, and showed so plainly that it would be his chief pleasure and consolation to do anything for Miss Ponsonby, that they did not scruple to take him into their counsels; and Mary looked on with exulting wonder at the ability and readiness displayed by Louis in the discussion of business details, even with a man whose profession they were. In remote space, almost beyond memory, save to enhance the present joy of full reliance, was the old uncomfortable sense of his leaning too much upon her. To have him acting and thinking for her, and with one touch carrying off her whole burthen of care, was comfort and gladness beyond what she had even devised in imagination. The only drawback, besides compassion for Mr. Ward, was the shock of hearing of the extent of the treachery of Robson, in whom her father had trusted so implicitly, and to whom he had shown so much favour.

They agreed that they would go to the Consul, and concert measures; Mary only begging that Robson might not be hardly dealt with, and they went away, leaving her to her overwhelming happiness, which began to become incredible as soon as Louis was out of sight.

By-and-by, he came back to the evening meal, when Rosita appeared, with her uncovered hair in two long, unadorned tresses, plaited, and hanging down on each shoulder, and arrayed in black robes, which, by their weight and coarseness, recalled Eastern fashions of mourning, which Spain derived from the Moors. She attempted a little Spanish talk with El Visconde, much to his inconvenience, though he was too joyous not to be doubly good-natured, especially as he pitied her, and regarded her as a very perplexing charge newly laid on him.

He had time to tell Mary that he was to sleep at the Consul's, whence he had sent a note and a messenger to fetch Tom Madison, since it appeared that the prosecution, the rumour of which had frightened the poor fellow away, had not been actually set on foot before he decamped; and even if it had been, there were many under worse imputations at large in the Peruvian Republic.

Fitzjocelyn had appointed that Robson should call on him early in the morning, and, if he failed to detect him, intended to confront him with Madison before the Consul, when there could be little doubt that his guilt would be brought home to him. He found that the Consul and Mr. Ward had both conceived a bad opinion of Robson, and had wondered at the amount of confidence reposed in him; whereas Madison had been remarked as a young man of more than average intelligence and steadiness, entirely free from that vice of gambling which was the bane of all classes in Spanish South America. Mary sighed as she heard Louis speak so innocently of 'all classes'—it was too true, as he would find to his cost, when he came to look into their affairs, and learn what Rosita had squandered. Next, he asked about the other clerk, Ford, of whom Mary knew very little, except that she had heard Robson mention to her father, when preparing to set out for Guayaquil, that in the consequent press of business he had engaged a new assistant, who had come from Rio as servant to a traveller. She had sometimes heard Robson speak in praise of his acquisition, and exalt him above Madison; and once or twice she had seen him, and fancied him like some one whom she had known somewhere, but she had for many months seldom left her father's room, and knew little of what passed beyond it.

Louis took his leave early, as he had to examine his prize, the pocket-book, and make up his case before confronting Robson; and he told Mary that he should refrain from seeing her on the morrow until the 'tug of war should be over.' 'Mr. Ward promises to come to help me,' he added. 'Really, Mary, I never saw a more generous or considerate person. I am constantly on the point of begging his pardon.'

'I must thank him some way or other,' said Mary; 'his forbearance has been beautiful. I only wish he would have believed me, for I always told him the plain truth. It would have spared him something; but nobody would trust my account of you.'

The morning came, and with it Madison; but patient as Fitzjocelyn usually was, he was extremely annoyed at finding his precious time wasted by Robson's delay in keeping his appointment. After allowing for differing clocks, for tropical habits, and every other imaginable excuse for unpunctuality, he decided that there must have been some mistake, and set off to call at the counting-house.

A black porter opened the door, and he stepped forward into the inner room, where, leaning lazily back before a desk, smoking a cigar over his newspaper, arrayed in a loose white jacket, with open throat and slippered feet, reposed a gentleman, much transformed from the spruce butler, but not difficult of recognition. He started to his feet with equal alacrity and consternation, and bowed, not committing himself until he should see whether he were actually known to his lordship. Fitzjocelyn was in too great haste to pause on this matter, and quickly acknowledging the salutation, as if that of a stranger, demanded where Mr. Robson was.

In genuine surprise and alarm, Ford exclaimed that he had not seen him; he thought he was gone to meet his lordship at the Consular residence. No! could he be at his own house? It was close by, and the question was asked, but the Senor Robson had gone out in the very early morning. Ford looked paler and paler, and while Louis said he would go and inquire for him at Miss Ponsonby's, offered to go down to the Consul's to see if he had arrived there in the meantime.

Mary came to meet Louis in the sala, saying that she was afraid that they had not shown sufficient consideration for poor Dona Rosita, who really had feeling; she had gone early to her convent, and had not yet returned, though she had been absent two hours.

Louis had but just explained his perplexity and vexation, when the old negro Xavier came in with looks of alarm, begging to know whether La Senora were come in, and excusing himself for having lost sight of her. She had not gone to the convent, but to the cathedral; and he, kneeling in the crowded nave while she passed on to one of the side chapels, had not seen her again, and, after waiting far beyond the usual duration of her devotions, had supposed that she had gone home unattended.

As he finished his story, there was a summons to Lord Fitzjocelyn to speak to Mr. Ford, and on Mary's desiring that he should be admitted, he came forward, exclaiming, 'My Lord, he has not been at the Consul's! I beg to state that he has the keys of all the valuables at the office; nothing is in my charge.'

Louis turned to consult Mary; but, as if a horrible idea had come over her, she was already speeding through the door of the quadra, and appearing there again in a few seconds, she beckoned him, with a countenance of intense dismay, and whispered under her breath, 'Louis! Louis! her jewels are gone! Poor thing! poor thing! what will become of her?'

Mary had more reasons for her frightful suspicion than she would detain him to hear. Robson, always polite, had been especially so to the young Limenian; she had been much left to his society, and Mary had more than once fancied that they were more at ease in her own absence. She was certain that the saya y manto had been frequently employed to enable Rosita to enjoy dissipation, when her husband's condition would have rendered her public appearance impossible; and at the Opera or on the Alameda, Robson might have had every opportunity of paying her attention, and forwarding her amusements. There could be no doubt that she had understood more of their plans than had been supposed, had warned him, and shared his flight.

Pursuit, capture, and a nunnery would be far greater kindness to the poor childish being, than leaving her to the mercy of a runaway swindler; and all measures were promptly taken, Ford throwing himself into the chase with greater ardour and indignation than even Madison; for he had trusted to Robson's grand professions that he could easily throw dust into the young Lord's inexperienced eyes, come off with flying colours, and protect his subordinate. If he had changed his mind since the Senora's warning, he had not thought it necessary to inform his confederate; and Ford was not only furious at the desertion, but anxious to make a merit of his zeal, and encouraged by having as yet seen no sign that he was recognised.

Regardless of heat and fatigue, Fitzjocelyn, Mr. Ward, and the two clerks, were indefatigable throughout the day, but it was not till near sunset that a Spanish agent of Mr. Ward's brought back evidence that a Limenian lady and English gentleman had been hastily married by a village padre in the early morning, and Madison shortly after came from Callao, having traced such a pair to an American vessel, which was long since out of harbour. It was well that the pocket-book had been saved, for it contained securities to a large amount, which Robson, after showing to Mary to satisfy her, doubtless intended to keep in hand for such a start as the present. Without it, he had contrived, as Madison knew, to secure quite sufficient to remove any anxieties as to the Senora Rosita owning a fair share of her late husband's property.

The day of terrible anxiety made it a relief to Mary to have any certainty, though she was infinitely shocked at the tidings, which Louis conveyed to her at once. Mrs. Willis, whom Mr. Ward had sent to be her companion, went to her brother in the outer room, and left the lovers alone in the quadra, where Mary could freely express her grief and disappointment, her sorrow for the insult to her father, and her apprehensions for the poor fugitive herself, whom she loved enough to lament for exceedingly, and to recall every excuse that could be found in a wretched education, a miserable state of society, a childish mind, and religion presented to her in a form that did nothing to make it less childish.

Mary's first recovery from the blow was shown by her remembering how fatigued and heated Louis must be, and when she had given orders for refreshment for him, and had thus resumed something of her ordinary frame, he sat looking at her anxiously, and presently said, 'And what will you do next, Mary!'

'I cannot tell. Mrs. Willis and Mrs. — — have both been asking me very kindly to come to them, but I cannot let Mrs. Willis stay with me away from her children. Yet it seems hard on Mr. Ward that you should be coming to me there. I suppose I must go to Mrs. — —; but I waited to consult you. I had rather be at home, if it were right.'

'It may easily be made right,' quietly said Louis.

'How!' asked Mary.

'I find,' he continued, 'that the whole affair may be easily settled, if you will give me authority.'

'I thought I had given you authority to act in my name.'

'It might be simplified.'

'Shall I sign my name!'

'Yes—once—to make mine yours. If your claims are mine, I can take much better care of the Dynevor interest.'

Mary rested her cheek on her hand, and looked at him with her grave steady face, not very much discomposed after the first glimpse of his meaning.

'Will you, Mary?'

'You know I will,' she said.

'Then there is no time to be lost. Let it be to-morrow. Yes'—going on in the quiet deliberate tone that made it so difficult to interrupt him—'then I could, in my own person, negotiate for the sale of the mines. I find there is an offer that Robson kept secret. I could wind up the accounts, see what can be saved for the Northwold people, and take you safe home by the end of a fortnight.'

'Oh, Louis!' cried Mary, almost sobbing, 'this will not do. I cannot entangle you in our ruinous affairs.'

'Insufficient objections are consent,' said Louis, smiling. 'Do you trust me, Mary?'

'It is of no use to ask.'

'You think I am not to be trusted with affairs that have become my own! I believe I am, Mary. You know I must do my utmost for the Dynevors; and I assure you I see my way. I have no reasonable doubt of clearing off all future liabilities. You mean to let me arrange?'

'Yes, but—'

'Then why not obviate all awkward situations at once?'

'My father! You should not ask it, Louis.'

'I would not hasten you, but for the sake of my own father, Mary. He is growing old, and I could not have left him for anything but the hope of bringing him his own chosen daughter. I want you to help me take care of him, and we must not leave him alone to the long evenings and cold winds.'

Mary was yielding—'I must not keep you from him,' she said, 'but tomorrow—a Sunday, too—'

'Ah! Mary, do you want gaiety! No, if we cannot have it in a holy place, let it at least have the consecration of the day—let us have fifty-two wedding days a year instead of one. Indeed, I would not press you, but that I could take care of you so much better, and it is not as if our acquaintance had not begun—how long ago—twenty-seven years, I think?'

'Settle it as you like,' she managed to say, with a great flood of tears-but what soft bright tears! 'I trust you.'

He saw she wanted solitude; he only stayed for a few words of earnest thanks, and the assurance that secrecy and quietness would be best assured by speed. 'I will come back,' he said, 'when I have seen to the arrangement. And there is one thing I must do first, one poor fellow who must not be left in suspense any longer.'

Tired as he ought to have been, he lightly crossed the sala to the room appropriated to business, where he had desired the two clerks to wait for him, and where Tom Madison stood against the wall, with folded arms, while Ford lounged in a disengaged attitude on a chair, but rose alert and respectful at his appearance.

Louis asked one or two necessary questions on the custody of the office for the night and ensuing day, and Ford made repeated assurances that nothing would be found missing that had been left in his charge. 'I believe you, Mr. Delaford,' said Fitzjocelyn, quietly. 'I do not think the lower species of fraud was ever in your style.'

Delaford tried to open his lips, but visibly shook. Louis answered, what he had not yet said, 'I do not intend to expose you. I think you had what excuse neglect can give, and unless I should be called on conscientiously to speak to your character, I shall leave you to make a new one.'

Delaford began to stammer out thanks, and promises of explaining the whole of Robson's peculations (little he knew the whole of them).

'There is one earnest of your return to sincerity that I require,' said Louis. 'Explain at once the degree of your acquaintance with Charlotte Arnold.'

Tom Madison still stood moody—affecting not to hear.

'Oh! my Lord, I did not know that you were interested in that young person.'

'I am interested where innocence has been maligned,' said Louis, sternly.

'I am sure, my Lord, nothing has ever passed at which the most particular need take umbrage,' exclaimed Delaford. 'If Mr. Madison will recollect, I mentioned nothing as the most fastidious need—'

Mr. Madison would not hear.

'You only inferred that she had not been insensible to your attractions?'

'Why, indeed, my Lord, I flatter myself that in my time I have had the happiness of not being unpleasing to the sex,' said Delaford, with a sigh and a simper.

'It is a mortifying question, but you owe it to the young woman to answer, whether she gave you any encouragement.'

'No, my Lord. I must confess that she always spoke of a previous attachment, and dashed my earlier hopes to the ground.'

'And the book of poems! How came that to be in your possession?'

Delaford confessed that it had been a little tribute, returned upon his hands by the young lady in question.

'One question more, Mr. Delaford: what was the fact as to her lending you means for your voyage?'

Delaford was not easily brought to confession on this head; but he did at length own that he had gone in great distress to Charlotte, and had appealed to her bounty; but he distinctly acknowledged that it was not in the capacity of suitor; in fact, as he ended by declaring, he had the pleasure of saying that there was no young person whom he esteemed more highly than Miss Arnold, and that she had never given him the least encouragement, such as need distress the happy man who had secured her affections.

The happy man did not move till Delaford had left the room, when Louis walked up to him and said, 'I can further tell you, of my own knowledge, that that good girl refused large wages, and a lady's-maid's place, partly because she would not live in the same house with that man; and she has worked on with a faithful affection and constancy, beyond all praise, as the single servant to Mr. and Mrs. Frost in their distress.'

'Don't talk to me, my Lord,' cried Tom, turning away; 'I'm the most unhappy man in the world!'

'I did not ask you to shake hands with Delaford to-night. You will another day. He is only a vain coxcomb, and treated you to a little of his conceit, with, perhaps, a taste of spite at a successful rival; but he has only shown you what a possession you have in her.'

'You don't know what I've done, my Lord. I have written her a letter that she can never forgive!'

'You don't know what I've done, Tom. I posted a letter by the mail just starting from Callao—a letter to Mr. Frost, with a hint to Charlotte that you were labouring under a little delusion; I knew, from your first narration, that Ford could be no other than my old friend, shorn of his beams.'

'That letter—' still muttered Tom.

'She'll forgive, and like you all the better for having afforded her a catastrophe, Tom. You may write by the next mail; unless, what is better still, you come home with us by the same, and speak for yourself. If I am your master then, I'll give you the holiday. Yes, Tom, it was important to me to clear up your countenance, for I want to bespeak your services to-morrow as my friend.'

'My Lord!' cried Tom, aghast. 'If you do require any such service, though I should not have thought it, there are many nearer your own rank, officers and gentlemen fitter for an affair of the kind. I never knew anything about fire-arms, since I gave up poaching.'

'Indeed, Tom, I am very far from intending to dispense with your services. I want you to guide me to procure the required weapon!'

'Surely,' said Tom, with a deep, reluctant sigh, 'you never crossed the Isthmus without one?'

'Yes, indeed, I did; I never saw the party there whom I should have liked to challenge in this way. Why, Tom, did you really think I had come out to Peru to fight a duel on a Sunday morning?'

'That's what comes of living in this sort of place. Duels are meat and drink to the people here,' said Tom, ashamed and relieved, 'and there have been those who told me it was all that was wanting to make me a gentleman. But in what capacity am I to serve you, my Lord!'

'In the first place, tell me where I may procure a wedding-ring! Yes, Tom, that's the weapon! You've no objection to being my friend in that capacity!'

Tom's astonished delight went beyond the bounds of expression, and therefore was compressed into an almost grim 'Whatever you will, my Lord;' but two hot tears were gushing from his eyes. He dashed them away, and added, 'What a fool I am! You'll believe me, my Lord, though I can't speak, that, though there may be many nearer and more your equals, there's none on earth more glad and happy to see you so, than myself.'

'I believe it, indeed, Tom; shake hands, to wish me joy; I am right glad to have one here from Ormersfield, to make it more home-like. For, though it is a hurry at last, you can guess what she has been to me from the first. Knowing her thoroughly has been one of the many, many benefits that Ferny dell conferred on me.'

There was no time for more than to enjoin silence. Louis had to hurry to the Consul and the Chaplain, and to overcome their astonishment.

On the other hand, Mary was, as usual, seeking and recovering the balance of her startled spirits in her own chamber. She saw the matter wisely and simply, and had full confidence in Louis, with such a yearning for his protection that, it may be, the strange suddenness of the proposal cost her the less. She came forth and announced her intention to Mrs. Willis, who was inclined to resent it as derogatory to the dignity of womanhood, and the privileges of a bride; but Mary smiled and answered that, 'when he had taken so much trouble for her, she could not give him any more by things of that sort. She must be as little in his way as possible.'

And Mrs. Willis sighed, and pitied her, but was glad that she should be off her poor brother's mind as soon as might be, and was glad to resign her task of chaperoning her.

Only three persons beyond the Consul's family knew what was about to happen, when Miss Ponsonby, in her deep mourning, attended the morning service in the large hall at the Consul-house; and such eyes as were directed towards the handsome stranger, only gazed at the unwonted spectacle of an English nobleman, not with the more eager curiosity that would have been attached to him had all been known.

Mr. Ward lingered a few moments, and begged for one word with Miss Ponsonby. She could not but comply, and came to meet him, blushing, but composed, in that simple, frank kindness which only wished to soften the disappointment.

'Mary,' he said, 'I am not come to harass you. I have done so long enough, and I would not have tormented you, but on that one head I did not do justice to your judgment. I see now how vain my hope was. I am glad to have met him—I am glad to know how worthy of you he is, and to have seen you in such hands.'

'You are very kind to speak so,' said Mary.

'Yes, Mary, I could not have borne to part with you, if I were not convinced that he is a good man as well as an able man. I might have known that you would not choose otherwise. I shall see your name among the great ladies of the land. I came to say something else. I wished to thank you for the many happy hours I have spent with you, though you never for a moment trifled with me. It was I who deceived myself. Good-bye, Mary. Perhaps you will write to my sister, and let her know of your arrival.'

'I will write to you, if you please,' said Mary.

'It will be a great pleasure,' he said, earnestly. 'And will you let me be of any use in my power to you and Lord Fitzjocelyn?'

'Indeed, we shall be most grateful. You have been a most kind and forbearing friend. I should like to know that you were happy,' said Mary, lingering, and hardly knowing what to say.

'My little nieces are fond enough of their uncle. My sister wants me. In short, you need not vex yourself about me. Some day, when I am an old man, I may come and bring you news of Lima. Meanwhile, you will sometimes wear this bracelet, and remember that you have an old friend. I shall call on Lord Fitzjocelyn at the office to-morrow, and see if we can find any clue to Robson's retreat. Good-bye, and blessings on you, Mary.'

Mary rejoined Louis, to speak to him of the kind and noble man who so generously and resolutely bore the wreck of his hopes. They walked up and down together in the cool shade of the trees in the Consul's garden, and they spoke of the unselfishness which seemed to take away the smart from the wound of disappointment. They spoke sometimes, but the day was for the most part spent in the sweetness of pensive, happy silence, musing with full hearts over this crowning of their long deferred hopes, and not without prayer that the same protecting Hand might guide them, as they should walk together through life.

By-and-by Mary disappeared. She would perhaps have preferred her ordinary dress—but the bridal white seemed to her to be due both to Louis and to the solemn rite and mystery; and when the time came, she met him, in her plain white muslin and long veil, confined by a few sprays of real orange flowers, beneath which her calmly noble face was seen, simple and collected as ever, forgetting in her earnestness all adjuncts that might have been embarrassing or distressing.

The large hall was darkening with twilight, and the flowers and branches that decked it showed gracefully in the subdued light. Prayer and praise had lately echoed there, and Louis and Mary could feel that He was with them who blessed the pair at Cana, far distant as they were from their own church—their own home. Yes, the Church, their mother, their home, was with them in her sacred ritual and her choice blessings, and their consciences were free from self-will, or self-pleasing, such as would have put far from them the precious gifts promised in the name of their Lord.

When it was over, and they first raised their eyes to one another's faces, each beheld in the other a look of entire thankful content, not the less perfect because it was grave and peaceful.

'I think mamma would be quite happy,' said Mary.

CHAPTER XXIII
THE MARVEL OF PERU

>   Turn, Angelina, ever dear,
>   My charmer, turn to see
>   Thy own, thy long-lost Edwin here,
>   Restored to love and thee,
>   GOLDSMITH.

Lord Ormersfield sat alone in the library, where the fire burnt more for the sake of cheerfulness than of warmth. His eyes were weary with reading, and, taking off his spectacles, he turned his chair away from the table, and sat gazing into the fire, giving audience to dreamy thoughts.

He missed the sunny face ever prompt to watch his moods, and find or make time for the cheerful word or desultory chat which often broke and refreshed drier occupation. He remembered when he had hardly tolerated the glass of flowers, the scraps of drawing, the unbusinesslike books at his son's end of the table, but the room looked dull without them now, and he was ready to own the value of the grace and finish of life, hindering the daily task from absorbing the whole man, as had been the case with himself in middle life.

Somewhat of the calm of old age had begun to fall on the Earl, and he had latterly been wont to think more deeply. These trifles could not have spoken to his heart save for their connexion with his son, and even Louis's tastes would have worn out with habit, had it not been for the radiance permanent in his own mind, namely, the thankful, adoring love that finds the true brightness in "whatsoever things are pure, whatsoever things are lovely, whatsoever things are of good report." This spirit it was which had kept his heart fresh, his spirit youthful, and changed constitutional versatility into a power of hearty adaptation to the least congenial tastes.

Gentleness, affection, humility, and refinement were in his nature. Mrs. Frost had trained these qualities into the beauty of Christian graces; and Mrs. Ponsonby and her daughter had taught him to bring his high principles to supply that which was wanting. Indolence of will, facility of disposition, unsteadiness of purpose, inconsiderate impulses without perseverance, had all betokened an inherent weakness, which the Earl's cure, ambition, had been powerless to remedy; but duty had been effectual in drawing strength out of what had been feeble by nature. It was religion that had made a man of Louis; and his father saw and owned it, no longer as merely the woman's guide in life and the man's resource chiefly in death, to be respected and moderately attended to, but never so as to interfere unreasonably with the world. No; he had learnt that it was the only sure and sound moving-spring: he knew it as his son's strengthening, brightening thread of life; and began to perceive that his own course might have been less gloomy and less harsh, devoid of such dark strands, had he held the right clue. The contrast brought back some lines which, without marking, he had heard Louis and his aunt reading together, and, albeit little wont to look into his son's books, he was so much haunted by the rhythm that he rose and searched them out—

> Yea, mark him well, ye cold and proud,
> Bewildered in a heartless crowd,
>   Starting and turning pale
>   At rumour's angry din:
>   No storm can now assail
>   The charm he bears within.
> Rejoicing still, and doing good,
> And with the thought of God imbued,
>   No glare of high estate,
>   No gloom of woe or want,
>   The radiance may abate,
>   Where Heaven delights to haunt.

The description went to his heart, so well did it agree with Louis. Yet there was a sad feeling, for the South American mail had been some days due, and he had not heard of his son since he was about to land at Callao. Five months was a long absence; and as the chances of failure, disappointment, climate, disease, and shipwreck arose before him, he marvelled at himself for having consented to peril his sole treasure, and even fancied that a solitary, childless old age might be the penalty in store for having waited to be led heavenward by his son.

It was seldom that the Earl gave way, and, reproaching himself for his weakness, he roused himself and rang the bell for better light. There was a movement in the house, and for some moments the bell was not answered; but presently the door was opened.

'Bring the other lamp.'

'Yes, my Lord.'

The slow, soft voice did not belong to Frampton. He started up, and there stood Louis!

'My dear father,' he said; and Lord Ormersfield sprang up, grasped his son's hand, and laid the other hand on his shoulder, but durst ask no questions, for the speedy return seemed to bespeak that he had failed. He looked in Louis's face, and saw it full of emotion, with dew on the eyelashes; but suddenly a sweet archness gleamed in the eyes, and he steadied his trembling lip to say with a smile,

'Lady Fitzjocelyn!'

And that very moment Mary was in Lord Ormersfield's arms.

'My children! my dear children, happy at last! God bless you! This is all I ever wished!'

He held a hand of each, and looked from one to the other till Mary turned away to hide her tears of joy; and Louis, with his eyes still moist, began talking, to give her time to recover.

'You will forgive our not writing? We landed this morning, found the last mail was not come in, and could not help coming on. We knew you would be anxious, and thought you would not mind the suddenness.'

'No, indeed,' said his father; 'if all surprises were like this one! But you are the loser, Mary. I am afraid this is not the reception for a bride!'

'Mary has dispensed with much that belongs to a bride,' said Louis. 'See here!' and, seizing her hand, he began pulling off her glove, till she did it for him; 'did you ever see such a wedding-ring?—a great, solid thing of Peruvian gold, with a Spanish posy inside!'

'I like it,' said Mary; 'it shows—'

'What you are worth, eh, Mary? Well! here we are! It seems real at last! And you, father, have you been well?'

'Yes, well indeed, now I have you both! But how came you so quickly? You never brought her across the Isthmus?'

'Indeed I did. She would come. It was her first act of rebellion; for we were not going to let you meet the frosts alone—the October frosts, I mean; I hope the Dynevor Frosts are all right?'

Frampton was here seen at the open door, doubtful whether to intrude; yet, impelled by necessity, as he caught Fitzjocelyn's eye, he, hesitating, said—

'My Lord, the Spanish gentleman!'

'The greatest triumph of my life!' cried Louis, actually clapping his hands together with ecstacy, to the butler's extreme astonishment.

'Why, Frampton, don't you know him?'

'My Lord!!!'

'Let me introduce you, then, to—Mr. Thomas Madison!' and, as Frampton still stood perplexed, looking at the fine, foreign-looking man, who was keeping in the background, busied with the luggage, Louis continued, 'You cannot credit such a marvel of Peru!'

'Young Madison, my Lord!' repeated Frampton, slowly coming to his senses.

'No other. He has done Lady Fitzjocelyn and all of us infinite service,' continued Louis, quickly, to prevent Madison's reception from receiving a fall in proportion to the grandeur of the first impression. 'He is to stay here for a short time before going to his appointment at Bristol, in Mr. Ward's counting-house, with a salary of 180 pounds. I shall be much obliged if you will make him welcome.'

And, returning in his glee to the library, Louis found Mary explaining how 'a gentleman at Lima,' who had long professed to covet so good a clerk as Madison, had, on the break-up of their firm, offered him a confidential post, for which he was well fitted by his knowledge of the Spanish language and the South American trade, to receive the cargoes sent home. 'In truth,' said Louis, coming in, 'I had reason to be proud of my pupil. We could never have found our way through the accounts without him; and the old Cornish man, whom we sent for from the mines, gave testimony to him such as will do Mr. Holdsworth's heart good. But nothing is equal to Frampton's taking him for a Spanish Don!'

'And poor Delaford's witness was quite as much to his credit,' said Mary.

'Ay! if Delaford had not been equally willing to depose against him when he was the apparent Catiline!' said Louis. 'Poor Delaford! he was very useful to us, after all; and I should be glad to know he had a better fate than going off to the diggings with a year's salary in his pocket!'

(Footnote. A recent writer relates that he found the near relation of a nobleman gaining a scanty livelihood as shoe-black at the diggings. Query. Might not this be Mr. Delaford?)

'Then everything is settled?' asked his father.

'Almost everything. The mines are off our hands, and the transfer will be completed as soon as Oliver has sent his signature; and there's quite enough saved to make them very comfortable. You have told me nothing of them yet?'

'They are all very well. James has been coming here twice a-week since I have been at home, and has been very attentive and pleasant; but I have not been at the Terrace much. There never was such a houseful of children. Oliver's room is the only place where one is safe from falling over two or three. However, they seem to like it, and to think, the more the better. James came over here the morning after the boy was born, as much delighted as if he had had any prospects.'

'A boy at last! Poor Mr. Dynevor! Does he take it as an insult to his misfortunes?'

'He seems as well pleased as they; and, in fact, I hope the boy may not, after all, be unprovided for. Mr. Mansell wrote to offer to be godfather, and I thought I could not do otherwise than ask him to stay here. I am glad I did so, for he told me that now he has seen for himself the noble way they are going on in, he has made up his mind. He has no relation nearer than Isabel, and he means to make his will in favour of her son. He asked whether I would be a trustee, but I said I was growing old, and had little doubt you would be glad enough. You will have plenty of such work, Louis. It is very dangerous to be known as a good man-of-business, and good-natured.'

'Pray, how does Jem bear it?'

'With tolerable equanimity. It may be many years before the child is affected by it, if Mrs. Mansell has it for her life. Besides, James is a wiser man than he used to be.'

'He has been somewhat like Robinson Crusoe's old goat,' said Louis. 'Poor Jem! the fall and the scanty fare tamed him. I liked him so well before, that I did not know how much better I was yet to like him. Mary, you must see his workhouse. Giving up his time to it as he does, he does infinite good there.'

'Yes, Mr. Calcott says that he lives in fear of some one offering him a living,' said Lord Ormersfield.

'And the dear old Giraffe?' said Louis.

'Clara? She is looking almost handsome. I wish some good man would marry her. She would make an excellent wife.'

'I am not ready to spare her yet,' said Mary; 'I must make acquaintance with her before any excellent man carries her off.'

'But there is a marriage that will surprise you,' said the Earl; 'your eldest cousin, whose name I can never remember—'

'Virginia,' cried Louis. 'Captain Lonsdale, I hope!'

'What could have made you fix on him?'

'Because the barricades could not have been in vain, and he was an excellent fellow, to whom I owe a great deal of gratitude. He kept my aunt's terrors in abeyance most gallantly; and little Virginia drank in his words, and built up a hero! But how was it?'

'You remember that Lady Conway would not take our advice, and stay quietly at home. On the first steamer she fell in with this captain, and it seems that she was helpless enough, without her former butler, to be very grateful to him for managing her passports and conducting her through Germany. And the conclusion was, that she herself had encouraged him so far, that she really had not any justification in refusing when he proposed for the young lady, as he is fairly provided for.'

'My poor aunt! No one ever pities her when she is 'hoist with her own petard!' I am glad poor Virginia is to be happy in her own way.'

'I shall send my congratulations to-morrow,' said the Earl, smiling triumphantly, 'and a piece of intelligence of my own. At H. B. M. Consul's, Lima—what day was it, Louis?'

Mary ran away to take off her bonnet, as much surprised by the Earl's mirth as if she had seen primroses in December. Yet such blossoms are sometimes tempted forth; and affection was breathing something like a second spring on the life so long unnaturally chilled and blighted. If his shoulders were bowed, his figure had lost much of its rigidity; and though his locks were thinned and whitened, and his countenance slightly aged, yet the softened look and the more frequent smile had smoothed away the sternness, and given gentleness to his dignity.

No sooner was she out of the room than Lord Ormersfield asked, 'And what have you done with the Spanish woman?'

The answer excited a peal of laughter, which made Louis stand aghast, both at such unprecedented merriment and at the cause; for hitherto he had so entirely felt with Mary, as never to have seen the ludicrous aspect of the elopement. Presently, however, he was amused by perceiving that his father not merely regarded it as a relief from an embarrassing charge, but as an entire acquittal for his own conscience for any slanders he had formerly believed of Dona Rosita.

Louis briefly explained that, the poor lady being provided for by Robson's investments in America, he had thought it right that the Ponsonby share of the firm should bear the loss through these embezzlements; and he had found that her extravagance had made such inroads on the property, that while the Dynevor share (always the largest) resulted in a fair competence, Louis had saved nothing out of the wreck of the Ponsonby affairs but Mary herself. 'Can you excuse it, father?' he said, with all the old debonnaire manner.

'You will never be a rich man, Louis. You and she will have some cares, but—' and his voice grew thick—'you are rich in what makes life happy. You have left me nothing more to ask or wish for!'

'Except that I may be worthy of her, father. You first taught me how she ought to be loved. You have been very patient with me all this time. I feel as if I must thank you for her—' and then, changing his tone as she opened the door—'Look at her now she has her bonnet off—does not she look natural?'

'I am sure I feel so,' said Mary. 'You know this always seemed more like home than anything else.'

'Yes, and now I do feel sure that I have you at last, Mary. That Moorish castle of yours used to make me afraid of wakening: it was so much fitter for Isabel's fantastic Viscount. By-the-bye, has she brought that book out?'

'Oh, yes, and James is nearly as proud of it as he is of his son. He actually wanted me to read it! He tells me it is selling very well, and I hope it may really bring them in something.'

'Now, then—there's the tea. Sit down, Mary, and look exactly as you did the morning I came home and found you.'

'I'm afraid I cannot,' said Mary, looking up in his face with an arch, deprecating expression.

'Why not?'

'Don't you know that I am so much happier?'

Before breakfast next morning Fitzjocelyn must visit his farm, and Mary must come with him.

How delicious was that English morning after their voyage; the slant rays of the sun silvering the turf, and casting rainbows across the gossamer threads from one brown bent to another; the harvest fields on the slopes dotted with rich sheaves of wheat; the coppices, in their summer glory, here and there touched with the gold of early autumn, and the slopes and meadows bright with lively green, a pleasant change for eyes fresh from the bare, rugged mountain-side and the rank unwholesome vegetation of

Panama. Shaggy little Scottish oxen were feeding on the dewy grass, their black coats looking sleek in the sun beyond the long shadows of the thorns; but as Mary said, laughing, 'Only Farmer Fitzjocelyn's cattle came here now,' and she stopped more than once to be introduced to some notable animal, or to hear the history of experiments in fatting beasts.

'There! they have found you out! That's for you,' said Louis, as a merry peal of bells broke out from the church tower, and came joyously up through the tranquil air. 'Yes, Ormersfield, you are greeting a friend! You may be very glad, old place! I wish Mr. Holdsworth would come up to breakfast! Is it too wet for you this way, Mary?'

This way was into Fernydell, and Mary answered, 'Oh, no—no; it is where I most wanted to go with you. We have never been there together since—'

'No, you never would walk with me after I could go alone!' said Louis, with a playful tone of reproach, veiling deep feeling.

In silence he handed her down the rocky steps, plunging deeper among the hazels and rowan-trees; then pausing, he turned aside the luxuriant leaves of a tuft of hartstongue, and showed her, cut on a stone, veiled both by the verdure and the form of the rock, the letters—

Deo Gratias,
L. F. 1847.

'I like that!' was all that Mary's full heart allowed her to say.

'Yes,' said Louis, 'I feel quite as thankful for the accident as for the preservation.'

'And that dear mamma was with us,' added Mary. 'Between her and you, it was a blessing to us all. I see these letters are not new; you must have cut them out long ago.'

'As soon as I could get here without help,' he answered. 'I thought I should be able to find the very spot where I lay, by remembering the cross which the bare mountain-ash boughs made against the sky; but by that time they were all leaf and flower; and now, do you see, there they are, with the fruit just formed and blushing.'

'Like other things,' said Mary, reaching after the spray, 'once all blossom, now—'

'Fruit very unripe,' as he said, between a smile and a sigh; 'but there is some encouragement in the world after all, and every project of mine has not turned out like my two specimens of copper ore. You remember them, Mary and our first encounter?'

'Remember it!' said Mary. 'I don't think I forgot a day of that summer.'

'What I brought you here for,' said Louis, 'was to ask you to let me do what I have long wished—to let me put the letter M here?'

'I think you might have done it without leave,' said Mary.

'So I might at first, but by the time I came here again, Mary, you had become in my estimation 'a little more than kin,' and less than—no, I wont say that, but one could not treat you as comfortably as Clara. I lost a cousin one August day, and never found her again!'

'Never?'

'Never—but the odd thing is, that I cannot believe that what I did find has been away these seven years.'

'Yes, that is very strange,' said Mary; 'I have felt it so. Wo do seem to understand and guess each other's thoughts as if we had been going on together all this time. I believe it is because you gave me the first impulse to think, and taught me the way.'

'And I know who first taught me to think to any purpose,' said Louis, smiling. 'But who is this descending on us?'

It was the Spanish gentleman, reddening all over at such an encounter, in mid-career towards her at the Terrace, and muttering something, breathless and almost surly, about begging pardon.

'Look here, Tom,' said Louis, lifting the leaves to show the letters. 'That is all I ever could feel on that matter, and so should you. There, no more about it,—you want to be on your way; and tell Mr. Frost that we shall be at Northwold in the afternoon.'

About half an hour after, Clara was delicately blowing the dust out of the wreath of forget-me-nots on the porcelain shepherdess's hat, when a shriek resounded through the house, and, barely saving the Arcadian in her start, she rushed downstairs. James, in his shirt-sleeves, was already on his way to the kitchen. There Kitty was found, too much frightened, to run away, making lunges with the toasting-fork at a black-bearded figure, who held in his arms Charlotte Arnold, in a fit of the almost forgotten hysterics. The workhouse girl shrieked for the police; Jane was at Master Oliver's door, prepared for flight or defence; Isabel stood on the stairs, with her baby in her arms, and her little flock clinging to her skirts, when Clara darted back, laughing too much to speak distinctly, as she tried to explain who the ruffian really was.

'And Louis is coming, and Mary! Oh! Isabel, he has her at last! Oh! Jem! Jem! did we ever want dear granny so much! I always knew it would come right at last! Jane, Jane, do you hear, Lord Fitzjocelyn is married! Let me in; I must go and tell Uncle Oliver!'

James looked at Isabel, and read in her smile Clara's final acquittal from all suspicions beneath the dignity of both. Uncle Oliver would have damped her joy, had it been in his power. He gave up his affairs as hopeless, as soon as he found that young Fitzjocelyn had only made them an excuse for getting married, and he was so excessively angry with her for being happy, that she found she must carry her joyous face out of his sight.

It was not easy to be a dignified steady governess that morning, and when the lessons were finished, she could have danced home all the way. She had scarcely reached the Terrace gate, when the well-known sound of the wheels was heard, and in another moment she was between the two dear cousins; Fitzjocelyn's eyes dancing with gladsomeness, and Mary's broad tranquil brow and frank kindly smile, free from the shadow of a single cloud! Clara's heart leapt up with joy, joy full and unmixed, the guerdon of the spirit untouched by vanity or selfishness, without one taint that could have mortified into jealous, disappointed pain. It was bliss to one of those whom she loved best, it was the winning of a brother and sister, and perhaps Clara's life had never had a happier moment.

Lord Ormersfield could have thanked her for that joyous, innocent welcome. He had paid her attentions for his son's sake, of which he had become rather ashamed; and as Louis and Mary hastened on to meet James and Isabel, he detained her for a moment, to say some special words of kindness. Clara, perhaps, had an intuitive perception of his meaning, and reference to her past heiress state, for she laughed gaily, and said, 'Yes, I never was more glad of anything! He was so patient that I was sure he deserved it! I always trusted to such a time as this, when he used to talk to me for want of dear grandmamma.'

Mary was led upstairs to be introduced to the five children, while the gentlemen went over the accounts in Oliver's room. Enough had been rescued from the ruin to secure, not wealth, but fair competence; the mines were disposed of to a company which would pay the value by instalments, and all the remainder of the business was in train to be easily wound up by Mr. Ward. Mr. Dynevor's gratitude was not overpowering: he was short and dry, privately convinced that he could have managed matters much better himself, and charging all the loss on Fitzjocelyn's folly in letting Robson escape. But, though James was hurt at his unthankfulness, and Lord Ormersfield could have been very angry, the party most concerned did not take it much to heart; he believed he had done his best, but an experienced eye might detect blunders, and he knew it was hard to trust affairs out of one's own hands.

Even the Earl was glad to escape to the sitting-room, though every one was talking at once, and Mercy the loudest; and Louis, as the children would call him in spite of their mamma, was at once seized on by Kitty to be introduced to 'our brother.'

'And what is his name, Kitty?'

'Woland!' shouted all the young ladies in chorus.

'Sir Woland is in the book that mamma did make,' said Kitty.

Louis looked at Isabel with laughing eyes.

'It was Uncle Oliver's great wish,' she said, 'and we did not wish to remember the days of Sir Hubert.'

Before Lord Ormersfield was quite deafened, Louis recollected that they must show Mary at the House Beautiful; and they took leave. The Earl begged James to come back to dinner with them, and Louis asked if Clara could not find room in the carriage too. It was the earnest of what Ormersfield was to be to her henceforth, and she was all delight, and earnestness to be allowed to walk home with James by starlight. And the evening realized all she could wish. The gentlemen had their conversation in the dining-room, and Mary and Clara sat on the steps together in the warm twilight, and talked of granny; and Clara poured out all that Mary did not yet know of Louis.

'I hear you have been in hysterics again,' had been Lord Fitzjocelyn's greeting to Charlotte. 'You are prepared for the consequences.'

Charlotte was prepared. The mutual pardon had not been very hard to gain, and Tom had only to combat her declarations that it was downright presumptuous for her to have more than master had a year, and her protests that she could not leave her mistress and the dear children in their poverty. The tidings that they were relieved from their present straits answered this scruple, and Charlotte was a pretty picture of shrinking exultation when she conducted her betrothed to Mrs. Martha, who, however, declared that she would not take his hundred and eighty pounds a year—no, nor twice that,—to marry him in that there black beard.

Mrs. Beckett made him exceedingly welcome, and he spent the chief part of his time at No. 5, where he was much more at ease than at Ormersfield. He confessed that, though not given to bashfulness before any man, there was something in Mr. Frampton's excessive civility that quite overcame him, and made him always expect to be kicked out of doors the next minute for sauciness.

Charlotte's whirlwinds of feeling had nearly expended themselves in that one shock of meeting. The years of cheerful toil, and the weeks of grief and suspense, had been good training for that silly little heart, and the prospect of her new duties brought on her a sobering sense of responsibility. She would always be tender and clinging, but the fragrant woodbine would be trained round a sound, sturdy oak, and her modesty, gentleness, and sincerity, gave every promise of her being an excellent wife.

Tom had little time to spare before undertaking his new office, and it was better that the parting should be speedy, for it was a grievous one, both to the little bride and to Isabel and the children. Friend rather than servant, her place could be ill supplied by the two maids who were coming in her room, and Isabel could have found it in her heart to sympathize with Mercy and Salome in their detestation of the black man who was coming to take away their dear Charlotte.

Clara's first outlay, on her restoration to comparative wealth, was on Charlotte's wedding-dress. It was a commission given to Mary, when with Fitzjocelyn, she went to London for one day, to put the final stroke to the dissolution of the unfortunate firm, and to rejoice Aunt Melicent with the sight of her happiness.

Good old Miss Ponsonby's heart was some degrees softer and less narrow than formerly. She had a good many prejudices left, but she did not venture on such sweeping censures as in old times, and she would have welcomed Lord Ormersfield with real cordiality, for the sake of his love to her Mary. Indeed, Louis's fascinations and Mary's bright face had almost persuaded her into coming home with them; but the confirmed Londoner prevailed, and she had a tyrant maid-servant, who would not let her go, even to the festival at Ormersfield in honour of her niece.

The Earl was bent on rejoicings for his son's marriage, and Louis dexterously managed that the banquet should take place on the day fixed for Tom's wedding, thus casting off all oppressive sense of display, by regarding it as Madison's feast instead of his own. Clara, who seemed to have been set free from governess tasks solely to be the willing slave of all the world, worked as hard as Mary and Louis at all the joyous arrangements; nor was the festival itself, like many such events, less bright than the previous toils.

The wedding took place in Ormersfield Church, on a bright September morning; James Frost performed the marriage, Lord Fitzjocelyn gave the bride away, and little Kitty was the bridesmaid. The ring was of Peruvian gold, and the brooch that clasped the bride's lace collar was of silver from the San Benito mine. In her white bonnet and dove-coloured silk, she looked as simple and ladylike as she was pretty, and a very graceful contrast to her Spanish gentleman bridegroom.

The Ormersfield bowling-green, which was wont to be so still and deserted, hemmed in by the dark ilex belt, beheld such a scene as had not taken place there since its present master was a boy. There were long tables spread for guests of all ranks and degrees. Louis had his own way with the invitations, and had gathered a miscellaneous host. Sir Miles Oakstead had come to see his old friend made happy, and to smile as he was introduced to the rose-coloured pastor in his glass case. Mr. Calcott was there, and Mrs. Calcott, all feuds with Mrs. James Frost long since forgotten; and Sir Gilbert Brewster shone in his colonel's uniform,—for Lady Fitzjocelyn had intimated a special desire that all the members of the yeomanry should appear in costume; and many a young farmer's wife and sister came all the more proudly, in the fond belief that her own peculiar hero looked in his blue and silver 'as well as Lord Fitzjocelyn himself.' And Miss Mercy Faithful was there, watching over Oliver, to make up for the want of her sister. And old Mr. Walby was bowing and gossiping with many a patient; and James, with his little brown woman in his hand, was looking after the party of paupers for whom he had obtained a holiday; and Mr. Holdsworth was keeping guard over his village boys, whose respectable parents remained in two separate throngs, male and female; and Clara Frost was here, there, and everywhere—now setting Mrs. Richardson at ease, now carrying little Mercy to look at the band, now conveying away Salome when frightened, now finding a mother for a village child taken with a sobbing fit of shyness, now conducting a stray schoolboy to his companions, now running up for a few gay words to her old uncle, to make sure that he was neither chilly nor tired. How pleasant it was to her to mingle with group after group of people, and hear from one and another how handsome and how happy Lord Fitzjocelyn looked, and Lady Fitzjocelyn quite beautiful; and, then, as they walked from party to party, setting all at ease and leaving pleased looks wherever they went, to cross them now and then, and exchange a blithe smile or merry remark.

No melancholy gaps here! thought she, as she helped her uncle to the easy chair prepared for him at the dinner-table; no spiritless curiosity, no forced attempts to display what no one felt!

There must needs be toasts, and such as thought themselves assembled for the sake of the 'marriage in high life,' were taken by surprise when Lord Fitzjocelyn rose, and began by thanking those assembled for assisting in doing honour to the event of the day—the marriage of two persons, for each of whom he himself as well as those most dear to him felt the warmest respect and gratitude for essential services and disinterested attachment, alike in adversity and in prosperity. Unpleasant as he knew it was to have such truths spoken to one's face, he could not deny himself the satisfaction of expressing a portion of the esteem and reverence he felt for such noble conduct as had been displayed by those whose health he had the pleasure to propose—Mr. and Mrs. Thomas Madison.

'There,' was his aside, as he sat down, 'I only hope I have not made him surly; poor fellow, I have put him in a predicament, but it could not be otherwise!'

Clara had tears in her eyes, but not like those she had shed at Cheveleigh; James gave Louis a look of heartfelt gratitude, bowed the lowest to the happy pair, and held up little Kitty that her imitative nod and sip might not be lost upon them.

Mrs. Beckett said, 'Well, I never! If ever a girl deserved it,' choked, and flourished her white handkerchief; Frampton saluted like my Lord and Louis XIV. rolled into one; and Warren and Gervas privately agreed that they did not know what was coming of the world, since Marksedge poachers had only to go to foreign parts to be coined goold in the silver mines. Mrs. Madison's pretty face was all blushes, smiles, and tears. Mr. Madison rose to reply with unexpected alacrity, and Louis was soon relieved from anxiety, at least, as far as regarded his eloquence, for he thought in the majestic Spanish idiom, and translated as he went—

'My Lords,' he began, 'gentlemen and ladies and neighbours, my Lord Fitzjocelyn has done my wife and myself an honour as unlooked-for as undeserved; and the manner of the favour is such that we shall carry the grateful remembrance to the end of our lives. He has been so condescending as to speak of such services as it was in our power to render; but he has passed over in silence that which gives him a claim to the utmost that I could place at his feet. He will forgive me for speaking openly, for I cannot refrain from disburthening my mind, and letting you know, even more than you are at present aware of, what your Senor—what your Lord truly is. Most of you have known me but too well. It is not ten years since I was a rude, untaught boy upon the heath, such as a large proportion of those present would deem beneath their notice: Lord Fitzjocelyn did not think so. His kindness of manner and encouraging words awakened in me new life and energy. He gave me his time and his teaching, and, what was far more, he gave me his sympathy and his example. It was these which gave vitality to lessons dimly understood, or which had fallen dead on my ears, when only heard in my irregular attendance at school. But the work in me was tardy, and at first I requited his kindness with presumption, insubordination, and carelessness. Then, when I had been dismissed, and when my wilful neglect had occasioned the accident of which the traces are still only too visible, then, did I not merit to be exposed and cast off for ever? I knew it, and I fled, as if I could leave behind me my grief and my shame. Little did I dare to guess that he was dealing with me as though I had been his own brother, and scrupulously concealing my share in the misfortune. When I returned, sullen and overwhelmed, he alone—yes! and while still suffering severely—spoke a kind word to me, and exerted himself to rescue me from the utter ruin and degradation to which despair would have led me. He placed me in the situation which conducted me to my present position; he gave me the impulse to improve myself; and, above all, he infused into me the principles without which the rest would have been mere temptations. If I have been blest beyond my deserts—if I have been prosperous beyond reasonable expectation—if, among numerous failures, I have withstood some evils—all, under the greatest and highest Benefactor, is owing to the kindness, and, above all, to the generous forbearance of Lord Fitzjocelyn. I wish I could testify my gratitude in any better manner than by speaking of him to his face; but I am sure you will all drink his health more heartily, if possible, for knowing one more trait in addition to your own personal experience of his character!'

Alas! that all things hidden, and yet to be proclaimed on the house-tops, would bear the light as well as Fitzjocelyn's secret! The revelation of this unobtrusive act of patience and forbearance excited a perfect tumult of enthusiasm among persons already worked up to great ardour for one so beloved; and shouts, and even tears, on every side strove in vain to express the response to Madison's words.

'Too bad, Tom!' was Louis's muttered comment.

'You are paid in your own coin,' retorted Mary, raising her glistening eyes, full of archness.

'I perceive it is no surprise to you, Lady Fitzjocelyn!' said Sir Miles Oakstead; 'and, I own, nothing from that quarter' (nodding at Louis) 'surprises me greatly.'

'She practised eavesdropping,' said Louis, 'when the poor fellow was relieving his mind by a confession to the present Mrs. Madison.'

'And I think Mrs. Madison and I deserve credit for having kept the secret so long,' said Mary.

'It explains,' observed Mr. Holdsworth. 'I did not understand your power over Madison.'

'It was the making of us both,' said Louis; 'and a very fine specimen of the grandeur of that rough diamond. It elucidates what I have always said, that if you can but find the one vulnerable place, there is a wonderful fund of nobleness in some of these people.'

'Do you take this gentleman as an average specimen?'

'Every ploughboy is not an undeveloped Madison; but in every parish there may be some one with either the *thinking* or the rising element in his composition; and if the right ingredient be not added, the fermentation will turn sour, as my neglect had very nearly made it do with him. He would have been a fine demagogue by this time, if he had not had a generous temper and Sunday-school foundation.'

'Hush!' said Mary, smiling—'you must not moralize. I believe you are doing it that poor Farmer Norris may not catch your eye.'

Louis gave a debonnaire glance of resignation; and the farmer, rising in the full current of feeling caused by Madison's speech, said, with thorough downright emotion, that he knew it was of no use to try to enhance what had been already so well expressed, but he believed there was scarcely a person present who did not feel, equally with Mr. Madison, the right to claim Lord Fitzjocelyn as a personal friend,—and an irrepressible hum of fervent assent proved how truly the farmer spoke. 'Yes,—each had in turn experienced so much of his friendly kindness, and, what was more, of his sympathy, that he could confidently affirm that there was scarcely one in the neighbourhood who had not learnt the news of his happiness as if some good thing had happened to himself individually. They all as one man were delighted to have him at home again, and to wish him joy of the lady, whom many of them know already well enough to rejoice in welcoming her for her own sake, as well as for that of Lord Fitzjocelyn.'

Again and again did the cheers break forth—hearty, homely, and sincere; and such were the bright, tearful, loving eyes, which sought those of Fitzjocelyn on every side, that his own filled so fast that all seemed dazzled and misty, and he hastily strove to clear them as he arose; but the swelling of his heart brought the happy dew again, and would scarcely let him find voice. 'My friends, my dear, good friends, you are all very kind to me. It is of no use to tell you how little I deserve it, but you know how much I wish to do so, and here is one who has helped me, and who will help me. We thank you with all our hearts. You may well wish my father and me joy, and yourselves too. Thank you; you should not look at me so kindly if you wish me to say more.'

The Earl, who had studied popularity as a useful engine, but had never prized love beyond his own family, was exceedingly touched by the ardour of enthusiastic affection that his son had obtained,—not by courting suffrages, not by gifts, not by promises, but simply by real open-hearted love to every one. Lord Ormersfield himself came in for demonstrations of warm feeling which he would certainly never have sought nor obtained ten years ago, when he was respected and looked up to as an upright representative of certain opinions; but personally, either disliked or regarded with coldness.

He knew what these cheers were worth, and that even Fitzjocelyn might not long be the popular hero; but he was not the less gratified and triumphant, and felt that no success of his whole life had been worth the present.

'After all, Clara,' said Oliver Dynevor, as his nephew and niece were assisting him to the carriage, 'they have managed these things better than we did, though they did not have Gunter.'

'Gunter can't bring heart's love down from town in a box,' said Clara, in a flash of indignation. 'No, dear uncle, there are things that can't be got unless by living for them.'

'Nor even by living for them, Clara,' said James; 'you must live for something else.'

Lord Ormersfield had heard these few last words, and there was deep thought in his eye as he bade his cousins farewell at the hall door.

Clara was the last to take her place; and, as she turned round with a merry smile to wish him goodbye, he said, 'You have been making yourself very useful, Clara, I am afraid you have had no time to enjoy yourself.'

'That's a contradiction,' said Clara, laughing; 'here's busy little Kitty, who never is thoroughly happy but when she thinks she is useful, and I am child enough to be of the same mind. I never was unhappy but when I was set to enjoy myself. It has been the most beautiful day of my life. Thank you for it. Goodbye!'

The Earl crossed the hall, and found Mary standing alone on the terrace steps, looking out at the curling smoke from the cottage chimneys, and on the coppices and hedge-rows.

'Are you tired, my dear?' he said.

'Oh no! I was only thinking of dear mamma's persuading Louis to go on with the crumpled plans of those cottages. How happy she would be.'

'I was thinking of her likewise,' said the Earl. 'She spoke truly when she told me that he might not be what I then wished to make him, but something far better.'

Mary looked up with a satisfied smile of approval, saying, 'I am so glad you think so.'

'Yes,' said Lord Ormersfield, 'I have thought a good deal since. I have been alone here, and I think I see why Louis has done better than some of his elders. It seems to me that some of us have not known the duties that lay by the way-side, so to speak, from the main purpose of life. I wish I could talk it over with your mother, my dear, what do you think she would say?'

Mary thought of Louis's vision of the threads. 'I think,' she said, 'that I have heard her say something like it. The real aim of life is out of sight, and even good people are too apt to attach themselves to what is tangible, like friendship or family affection, or usefulness, or public spirit; but these are like the paths of glory which lead but to the grave, and no farther. It is the single-hearted, faithful aim towards the one thing needful, to which all other things may be added as mere accessories. It brings down strength and wisdom. It brings the life everlasting already to begin in this life, and so makes the path shine more and more unto the perfect day!'